MY FERAL ROMANCE

FAE FLINGS AND CORSET STRINGS

TESSONJA ODETTE

Cover and interior illustrations by Tessonja Odette

TESSONJA ODETTE

FAE FLINGS AND CORSET STRINGS

For anyone who'd prefer to curl up inside with a smutty book rather than put on "real" pants and leave the house.

A NOTE ON CONTENT

My Feral Romance may be an adorable, low-stakes, fantasy romcom, but it does contain some topics that may be upsetting to some readers. Below is not an exhaustive list, but please note the following content:

- Adult situations
- Explicit language
- Characters overindulging in liquor
- Fantasy drug use
- Childhood trauma, family discord, and painful secrets
- Descriptive on-page sex scenes (medium spice) including light consensual biting during intercourse; a bloody kiss—it will make sense, I promise. This is ***My FERAL Romance*** after all. These two like it a little rough and messy.
- Sexual activity in public spaces (without an audience)
- Violence, blood, and mild gore
- Illegal fighting sport

Welcome to Faerwyvae

The only part of the world inhabited by fae. An isle united under fae rule where humans and fae live side by side. Faerwyvae is protected by a barrier of fae magic. Fae never leave the isle, and humans are only permitted to cross the border under strict regulations.

Eleven Courts of Faerwyvae

WINTER SPRING SUMMER

AUTUMN EARTHEN

WIND FIRE SEA

SOLAR LUNAR

STAR

Seelie and Unseelie Fae

Most fae have two physical manifestations: an unseelie form and seelie form. Unseelie form is a fae's natural manifestation, whether animal, elemental, or spiritual in nature. Seelie form is a manifestation modeled after human likeness. Some fae shift effortlessly between the two forms. Others claim one form and rarely shift. While there are many exceptions, seelie fae tend to live in human societies, while unseelie fae tend to favor the wilds.

Fae Monarchs

Each court is ruled by two fae monarchs: one seelie and one unseelie, each responsible for separate aspects of leadership. The seelie monarchs oversee day-to-day operations of modern society for humans and seelie fae. The unseelie monarchs advocate for the wild fae and preserve their way of life according to ancient traditions.

Locations

- ◇ JASPER, EARTHEN COURT
- ◇ CYPRESS HOLLOW, EARTHEN COURT
- ◇ CYLLENE HOTEL, STAR COURT

Faerwyvae
Lunar
Star
Fire
Autumn
Spring
Wind
Winter
Solar
Earthen
Summer
Sea
Bretton

PROLOGUE

DAPHNE

Flippant. Brash. Arrogant. Reckless. I have several choice words to describe Monty Phillips, and none of them are flattering.

My opinion was set the day I began my internship at Fletcher-Wilson Publishing. The first thing Monty said to me was not *Hello, how do you do,* or *Nice to meet you.* It was, "I must inform you my personality is twisted. Don't take me too seriously." All the while he had a crooked, dimpled grin on his too-handsome face. I simply stared at him, canines bared in disgust. Because, unlike him, I was taking my new job *very* seriously. As the only four-legged fae employee at Fletcher-Wilson, and perhaps the first pine marten any of my coworkers had seen in person, I needed to make a good impression. Do the right things. Say the right words. I'd failed at integrating into seelie society once before. I wouldn't fail again.

And there Monty Phillips was, joking around with ease, flipping a cigarillo between his fingers as if work was just a brief interlude between smoke breaks.

"We're going to have a lot of fun working together, Daffy Dear," he said, then sauntered off to do who knows what. I didn't take him for someone who got any work done.

I was stunned. While all the other coworkers I'd been introduced to stammered over having to address me by first name instead of a proper surname like humans have, he didn't bother to use my name at all. He called me *Daffy*, not Daphne. The nerve!

My assessment of his work ethic hasn't improved over the last year we've been colleagues. He's still the same flippant rake he was the day we met. But I've gotten to know him a little better. We even managed a book tour together, with him as the publicist and me as his assistant.

Now I catch sight of him in Fletcher-Wilson's lobby for the first time in what feels like ages, and there isn't an ounce of annoyance in my heart at seeing him again.

Only joy.

For all my talk about Monty Phillips' flaws, I've come to consider him one of my favorite people. Odd how the most annoying personalities can wriggle their way into your heart. Like a parasitic bug.

Yes, that sums up Monty nicely.

A heartworm.

One that's slithering away from me.

My joy shifts, tightening my lungs, as I watch the space growing between us. I've just stepped into our workplace's lobby from upstairs, while he's making a beeline for the front door. Sunlight streams through the large windows, which display a view of horse-drawn carriages and suit-clad pedestrians. My eyes, however, are locked only on Monty. His retreating back reminds me how long it's been since we've had a full conversation. Since we chatted and laughed like friends.

At least...I thought we were friends.

Can two people still be friends even if they rarely see one another?

It's been a year since we managed The Heartbeats Tour together, a wildly successful event for two of Fletcher-Wilson's most popular authors, Edwina Danforth and William Haywood—both of whom became our dear friends by the end. That was the last time Monty and I worked so closely together. I was still an intern then, but now that I've been promoted to an editorial assistant, I spend most of my time working on the editorial floor. I haven't assisted on a single book tour since, while Monty has done nothing but manage one after another.

The thought that I might not see him again for months on end has his name leaping from my lips, twisted into a question.

"Monty?"

He pauses before turning around, and when he does, another spark of joy warms my chest. He looks the same as ever. Same charming grin, same pair of dimples in his cheeks, same pale blond hair falling in loose curls that makes him look every inch the devilish rake I know him to be. Same haphazard state of dress with his loose cravat, open collar, and a waistcoat without a jacket. Same casual grace, his hands tucked into his trouser pockets and an unlit cigarillo perched over the rounded shell of his ear.

His eyes sweep over me, and I'm reminded that he may look the same as ever, but I don't.

The last time he saw me, I was a pine marten. A small creature with a fluffy tail that frolicked on four paws.

Now I look like a woman.

As a fae, I have the ability to shift between two physical manifestations. Unseelie form is a fae's natural manifestation—a pine marten, in my case—while seelie form is a body modeled after human likeness, save for the telltale angled tip of our ears. Monty has only seen me in my seelie form once. He doesn't know I've recently adopted this body full-time.

I shift from foot to foot, my stomach clenching as I await his reaction. Is it strange for him, seeing me this way? Does he think my clothing suits me? I'm dressed in flowing slacks, a blouse, and a waistcoat. It's a far cry from the yellow dress I wore the last time he saw me in this body. An even farther cry from my fluffy gray-brown fur and mustelid figure. Then again, I'm not sure why I should care what he thinks. I may no longer despise the man, but he's still the same ridiculous rake he always was. He's still just my friend. And yet I can't help hoping he'll…I don't know. Say something nice? Compliment me?

Then the most mortifying realization dawns. What if he doesn't even recognize—

"Hey, Daffy." There's no hesitation in his voice. No uncertainty.

He recognizes me after all.

I blow out a relieved breath, though I'm still apprehensive as I make my way toward him. I'm too aware of the way I walk, the careful steps I take that are so unlike the way I used to scamper about. I don't recall ever being this self-conscious around him before. "I haven't seen you in a while," I say.

"Well, this is hello and goodbye," he says, tone dry. "I got fired."

Disappointment sinks my gut. My eyes fall to the broadsheets folded under his arm, which gives me some clue as to why he may have lost his job as a publicist at Fletcher-Wilson. I read his interview in the *Cedar Hills Gazette* this morning, so I'm sure our boss did too. Monty was an idiot to agree to the interview in the first place, and an even bigger one for the things he admitted to in it. The interview revolved around The Heartbeats Tour, specifically the whirlwind romance that developed between its headlining authors. Monty claims he played matchmaker for Edwina and William during said tour...and detailed every one of his outrageous actions during his so-called matchmaking.

My lips peel into a grimace. "Why doesn't that surprise me?"

"You did warn me," he says with a chuckle, though his mirth seems forced. I suppose losing his job isn't a laughing matter.

He's right, though; I did warn him. I warned him every step of the way not to do anything he could get in trouble for. *Don't get involved in a seduction bet between Edwina and William. Don't flirt with Edwina. Don't take your authors to bawdy parties. Don't sneak off at every chance you get for a smoke break. Don't spend the company budget on stupid things. Don't treat your job like a playground.* Did he listen to me? No, of course he didn't.

I want to say it serves him right, but before I can speak again, he takes a step away. "Well, I'm off."

"Wait, that's all?" He pauses at my panicked tone. If I wasn't so shocked at his attempt at a swift exit, I might be more embarrassed.

And yet...

There's so much I've wanted to say to him. So many things I want to catch up on. I want to tell him why I've taken on seelie form full-time. That I've started painting. That I've found a passion for a career I want, if only I can grow my confidence to become an illustrator. That I've been drawing in secret all this time. That Edwina recently found one of my sketches...and liked it.

He shifts back to face me, and the wildest idea of all comes to mind.

What if I invite him to come with me when I make my annual visit back home? Every year I attend the Lughnasadh celebration in Cypress Hollow, my former hometown in the Earthen Court's unseelie forest. This year's festival is just a few weeks away, and I've been meaning to invite a friend. I've never taken a friend back home, but this year is different. This year I want a tether to my *new* life. Someone to remind me that even though Cypress Hollow is comfortable and peaceful and I fit in so well, there's a reason I chose my new life. There's a reason I strive to belong in seelie society, even when I make mistakes. Even when I embarrass myself. Even when I get things wrong. And that reason is the friends I've made, the life I'm starting to build for myself, and my renewed passion for painting.

The trip could benefit him too. My village specializes in a Lughnasadh matchmaking ritual he'd find quite amusing. Perhaps he'd even play guest matchmaker since he's so obsessed with bringing couples together.

"Do you maybe want to..." The invitation is on the tip of my tongue, but I can't summon the courage to voice it. Perhaps that's too much to ask of someone I haven't seen in so long. So I try something easier. Less daunting. "Share a meal? Catch up?"

Monty's expression shifts, an unreadable emotion crossing his face. Is he surprised? Offended? This wouldn't be the first time I've misunderstood a social cue. However, I'm not convinced that's what this is. Because there's a vicious little beast who's always awake inside me, no matter what I look like on the outside. She's a hunter. A killer. She can always recognize easy prey.

And she's sensing fear.

Fear.

But why? Monty has never been afraid of anything. He's reckless, bold, and unapologetic. He's annoying and hilarious and surprisingly caring at times. But I've never sensed fear in him.

Before I can assess it further, it's gone, making me wonder if it was ever there to begin with. Monty's expression turns smug as he saunters up to me. I freeze at his sudden proximity, my breath catching as he lifts his hand…

And pats me on the top of the head.

Like an animal.

A creature.

My heart collapses in my chest. I meet his eyes and the condescending look he stares down at me with. It's the last thing I expected from him.

Or maybe it's the last thing I hoped for.

I thought he'd look at me differently now that I'm in seelie form. I'm not sure how exactly I *wanted* him to look at me, but maybe I expected something more like the wide-eyed awe he held when he first saw me in this body during The Heartbeats Tour. At the gala, when I wore a yellow dress and he shared a dance with me. A clumsy one, but a dance nonetheless. The way he looked at me then made me feel like maybe I was worth looking at.

But this isn't anything like that. This is patronizing.

I pull my head from under his hand, baring my teeth. "You really do think of me as a pet, don't you? Even when I look like this?"

There's no warmth in his eyes as he gives me a wink. "A really cute pet."

My heart crumples tighter. "You're an asshole."

"And here I thought we were friends," he says with a mocking pout. "See you around."

I don't try to stop him as he turns away with a halfhearted wave.

I only try to stop myself from crying.

Because Monty Phillips doesn't deserve my tears. Or my friendship.

I swipe roughly at my cheeks and the traitorous moisture there. Then I storm in the opposite direction without giving that asshole a second glance.

Lesson One

FRIENDSHIP AND THE MORTIFYING PROSPECT OF SOCIALIZING

CHAPTER ONE

ONE YEAR LATER

DAPHNE

A lady of gentle breeding must be accomplished in a myriad of skills: dancing, polite dining, witty conversation, music, and fine art. I only ever excelled at the latter skill while failing at all the rest. Maybe that's because I don't come from gentle breeding. In fact, my conception was rather violent indeed. My mother is famed across the unseelie forest for having bitten my father's ear clean off after their mating session. I suppose that's what he gets for trying to cuddle the surliest pine marten in the Earthen Court and asking her to move into his tree with him. Pine martens are solitary by nature, even the fae ones. I know because I lived alone for much of my three centuries of life.

Until I learned to shift into my seelie form and made the hapless decision to enter human high society as a debutante.

That experience ended the same way my parents' short-lived coupling did.

With a bitten-off ear.

And I was the one doing the biting.

While my mother's bite earned her respect and notoriety amongst the local fae creatures, mine got me cast out of society, after which I retreated to the safety of my unseelie hometown for the next decade.

Now I'm on my second attempt at integrating into human society, via the working class this time, and things have gone smoothly. I have a job, a functional human body, and even a few friends. Yet I'm constantly waiting for the proverbial severed ear to drop.

As I stare at the canvas perched on the easel before me, I wonder if this is that day. The day it all goes to shit.

I grimace at my sketch. It looked fine this morning when I gave my canvas a proud once-over before hefting it under my arm and escorting it to my workplace. Now that my piece sits beside several other artists' in-progress illustrations, it's painfully clear I made a mistake in bringing it to the studio today. Never mind that my final sketch is due for my supervisor's approval in less than an hour. I'm going to need an extension.

A wicked cackle sounds over my shoulder. "That is so ugly."

I swat at the fluttering fae creature, who is thankfully *not* my supervisor.

The sprite only laughs harder, zipping over my head to the other side. Her girlish voice climbs to a feverish pitch. "You must be soooo embarrassed."

"I would be," I say through my teeth, "if anyone saw it."

"I'm seeing it."

"Anyone who counts," I amend. "Which you don't."

I glance once more at the other canvases, illuminated by

the morning glow streaming through the studio's arched windows. Is it just me or is the sunlight refusing to grace my easel? Not that I can blame it. At least none of the other artists have arrived to witness my mortification, though they will be here soon. While I've only been commissioned for a single project, four in-house illustrators work at Fletcher-Wilson full-time, all of whom have been in this field far longer than I have.

The sprite tiptoes on air into my field of vision, tilting her head to the side. She's about the size of my palm and resembles a pixie with her tiny body and buzzing wings. What sets her apart from a regular pixie is that she's made entirely of paper, from her four slender limbs to her hair, wings, and skin. With a flutter of her cream-colored parchment lashes, she says, "I bet you're thinking about how much better the other artists are than you."

I swat at her again. "Why are you here? This is a publishing house and you're a book sprite. Surely there are more interesting departments to invade. Wouldn't you rather insult a new manuscript?"

"I prefer to insult the manuscripts *you're* reading," she says.

"Why?"

"Because we're friends."

"Since when? I don't even know your name."

"Well, I only named myself this morning. I've decided to be Lady Araminta of the Shining Waters."

I scoff. "That's certainly a name."

"Isn't it? What's yours again? Daffy?"

"Daphne," I snipe back, but her mispronunciation sends an unexpected spear through my heart. Only one person has ever dared to call me Daffy. If he were here now, I'm sure he'd have something annoying to say about my situation. And yet...it would probably cheer me up too.

You can't weasel *your way out this pickle, Daffy Dear,* is what I bet he'd say. He always loved his stupid puns.

To which I'd argue that I'm not a weasel; I'm a pine marten. Furthermore, I'm in seelie form now and—

Why am I arguing with an imaginary Monty Phillips? That idiot got himself fired almost a year ago and I haven't seen my former colleague since.

"I waited at your desk since dawn," the newly christened Araminta says, "ready to read queries over your shoulder, but you never showed at your usual time."

"Yes, well, I'm not working in editorial today," I say under my breath as I take up a stick of graphite and rework some of the lines on my canvas. Fridays are the one day of the week I get to work on my commission. A commission I'm growing increasingly convinced I don't deserve.

"You should have stuck to editorial. You're really, reeeeeally bad at art." Araminta tumbles through the air in a renewed fit of cackles. "I'm glad I found you today. This is so much better than reading queries."

I glower at the tiny creature. Who knew an infestation of harmless bookworms would grow so troublesome? When the bookbinders first spotted the adorable fae worms napping on stacks of paper at Fletcher-Wilson's printing warehouse, they were charmed. Bookworms are a type of book sprite—the spirit of fiction made physical—and are drawn to spectacular prose. We saw it as a blessing. None of us knew some of the bookworms would find their way to our main office and metamorphose into absolute terrors. For weeks now these evolved winged book sprites have been tormenting us with misdemeanors ranging from dog-earing pages to cracking spines to absolute war crimes like spoiling the endings of manuscripts or—like the sprite who plagues me now—fancying themselves critics.

One would think I'd have more patience for the wicked

creatures, considering I'm fae myself, but I don't. Were I in my pine marten form, I'd have eaten this snack-sized menace without remorse. The fact that I haven't snatched her from the air and bitten off her tiny cackling head is a miracle.

I eye her through slitted lids as she points and laughs at my canvas with gusto, wondering if perhaps I might be a *little* hungry. But, alas, murder is not on today's agenda. Maybe it's because I prefer cooked food when I'm in seelie form.

Or maybe it's because the sprite isn't wrong. My sketch *is* ugly.

Ignoring Araminta as best I can, I make a few more corrections with my graphite, then step back to assess my work again. My eyes wander over the delicate lines that form the two partially undressed figures I've drawn. The female looks gorgeous with her windswept hair and languid posture. Her lips are parted in a sensual *O*, the bodice of her gown pooling around her waist to reveal a heaving bosom nearly spilling from her corset. The hem of her ballgown is hiked up to reveal gartered stockings encircling thick thighs. She's everything a cover-worthy heroine should be. I shift my attention to the male figure and my mood sours. "It's the hands," I say, pointing to where the hero grips the heroine's hips.

Araminta taps her chin as she hovers in front of the canvas. She tilts her head this way and that before another burst of mirth escapes her lips. "Those aren't hands. Those are *paws*."

Alarm rushes through me as I inspect my work closer. She's right. My hero has not human metacarpals and phalanges but thick meaty paws.

"How the hell did that happen?" I set about frantically reworking his digits, desperate to turn them into the strong groping hands I was aiming for. My efforts result in an indecipherable blur of graphite.

"Before you stress solely over his paws, you should probably save some anxiety for the rest of him."

"The rest of him is—" I swallow my words as I take in further evidence of the monstrosity I created. I blink several times, hoping that the next time I open my eyes I'll see something else on the canvas. Instead, I only see more and more flaws. Not only does my hero have paws, but his torso is too long. His legs are too short. Overall, he's rather bendy and fleshy. Almost like...

"A weasel," Araminta says. "You drew a man shaped like a weasel."

I stammer before I manage to find coherence. "Not entirely. He...he is almost human-shaped."

"Almost?" The sprite flutters to the corner of my canvas where she lands. Sprawling on her belly, she kicks her legs in time with the flap of her papery wings. "You've clearly never been with a man if that's what you think they look like naked."

I give her a withering look. "Like you know any better than I do. You only emerged from your chrysalis, what, two weeks ago?"

She shrugs. "I've read a lot of interesting books since then, so I know plenty. What's the word you use to describe them? Smutty?"

"Yes, well I've read even more smutty books than you. And I *have* been with a man. *Plural* men."

Araminta looks impressed for once. "At the same time?"

"No, not at the same time." I purse my lips, sealing away the fact that none of my sexual exploits involved much time assessing my lovers' goods. Or pleasure, for that matter. Nothing worth inspiring art.

"How did you even get this job?"

"I'll have you know I was personally recommended by Edwina Danforth." I turn my nose up at the sprite before whirling on my heel to rifle through my leather satchel. Once I find my sketchbook, I flip through the pages. "She's one of my dearest friends and asked me to illustrate the new covers for her most popular book series."

"Favoritism, then? Not talent?"

"It wasn't just her. Mr. Fletcher approved of her suggestion." Mr. Fletcher is both Edwina's publisher and my boss. I never would have been considered for the commission were it not for Edwina's pleading on my behalf, but the fact that Mr. Fletcher agreed to hire me must count for something.

"And he had so much faith in you that he's only allowing you to work in the illustration department one day a week."

I give her a warning growl and finally locate the page I'm looking for. It's the rough sketch I drew before I reproduced it as a clean sketch on my current canvas. I glance from the paper to the easel and back again, comparing the two drawings. The blood leaves my face as I realize the flaws were there from the start. How did I look at this sketch and think it was satisfactory enough to be replicated in my final piece? How did my supervisor do the same?

Araminta studies the page in my sketchbook. "Did your friend even look at your artwork before she recommended you?"

"Of course she did," I say, flipping dozens of pages back to the very piece that convinced Edwina I'm a capable artist. My panic eases as I study it. Two mostly nude figures are entwined in a passionate embrace, every intricate line alive with movement. The emotion practically leaps off the page, the sexual tension palpable in the placement of the figures' hands, the breath of space that separates their lips.

"This is why she recommended me," I say, every word brimming with pride. Even under my most critical assessment, the sketch is beautiful.

So how did this piece turn out so perfect, while my

current one is a thing of nightmares? This sketch is more than a year old, which means I should have gotten better since then, not worse. Was it the lack of pressure that made this one so easy? I never intended for a soul to see it, for sketching has always been my secret hobby. The one activity I carried with me from my brief time as a debutante. I never imagined Edwina would discover my sketchbook during one of her visits. Yet discover it, she did.

And humiliated I was.

Not only was my sketchbook and all its contents never meant for anyone's eyes but mine, but the sketch Edwina saw was inspired by her most recent manuscript—which wasn't meant for anyone's eyes but Mr. Fletcher's. She'd just turned it in that week, and I had to confess I'd *borrowed* it from his office one night, sneaking an early peek.

She didn't so much as balk at my furtive actions. Furthermore, she refused to hear a word of apology and instead begged me to reproduce the sketch in full color. I wanted to refuse. I hadn't picked up a paintbrush since my disastrous debut season when I found solace painting landscapes and portraits while the other debutantes engaged in gossip I was firmly excluded from.

But how does one say no to the woman who is not only your dear friend but also your favorite author?

One doesn't.

"I see the problem," Araminta says, pulling me back to the present.

"What problem?" I snap, tapping the sketch with my graphite. "This is perfect."

"It is, which is precisely my point. This piece is perfect because it involves two *women*."

I frown, staring down at the sketch once more. I mean, of course it involves two women. The couple from the borrowed manuscript was a water nymph and a banshee.

Their chemistry was so titillating, I couldn't *not* draw them—

That's when understanding dawns.

"You are absolute rubbish at drawing men," Araminta says, putting words to my realization.

My stomach drops to my feet, as does my sketchbook. I crouch down to pick it up, but it's now splayed open to reveal a page that only further solidifies my terror. It bears several quick sketches I made months ago while I was practicing male anatomy. They looked decent enough at the time, but now that I've become intimately acquainted with my flaws, they're all I can see. Too-long torsos. Fingers that look more like paws. Beady eyes. Muzzles instead of mouths.

"No, no, no." I snap the sketchbook shut but remain hunched by the floor. "I can't draw men."

Which is a problem. A big fucking problem.

Because I've been commissioned to paint four covers in the next three months, and each features a male-female pairing. If I succeed, Mr. Fletcher may promote me to full-time illustrator during my next performance review at the end of July.

But if I fail…

My eyes unfocus. "This can't be happening."

The buzz of paper wings reaches my ears, but I don't bother looking at the sprite. She flies around my head three times before landing on the puffed sleeve of my ivory blouse. "Ugh. It's no fun when you're all sad about it. It's only amusing when we make fun of your art *together*."

My lungs tighten, my fingers curling into fists. Everything inside me yearns to shrink down into the comfort of my unseelie form. To return to my tiny stature, so easy to overlook, and a furry face that hides emotion.

But I can't shrink down and hide. I promised myself I wouldn't anymore.

When I returned to seelie society for the first time in a decade, still reeling from my awful experiences as a debutante, I hid in the comfort of my unseelie form. Even when I entered the workforce, I did so as a pine marten, only shifting into my humanoid body in secret when I wanted to draw.

Bit by bit, I've gained more confidence over the last couple of years. The working class isn't nearly as judgmental as high society was. I secured a job and gained a few close friends. I was navigating my life with ease in the busy city of Jasper, Earthen Court, which is rather different from the small unseelie village I left behind. I was blending in with the humans and seelie fae around me.

Yet *blending* isn't *belonging*, and the latter was what I lacked.

Then Edwina gave me the nudge I needed.

I picked up my paintbrush for the first time in years and it felt like coming home. A new home. A *real* home. Not the one I'm honor-bound to return to in three months for my village's annual Lughnasadh celebration. Thanks to a magically binding ritual I drunkenly participated in during last year's festivities, I now have to prove I've dug strong roots in Jasper, or I'll be stuck in Cypress Hollow for good.

I might not have minded that before. Half my heart has always been tethered to safety, always yearning to give up on society and go back to the forest where it's easy and predictable and I never have to be anyone but the furry little mustelid I am.

But that was before I rekindled my love for painting, before I remembered the true joy of opposable thumbs. Discovered a career I'd do anything to make my own—illustration.

I can't give that up now. I can't be trapped in Cypress Hollow where not a single art gallery exists and the sultry paintings I love are as unappreciated as indoor plumbing. I can't relinquish my dreams due to last year's drunken mistake fueled by too much berry cordial and a dash of heartache.

Araminta pats my sleeve. "There, there." When I don't respond, her tone turns impatient. "I said *there, there*. Come on. Enough feeling sorry for yourself. You're not the worst artist ever. Only really bad."

"Is that supposed to be comforting?"

She rolls her eyes. "The solution is right in front of you. Your female figures are good because you can draw what you see." She points at the woman on my canvas. "You think I don't recognize that pretty lady? It's you! You lounged before the mirror and made that sexy little *O* face, didn't you?"

My cheeks blaze as my eyes dart to the figure in question. How did Araminta know? The heroine looks nothing like me. Her hair is long, pale, and streaming while mine is short and black, cropped just below my chin. She is supposed to be tall while I'm on the petite side. Her eyes are meant to be blue while mine are dark brown. Her ears are round while mine have angled tips. Her figure—well, her thighs are as full as mine, I can say that much. As for her orgasmic expression...

I avert my gaze from both the canvas and the sprite, feigning nonchalance. "Well, why shouldn't I use myself as a model?"

"Exactly. You used a model, which is why she turned out well. Don't you see? What you need is..." Araminta does a little twirl, then flourishes her arms in a wide arc. "A naked man."

I blink at her.

"You know. To draw."

She's...maybe not wrong. I've considered using a model for my male figures, yet my options are limited. First, he needs to have the kind of physique Edwina's heroes possess —tall, muscular, and dripping with sex appeal. Second, I don't have time to enroll in drawing classes, what with my full-time work schedule and no arts colleges in the city of Jasper. Or anywhere in the Earthen Court. Third, I'm anxious around crowds and strangers.

Yet Araminta is right. Unless I want to give up my dream career before it's even begun, I need a model. And if drawing classes and strangers are out of the question, I suppose that leaves me one choice. A choice that might solve more than one of my problems.

Bolstering my courage, I rise to my feet and flip my sketchbook open to my most recent drawing. Without letting myself dwell on my monstrous weasel-man, I tear out the page and fold it into my waistcoat pocket. Then, with my head held high despite the nerves swarming in my belly, I march toward the door.

Araminta flies after me. "So you're going to find a model?"

I swallow hard. "I'm going to get a husband."

CHAPTER TWO

MONTY

A man never forgets his first. The pleasure. The pain. The tangle of emotions. And while Fletcher-Wilson isn't the first job I was fired from, it was the first job I liked.

Now I'm back in the very office I was let go from almost a year ago. The room looks the same as it did then, with its oak-paneled walls, the neatly organized bookshelves, and the enormous portraits of two unsmiling human men—the original founders of Fletcher-Wilson, rest in peace. Their son, Mr. Fletcher, sits before me now, inspiring the same sense of dread I felt before he fired me last year. I'd kill for a cigarillo, if only to have something to fidget with, but I suppose that's how I felt then too.

The key difference between then and now is that I'm no longer Junior Publicist at Fletcher-Wilson. I'm not one of Mr. Fletcher's employees at all.

This time I'm here to plead for a publishing deal.

I resist the urge to loosen my cravat, shrug off my jacket,

and roll up my sleeves. I wore a fine suit for this, every button properly secured in all the proper places, even though I prefer more casual attire for work. Suits like this remind me too much of when I was an aristocrat. If I wanted to wear a pompous ensemble every day, I wouldn't have gotten myself disinherited. But this is an interview with a man who I'm pretty sure hates me. I should make the best second impression I can.

Mr. Fletcher leans forward in his oversized chair, propping his elbows on his mahogany desk as he eyes me beneath bushy brows. He's a stoic man with a heavy build, dark hair, and an impressively thick mustache; not the kind of face you'd picture as the publisher of the isle's most popular steamy romance novels. Though he doesn't publish primarily smut. Fletcher-Wilson publishes everything from romance to poetry to how-to guides, the latter of which is the genre I hope to enter.

He makes a grunt of some indecipherable emotion, then taps the front page of my manuscript. It's the exact same thing he did when he confronted me with the newspaper interview that led to my termination. I can't help but expect my manuscript to be as thoroughly obliterated as my employment was back then, but why would Mr. Fletcher schedule a meeting with me if he was simply going to reject me?

"It's good," Mr. Fletcher says.

"It is?" My body stills, and only now do I realize my knee had been jiggling. I blow out a heavy breath and shift in my seat, curling my lips into a grin. "You truly like my manuscript?"

"It isn't perfect," Mr. Fletcher says, holding out his hands to temper my excitement, "but I can see its appeal. You've done well at the *Cedar Hills Gazette*."

I tip an imaginary hat. "I am grateful for your recommendation to the position." Despite having fired me, Mr. Fletcher was kind enough to get me my new job at one of the local papers. He may not have been thrilled about the actions I confessed to in last year's interview, but my matchmaking claims convinced him I'd do well as a romance columnist. Hence my current vocation writing under the pseudonym *Ask Gladys*.

He gives me one of his rare smiles. "You may not have followed my advice about keeping your articles appropriate, but I must admit, the *Cedar Hills Gazette* has never been more popular. Readers love what you've done with the *Ask Gladys* column."

I nod. "My article 'Fifteen Steps to Fantastic Fellatio' sold so many copies, the paper had to print an extra run by ten in the morning."

Mr. Fletcher's grin turns into a grimace at the word *fellatio*. Again, how does this man publish the isle's smuttiest smut author? He rubs his brow. "Yes, well, it may not be my reading material of choice, but romance columnist suits you."

He's right, it does suit me. I've always had a bit of an obsession with matchmaking—with my own twist, of course, which usually involves annoying the hell out of two people until they realize they like each other. That obsession translates well into answering romance queries and penning mildly inappropriate articles. My new boss has been so impressed with my work that he requested I compile my best romance advice into a how-to guide and publish it under the *Ask Gladys* pseudonym. I've never wanted to be an author, but my boss posed a challenge I couldn't refuse. If I land this publishing deal on behalf of the *Gazette*, he'll contract me as Gladys for six more years. Not only that, but he'll offer a signing bonus on top of my portion of the publishing advance. Normally, the *Gazette* only contracts their columnists for a year at a time, so this kind of opportunity won't likely come around again.

I live for challenges, particularly if they feel like a game. What better game to play than proposing a book to the man who once fired me?

Not to mention I really fucking need the money.

"So..." I spread my hands and give him my most charming grin. "What do you say? Does Fletcher-Wilson want to carry me to fame?"

Mr. Fletcher's expression shifts from amused to exasperated. "Don't get ahead of yourself, Mr. Phillips. I already said it wasn't perfect."

"Well, do tell."

"Your book compiles the most sensible advice you've given on modern courtship."

I smirk at his emphasis on *sensible*. He's right to differentiate my book's contents from my usual fare, though. Most of my *Ask Gladys* articles are humorous if not a touch obscene. "How to Lace a Corset for the Ultimate Breast Buffet." "How to Unlace a Corset for a Titillating Striptease." "How to Flap a Fan to Draw Attention to Your Assets." "How to Get Off When Your Fae Lover is Incorporeal." But I alternate those topics with true gems regarding everyday courtship. As someone who's been courted, flirted with, eye-fucked, and nearly mauled by eager lovers, I know what turns a man off or on. What tempts a suitor into long-term commitment and what sends him running for the hills. These are the topics that form the bulk of my manuscript.

Mr. Fletcher continues. "It is unique in that your audience is working-class women but you utilize your perspective as a former aristocrat. You merge modern feminine freedoms with the rules of courtship that normally only apply to highborn ladies."

"It's brilliant, isn't it?" I lean forward in my chair,

ensnared by his praise and ready to be reeled in with more. "What else do you like about it?"

He ignores my commentary. "But what it lacks are real-life examples. As of now, you're merely spouting advice without concrete proof that your words are worth their salt. It comes across as pompous and belittling."

I settle back into my seat, fighting my urge to extract a cigarillo from my jacket pocket. Writing behind a pseudonym has protected me from the horrors of face-to-face criticism of my work, so his assessment stings. "I intended for the tone to come across as grandmotherly and wise."

"You are neither a grandmother nor wise."

"But Gladys is."

He cuts me a withering look. "Gladys is a pen name, and I will not publish a romance guide for women written by a man under a woman's name without disclosing it as such."

I purse my lips. This shouldn't surprise me, considering what a stickler Mr. Fletcher is. One of his most popular titles is a book written by a woman under a male pseudonym. He only agreed to publish it if the copyright page disclosed both the writer and performer of the work. I do hope he doesn't expect me to reveal my real name as the author. Then again, it would be hilarious if my father found out I'd written a book involving such unrefined topics as sex and courtship. But if my career reaches a higher level of success, I risk him being proud of me. I'll be damned if I give him a reason to try and bring me back into the fold.

"We don't have to disclose your identity," Mr. Fletcher says as if my worries were written on my face, "but we will make it clear that Gladys is a pen name and property of the *Cedar Hills Gazette*. Regardless, Gladys needs to back her advice with proof, whether she's a wise grandmother or not."

I shrug. "Fair enough. I can post a request for testimonials from my readers. I'll have it published in Monday's issue."

"That may add legitimacy to your advice, but your readers write to you anonymously. You can't guarantee your testimonials will come from the same people, or just those eager to see their words published. I want *real* examples."

"Can I use Edwina Danforth and William Haywood?" As his expression darkens, I rush to add, "I know it's a touchy subject, considering I was fired for matching them—"

"You weren't fired for playing matchmaker between them. You were fired for the unseemly behavior you demonstrated as a publicist when you managed their book tour. More so for admitting to it in a rather detailed interview."

Oh, that fateful interview, published in the very paper I now work for. I suppose I could have acted with more foresight when I relayed the events of The Heartbeats Tour. A year had already passed since the tour, so I didn't see the harm in sharing some of the most entertaining moments. Apparently, Mr. Fletcher didn't feel the same way. Particularly about the part where I propositioned Edwina for casual sex. In my defense, it was a ruse to spark William's jealousy.

"But you do agree I matched Weenie and Will, right?" I say. "To this day, they insist I played no part in their relationship."

Mr. Fletcher squeezes the bridge of his nose. "Did either of them knowingly utilize the advice you've written about?"

I open my mouth to say yes, but I suppose that would be untrue. While I could lie, I'd prefer to win this challenge fair and square. And while I may have encouraged Edwina and William to notice the feelings they were already developing through my strategic use of jealousy and misdirection, I hardly gave them any real advice.

"No, they didn't," I confess.

"Playing matchmaker from the shadows is different from laying down rules for someone to follow of their own accord. You need a case study specifically for this book. Someone to prove your advice works."

My stomach bottoms out. One thing I've liked about writing as Gladys is the anonymity. The separation between me and the readers who ask for my advice. There's no one to directly hurt. No one to look at me with disappointment in their eyes. If someone takes my advice and uses it, the responsibility is theirs, not mine, no matter how it turns out. Similarly, when I play matchmaker for unsuspecting friends or acquaintances, their actions and decisions are theirs alone. They never know what I'm scheming in the moment, for that would defeat the purpose.

Which means Mr. Fletcher is right. I have no proof.

He continues. "Coach an unattached woman seeking love. Teach her your most important principles and have her demonstrate them in real life. Put her in the same situations your readers have written to you about and have her execute your advice the right way. If she forms a favorable attachment by the end of your experiment, you'll have a successful case study with a happy ending and a promising manuscript on your hands."

I drum my fingertips against the arms of my chair, still wary at the thought of working so closely with a woman. A bachelorette at that. I'm not so vain as to consider myself the ultimate catch, and I am quite proficient at making myself unlikable when it serves my purposes. But still. There's a reason I keep most people at arm's length. A reason I never engage in any romantic entanglements other than the occasional tryst. And those trysts have rules. No kissing. No encores.

Mr. Fletcher speaks again. "I won't guarantee a publishing contract now, for I want to see the results of your case study first. I'll give you four months. Are you up to the challenge?"

Something bright and wicked ignites in my chest at the

word *challenge*. When he puts it that way, how can I refuse? If I treat this case study like a game…

"Deal," I say, "but let's make it three months."

Mr. Fletcher arches his brows as if impressed by my ambition.

Little does he know it's not an ambitious work ethic that motivates me but a massive chunk of debt and a money-lender to appease.

He taps my manuscript again. "I'm serious when I say keep things appropriate. If I'm going to put the Fletcher-Wilson name behind this, I need all your face-to-face interactions on behalf of this book to be exemplary. No drugs, no orgies, no philandering."

I quirk my lips at one corner. "You know you're taking all the fun out of it, right?"

His eyes narrow to a glower.

"I'm kidding. I can be appropriate."

He heaves a sigh. "I hope you're right. The only reason I didn't throw your query in the rubbish bin the minute I saw your name was because your column has done so well, salaciousness and all." He pushes my manuscript across the desk. Lowering his voice, he adds, "That and the fact that your interview didn't end up causing any backlash for Fletcher-Wilson."

"Does that mean you regret firing me?"

"No. Now get out of here before I change my mind. Come back in three months with that case study."

My mood is buoyant as I leave Mr. Fletcher's office and reach the editorial floor. Here the sounds of shuffling paper and the scratch of pens on parchment fill my ears. It's so much like the *Gazette* with its open floor plan bearing rows upon rows of desks, its high ceilings, its exposed brick walls dressed in climbing ivy. Yet this place holds a spark of nostalgia I don't have at my new place of employment.

Not only was Fletcher-Wilson the first job I liked, but it was also the first job where I made friends.

William and Edwina, thanks to The Heartbeats Tour.

Zane, William's best friend who conspired with me in my matchmaking efforts.

And...

Daphne.

I stroll down the center aisle between the multitude of desks, nodding at the few familiar faces I see. None of them belong to her. None of them belong to the woman I hurt with my cold farewell the day I got fired.

I've never made peace with that. Never decided whether putting distance between us was the right thing to do.

Nice knowing you, Daffy Dear.

See you around.

Part of me hoped I'd see her today.

Part of me was terrified I would.

I take another glance across the editorial floor without seeing any sign of her, unsure if my relief or disappointment is stronger. I hate that I can't recall which desk is hers.

This is for the best, I tell myself as I force my gaze to the back of the room and make a beeline toward the stairwell. What would I have told her anyway? That I'm sorry? That I wish we were still friends?

My insides writhe with a discomfort I can't name, the kind that makes it hard to breathe. I reach for my cravat, loosening it along with the top buttons of my shirt. That only offers meager relief, so I extract a rectangular case from inside my jacket, remove a cigarillo, and place it between my lips. Even without lighting it, the promise of calming lavender, sage, and Moonpetal soothes the fraying edges of my nerves.

Finally, I reach the stairwell, only to pause as an unfamiliar male stomps up the steps. He pays me no heed, his attention fixed on the paper pixie he's muttering to. "You don't need to ruin the fucking ending, Reginald. I never asked you to read the last page..."

I arch a brow at the odd but amusing sight, then turn back toward the stairwell—

That's when something catches my attention from my periphery.

Short black hair, petite stature, curving hips.

I whirl back around, my eyes locking on the figure. I know it's her, even with her back to me as she strides down a narrow corridor at the other end of the editorial floor. Even in that body that's so different from the slinky little pine marten I spent so much time with. Even in flowing slacks, a lace blouse, and a brown waistcoat, so different from the cute yellow dress she wore the last time I let myself get close to her.

When our friendship started to feel real.

Too real.

I shift to the side, one foot ready to bolt down the stairwell, the other drawing me toward the other hall.

I pull the cigarillo from my lips.

Flip it between my fingers.

And take a step in a direction I might regret.

CHAPTER THREE

DAPHNE

I press myself close to the wall outside the break room door. Angling my body to the side, I peer through the door's glass window. Thankfully my target is alone, sipping tea at one of the many tables inside. He's half turned away from me, his focus locked on the broadsheets he's reading. I untuck the piece of paper from my waistcoat pocket and unfold it. Holding it out before me, I look from my sketch to the man.

My target is Brad Folger from marketing. He's tall, I suppose, with expertly styled dark hair, a decent build, and—most importantly—human hands. I haven't a clue what he looks like naked or if he has a rippling abdomen and excessive sex appeal, all of which are essential for Edwina's heroes, but at least he'll look suitable next to the heroine in my sketch. More so than the weasel-man.

"Yeah," I mutter, "he'll do."

"He'll do?" Araminta echoes, her voice a sharp whisper.

"That's how you refer to your future husband? Remind me how you made the leap from male model to matrimony?"

"I'm doing what the humans call *killing two birds with one stone.*" Not that I've ever used stones to kill birds, for my teeth have always been sufficient. When I was a pine marten, that is. Now I go to the butcher on Third Avenue. Their smoked chicken breast is delicious.

Araminta's mouth falls open. "You're going to kill Brad from marketing? There are easier ways to procure a model without resorting to murder."

I cut her a glare. "It's an expression. It means I'm taking care of two problems at once. One being my need for a model."

"What's your second problem?"

My second problem is a magically binding ritual I drunkenly participated in last Lughnasadh with a honey badger named Clyde, but Araminta doesn't need to know about that. All that matters is that marriage will solve both issues. And since Brad is the last man who has asked me out on a date, I might as well start with him.

I tuck the sketch back in my pocket. Then, with a bracing breath, I push open the break room door and stride toward Mr. Folger's table. In my head, I rehearse the right things to say.

Good morning.

How do you do?

How is your tea?

What do you think of the weather?

Interesting news in the paper today?

Small talk is essential groundwork before broaching important topics. Like accepting dates. Or asking men to model for you. And eventually getting married. Society has rules and a correct order of doing things. While I may struggle with some of the finer points of propriety, I've always been good at following rules.

Save for that time I bit my fellow debutante, but that was a special circumstance.

I stop before Mr. Folger's table. He looks up from his broadsheets and gives me a polite smile. I wish I could say his grin makes my heart palpitate, the way it does in books when a character glimpses such an expression on their paramour's face, but it does no such thing. Then again, fictional courtships never happen this way. Fictional courtships are full of big emotions—the good and the bad—and they unfold in dramatic ways in dramatic settings. A ballroom. A heist. Not a contrived meeting in the break room at work on a typical Friday.

But I don't need a whirlwind romance. I only need easy and continuous access to a man's body. Which means I need Brad Folger.

"Good morning, Mr. Folger," I say, aiming for a light and feminine tone. Instead, my voice comes out flat. I've never been great at inflection. So I tack on a smile, unsure if showing my teeth would make it look more genuine. I alternate between the two before I settle on what I hope is a demure closed-lip grin.

"Good morning, Miss...Daphne." I'm used to the pause he makes before saying my name. Unlike him, I don't have a surname, which makes humans uncomfortable when we aren't yet on a casual first-name basis. Surnames are a human tradition, so fae don't naturally have them. Many fae choose surnames when they enter society, but I still haven't.

"How is your day?" I ask, doing my best to maintain eye contact as is expected of someone engaging another in conversation. Locking eyes with another person is a sensation that makes my skin crawl when I'm not genuinely interested in assessing what I'm looking at. In the forest, prolonged eye contact is often a sign of threat. Why the hell do humans insist that staring deep into another's eyes is polite?

From my periphery, I notice a bookworm inching across the long counter that spans the far wall and I can't help but slide my gaze to it. They're such cute fat little creatures, about the length of my foot and several times more rotund, with pearlescent white flesh and no visible eyes. Best of all, they don't talk. I'd much rather snuggle its chunky silent body than chat with Mr. Folger, but he is the reason I'm here, not cuddly worms.

I pull my gaze back to him as he answers.

"It's pleasant," he says. "And yours?"

"Mine is...also pleasant." Was that enough small talk? My fingertips flutter at my sides, drawing my awareness to my hands. What should my hands even be doing right now? Do I ball them into fists? Hold them straight and loose? Fold them at my waist? I opt for fiddling with the buttons on my waistcoat instead as I blurt out, "I'm ready to give you my answer."

His eyes widen, then he tilts his head to the side. "About what?"

"Your inquiry."

He shakes his head. "I'm...not sure I follow."

Heat fills my cheeks. Did I take the small talk too far? Maybe I was being too subtle after all. "You asked me to join you for drinks. I said I'd think about it and I have. I would be honored to take you up on your offer. I like berry cordial and I'm free this weekend."

A tittering laugh followed by a flash of movement snags my attention, but when I glance at the doorway, it's only Araminta peering at me from around the corner. Thank the All of All she didn't follow me inside.

I turn back to Mr. Folger with a hopeful smile, but the

apology on his face crushes my expectations before he even says a word.

He folds his broadsheets upon his lap. His mouth opens to silence, as if he can't find his words. Finally, he furrows his brow and speaks. "I asked you out for drinks two months ago."

"So you do remember. What a relief. I thought you forgot."

His expression turns apologetic again. "Two months may not seem like a long time to a fae with a lengthy lifespan like yours, but it can be for a human like me. I...I'm already courting someone else. No, to be fully transparent, I'm engaged."

"Engaged." I don't know why I'm so surprised. Courtships progress quickly in seelie society, once two courting people set their minds on marriage. And Brad is right. Two months is too long to wait to answer a man's offer for a date. I should have figured that out on my own. I flap my hands in a dismissive gesture, trying my best to maintain my smile. "That's totally fine. But perhaps you could help me with something else. Would you, by any chance, model for me? Temporarily."

"Model?"

"I need a male model for my illustration commission. If you haven't heard, I'm illustrating the brand-new covers for Edwina Danforth's *Governess in Love* series."

"The, uh, sexy covers?" His complexion turns slightly green as he asks this. At my nod, he shifts uncomfortably in his chair. "Miss...Daphne, I'm afraid I can't do that."

"No?"

"No, because it would be highly improper. My fiancée wouldn't feel comfortable with that, and neither would I. You and I hardly know each other."

"That's why I figured we'd go on a date first, but if you're already taken—"

"If you wanted to go on a date with me, you should have said yes two months ago."

"Well...I wasn't sure I wanted to." The truth is, even though I find Brad aesthetically pleasing, I'm not personally attracted to him. Maybe it's because I don't know him. But isn't that what dating is for? Whatever the case, my stomach turns at the thought of going on dates with people I'm not yet comfortable with.

His expression hardens, and too late I realize I've offended him. "Just because pureblood fae are incapable of lying doesn't mean you should speak so bluntly. Regardless, it's clear neither of us have what the other is looking for."

"Right. You're right. I should...go. I'm going to go. Good day."

I rush out of the break room as fast as I can, resisting my desire to shift into my unseelie form so I can scamper off on four paws. Instead, I find solace by closing the break room door, placing some tangible divide between me and the man who just rejected me. Pressing myself against the wall beside the doorframe, I cover my face in my hands. I only hope no one is looking down this hallway from the editorial floor. I can't bear to face a soul right now. The only thing that could make this worse is if Brad Folger ends his tea break early and finds me out here. As soon as I gather my bearings and regain the strength in my legs, I'm running back to the studio.

Araminta's laughter circles my head. "That was so embarrassing."

I'm about to utter a groan of agreement when a male voice shatters my every thought. "Tell me about it."

Dropping my hands, I turn to find a figure leaning against the wall on the other side of the doorway.

I may have thought the only thing that could make this situation worse was if Brad emerged from the break room, but I was wrong.

This is the worst thing that could happen.

Because the last person I would have wanted to witness my humiliation is Monty Phillips.

"Hello, Daffy Dear," he says with his most annoying grin, one that puts a dimple on full display. I blink, willing for him to disappear, for this all to be some awful hallucination, but his presence only grows more certain. My eyes sweep over him, taking in his navy suit, his loosened cravat, and the open collar of his shirt that reveals the base of his throat. His gray eyes glitter with mischief while his pale blond hair settles in loose messy curls around his face. He leans against the wall with an air of indifference, ankles crossed, one shoulder propped against the door frame. He holds a stack of papers under one arm and flips an unlit cigarillo between his fingers with his free hand—a habit I know well.

For a moment, it feels like nothing has changed. That we're back where we were two years ago, managing The Heartbeats Tour together and forging a bond that felt at least a little like friendship.

My heart stutters and then starts into a stampede, emotions clashing within me. I don't know what to process first. My embarrassment over what he just witnessed? My anger that he has the audacity to stand there so casually, as if we haven't been estranged for almost a year? Or that tiny spark of excitement that leaps at seeing him again?

"What the hell are you doing here?" I snap. I'm surprised at how quickly the words leave my lips. There's no thought. No need to rehearse the right thing to say. Probably because I've never worried about that with Monty.

His dimple deepens as a corner of his mouth lifts higher.

"There's that charming little spitfire I remember. Pray tell, who was that awkward woman in the break room just now?"

I shrink down. "Did you see the whole thing?"

"Every filthy inch."

"Why do you have to put it that way?"

He chuckles. "I've never seen you like that."

I doubt that's entirely true. While I may not have trouble being myself around him, he's witnessed a handful of uncomfortable moments. Maybe they were only uncomfortable for me.

"She was soooo awkward, wasn't she?" Araminta says.

He tilts his head at the sprite. "Who is this? A new hire?"

"A pest," I mutter.

Araminta curtsies in midair. "Lady Araminta of the Shining Waters. I'm Daphne's best friend."

Monty puts a hand to his chest as his eyes lock back on me. "Ouch, I see you've already replaced me, Daffy Dear."

His words set off some dark sharp part of me. The hunter. The killer. The tiny beast with deceptively sharp teeth. It chews up every tangled emotion brewing inside me until only anger remains. I scoff. "Were you ever my friend?"

The hand that has been flipping his cigarillo goes still and his grin falters.

The sight reminds me of a small rodent catching the first glimpse of the shadow in the underbrush. The predator stalking its prey. It emboldens me. "I don't know what kinds of friends you have these days, but mine don't ignore my offer to catch up and then forget about me for a year, only to show up to laugh at me." I fold my arms and turn on my heel, echoing the same cold words he said to me all those months ago. "Nice knowing you, Monty. See you around."

Araminta lets out a low whistle, followed by her tittering laugh. "Wow, she hates you."

A satisfied grin tugs my lips as I stride down the hall. Is

this what it feels like to get the last word in? To be bold and brave and clever? To be—

"Daph."

I'm almost at the end of the hall when Monty's voice roots my feet in place. It's not merely him saying my name that makes me stop. It's his serious tone. The edge of desperation in that single syllable. I'm still halfway in hunter mode, my senses attuned to easy prey. Monty's voice triggers that awareness, urging me to strike the killing blow, but it no longer feels satisfying. Now it only fills me with guilt.

I keep my arms folded protectively over my chest as I turn around.

"I didn't for—" Monty's words are interrupted by the opening of the break room door.

Brad Folger steps into the hall, a startled sound escaping his lips as he finds Monty beside the open door. He recovers from his momentary fright with a look of recognition. "Ah, Mr. Phillips. It's been a while. How do you do?"

Monty's eyes remain locked on mine. "Fuck off, Brad. I didn't forget."

Brad blanches, his gaze swiveling from Monty to me and back again, before he scurries down the hall, shoulders hunched.

"I didn't forget," Monty repeats once Brad is out of sight.

Silence stretches between us, punctuated by the buzz of Araminta's wings. She hovers in the air, gaze volleying back and forth much like Brad's did, but without an ounce of his sheepish self-awareness.

The hunter in me lowers her defenses. "All right."

He takes a step closer, his expression wary. Questioning. I've hardly ever seen him looking anything but confident. A corner of his mouth quirks, but it isn't his usual dashing smirk. This smile is softer. Less sure. "I'm sorry, Daph. I was an asshole the last time we saw each other. Let me make it up to you."

I squeeze my arms tighter, hoping I can hide how much his words soften my heart. "How do you intend to do that?"

He takes his stack of papers out from under his arm and extracts a fountain pen from his jacket pocket. I watch as he leans against the wall, tucking his cigarillo behind his ear and uncapping his pen with his teeth. My lips part involuntarily as my eyes narrow on what I can see of his canines. Why does the sight of them make my heart quicken so pleasantly? He scribbles something on the back of one of his papers, drawing my attention to the flex of his knuckles, the length of his fingers, the ease with which he holds his pen.

Were Monty's hands always so...handlike?

He stops writing and thrusts the paper toward me, snapping me out of my reverie.

I accept the page and assess his messy scrawl. It's an address for somewhere in town.

My gaze lifts to his. "What the hell is this?"

"I overheard what you said. You're looking for a model, right? I have a solution that's far better than anatomy classes or propositioning random coworkers. Go to this address tonight at nine."

I shrink down, hackles raised. "This isn't an orgy, is it?"

"What's an orgy?" Araminta says, landing on my shoulder. "Can I come?"

"Why does everyone expect me to take people to orgies? No, Daph, it's...better than that. Just trust me."

"I'm not going to some unknown address alone."

"Bring a friend."

"I don't..." I can't bring myself to admit I don't have many friends. None that live in town, at least.

Monty tucks his bundle of papers back under his arm and

recaps his pen. Holding my gaze, he steps closer. So close I can almost smell the clean linen of his shirt.

I bristle, expecting him to pat my head the same way he did when we last saw each other.

Instead, he keeps his hands to himself. "I'll see you tonight. We'll catch up, all right?" He doesn't wait for me to answer. He just winks and saunters off.

I frown as I watch him walk away. Even after he's gone, I'm unsure what to make of everything that just happened.

I saw Monty again.

He was…nice to me.

And he has a solution to my model problem?

I stare at the address again, noticing the faint lettering coming from the other side. I turn the paper over and find the title page of a book called *Ask Gladys: How to Play the Game of Love and Win.*

I tilt my head to the side. Isn't *Ask Gladys* a romance column in the *Cedar Hills Gazette*? I know Monty works at the paper now, but I never learned what his position is. Whatever the case, this must explain why he was here.

What exactly has Monty been up to this past year?

A burning desire to uncover the answer takes root in me. I turn the paper back over, studying the address again. Wherever this place is, there might be crowds. Strangers. Socializing. Everything I hate and everything I'm terrible at.

But do I dare miss out on discovering what Monty's supposed solution is? Courage and curiosity fight to overtake the terror inside me. But still…

"I'm not going here alone," I say under my breath.

Araminta flutters from my shoulder to the paper in my hands. "Then I guess it's you and me, bestie."

CHAPTER FOUR

MONTY

Every step that takes me away from Daphne fills me with the most soothing relief. Not because I'm leaving her but because…I did it. I took a step toward mending something I never should have broken. That doesn't mean I want to linger, for I do tend to ruin good things. Might as well leave before I make an ass of myself.

I exit the lobby of Fletcher-Wilson to the streets of downtown Jasper, untucking my cigarillo from behind my ear and placing it between my lips. The late morning sun warms the air to the perfect climate, and I make haste to doff my jacket and roll up my shirtsleeves.

Verbena Street is in the heart of the business district, lined with modest brick offices interspersed with the occasional public house or restaurant, catering to professionals on lunch breaks or out for meetings. The sidewalk bustles with activity from those like me going about their workday. Meanwhile, coaches fill the streets with sounds of horse hooves and wagon wheels on cobblestones. Most everyone is dressed in semi-casual work attire, though there are a few fine suits and top hats in the crowd.

Jasper is primarily a human city, but there are plenty of seelie fae too, noted either by their pointed ears, animal features, or other notable fae characteristics. Fae in their unseelie forms can be elemental, spiritual, or animal in nature, and evidence doesn't always carry over to seelie forms. Many fae show no physical change between the two forms—or can't shift at all—and merely have access to their own unique magic. The hardest to differentiate at a glance, however, are those who were born with both human and fae blood. Human-fae hybrids bear rounded ears and rarely show any outward signs of their fae lineage. They can blend in, lie, and heal slightly faster than a pureblood human. Some can even shift between forms. One can be acquainted with a human-fae hybrid their whole life and never know it, should the other person choose to keep it a secret.

As I move through the crowd, I extract my cylindrical silver igniter—a handy new invention, thanks to Star Court technology—from my waistcoat pocket. I press the wheel that strikes the yellow crystal, creating a spark. Then a flame. I bring the flickering warmth to the end of my cigarillo. With a long drag, I draw in the soothing lavender-flavored herbs that mingle with the fresh Earthen Court air. Every muscle in my body relaxes.

I blow out a breath of smoke, and my mind returns to thoughts of Daphne. A smile spreads over my lips, even as I take my next drag.

So she's an illustrator now, and for Edwina's new book covers. How did that happen? I always knew she liked art, particularly the sexy kind, as I often caught her salivating over the illustrations in Edwina's books. But I had no idea she possessed artistic talent of her own. A pang of regret weighs down my chest, disrupting my sense of calm. It's my fault I've missed out on whatever she's been through over the past year. Even before that, in the months that followed The Heartbeats Tour, I never made much of an effort to see her. In fact, I avoided her.

A purposeful distancing. A habit. A necessity.

I've learned the value in cutting ties with those around me, from friends to enemies and everything in between. My father. My first paramour. My former fiancée. Lovers who cling too tightly. Those who get too close. Those who want more from me than I can give. Those who deserve better than me. Those who hurt me and call it love. Those *I* hurt and call it love.

There was a time, near the end of the tour, when I feared Daphne was becoming one of those people. Someone who wanted too much. Someone who looked at me with an innocent hope that made me painfully aware of the vast discrepancy between the man I am in her eyes and the man I really am. She was the kind of person I wanted to tell all my secrets to—the most dangerous kind of person. Because sharing my secrets would mean breaking a bargain. And breaking bargains means death.

I take another drag of my cigarillo, the Moonpetal working wonders on my nerves. Blowing out a breath, I shake my head. There's something different about Daphne. I feel *better* after having apologized to her. Better after seeing her. Very few people whom I've distanced myself from have sparked such regret. Or such elation upon seeing them again. It was like no time had passed at all.

Small things have changed, of course. She seems more comfortable in her seelie form than she did before, though I can still see the uncertainty in the way she holds her hands, her arms. The slight hunch of her posture. Like she's constantly battling a yearning to be smaller. Apparently she's entered the world of courtship, or has at least tried to. What the hell was that with Brad? Who waits two months to answer a man's request for a date?

There was a slim moment, as I witnessed her awkward interaction, when it struck me that Daphne could be the perfect subject for my case study. I didn't humor that idea long. She may be naive when it comes to courtship, but the thought of coaching her with my advice makes my blood boil and my stomach churn. It just feels...I don't know. Exploitative, or something.

One thing that hasn't changed is how she speaks to me. That wry tone, always ready to lash me, berate me, scold me. She has always been brutally honest with me in a way very few people have ever dared to be. Yet her jabs have always come with a dash of care, a barbed whip meant to bring me to heel and let me know when I'm taking my often-twisted proclivities too far. She tames me in a way that feels like a hug.

I've missed that in my life. Desperately.

Because it's the opposite of how my father has always tried to tame me.

My mood sours a little at the thought of my father, so I take another long drag of my cigarillo. The *Cedar Hills Gazette* is across the street on the next block, and it's about time I started my workday. As I join the pedestrians waiting for a break in coach traffic to cross the street, I catch a dreaded yet familiar sight from the corner of my eye. Two fae males in bowler hats, one with a cane, the other with meaty fists, approach from several feet back, their eyes on me.

"Fucking Friday," I mutter under my breath. "Of course."

Every Friday I have the displeasure of chatting with these unfriendly blokes, neither of whom I know by name.

I cross the street, not bothering to outpace my stalkers.

Instead of heading for my workplace, I slink into the quiet alleyway behind the building. The last thing I want is to invite thugs into the *Gazette*. Not that they're the most intimidating folks, considering one knits scarves in his free time and the other is as skinny as a pole, but they aren't exactly friendly either.

With a deep inhale, I finish my cigarillo and crush the butt under my heel just as the two men slink into the alley. I give them a humorless grin. "What kind of warning is it today? Fists or words?"

"Words, you fucking ingrate," says the one with the cane, a lanky bloke with tufts of red-brown hair that peek from beneath his bowler hat. From his fidgety movements paired with his beady eyes, I'd guess he's a squirrel fae. "Payment's due today."

"You truly don't need to remind me."

"How are you going to pay?" asks the one with meaty hands. This one has no unseelie characteristics to suggest what kind of fae he is, but he's a broad, bulky fellow with a fleshy face and a thick neck that's always hidden beneath a knitted scarf. Today it's a blue scarf patterned with rows of little white daisies.

"The usual way," I say with a sigh.

"Right," says Cane. "You know what to do then."

"I do. I'll be there tonight as fucking usual. So do we really need to do this every week?"

"Boss' orders," says Meathands.

"Well, it's been a pleasure," I say, tone flat, "but I've got places to be. Kindly fuck off, dear gents, and I'll do what I'm supposed to do."

The two give me menacing glowers—which might be unnerving if I hadn't been on the receiving end of them every week for months on end—before skulking off.

Meathands, however, peers back around the corner. "Do

you want to buy a scarf?" he rushes to ask, pointing to the one around his neck. "Eight emerald rounds, special deal for ya."

"For the hundredth time, no."

His face falls, and he curls his lips into a parting snarl. Siegfried Financial must not pay its cronies well, considering one is desperate to launch his handmade scarf business.

I lean against the alley wall and release an aggravated breath. It's been almost three years since I took out a loan from an admittedly unsavory source, and the rising interest has made my weekly payments impossible to maintain for the past year. Had I understood just how long it would take to pay back said loan, I wouldn't have resorted to taking one out in the first place. Yet I didn't have many options. I was newly disinherited without a single emerald chip to my name and asking my father for aid was out of the question. Turns out one needs money to function in the world. I needed fine clothing to get a job, food to survive. I didn't exactly *need* the luxury apartment I leased for a year or a high-spending lifestyle like the one I grew up with, but that's only in retrospect. At the time, opulence was akin to breathing. My idea of a downgrade was another man's picture of perfection.

Regardless of what I wanted to spend my loan on, most reputable lenders weren't keen on handing funds over to a disinherited aristocrat without a guarantor. I was grateful when I came across Siegfried Financial, which only needed collateral.

Not just any kind of collateral, but its specialty of choice.

Secrets.

After being raised amongst the elite, I'd gathered my share of secrets over the years. Who's sleeping with whom, whose business is crumbling, who dabbles in illegal investments, who harbors amusing kinks. I entered the lender's office fully prepared to hand over any number of these minor yet shocking secrets. None would cause direct harm to me or anyone I truly cared about, so they were fair game as far as I was concerned. There was only one secret I kept that could wreck the lives of those I loved, but it was locked behind a bargain. I was magically bound to never tell that secret to anyone. Which meant it was safe.

Or so I thought.

It turned out the goblin in charge of Siegfried Financial could read one's deepest, most closely guarded secret with a single look. I didn't have to say a word or break my bargain. Just like that, my lender had control over the only secret I wanted to keep safe.

So here I am, twenty-some-odd thousand emerald rounds in debt, the original funds from my loan long since spent. I'm stuck with a weekly payment I can't afford, interest that increases at an astounding rate, and only three months left before my lender cancels the remainder of my debt in exchange for spilling my secret. A secret that could destroy my family.

I can't let that happen.

Not for my father's sake. Not even for mine.

It's my sister's reputation I care about. Mother's. Our estate's staff. All the lives that could be thrown into turmoil should this secret get out and drag the Phillips name into scandal.

That's the real reason I need the publishing deal and the six-year contract of employment at the *Gazette*. With proof of long-term employment, I can secure a legitimate loan with a reputable bank. I can use my signing bonus and publishing advance as collateral. I can free myself from this awful loan before my secret gets out.

Curling my fists, I exit the alley and head toward the *Gazette*. All the relief and pleasant feelings from seeing

Daphne evaporated during my chat with Cane and Meathands. Yet the reminder that I'll see her tonight sets the most jagged edges of my nerves at ease. I won't be able to impress my friend as thoroughly as I wish, thanks to the job I have to do tonight, but it's not about me anyway.

It's about Daphne. The problem that I hope I have the solution for.

If I focus on that, I can ignore the fact that this life I've built—this life of my own, regardless of debts—is at risk of getting royally fucked.

CHAPTER FIVE

DAPHNE

Later that night, I return to Fletcher-Wilson, pausing on the sidewalk outside the office. Fletcher-Wilson is closed now, as are most of the other buildings on Verbena Street. There are a few other pedestrians around, along with plenty of coach traffic, but I can't fight the tightness in my shoulders. I rarely go into town at night. Certainly not to mysterious locations alone.

Though...I supposedly won't be alone.

I cast my gaze around, keeping my ears attuned in anticipation of fluttering wings. Araminta said to meet her outside the office at a quarter to nine, and since I don't have any other close friends in town, she's my best option for company. Hopefully I don't regret it.

I step closer to the building, peering through the wide front window that reveals a pitch-black lobby. I'm not too concerned that Araminta has been locked inside. She may look like a pixie and her body and wings may be comprised of paper, but she is, at her barest essence, a book sprite. And since sprites are spiritual creatures, she can probably float through walls if she chooses to.

"Looking for me?"

I bite back a yelp and whirl around. A young woman stands there, towering over me by several inches. She has pointed ears, pale lilac hair arranged in a single long braid, and the most extravagant black gown in a style that hasn't been fashionable for at least a decade. Her sly grin is all that sparks recognition.

I pull my head back. "Araminta?"

"Why are you surprised? I said I'd be here." Her voice retains some of its girlish quality but with a depth it didn't possess in her tiny body.

"I'm surprised because you look like this," I say, gesturing from her head to the hem of her gown.

She titters, which tells me this *is* Araminta. "I'm not going to enjoy a night on the town in my unseelie form. Honestly, Daphne, what a silly concept."

I assess her again, still trying to reconcile the tiny paper sprite with this eccentric beauty who stands before me now. There's no sign of her wings, no parchment lashes. Is this how my friends and acquaintances felt when they first saw me in seelie form? "Why is your hair purple?"

She gives me a confused half smile. "I don't know. Why is your hair black?"

I open my mouth only to snap it shut. I see her point. While I expected her hair to resemble the paper strands she has in her unseelie form, I can't say my hair looks like my pine marten fur either. I'm gray-brown in my unseelie form with a cream throat and underbelly. Even though some fae retain similar features from one form to the other, not all do. Apparently, Araminta and I are the kinds of fae who don't.

I turn my attention to her black dress, scanning her

overly puffed leg-of-mutton sleeves and the ridiculously high neck of her bodice. "You look like an old widow."

"Why, thank you."

"Where did you even get a mourning gown like that?"

She pulls a face like I'm daft. "An old widow, obviously. I would have been naked if I hadn't procured a dress."

I narrow my eyes. "Where did you happen to get a dress from an old widow?"

"I didn't get it from *her*. I got it from her house. She was very dead, so I don't think she minded much."

"You stole a gown. From a dead woman."

"Her will hasn't been read yet. Until then, her things don't belong to anyone."

"I don't think that's how it works. Furthermore, how did you come to know about a newly dead widow and the status of her will?"

"The *Cedar Hills Gazette* obituaries, of course. Such an informative publication." She does a twirl, showing off her voluminous skirts. As she faces me again, she takes a whiff of her sleeve, lashes fluttering. "You know, the clothing of dead people smells almost as good as paper."

"You are positively morbid. Is it too late to cancel my night?"

Ignoring me, Araminta links her arm through mine. "I can't tell you how excited I am to be out on the town with my best friend."

I grumble under my breath as she starts skipping, dragging me along in her wake, and drawing the judging eyes of a dour-looking businessman.

Despite how my cheeks flush, it's oddly refreshing not being the most socially inept person around. At the very least, my current embarrassment distracts me from my anxiety over our unknown destination.

I DOUBLE-CHECK the address on the piece of paper. Then triple-check it for good measure. Yet there it is, the location of Monty's mysterious solution to my model problem. It's a blocky three-story building of crumbling brick nestled in the industrial district not far from Fletcher-Wilson's printing warehouse. The only reason I know we're in the right place is because the crooked sign at the top of the building that reads *Tamisen's Textiles* also bears the address. Yet I know Tamisen's Textiles closed last year after a fire swept through the interior, burning up every scrap of fabric and resulting in the company's bankruptcy. Not to mention the wire fence that surrounds the building's property with warning signs stating it's been condemned. So why the hell are there so many people here?

A crowd gathers before the door as figures enter the building one at a time. Most of the patrons are men, though there are several women amongst them too, many of which are dressed like me in casual slacks and blouses. Not a soul is outfitted in a mourning gown, but Araminta doesn't seem at all concerned that she's overdressed.

"There are so many people here," she says, her eyes alight with wonder as we hover on the sidewalk, neither of us daring to take a step through the gap in the wire fence that will lead us to the building. "Do you think it's an orgy after all? I looked that word up in the dictionary this evening. It sounds fun!"

"No," I say, a note of scolding in my tone. Not for the first time, I think of turning back. Yet my curiosity is too strong. I may be anxious around crowds and strangers, but my fascination with the unknown has always been prominent. It's what drew me to human society in the first place. After the fae won the last human-fae war and united both peoples for the first time in over a thousand years, I got my first look at a human city. It was terrifying. Enormous. All hard lines and clashing noise. Fleshy bodies, strange scents, undetectable dangers all around. But there was something else I discovered, amidst all the grotesque new sights.

Art.

Stunning statues, hand-painted pottery, galleries filled with paintings with gilded frames, each piece capturing a moment in time or a scene only one's imagination could convey.

What a beautiful terror that was to behold.

That terror stuck with me, even after I returned to my village in the unseelie forest. It burrowed deep inside my heart until it transformed into a thrill. A thirst. An unrelenting hunger. I needed to see that art again. To understand it. Like the first time I sought to hunt prey larger than a squirrel, I was invigorated.

I feel some of that now. A need to know what's inside that building. A pull drawing me closer to my source of fear and fascination.

Before I can lose my nerve, I take a step toward the gap in the fence. "Let's go."

We follow a pair of seelie fae with humanoid bodies and mossy hair through the fence and head toward the building until we merge with the back of the crowd. I flutter my fingers at my sides, expelling some of my anxiety. I'm tempted to shrink into my pine marten form, an urge I always get when I'm nervous, and it grows when I spot a pair of raccoons—fae in their unseelie forms—darting between ankles and sneaking toward the front. So badly I want to shift and call after them, *Wait, I'm like you! We're the same! Let's go together.*

But we're not the same, and I'm not going to shift. When I

decided to adopt seelie form full-time, I vowed to stop shrinking when I'm scared.

We reach the front of the crowd, and a fae male greets us from behind a ragged podium perched just before the closed door. So far I've only glimpsed a sliver of dim light during the short intervals when the door opens to allow guests, so I still haven't a clue what lies inside. The buzz of conversation around me hasn't given me any indication either, as most are talking about their workday or other casual topics.

The fae male extends his hand over the podium. I glance from his open palm to his face. He's slightly taller than me and covered entirely with golden-brown fur. His ears are pointed, though in a completely different way from most seelie fae. Instead of a fleshy angled shell, he has elongated fur-covered ovals, shorter than a rabbit's but longer than a mouse's. Like a kangaroo, perhaps? That would explain his broad torso and the bulge of his biceps beneath his shirt. It suddenly occurs to me how much he looks like the male figures I draw. Human-shaped, but quite animal in nature.

If only Edwina wrote about heroes like him, I'd be a stellar artist.

I assess his open hand again—his very human-shaped hand, albeit a hairy one, so maybe I can't draw heroes like him after all—but still don't know what he wants. A handshake? I hesitate before placing my palm in his, then startle as a chuckle escapes his lips.

"Payment," he says. "It's six emerald chips tonight."

I snatch my hand back. Damn it all. Leave it to me to misunderstand such a gesture. I smooth my palms over my waistcoat, seeking which pocket I might have put my chip purse in. Did I even bring it? "I, uh, I wasn't aware this was a paid event. I was invited by someone, and he didn't tell me—"

"You're on the guest list then? What's your name?"

"Oh, uh, it's Daphne."

"Right," he says, nodding at a list upon his podium. "There you are. A special guest indeed. You've even got your own table. Number eight on the second floor. And your friend?"

Araminta flutters her lilac lashes and sinks into a formal curtsy. "Lady Araminta of the Shining Waters."

His mouth quirks sideways. "I don't see a Lady Araminta, but Miss Daphne has a plus-one. Go ahead." He raps his knuckles on the closed door, and it swings open.

I exchange a glance with Araminta, who beams back at me. Before I can think better of it, she ushers me inside the building. The lighting is so dim I almost miss the enormous fae male who stands beside the door, curling horns on each side of his head. "Enjoy your night," he says in a surprisingly sweet tone.

Araminta links her arm through mine like she did on our walk here, and this time I don't mind. Because I need to hold onto something as the narrow hall opens to an enormous space. Chatter and laughter fill the air, along with shouts of "Place your bets here!" from figures holding large rectangular boxes. The scent of sweat, ale, tobacco smoke, and the distinct aroma of year-old cinders invades my nostrils, yet there's no sign of the burned-down textile factory this place once was. Instead of being crowded with machinery, the floor is open save for the bodies mingling animatedly, an air of anticipation sizzling around them.

My shoulders climb high as I fold in on myself, my senses overwhelmed by all the new sights, sounds, and smells. Araminta's arm through mine is all that keeps me from covering my ears.

"Second floor," Araminta says, pointing to the side and dragging me toward a rickety metal staircase. We weave through bodies until we reach a balcony that lines the interior walls of the building. There's a third-floor balcony overhead, and neither this floor nor the one above offers more than a flimsy metal railing to keep its occupants from spilling over the ledge. I give the edge a wide berth, pressing myself close to the safety of the wall as we proceed down the walkway. My pulse increases the further we go and the more people I brush against in my attempt to reach our destination. The kangaroo fae from the entrance said I have a reserved table, but the only tables I see are farther down. Thankfully, that's also where the crowds are thinnest.

My nerves settle somewhat once we reach a faded velvet rope that partitions the table area. I have to give my name to a human female dressed in a black suit before we can pass it. I'm sweating by the time we settle in at table eight, a crooked piece of furniture with a tattered red tablecloth. My pulse begins to calm now that I'm seated, but I'm still struggling to process the sounds, sights, and smells that assault me from every angle.

I pull my attention to my immediate surroundings, seeking a narrower range of view to give me some semblance of comfort. My gaze lands on a glass lamp at the center of the table. It's filled with fluttering orbs of yellow light—fire sprites. As I lift my eyes, I find more flying overhead or filling the enormous glass orb that hangs from the ceiling, providing the only source of illumination. Only now do I realize there's no electricity in this building. Electricity is a relatively modern invention, harnessing the magic of the ley lines that crisscross the isle of Faerwyvae, yet most modern establishments use it. Certainly Tamisen's Textiles does.

Or...did.

Wouldn't the electricity still work despite the fire, since all that burned down was cloth?

Then it hits me. We're in an illegal operation.

The rundown building, wire fence, and lack of event signage should have tipped me off.

I leap up from my chair, sending its legs screeching behind me. "We need to go," I hiss at Araminta.

"What? Why?"

"We might get arrested."

"Oh, how novel!"

"No one is getting arrested." The familiar voice accompanies a gentle hand that lands on my shoulder. I angle my head to find Monty Phillips beside me, his dimpled grin on full display. "I assure you, this is all perfectly legal."

"Yes, well, what exactly is *this*?"

"You'll see." His palm leaves my shoulder, and his other comes forward, bearing what I at first think is a bouquet. Instead, it's a puff of pink candy floss on a stick. With a mocking bow, he extends it to me and adopts a haughty tone. "For you, miss."

I can't help but humor him with a grin. As I accept the confection, he nods toward the railing. "You'll want a closer view. Trust me."

CHAPTER SIX

DAPHNE

Apprehension crawls up my spine as I follow Monty to the metal balustrade. As I reach it, I stare down at the crowded floor. Good thing I'm not afraid of heights, for climbing trees and other scalable objects was my specialty as a pine marten. That doesn't mean I fancy taking a tumble in my seelie form, so I maintain a healthy distance from the ledge, unlike some of the young people at the busier end of the balcony who are perched upon the rail with their legs dangling in midair. At the very center of the floor below is a raised platform. The crowd is dense around it, but the stage is unoccupied. Will this be a performance of sorts? My fascination has grown now that Monty's here, but the cacophony of chatter and laughter continues to assault my senses.

"You haven't tried it yet," Monty says, drawing my attention to where he stands beside me. He leans with his forearms propped on the railing, shirtsleeves rolled to his elbows, his collar open, no cravat or waistcoat. It's strange being this close to him, with our eyes nearly level. I was a tiny mustelid during most of our interactions and got used to viewing him from the ground. Only once have I been so near him while in my seelie form—on one of the last stops of The Heartbeats Tour, when I donned my humanoid body to participate in a charity gala—but I've forgotten how strange it is to look at him head-on.

I've also forgotten his question.

"Pardon?" I say, blinking at him.

An amused grin tugs his lips, and he nods at the pink candy floss clutched in my hand. "Your treat. You haven't tried it yet."

"Oh, right." I tear off a piece of the fluffy confection and bring it to my tongue. It's more flavorful than I expected, blackberry with a hint of something else that warms my stomach…

"Blackberry cordial," Monty says. "It's boozy candy floss."

My eyes widen. Did he remember my favorite drink, even after all this time? He always was thoughtful in that regard, indulging me in my love for sweet liquor even when he himself doesn't imbibe. Then I recall that he witnessed my conversation with Brad Folger today, to whom I relayed my preference for berry cordial. Maybe that's the only reason Monty remembered.

He speaks again. "It's spun with an enchantment that cuts out excess noise. For those with sensitive fae hearing. Or… those who don't like crowds."

Now I'm truly impressed. Both reasons apply to me, though the former is less of an issue in my seelie form. The softness in his grin tells me he was more concerned about the latter, and as the remnants of my sugary bite dissolve fully over my tongue, I begin to feel its magical effects. The clamor around me lowers to a muted hum, not obscured in any way, just less piercing. Tension eases from every muscle, filling me with calm.

"You like it?" Monty's voice remains as clear as before, so the enchantment must not alter sounds in one's immediate proximity.

"I do, but where did you get it? You didn't steal it from a sugar sprite on your way here, did you?"

He gives me a wry look, then points to the far end of the building. "Concessions, Daffy Dear."

"Oh, I want to go!" Araminta leaps between us. "I've always wanted to try booze. Might you be so kind as to loan me a few emerald chips?"

I narrow my eyes to slits. "Are you even old enough to drink? And why the hell would I give you money?"

"I may have freshly emerged from my chrysalis," Araminta says with a huff, "but I was a bookworm for one hundred and twenty-seven years. I'm an adult, thank you very much. And I need money because I don't yet have a job. Today is my societal debut, after all."

"Here," Monty says, handing her a few emerald chips. "Have a blast."

Araminta squeals as she accepts the currency and darts off. I stare after her as she disappears into the crowded end of the balcony, and I'm struck with a pang of worry mixed with envy. How is she so much braver and more self-assured than I am?

"So, you got yourself a bookworm." Monty extracts his cigarillo case from his trouser pocket and places one of the slender joints between his lips. He holds my eyes as he lights it with a cylindrical igniter. My gaze falls to his mouth as he takes a long drag and blows out a smoky breath, the air between us filling with a sweet floral aroma. It's much more pleasant than the cloying tobacco coming from the other patrons.

I realize I'm still staring at his mouth and force my attention back to his eyes. "Infestation at the office. Our bookworms have figured out how to grow wings."

He chuckles. "I had no idea bookworms metamorphosed."

"Neither did we," I say. "We had to bring in a faentologist to consult on where the papery sprites were coming from. We knew bookworms were a type of sprite, so it made sense the paper pixies were book sprites too. Apparently, metamorphosing is a new development for bookworms, and not all of them choose to do so. Thank the All of All."

He laughs again, but the sound is drowned out by a clanging bell, followed by a cheer. The clamor is so alarming that my entire body goes rigid. Belatedly I realize the enchantment has begun to wear off. I stuff another piece of candy in my mouth, just as Monty's hand gently braces my lower back.

He points to the floor, cigarillo between his fingers. "It's starting."

Something about Monty's touch settles my nerves and I look to where he's indicating. A fae male with green skin and a ridiculously tall top hat stands at the center of the stage. If this is about to be a performance, he must be the Master of Ceremonies.

The enchanted confection soothes the harshest edges of sound once more.

The kangaroo fae from the front door steps onto the stage with a glass fishbowl containing folded pieces of paper. The Master of Ceremonies raises a hand above the bowl. Then, with a snap of his fingers, a slip of paper appears in his hand. "Our first combatant," he says, his voice carrying lightly over the now-softened din as he reads what's written on the paper, "is Gabby Stabbington!"

A cheer I can only partially hear erupts in the room and the crowd parts to reveal a broad-shouldered fae female dressed in slacks, a short-sleeved linen shirt, and an apron splattered with what looks like blood.

I glance at Monty. "Her name is Gabby Stabbington?"

"No one uses their real names here. Though you might recognize her from the butcher shop on Sixth and Loam."

I've never been to a butcher on Sixth and Loam, for I prefer the one on Third, since it's closer to home. That does, however, explain the bloody apron. And yet...what am I about to watch? The Master of Ceremonies called her a combatant.

I pluck a fresh piece of candy floss from the fluffy bundle and pop it in my mouth. The announcer places his hand over the bowl again, quieting the crowd once more. With another snap of his fingers, a second slip of paper appears in his palm. "Our second combatant, Marshall Bruisemaker!"

"This is perfect," Monty says. His forearms are propped on the railing again, which means he's no longer bracing my back. I'm not sure why that disappoints me. It's not like I *need* his touch to calm me when I have my tasty confection to do just that. He flashes me a wide grin. "You're going to like him."

I glance back at the stage as a towering man steps upon it, his bare torso rippling with muscles in places I never knew *had* noticeable muscles. His jaw is square, his cheekbones high. He's...

"A sexy storybook hero, yes?" Monty takes the words straight from my mouth. The stage clears of everyone but the two combatants and the clanging bell sounds again. At once, the two figures race toward each other. Gabby Stabbington sends a punch to Marshall Bruisemaker's gut, but he hardly falters, swinging his fist into her ribs.

My mouth falls open. No wonder this is being held in such a suspicious location, on the fringes of the city. I've never heard of mixed-gender boxing matches—which is what I'm guessing this sport is. I've only watched a few friendly matches and always grew bored when there wasn't enough blood. I'd seen more violent entertainment on an average Tuesday in the unseelie forest. But this...

This is something else. I'm about to ask why Monty brought me here when my eyes lock on the male fighter again. My focus settles on the flex of his muscles, the intricate dance of the veins that rope his forearms. The fighters turn, exchanging vicious blows, which gives me another angle to admire.

My head swivels toward Monty, my lips spread in an amused grin. "*This* is the solution to my model problem?"

"Bare-knuckle amateur boxing," he says. "A great way to study anatomy, am I right? It's fantastic entertainment besides. Less rules than a typical boxing arena, save for the obvious: no weapons, no magic, and no fatal blows. But like I said, this is legal. Mostly."

I almost don't catch the last part. "Mostly?"

He takes a final drag from his cigarillo, then leans in close, his chest almost brushing my shoulder. I freeze, my pulse quickening at his sudden proximity, until I realize he's only reaching for the glass tray on the table behind us. He discards the butt of his cigarillo and returns to face the balustrade, oblivious that he gave me a momentary loss of breath. "The organizers behind this operation donate hefty sums to the patrol force, so the officers turn a blind eye."

I stuff another piece of sugary fluff into my mouth. "Do you come here often?"

"Every Friday. What better way to release the stress of the work week?"

My chest warms as I recall that about him—his love for boxing. I can't count the number of times he snuck away during The Heartbeats Tour to catch a match. I also remember him getting into a scuffle or two himself. There was even an incident I was involved in, when Monty confronted a lion fae who'd tried to take advantage of an inebriated Edwina Danforth. I'm still proud of the yelp that bastard made when I bit his ankles.

I face the stage again, just in time to catch a spurt of blood flying from Gabby Stabbington's face as Marshal Bruisemaker's fist collides with her nose. The crowd gasps, and I wonder if she's done for. But she doesn't so much as stumble back. Instead, she swings for his face in return. As he throws up his arms to block her, she pivots and jabs her other fist straight into his gut. Then another. He lowers his arms to retaliate, but her next punch strikes his cheek, sending his head snapping to the side. A final jab to the gut knocks him on his back.

The kangaroo fae hops onto the stage, acting as referee. He leads the crowd in a chant of counting. When Marshall fails to stand by the count of ten, Gabby throws up her fists in victory.

"Good ol' Gabby," Monty says. "Always reeling her opponents in by making them feel like they've got the upper hand. Only to utterly destroy them in a series of incredibly painful blows." He cradles his ribs, as if Marshall's pain is his own.

Applause erupts all around as Marshall slowly eases to his feet and meets Gabby at the center of the ring for a friendly handshake. I frown, watching Marshall and his magnificent muscles climb down from the stage and disappear into the crowd.

I cast a pleading look at Monty. "Wait, that's all?"

"The night is far from over. Matches continue until midnight, but we have a few minutes until they select the fighters for the next bout."

That sparks excitement in my chest, and I bounce on the balls of my feet, gobbling up another piece of blackberry-flavored fluff.

Monty chuckles. "I'm glad you're enjoying yourself. Does that mean I'm right? Will this help with your illustration work?"

My excitement dims a little. Even though I found a lot to admire about Marshall's physique, I'm not sure I'll be able to recreate it from memory once I'm at my canvas again. Still, I must admit this is the closest I've gotten to studying a male body in quite some time. And not just any body. Marshall is a perfect example of one of Edwina's heroes.

But is that enough to improve my skill?

"I hope so," I say.

"How did you end up illustrating book covers for Edwina, anyway?"

My cheeks flush. "She found my secret sketchbook."

"You had a secret sketchbook? Was it smutty?"

My cheeks heat. "Yeah."

"And you never showed me?" He shifts, leaning his side against the balustrade so he can face me.

Like this morning, I get that strange sensation that nothing has changed. That we're right back to the easy banter we had two years ago. "I never showed anyone. And she only saw my best sketch. If she saw any of the others…"

With a grimace, I tuck my free hand into my waistcoat pocket and extract the folded-up sketch I placed in there when I went to find Brad Folger. Before I can convince myself not to, I hand it to Monty.

He snorts a laugh as soon as he lays his eyes on it. Then he studies it closer and throws his head back for an even heartier laugh. I don't know if I've seen his eyes crinkle at the corners like that. His cheeks dimple deeper than ever. "This is fucking terrifying," he says, voice rich with mirth.

I snatch the sketch back, but there's only wry humor in my tone when I say, "Now you know why I need a model."

He gestures toward the stage, looking rather proud of

himself. "Marshall was perfect, wasn't he? Did you see those forearms?"

"Oh, I saw them." My eyes unfocus as I picture Marshall as Alexander from *The Governess and the Rake,* the book I'm currently working on illustrating. I imagine him in some of my favorite scenes, the way he hoists his lover, Dolly, onto his desk. The way he pins her arms over her head as he thrusts into her, papers spilling to the ground. "He could pin me down so hard with those."

"Could he, now?"

My cheeks blaze as I realize I said that out loud. That's something I'd say to Edwina, not Monty. Then again...isn't Monty supposed to be my friend? The same way Edwina is? Why should I get so flustered over what I say to *him*?

I fight my urge to shrink down and meet his eyes with feigned confidence. "Yes, he certainly could."

For a moment he simply stares at me, as if seeing me for the first time. I note that one of his palms is clenched around the railing, knuckles white, the veins on the back of his hand on full display. That's the second time I've caught myself admiring his hands. They are very much *not* paws. Come to think of it, Monty's forearms aren't too different from Marshall's...

I tear my eyes away, desperate to change the subject. "How is your new job? And why were you at Fletcher-Wilson with a manuscript for *Ask Gladys*?"

"Well, you might not believe this, but I am—"

The bell sounds again but less piercing this time, thanks to my candy, and the Master of Ceremonies returns to the ring, along with the kangaroo referee and his fishbowl. My excitement returns and I stuff an even bigger mouthful of candy between my lips. This enchanted boozy fluff sure is something. My stomach is warm, my head is light, and the riotous sounds around me are tolerable. Who knew spending an evening out in a crowded, sort-of-illegal venue could be so much fun?

"For our next bout, let's welcome Grave Danger!" the announcer shouts. A slender male with scaly skin and pointed ears steps onto the stage.

Monty curses under his breath. "Damn. He always fights dirty."

"As for his opponent…" The announcer snaps his fingers. Opens his folded paper. "Lucky Lovesbane!"

"What a boring name," I say, peeling an enormous chunk of fluff from my treat.

"Shit," Monty says. "I'm up!"

I frown, unsure what he means by that. I bite into my candy floss as I glance his way, only to find his face hidden behind his shirt.

The shirt he's pulling over his head.

My mouth remains stuck open, blackberry cordial and whipped sugar melting over my tongue as my eyes rove over the expanse of skin displayed before me. I've always known Monty to be tall and I assumed he was slender. Which he is. But he's also…

"Muscles," I say, forgetting the candy floss I was in the process of eating, which now adheres to the front of my lips and dangles over my chin.

Of course, Monty chooses that moment to finish stripping off his shirt and catches me ogling him. Ogling…every inch of his very impressive, very rippling physique. He's somehow lean yet chiseled, all hard angles, dips, and rises. He even has that V-shaped muscular configuration above the low waist of his trousers, something I've only ever read about. I force my gaze to his and find his gray eyes glittering with amusement. His lips quirk at one corner. Then he tosses his shirt onto the table and swings his legs over the railing. I expect him to jump down, but something draws his attention back to me. He shifts to face me from the other side of the balustrade, feet perched on the outer ledge of the balcony.

"You've got something, right here..." His fingertips come to my face. To my lips.

I'm frozen in terror as he plucks the chunk of candy floss I had stuck to me. With his half grin still on his face, he brings the fluff to his mouth. Then pauses.

"Ah, right. Booze." He holds his fingers out to me, the pink fluff between them.

I'm so shocked, so mortified, that I act on instinct alone, leaning in to take the candy from his fingers.

It happens so fast, I can hardly process what I'm doing...

Then my mind catches up with the lips I have wrapped around the tips of Monty's forefinger and thumb. The tongue that sweeps excess sugar off his skin. I pull back at once.

For the love of the All of All, what did I just do? Should I disappear forever? Should I shift into my unseelie form and run away, never to return?

"Root for me, Daffy Dear," he says as if we'd just had the most normal exchange in the world. Then he does the last thing I expect.

He licks his fingertips—the very place my mouth was mere seconds before.

A ball of heat burns low in my belly at the sight.

With that, he releases the railing, steps back, and drops from the balcony.

CHAPTER SEVEN

DAPHNE

My heart crashes in my chest as I watch Monty land in a partial crouch on the floor below. The audience claps as he approaches the ring, and I internally beg him not to turn around and look at me.

For if he did, he'd see the furious tint of red in my cheeks.

I still can't comprehend the fact that I just sucked candy off his fingers. In public. And that he licked my saliva off in turn. It was vulgar. Improper. Something that could get a woman cast out of gentle society, regardless of whether she's human or fae.

But…this isn't gentle society, and I've already accepted that I am not a lady of gentle breeding. A quick glance at those who occupy the tables around me shows not a single judging eye looking my way. Everyone is far more interested in the sport. Now that I'm truly assessing my surroundings, I notice far more scathing sights than what I just did. A human male stands on one of the tables, shaking his hips in a drunken dance, his pint of ale sloshing over the rim of his glass. An elegant human woman wears a silky pink evening gown…that's entirely see-through. A couple kisses passionately against a wall, only half hidden by shadows—wait, is that Araminta? Before I can know for sure, another burst of applause drags my attention back to the center of the room.

Monty climbs upon the stage. His feet are bare, the cuffs of his trousers rolled up to his lower calves. He and his opponent stand at opposite corners of the ring, preparing for their fight. Monty swings out his arms, rolls his shoulders, shuffles his feet. My eyes are locked on his every move, every flex of his muscles. The cords in his neck, the bob of his throat, the curl of his lips…

I lift my gaze slightly to find his eyes are already on mine. He points at me, and damn it all, I can't help but recall licking that very finger. Then his lips move, and though his voice doesn't carry past my candy's enchantment—and perhaps the crowd is too loud regardless—I can read the shape of each word. *Root for me.*

I don't know exactly what rooting for someone entails, but if it means hooting and hollering like those around me, I'd rather eat raw broccoli. Which I despise. But I do want to encourage him. Show my support. So I raise my fist with a quiet and uncertain "Yay?"

He emits a laugh I can't hear.

Then I notice another pair of eyes on me.

His opponent—Grave Danger, I think the announcer referred to him as—swivels around, eyes narrowed as he assesses me. His skin is coated entirely with amber scales, his green eyes bearing slitted pupils, his grin showing off pointed teeth. I'm startled by his attention at first, and I'm tempted to shrink from his sight. But a stronger instinct takes over. My inner hunter, emboldened by the liquor in my belly, curls my lips in a snarl as I stare down my nose at him like he's nothing more than a field mouse. Holding his gaze, I tear off another bite of candy floss.

He turns back around and appears to shout something at Monty. Monty visibly stiffens, expression darkening as he flexes his fingers. Balls them into fists.

The bell rings again, and the two fighters step out from their corners. Where the previous combatants immediately swung for each other, Monty and his opponent start slow, assessing as they circle each other. They exchange a few experimental blows that are dodged with ease. Even without knowing much about this sport, I can tell they're merely testing each other. Sizing up the competition.

Finally, Monty lunges forward and swings for his opponent's ribs. Grave Danger returns the punch, and the two practically fly at each other, punching, blocking, dodging, their moves so quick I can hardly follow them. The previous match was raw and brutal, but this one is more like a dance. Perhaps the two fighters are simply matched in skill and speed. Though the longer I watch, the more I come to understand they each possess their own style.

Grave Danger moves in sharp, sudden bursts, normally in straight punches or quick jabs to the face or neck. He strikes with ferocity and speed, his dodge as fast as his attack. That paired with the amber scales coating his skin tells me he must be some kind of serpentine fae.

Yet where Grave Danger punches faster and more frequently, Monty's throws are harder, more decisive. I drink in the sight of my friend, the way his shoulder blades glide beneath his skin with every punch, the way his abdomen contracts. My heart stutters with every blow Grave Danger lands on him, but I feel something else entirely when Monty throws a punch. When his knuckles split after a vicious jab to his opponent's jaw.

It's the thrill.

The same one I felt when I saw my first human city. The first time I saw the marvels within an art gallery. Or when I stood outside this building, eager to discover what it contained. Or when I prowled the forest in my unseelie form, stalking unwitting rodents and small birds.

I grip the railing and lean partially over it, no longer caring about the ledge or the dangers of falling in my seelie form. I'm too drawn in to what I'm watching to worry about that. All I want is the closest look I can manage.

Because this violence…

It's beautiful.

A work of art. A canvas awash with the muted hues of the crowd, flecked with crimson blood, highlighted with golden illumination from the sprites that glow overhead. At the center of this masterpiece is Monty. He's amazing. The way he moves. The way he strikes. The sweat that coats his skin. The blood on his knuckles.

His hands are more than handlike.

They are godly, fierce, and everything inside me burns to draw them.

The bell sounds, and the fighters break away, darting back to their respective corners. My stomach drops with disappointment until I realize they're only taking a break. Still, I could hiss in my impatience, but at least I can take this time to study Monty's form without Grave Danger obscuring my view. His chest heaves as he downs a glass of clear liquid. My lips part as I watch his throat bob with every swallow. Rivulets escape the corners of his lips, mingling with the sweat that paints his jaw, his neck, his impressive pectorals. Monty hands the empty glass to someone beside the stage, then rolls his neck and swings his arms. When he catches my gaze, he offers me a nod, but he's less flippant than he was earlier. There's a serious look on his face, a hardness in the line of his jaw.

The bell rings again, and the fighters return to the center of the ring, attacking each other at once. The break seems to have given them renewed vigor as they whip into a frenzy of punches, blocks, and dodges, neither gaining the upper hand nor backing down.

This goes on for three more rounds. By the fourth round, both fighters are visibly losing stamina. Their moves are slower, heavier, though they continue to be matched in damage, both in what they take and what they receive.

At one point, they exchange blows to the ribs that result in a clinch, both staggering to maintain their defense. Monty's expression is intense yet weary around the edges while he throws another punch to his opponent's ribs. Grave Danger's teeth are bared, eyes narrowed, a snake cornered, yet he keeps Monty locked in the clinch.

The fae male's gaze flicks up, flashing toward me for the briefest moment. Then his lipless mouth pulls wide and he hisses words I can't hear. Grave Danger releases the clinch and darts back, but Monty roots himself in place, gaze murderous. I don't know what the male said to him—

The next thing I know, Monty lunges forward, fingers wrapped around Grave Danger's throat. The fae does nothing to fight Monty off, even as his fingers wrap tighter.

Then the referee charges into the ring, shoving Monty back. Monty releases his opponent at once, just as the Master of Ceremonies steps onto the stage to shout, "Disqualified!"

Monty whirls around, hands on his hips as his lips form the word *fuck*. His disappointment is palpable enough to feel to my core. It isn't hard to guess choking isn't allowed. Monty would have known that. So what did Grave Danger say to upset him?

Monty's gaze lifts to mine, and he gives me an apologetic half smile that doesn't reach his eyes.

Behind him, the referee raises Grave Danger's hand to

show him the victor, but in a flash of motion, the fae shrugs out of the kangaroo fae's grasp and takes a step toward Monty. Then, pivoting back on one leg, he lifts his knee…

My eyes go wide, my heart leaping into my throat. I shout Monty's name in warning. He shifts to the side—

Just as Grave Danger extends his leg in a sharp upward kick that strikes Monty on the jaw.

He lands hard on his back.

CHAPTER EIGHT

MONTY

There are few better ways to wake up than in the arms of a beautiful woman. Or, in my case, the lap, which I only surmise due to the telltale silhouette of breasts that hover above my face. Clothed breasts, unfortunately, which tells me I'm not regaining consciousness in the middle of a particular kind of good time. Then again, it's been a couple of years since I've last had *that* kind of good time, so what do I know?

That's when a pair of dark eyes peer over those clothed mounds and pain erupts in my jaw.

I blink through my hazy vision until Daphne's face becomes clear. When I see the faded green upholstery behind her, I recognize it as belonging to the settee in the club's makeshift recovery room. A few glass orbs filled with fire sprites dangle from the ceiling, casting the dreary walls of peeling paint and partially singed wallpaper in a green glow. These particular fire sprites are known for their healing energies, as are the clusters of shelflike mushrooms that grow in the corners of the room.

My memories sharpen, reminding me of where I am and why I'm here. The match. My disqualification. The prohibited kick that knocked me out.

Daphne's furrowed brow smooths with relief and she heaves a heavy sigh. "Thank the All of All you're not dead."

I shift my head in a weak attempt to rise but think better of it when my vision starts spinning. "I expected tears, Daffy Dear," I say, my voice coming out weaker than I intend.

"What?"

"Tears. You once told me you'd cry if I died."

She pulls her chin back, a perplexed look on her face. Then her eyes widen. "Are you talking about the time on the tour when I said I'd weep over your remains? That's different."

"How so?"

"The subject of your demise began with me stating I'd pay to see you get struck down by lightning. Then I said I'd laugh if you got hit by a train."

I release a halfhearted chuckle that sends a spear of pain through my jaw. "Ah, right. Only then would you weep over my remains."

"Only then," she echoes. "Seriously, though, are you all right? Are you...concussed, or whatever that horrible thing is that happens to human brains?"

"I'm not concussed," I say, though maybe I am. I've been concussed before, during one of the first boxing matches I participated in, long before I'd developed any skill in the sport. Even if I am, she need not concern herself too much. I feel fine now and heal relatively quickly, with or without the aid of the green sprites or the medicinal mushrooms in the room. But I don't tell that to Daphne. "How long was I out?"

"A minute or two maybe? The referee and Master of

Ceremonies dragged your pathetic corpse in here, and I rushed down to see if you were all right."

I give her a coy look. "And you decided to offer me your lovely thighs as a pillow?"

She narrows her eyes to a glare and pokes me hard in the arm. "I sat next to you, that's all. You're the one who reached for me and wormed your way onto my lap."

The blood drains from my face. I don't recall doing that. Thank fuck it was Daphne beside me and not Grave Danger. Speaking of...

"Did that asshole get disqualified too?"

"Yes," she says through her teeth, poking me in the arm again—my bicep this time. "What the hell did you say to him that made him want to kick you in the head? And why did you choke him?"

"What did *I* say? Me? He's the one who..." I trail off, not wanting to admit the truth.

But Daphne can read it on my face. Her glare softens. "Then...what did *he* say?" She lowers her voice. "Was it my fault?"

I angle my head in her lap to pin her with a serious look. "Why the hell would you think it's your fault?"

Her lips pull into a grimace. "I sort of...snarled at him."

I purse my lips to hide my grin. "Did you now?"

"I did. He looked at me and I just...snarled. Teeth and all."

Why am I so flattered by that? "It's not your fault." If I relayed the vile words my opponent spat at me, she *would* think it's her fault, but it isn't. It's mine. I knew Grave Danger was goading me. That's what he does when he's in the ring. He riles up his opponent and makes them sloppy.

But I don't get sloppy.

I get bloody angry.

At least I did this time. His words have never gotten to me during any of our previous matches because I've never given him the right fuel. All he's had at his disposal before are petty jibes at my past, calling me *rich boy*, ridiculing me for being cast out of the aristocracy, disinherited by my father, fired from almost every job I've had.

Fucking laughable. Even more so because everyone knows Grave Danger is a rich boy too. A menace to the aristocracy I was ousted from.

Then tonight…

Tonight, I unwittingly gave him the right kind of fuel. Tonight, I gave him Daphne.

Is she your girl? No? Mind if I fuck her senseless after our fight?

Rage boils my blood at the memory, and that was only the beginning. What really set me off was what he said last.

She looks a little feral. Bet she likes it rough. How rough do you think she'd take it? A little teeth? A little blood? Some light choking—

All I could think was to silence him. Destroy every part of him that could form another word about her.

My only consolation is that perhaps my disqualification was all part of the plan. Not *my* plan, but my moneylender's. Siegfried Financial has a heavy hand in fixed boxing matches, which is how I make my weekly payments—the ones I can no longer afford to pay on my own, thanks to the overwhelming interest that continues to rise. Each Friday I enter the roster of fighters, get called to fight a mystery opponent, and lose before the final round. Sometimes I receive instructions on which round to lose during, and on rare occasions, I'm even ordered to win. Tonight, I received no demand to get disqualified, only to lose.

If I fucked up this week's payment, I'll receive a penalty: the date on which my lender plans to reveal my secret will be moved up one week earlier. That's my penalty whenever I miss a payment.

"Monty." Daphne pokes me in the bicep again. Once. Twice. "Are you all right? Are you sure you're not dying?"

Her voice mellows my distress. I heave a sigh and close my eyes. "I'm fine."

"Do you want to put this on?" She drops what I assume is my shirt onto my torso. I clasp it to my chest without making any move to dress. "Your shoes are here too. They're on the floor."

"Thanks, Daph. Just give me a moment."

We settle into silence, though after a few long moments, I feel another poke to my arm. And another. Then she lays her hand flat over my bicep...and squeezes. The softness of her palm mixed with the firmness of her grip and the fact that I'm lying in her lap...

My heart stutters and my eyes fly open. I catch her staring intently at where she's groping me. "What are you doing?"

Her eyes whip to mine, and a deep blush infuses her cheeks. She snatches her hand back. "I was...uh...investigating."

Her embarrassment calms that strange hitch in my heartbeat. "Investigating what?"

She pulls her bottom lip between her teeth, giving it an anxious nibble. My eyes lock there, and I realize I've rarely seen her mouth this closely. Not her human mouth, at least. I'm still more familiar with her furry pine marten face than this pretty visage with its dark eyes framed by black lashes, the coral rose tint to her cheeks, the plumpness of her lips.

"Monty," she says, and I watch the way she shapes my name. The way she breathes it. "I need your body."

My heart stutters all over again, taking the breath from my lungs. Her face is suddenly too close, even though she hasn't moved an inch. Her breasts are even closer, and I can't fathom how I sat here with them hovering over me all this time without an ounce of self-awareness until now. Not to mention the fact that I'm still fucking shirtless.

I sit up so fast it sends my vision spinning, and I grip the back of the settee to steady myself. "You…what?"

She angles herself toward me, eyes pleading. "Your body. I'm begging you to let me draw you."

My mind takes several moments to catch up with her words. That's what she meant? I can't tell if I'm relieved or disappointed.

What the fuck am I talking about?

Of course I'm relieved. Daphne and I can't go down that…other road. I can't go down that road with anyone. I only managed to get myself disinherited by convincing my father I'd never marry or even court someone publicly. And while I've engaged in the occasional bout of casual sex, Daphne is not a candidate for such acts. Because she's my friend. She deserves better. Besides, I've lost interest in dalliances the last couple of years. No matter how I try to make it clear that's all I'm emotionally available for, I still end up breaking hearts when I fail to want more from my partners. It really takes the pleasure out of fucking.

I run a hand over my face, wincing at the sharp ache in my jaw. At least the pain manages to shoot some sense into me and allows me to regain my composure. Adopting a casual demeanor, I pull my shirt over my head and begin rolling my sleeves up to my elbows. Her eyes follow my every move, locked onto my forearms. "You want to… draw me?"

"I need a model for my covers."

"Which is why I invited you to tonight's match."

"But drawing from memory only works so well. I draw best when I have a live subject."

I finish arranging my sleeves and settle against the far end of the settee, throwing my arm over the back of it. My heart continues to pound slightly faster than normal, though I do my best to pretend no such thing is happening inside my body. "Who do you use for your female models?"

She shrinks down a little, a shy smile curving her lips. "Me."

And now I wish I never asked because all I can see in my mind's eye is the sketch she showed me earlier. The one with the terrifying fleshy weasel-man, yes, but more pressingly, the sexy female in his arms. The one with half her clothing torn off, head thrown back in titillated rapture. My inner perverted asshole rears his ugly head and wonders if *that's* what she looks like half dressed. When she's drowning in the throes of passion.

I grip the back of the settee so hard I fear I might break the damn thing. This is dangerous. Really fucking dangerous.

I'm struck with a familiar panicked instinct. A need to pull away in every shape and form. To place several more feet of space between us. To say something cold and cutting to drive an emotional wedge alongside the physical one. Then, finally, to spread time between us and keep myself away from her.

It's what I've always done when people get too close.

It's what I've done to her several times already, to varying degrees, until the day I took it too far.

Nice knowing you, Daffy Dear.

I've replayed that farewell again and again since the day it happened, and I've regretted it every time. I can't repeat that mistake. I can't hurt her. Or maybe it's myself I can't hurt. Maybe I'm being selfish in wanting to revisit our friendship. To maintain a relationship I can only participate in so far. Not too deep. Not too honest. Just enough to satisfy the piece of me that's felt so fucking empty since The Heartbeats Tour.

She brings both legs underneath her and faces me fully on

the settee, hands clasped in a gesture of desperate pleading. "Please?"

My mind is busy erecting mental walls, but the echo of that single word halts their frantic construction.

"This commission is important to me. I…I need it." Her throat bobs. "Will you help me?"

Was Daphne always so persuasive? Did she always have the ability to strip me of all my good senses and instill a desperation to say anything—do anything—to keep such a sad look off her face?

Yet there is a sly and calculating beast within that reminds me this is still a dangerous situation. I can't give in completely. Not without some sort of safeguard.

And I know just the thing.

It gives me no satisfaction to consider this option, and I already rejected the idea once today. Yet, with cold resignation, I realize how necessary it is. We need the right kind of boundary between us, and I need a solid lead in securing the long-term employment and signing bonus my boss offered. I must pay off my debt with a legitimate loan and free myself from my lender. And I only have three months left to do it.

It takes all my restraint to speak with control. To force a taunting grin to my lips and pretend my every word isn't contrived. "You need help with your career? It just so happens I do as well."

"You do? Does it have to do with why you were at Fletcher-Wilson this morning?"

"It does indeed. You need a model. I need someone who's a disaster at dating."

Her eyes narrow. "What exactly are you implying?"

"Be my feral little muse, Daffy Dear, and I'll be yours."

CHAPTER NINE

DAPHNE

No matter how long I stare at Monty, I can't make sense of his words. "Be your muse for what? And what do you mean by *disaster at dating*? I…I'm…"

"You can't finish that sentence without lying, can you? Oh, the woes of being pureblood fae. Such an inconvenience that you must tell the truth all the time, isn't it?"

I level a hard stare at him. "I know the rules of courtship."

"Brad Folger would say otherwise." When I open my mouth to argue, he speaks again. "Do you want my body or not? I won't give it away for free."

My gaze sweeps over his form. Even though he's donned his shirt again, I can't get the sight of him fighting out of my mind. A dance of muscle and sinew. A portrait of beauty and violence. I heave a resigned sigh. "Yes, but I'm not agreeing until you explain—"

"There you are." Araminta's voice accompanies a rush of sound, courtesy of the now-open door. The roar of shouts and cheers tells me another match has started, and the racket has my hackles raised until Araminta closes the door behind her. I left the rest of my candy floss at my table and its effects have worn off.

Araminta flounces toward us, the black ruffles of her mourning gown bouncing with every step. And she's not alone. She's latched onto the arm of a young human male—in his early twenties, perhaps—who greets Monty and me with a bashful smile. Now that I see the pair together, I'm sure they're the couple I spotted kissing in the shadows before Monty's match.

"I've been looking for you everywhere," Araminta says. Her black bonnet hangs down her back, and loose wisps of her lilac hair have come free of her braid to flutter around her face.

I scoff. "You're the one who ran off, never to return. I thought you were only getting candy floss."

Araminta grins. "Well, I did, but I wanted to try ale too. So David helped me out and bought me a glass. Now we're in love and I'm spending the night with him."

"You're in love." I nearly choke on the words, my eyes volleying between the two figures who stand before us. "With David. A man you just met."

Araminta beams.

I shift my full attention to her partner. "And what do you have to say about this, David?"

The young man hinges at the waist in an overly formal bow. "I'm fond of your daughter, ma'am. I hereby make a binding vow to take good care of her tonight and treat her with the utmost respect. I'll have her home first thing in the morning."

My face flushes with a shock of heat. "Daughter… what? No."

Monty snorts a laugh, and I cut him a glare.

David pales as I turn my attention back to him, which tells me my expression must be murderous. I can't believe he thinks I'm Araminta's mother. In his defense, it is often impossible to determine the ages of pureblood fae, and with over three hundred years of life behind me, I am *technically* old enough to be her parent. Yet I'm happy to say I've not once had a litter of kits, despite the many mating seasons I participated in as a pine marten. I'm about to say as much, but something tells me this is one of those times where I should *not* admit what's on my mind.

"I know you were looking forward to spending more of the evening with your best friend," Araminta says. At first I think she means Monty until I realize she's referring to herself. For the love of the All of All, this creature is truly delusional. If she can state such falsehoods without a single repercussion from the fae magic that keeps us from lying, she must believe every word she says. "I'll stay at your place another time."

"I never once invited you to my place," I say.

She ignores me and bats her lashes at Monty. "You'll walk her safely home, won't you?"

I meet his eyes, finding hesitation in them. In all of him, written in the tight line of his shoulders, his jaw. Then he looses a breath that dissipates every sign of tension, making me wonder if I imagined it. "Of course I'll walk her home. There's no way in hell I'm letting her stroll the streets of Jasper alone this late at night."

"It's settled then." Araminta squeals and hugs David's arm tighter. They're already halfway out the door when she gives me a parting wave. "See you at work Monday!"

The door slams, and only then do I notice the tightness in my chest. The way my hands ball into fists as I resist the urge to run after them and give David a proper warning. I don't know why I care. Araminta isn't a child and can do whatever she pleases. Furthermore, didn't I consider eating that horrid little sprite this morning? But still. I've always had a weakness for worrying over the people who annoy me most.

Case in point being the man beside me.

I glance at him sidelong.

"They grow up so fast, don't they?" He chuckles. "Come. I'll walk you home."

I rise from the settee, arms crossed. "Fine, but you're telling me all about this muse business."

"You're Gladys?" My shocked tone echoes through the silent streets as we make our way from the industrial district toward the heart of the city. I slap my hand over my mouth, glad there aren't any residences nearby with slumbering souls to wake. I lower my voice. "You're Gladys? As in *Ask Gladys*? As in 'Fifteen Steps to Fantastic Fellatio'?"

Monty's lips pull into a smug grin. "You've read my column."

"Let me get this straight. You give love and sex advice to women. As a man."

He shrugs. "Who better to write about fantastic fellatio than the one receiving it?"

My pulse rackets at the influx of images invading my mind, of Monty sprawled on his back, those gorgeous muscles on full display, his lover between his legs, tongue working over the length of his cock—

I force the pictures from my mind.

Though I kind of want to draw them when I get home...

"Scum," I mutter, and I'm not entirely sure which of us I'm speaking to.

"What's that?" Monty leans close, bumping his shoulder

into mine, expression taunting. "I believe the word you meant was *genius*. Or maybe *generous*. I seem to recall you needing a favor from me, after all. Shouldn't you be kinder?"

"I seem to recall you proposing an equal exchange, so I'd hardly call that a favor. Now explain what this is all about."

He straightens and takes a step away from me, returning to a proper distance. It's times like these I remember Monty is highborn. His parents are two of the most respected humans on the isle. His father is Lord Phillips, the Human Representative of the Earthen Court, and his mother is Lady Phillips. I don't know much about Lady Phillips, but Lord Phillips is rather famous, considering he's one of the eleven Human Representatives—the only governing position a human can have in Faerwyvae. It's strange to think of Monty as his son, yet every now and then I glimpse the part of him that was raised in refinement. This is a man who knows what society expects of him. When he breaks the rules, it's deliberate.

When I do, it's an accidental bloodbath.

"Now that you know I'm Gladys," Monty says, "you may have surmised I'm writing a book."

"Yes, you wrote the address to the club on the back of your title page."

"Are you impressed?"

"That you own a fountain pen? Or that you know how to use it? Believe it or not, I always knew you were literate."

He gives a good-humored roll of his eyes. "No, that I've written an entire book. Well, to be more precise, it's a compilation of my best courtship advice I've written for the *Ask Gladys* column, bound in a single volume. I've added anecdotes regarding how to apply said advice to similar scenarios my readers might be experiencing. It's brilliant as it stands, truly, but Mr. Fletcher insists I need a case study."

"Which is what you want me to be? What would I have to

do?" We reach the heart of the business district on Verbena Street, just a few blocks from Fletcher-Wilson. My apartment isn't too far from there.

"You would let me coach you through a myriad of the scenarios I've written about," Monty says. "Then you'll act out my advice in applicable situations. If you make a promising match, you'll prove my advice works, which will in turn give my book credibility."

My heart climbs into my throat. "You mean...I'll have to go on dates? With strangers? That sounds humiliating."

"It won't be."

"You don't understand. I'm not good in those situations. Without clear rules—"

"That's what you have me for. I wrote the rules. Remember?"

"So, what, you're going to teach me the rules and send me out on my own?" I twist my fingers at my waist, my hands trembling at the mere thought of what he wants me to do.

He slows his pace and stares down at my twining fingers. His voice softens. "If you're anxious about being alone, we can do it together. I can construct scenarios where it's appropriate that I accompany you. That way I can coach you in real time. It will be like having my book in your purse, something all the single ladies on the isle will someday do. But in your case, I'll be beside you. Furthermore, we can alternate who gets to choose which piece of advice to act out. That way you get plenty of say in what you participate in."

The thought of him being with me eases some of my anxiety. Still, I hate the thought of interacting with strangers. I pull my lips into a grimace. "Couldn't we...you know...act out your advice together?"

"No." He utters the word so fast I almost miss the way my heart sinks.

Then I realize the implications of what I just suggested

and pull up short. "I didn't mean *together* together, because… ew."

"Ew? That's your opinion of me?"

I shrug. He's the one who flirts like it's the official sport of Faerwyvae and who propositioned Edwina for casual sex. Not to mention all his bawdy jokes about having sex with pirates and breasts that look like whipped cream, or whatever it was he teased William about on tour. And then there's his broody anecdotes about how he's not a hero and will never settle down. Does he think I've forgotten? Ew indeed.

"When I said together, I meant as pretend," I say. "And I didn't mean we'd act out things like the 'Fifteen Steps to Fantastic Fellatio'—wait." The blood leaves my face as my terror dawns. "That's not the kind of advice I'm supposed to demonstrate, is it? Not that I mind doing that or consider myself unskilled, but I'd rather you weren't watching—"

"Of fucking course it's not," he says, and I'm surprised at the sharpness of his tone. His jaw is tense, a flush of pink creeping up his neck—something I probably wouldn't be able to see beneath the dim glow of the streetlamps were it not for my excellent nocturnal eyesight. My current senses may not be as keen as they are in my unseelie form, but I retain some of those advantages in this body. He clears his throat, though it seems to take him considerable effort to gather his composure. "You're not…I'm not…"

He runs a hand over his face, wincing like he did earlier once he reaches his jaw, as if he keeps forgetting about his injury and the ever-growing bruise there.

"You are not fellating anyone in front of me, all right?" he manages to say through clenched teeth. "That's not going to fucking happen. This is about courtship for the modern working-class woman, and I promised Mr. Fletcher this case study would be real and appropriate. Moreover, it needs a happy ending."

Relief settles over me, and we proceed walking. "Then why can't you be the test subject?"

"Me?"

"Yes. If the case study needs to be real, then why not chronicle your own courtships and how others have won your heart?"

Some strained emotion crosses his face that almost looks like grief. Then, with a shake of his head, it's gone, replaced with a smirk and a self-deprecating tone. "I will not marry, and my case study needs a dazzling conclusion. A happy ending. What kind of happy ending can I provide, when I'm not marriage material? I'm hardly even courtship material, and I know you'll agree, based on your *ew* assessment of me."

I give him an apologetic wince.

"You, on the other hand..."

"You think *I'm* marriage material?" Maybe I can forgive him for calling me a disaster at dating.

He gives me a pointed look as if to tell me not to get ahead of myself. "With my aid, yes. I'll help you find the right partner to demonstrate my advice with. You know I have no patience for assholes. I'll ensure you only interact with the most respectable of specimens. Besides, I'm something of a matchmaker, remember? If we do this well, you'll be the one who gets a happy ending. You'll have a partner who can serve as your model long-term. Not just a temporary fix like me."

It never occurred to me that Monty would only model for me temporarily, though I never considered him a permanent solution either. I was only thinking of *now*. Of how desperate I am to successfully complete my commission. He has a point, though, doesn't he? What better way to secure a model —a valuable resource for my art—than from the safety of a committed relationship?

And that's not the only benefit I'm positioned to reap. As I've already determined, marriage will solve my most dire problem. The one that will force me to stay in Cypress Hollow if I can't prove I've set down deep and indisputable roots here in Jasper. Lughnasadh is only three months away, which means I need tangible proof by then. My short-term cover commission isn't enough to constitute *strong roots*. Only a promotion to full-time illustrator will. But if I don't get the promotion, marriage is the surest bet.

"You think you can help me find a husband?" I say, a tremor in my voice.

He raises his brows. "Is that what you want?"

"It's what I need. For...reasons." Stupid drunken magical ritual reasons that I'd rather not tell him about yet.

A grin spreads his lips, though I can't help but think it looks a little forced. "If that's what you want, I can make it happen. I'll arm you with the skills to find the perfect match. A man with marriage in mind."

"A quick marriage," I add. "It has to take place before Lughnasadh."

He cocks his head. Even though my glare warns him not to ask, he opens his mouth anyway.

Thankfully, I'm given the perfect distraction.

"Oh, look, we're here," I rush to say. We've reached the corner opposite a street lined with brick row houses. "My apartment is just across the way, so you've done your duty as my escort. Thank you for walking me home. I should really get to bed—"

"Not so fast." Monty's words halt me in place just as I'm about to take a step. "What about our arrangement? Shall we seal our bargain?"

"A bargain?" My breath catches. Fae bargains are not something to enter lightly and breaking them leads to serious consequences for both parties, often death. I'm already suffering the ramifications of the last binding ritual I participated in. Do I dare partake in another? Consequently, as the fae party between us, our bargain will be fueled by *my* magic. That's a big responsibility, if only mentally. "You want our arrangement to be magically binding?"

"Of course. This is a matter of both our careers. Without stakes, why put in effort?" He says this with an easy wink, yet there's a hint of desperation at the corners of his eyes. Or perhaps it's my inner hunter alerting me of prey. Whatever the case, Monty needs this for reasons that might be deeper than he's stated aloud.

Yet the same goes for me, doesn't it?

I need a model, and I could benefit from his courtship lessons, particularly if they work.

If they can land me a husband.

If they can help me sever my permanent ties to my home village.

"Here are my proposed terms," Monty says. "For every courtship lesson you successfully complete using my advice, I will pose as your model for one session. Each lesson or session will last for up to a full day. Our bargain will be deemed fulfilled upon whichever of the following conditions is first met: we exchange a total of four courtship lessons for four painting sessions; we conclude my case study with you demonstrating all of my most important principles; you enter a committed partnership; we reach the thirty-first of July."

I assess each of his conditions, surprised by how thorough he's being. And that our arrangement will only last for three months—until the end of July. That works perfectly with my need for a husband by Lughnasadh on August 1st.

My shoulders tense as I stare down at his hand. I'm still wary about making a formal bargain. But as my gaze wanders up the length of his forearm, taking in its chiseled shape, the veins that rope it, I'm reminded all over again how badly I need to draw this man. Steeling my resolve, I take a deep breath and place my palm fully in his. Just before he can shake my hand, I pull mine back and say, "Only if we reverse the order. For every session *you* model for *me*, I'll perform one of your courtship principles. And we'll start this weekend."

"I didn't know you were such a fierce negotiator."

He also doesn't know I was only granted an extension on my sketch until Monday. I need him to model for me as soon as possible.

"Fine then," he says with a shrug. "I agree to *your* terms and enter this bargain. And you?"

I take a deep breath and place my palm fully against his. "I agree to it as well."

He squeezes my hand in a firm shake. Just like that, it's done. There's no spark of magic. No rush of awe. I sealed a binding bargain without any effort but a few words. It was as easy as buying meat from the butcher.

As we separate our hands, I notice a surprising warmth in my palm, tingling from where our skin touched. It has nothing to do with magic and everything to do with the fact that I touch very few people. And yet, where I normally recoil at unwarranted touch, I don't find Monty's at all unpleasant.

His lips pull into a sly smirk. "Tell me, Daffy Dear, where would you like to paint my half-naked body this weekend?"

Lesson Two

COURTSHIP AND THE ART OF AN UNEXPECTED ATTRACTION

CHAPTER TEN

MONTY

Holding still is not a skill I possess. Perhaps I should have thought of that before I made a binding bargain to pose as a model. Though I suppose I expected a little more time to prepare. I certainly didn't anticipate being told to freeze the moment I stepped into the parlor of Daphne's apartment. Furthermore, I'm fully clothed. This is probably the most surprising, considering the weasel-man on the sketch she showed me was bare-chested.

My muscles twitch with restless energy, even though it's only been five minutes."Can I—"

"Don't even open your mouth," Daphne says, standing on her settee with a sketchbook in hand, a look of pure madness in her eyes. She's dressed in loose gray slacks with a white blouse and suspenders, her short black hair tucked behind her pointed ears. I didn't know what to expect of her living space, but as my eyes wander the interior, I can't imagine any dwelling suiting her better.

Her apartment is located on the third floor in one of many identical row houses on her street. Though there is one marked difference between her apartment and all the rest—the tree growing through the center of it. From the outside, it simply looked like a large tree was growing directly behind the house. But now I find it's growing straight through Daphne's apartment. Its trunk serves as a central pillar, the roof composed of tightly knit branches hung with an eclectic array of lamps. Though the outer walls are brick like I imagine the rest of the apartments are, boasting large windows that let in the morning sunlight, the interior walls are more like partitions. A wall of loosely knit vines here, a drape of ivy there. From where I stand, I can see her kitchen off to one side of the parlor and what I assume is her bedroom on the other.

I drag my gaze back from her bedroom, not daring to stare at her most private quarters.

"There!" She grins down at her sketchbook. "It's finished."

I throw my head back with relief. Thank fuck I can move now. "I'm surprised," I say, shaking out my arms and legs. "That may have been torture, but I expected to pose much longer."

She looks up from her sketchbook, brow arched. "We haven't even begun. That was just practice."

"Practice? For what?"

"I'll show you." She steps from the settee to her tea table and down to the floor in a matter of a few graceful hops. It reminds me of how she moves when she's a pine marten, leaping onto furniture and climbing with ease. I've only seen her acting reserved and self-conscious in her seelie form before, so I must admit I'm pleased to see her in such an energetic mood. She must be more comfortable in this body when she's in the safety of her own home.

She scampers the rest of the way to me and shows me the sketch. It's rough, merely an array of messy marks and hasty shading, yet it's clear what she's drawn.

It's me. My face. A shaft of sunlight falling over the bottom half, marred slightly by the faint bruising that colors my jaw. The contusion healed mostly overnight, but there is still evidence of the kick that knocked me out.

"As soon as you stepped into the parlor," Daphne says, "the light fell over you just right. I had to draw it."

My chest warms as I study the sketch once more. I can't be mad about holding still for so long now, can I? "What are you going to do with this sketch?"

She shrugs. "It's just a practice sketch. I don't do anything with them. I just...do them."

"May I keep it?"

Her eyes turn to mine as if it's only now dawned on her that I'm here. She takes a step away and averts her gaze, a coral tint to her cheeks. "I suppose," she says, tearing the page from her book. Instead of handing it to me, she sets it on the tea table. "But only if you hold still and be a good model for me."

"Don't we already have a bargain in place for that?"

"This," she says, tapping the sketch, "is collateral. Our bargain only stated you'd pose for me, not that you'd pose *well.*"

I infuse my tone with mock excitement. "You mean I can perform my side of the bargain terribly and still fulfill our terms?"

She gives me a withering stare.

"I'm kidding. I can behave and...stand still for a goddamn eternity, if I must. Just tell me what to do."

Daphne directs me to the far end of her parlor, past her

sitting area near one of the bright windows that line the walls. There, her easel is set up before a waist-high bureau. Upon the bureau is a plush pillow draped in a knitted shawl.

She steps up to the pillow-shawl combination and grips it. "Your hands will go here," she says, giving the pillow a squeeze. Then she darts to her easel and turns the canvas to me. Upon it is the woman she showed me in her sketch last night. She gestures toward the blank space beside her. "And you'll stand in this general area. Pretend the pillow is her hips and the shawl is her skirt."

As I approach the pillow, I'm overcome with a sudden wave of embarrassment. I can normally take on professional levels of humiliation, for what do I care for my reputation? Yet with Daphne's hopes pinned upon me, I want to get this right. I want to be of use to her and her art.

My motions are stiff as I get into place. "Like this?" I ask, my voice cracking slightly.

She studies me for a few beats before coming to position me herself. With a few decisive touches, she moves my hands, orders me to splay my fingers, and helps me shift my stance. My pulse quickens at how easily she touches me. She's not an overly affectionate person and only accepts touch from those she knows. Anyone who tried to pet her in her pine marten form risked losing fingers. Yet she moves me around like I'm a prop.

I suppose that's what I am in this moment.

She steps back and gives an approving nod. "Now hold that—wait." Her gaze sweeps over me. "You're still wearing a shirt."

"There it is," I say with an amused grin. I was wondering when the demand to remove my clothes would come. "Don't worry, Daffy Dear. I'll strip with haste."

"Just your shirt," she mutters as she scurries back to her easel.

I step back from the bureau, though I try to keep my previous position at the fore of my mind as I loosen the buttons of my waistcoat and undo my already loose cravat. Once I shrug out of my shirt, I toss my clothing to the side and step back into place. As I grasp the pillow, I cast a questioning glance at Daphne, seeking her guidance—

I nearly choke on my urge to laugh.

Daphne's expression is so comical, so fucking cute, I can't stand it. She's somehow managed to embody the sweet innocence of her pine marten face but with an expression she could only make in seelie form. She stares unabashedly at me from behind her easel, neck craned to get a full look. Her eyes are round, her lips pursed in a tight knot as she attempts to hide her smile.

"Like what you see?" I ask, shifting in place to better get into position.

"You'll do," she says, lips still pursed, and then darts back behind her easel. "If I ignore your bruises. You know, you should be more careful not to damage my merchandise for the duration of our bargain."

"Merchandise," I echo with a chuckle, though my stomach plummets. If she asks me to stay away from the club, I won't be able to grant her wish. A visit from Cane and Meathands this morning confirmed that getting disqualified was not part of the plan, which means I didn't make last week's payment. Subsequently, my secret is set to come out one week earlier—the end of July instead of the beginning of August. I can't miss any more payments, and since I can't afford the ridiculous amount of interest, I have to participate in the fixed matches.

She begins to draw, the sound of graphite on canvas filling the air. Once again, I feel like I'll lose my mind after what can only be several minutes.

"Can we talk while I stand here? I need a distraction. Either that or an abundance of smoke breaks."

"Fine, we can talk," she says, tone begrudging. "I'll do your face last. But don't you dare move anything else."

"As you wish, Daph. Let's talk about my case study, then."

The grumble she makes tells me she'd like to talk about anything else. Too bad for her.

"I told you we could alternate choosing which principle to follow," I say, "so I've brought my manuscript with me for you to read. You can familiarize yourself with the topics we could address."

"Ah, is that what that stack of papers is all about?" She tilts her head at the stack I left on the small table near her parlor door when she told me to freeze upon entering.

"It is, but you don't need to rush to read it. I already know which topic we can start with. It's a foundational principle for everyone seeking a mate. And that is: to find a partner, you must go to where your potential partner is. In other words, socialize. So our first experiment will be a social one."

She releases another displeased grumble.

"Is there anywhere specific you might like to go? If you're looking for a husband, we need to go where you might meet him."

"Mmm. Meat," is all she says.

I scoff. "Don't *mmm meat* me and ignore my question."

Another grumble. "I don't socialize. I don't even know where people go."

"Fair enough. I suppose I'll pick our location. What kind of husband are you looking for?" The question makes my pulse quicken, though maybe it's merely my nerves fraying as I continue to force my body to hold still.

"He must be tall and muscular with a rippling abdomen and excessive sex appeal." She says it in a rush, as if it's rehearsed.

"Is that just what you want in a model?"

"The bare essentials."

"Model work aside, what do *you* want in a husband? Personally?"

"Someone who will marry me by Lughnasadh. And, if I allow myself to be particular, he should have no qualms about me continuing my career after we marry. And I suppose he shouldn't insist on having children for at least a few years, as I intend to enjoy my career thoroughly first."

My heart falls. She has yet to state a single quality that has to do with her wants. Only her needs. Her work. And why the hell does she need to marry someone by Lughnasadh? I state the question out loud.

She glances up from her canvas to meet my eyes. Her lips pull into a grimace. "Well, as it turns out...I'm sort of... engaged."

My breath catches in my throat. It takes me several long moments before I realize how tightly I'm squeezing the pillow. With a slow exhale, I loosen my grip and splay my hands in their proper position. "You're engaged," I say, doing my best to control my voice. Why am I so worked up over this surprising discovery? "To whom?"

She rubs her brow, leaving a smear of graphite on her forehead. "A honey badger named Clyde. It's not a real engagement. Well, it's sort of real. Sort of not. I can get out of it."

"I think I'm going to need a better explanation than that."

Her shoulders slump. She rubs her brow again, darkening the smear on her skin, and returns to her sketch. "Every Lughnasadh I return to visit Cypress Hollow, an unseelie village in Earthen Court's northern forest. I consider it my hometown, as it was the first communal place I lived in. One of the most popular celebrations during Cypress Hollow's Lughnasadh festival is matchmaking. And the primary matchmaking ritual is handfasting. Not the kind of ceremony modern couples act out during their weddings these days but an older version. One that serves as a trial mating—an engagement of sorts—for a year and a day. After said year and a day, during the following year's Lughnasadh festivities, the couple may permanently seal their vows or dissolve them. But they must agree one way or another, or the village elder will make the final choice. And I can't trust Elder Rhisha to take my side because Clyde is her damn nephew. Cypress Hollow has strict rules about mates and commitment, so if I end up mated to him, I'll have to stay in my village with him and give up my life here."

"You don't want that, right?" I ask, and my pulse kicks up in anticipation of her answer. Why does it feel like my heart will crumble if she's impartial to staying in Jasper versus marrying a honey badger?

"Of course not," she says, and my lungs loosen. "I regretted performing the ritual as soon as I awoke the next morning. Especially when I remembered I can't paint as a pine marten."

"You can't?"

She flourishes her free hand. "I need thumbs. I tried my best with paws, but my art was atrocious. Even more so than weasel-man." She says the last part under her breath. "Besides, the residents of Cypress Hollow have no interest in the kinds of paintings I like. They favor functional art or woodworking, not illustrations of scantily clad ladies and gents on the verge of coitus."

"Ah." I chuckle. "I can see how limiting that would be for you."

"Quite so. And my dream to be an illustrator had already taken root by then. The roots were thin, but they were there."

"Then how did this happen? Were you forced into it?" It

takes all my restraint not to strangle the pillow again at the thought of her being coerced.

"I wasn't forced. I was drunk."

"Drunk? I've never known you to be unable to handle your liquor."

"Yes, well, it was your fault," she mutters.

"My fault? How so?"

"Hmm? No talking. Hold still."

My mouth is stuck open. I know I heard her right. She said her inebriated state was my fault. But if this happened last Lughnasadh, we weren't…

The truth strikes me like a blow to the chest. Last Lughnasadh was shortly after I was fired from Fletcher-Wilson.

When I hurt Daphne with my dismissive goodbye.

Could it be that she was so upset by my cold words that she drowned her sorrows in booze and wound up engaged to this Clyde bastard?

"Doesn't the fact that you were drunk negate the bond?" I ask. "You couldn't have been in the right mind to consent."

"This is a matter of magic, not law," she says. "My best bet to dissolve the handfasting is to bring proof that I can no longer fulfill mating vows. I must state, in full truth, that I have strong ties here in Jasper. Hence marriage."

"Aren't your ties already strong enough? You have a job and an apartment."

"I can exit both without much lingering attachment. I must be able to state that my roots in Jasper are strong. I hoped advancing my career would serve that purpose. My next performance review is at the end of July, and Mr. Fletcher may promote me to full-time illustrator. If that ends up happening…" She heaves a wistful sigh. "Then I can say, without an ounce of deception, that my career is important enough to keep me here."

"But you're afraid that won't happen," I say. "Which is why you're considering marriage."

She nods. "Mr. Fletcher didn't promise to promote me, only that he'd consider it based on my performance with this commission. And I can't rely on any hope that Clyde will agree to dissolve our bond of his own accord. He's always been in love with me, and I never gave him the time of day. Until last year."

"Did you...uh..." Why the fuck am I asking this? I shouldn't ask. Don't ask. "Did the two of you...what I mean is, did he take advantage of your inebriation? Physically?"

She gives me a look of pure horror. "You mean did we mate? No. He's like a brother to me. For one reckless moment, he seemed safe, that's all. Someone who would... stay with me. No matter what, even if it could never be romantic on my side."

Another invisible blow strikes my chest. He'd stay with her. Unlike me, who left her in such a curt manner. I swallow the lump in my throat. "You've gotten yourself in a proper pickle, Daph."

"That's what I have you for." She gives me a halfhearted grin. "Now I mean it when I say no talking. It's time for your face."

I groan. Thankfully, she lets me shake out my arms and legs. But when it's time to return to my position, she presents a greater challenge.

"Look at your invisible lover like you want to ravish her."

I frown at the blank space before me, then rework the muscles in my face to form something like a passionate stare.

She snorts a laugh. "You look constipated."

"Daph!" Heat crawls up my neck, though I can't help but laugh too. "This is harder than you think."

"Can't you pretend you're looking at something you desire?"

"I'm not an actor," I say, though I've been a capable pretender in the past when it has served my purposes. When I want someone to dislike me, I act unlikeable. When I want someone to see me as a heartless rake, I give them a heartless rake. Yet, for some reason, when it's just Daphne and me, it's hard to put on any kind of false persona.

"I'll see what I can do." She leaves her easel and scampers into the kitchen. I watch her through the partition of ivy, witnessing as she climbs onto her countertop and kneels before a bowl of fruit. Again, I'm amused at how much of her unseelie behavior she's revealing. "Do you like apples?" she calls out to me.

"They are...adequate, I suppose. As far as fruits go."

She skips into the parlor, a red-gold apple in hand, which she holds in front of my face. "Look at this like you want to ravish it."

I lick my lips, and that's as far as I get before I burst into laughter. "This is ridiculous. How am I supposed to look at an apple desirously?"

Her grin tells me she's greatly enjoying my discomfort. "What else can we use? Something to inspire a serious yet desirous expression." She wanders to a table strewn with loose papers. "Oooh! Want to see my breasts? I'm not sure they're much to look at, but they might do the trick."

Heat floods my face as I struggle to process her question. I'm stammering by the time she returns to me, a piece of paper in hand. I drop my gaze...

And it all makes sense.

My panicked shock shifts into amusement. "*Drawings* of breasts. Not *your* breasts."

Her eyes go wide. "Well, they're my drawings. I didn't mean mine as in *mine*. Though...some of these are mine."

I ignore that last part and study the sketches that crowd nearly every inch of space on the paper. Breasts in all shapes and sizes grace it from every angle. "You're trying to arouse me."

"If it makes you look less constipated, yes."

"They're nice," I say, returning the paper to her, "but it's a little strange trying to get aroused by drawings of breasts in front of my friend while she sketches me."

She nibbles a thumbnail as she stares down at the paper. "Would it help to see real ones? To see mine?"

I'm struck dumb all over again, my mind draining of its faculties.

"Maybe that's not appropriate," she rushes to say. "Nudity is confusing to me. I'm not covering anything in my pine marten form. If I lift my tail, my entire sphincter is on display and no one is offended by it."

I lower my head, relinquishing my pose to brace my hands at the edge of the bureau, stuck between a fit of laughter and my stupor over the subject matter at hand. Good God, Daphne is destroying me. Did she always have such an unfiltered way of speaking?

She continues. "What I mean is, why could Marshall Bruisemaker fight shirtless but Gabby Stabbington couldn't? I understand it's all part of the rules of seelie society...but I don't truly *get* it. It doesn't seem fair."

"Welcome to misogyny and the good old double standard," I manage to say, my head still hanging low, eyes closed as I fight to regain my decorum.

"So you agree? I can see your nipples. They're right in front of me. So why can't you see mine?"

I push away from the bureau, forcing myself to straighten. If we don't change the subject soon, I'm going to lose my composure entirely. "Can we change—"

My gaze locks on her right as she shrugs free of her suspenders and tugs her blouse over her head. I expect to see layers of clothing beneath it. A chemise. A corset. Yet there's none of that. Instead, I find her bare, broad shoulders, her soft abdomen, and a flimsy layer of pale blue silk covering her breasts in two meager triangles lined with lace. This is very much a fae-style undergarment—a bralette, I believe it's called—and not anything I've seen in person.

My heartbeat pulses to a crescendo, a rush of blood pounding through my ears. I need to tear my gaze away from that silk, from the small dip of cleavage above it and the peaked buds of her nipples behind it, but my eyes won't obey.

"This should work, right?" she asks, oblivious to the cacophony my heartbeat is making in the space between us. The way my chest lurches with every beat. She rambles on. "Just pretend they're someone else's. Someone you like."

Her fingers move to the bottom hem of her bralette, ready to tug it upward.

I step forward in a rush, my hand landing firmly on top of hers.

She freezes.

I freeze.

The whole fucking world freezes around us save for the riotous slam of my heart. Her eyes lift to mine, and color flushes her cheeks as if she only now realizes what she was about to do. Meanwhile, I'm too aware of her nearness. My hand on hers, the bottom of my palm skimming the lace hem she was about to lift. My other hand...on her hip. When the fuck did I put it there?

And her face. So close I could count every one of her dark eyelashes. The freckles I never knew she had.

That's when I feel it. The tightening in my trousers. The desire pulsing low in my abdomen. The pleasure and pain that comes from want.

This is dangerous.

"Daphne." My voice comes out in a strained whisper.

"Stop," she says, and my terror is so strong I'd give anything to disappear.

She must feel it. She must know I'm hard right now. Hard for *her*—

"Don't move an inch," she says, a smile curving her lips. "That's it. That's the look. Hold still."

She darts out of my arms and scampers to her easel so fast, I'm left frozen in place. The sound of graphite moving over her canvas mingles with my still-raging pulse.

"Damn you, Monty," she says, her tone light despite her chastisement. "You lost it. Don't worry, I can still picture it. There was an intensity in your eyes that was perfect. Don't move though. The rest of your face is just right."

My breaths come out erratic as I try to calm my nerves and convince my cock to stop straining the front of my trousers. And pretend that Daphne isn't standing there, drawing me from a mere few feet away in that tiny lacy bralette. Pretend I've forgotten the feel of my hand on hers, stilling her as she was about to lift the hem.

Pretend I don't wish—at least a little—that I hadn't stopped her.

CHAPTER ELEVEN

DAPHNE

When I bring my canvas to work on Monday, it's with a light heart and a skip in my step. Not even the sight of it perched beside the other illustrators' work in the studio can break my confidence. This time I know it's ready. I am, however, surprised at how quickly I get my supervisor's approval. The art director barely glances at it before she deems it ready for the painting stage, which makes me wonder if she'd have approved weasel-man after all. But just before she's about to leave the studio, she casts a thoughtful look at my sketch and adds that she's particularly impressed with the hero's lustful expression.

That of course reminds me of what happened to encourage said expression on Monty's face.

My cheeks flush at the memory as I make my way from the studio to the editorial floor. I was so wrapped up in the excitement of my art, the comfort of working in my own home, that I didn't register the weight of our interaction until after he left my apartment Saturday afternoon. Only then did I realize I'd finished my sketch and bid him farewell in nothing but my bralette. No wonder he struggled to fully look at me.

Aside from that one time, that is.

When his hand stilled mine, his chest heaving, eyes heavy.

I'd told him to pretend I was someone else. That my breasts belonged to someone he liked.

He was merely obeying my directive, wasn't he?

I reach my desk and slap my hands to my burning cheeks to distract myself from the strange flutter in my stomach. One that might be embarrassment or...who really knows? Whatever the case, my arrangement with Monty is already proving fruitful.

Though, as I settle into my seat, I can't help wishing Araminta were here. Which is ludicrous because why would I want her verbally tearing apart my perfect sketch? I suppose the challenge of earning even the slightest hint of her praise would feel more fulfilling than my supervisor's too-fast approval.

A flicker of worry settles in my gut. I haven't seen Araminta since the boxing match when she left with that man named David. If he hurt her in any way—

I bite back a yelp as I open my desk drawer to find a small body lying motionless on my stationery. My heart climbs into my throat until I note the slightest flutter of paper wings, the steady rise and fall of the creature's chest.

"There you are," I say, nudging Araminta in the leg with my forefinger. The rhythmic noise of my coworkers going about their own duties keeps my voice from carrying too far. Not that it matters. With the paper pixie infestation growing so rapidly, chatter has increased in tandem. Still, I'd rather not draw much attention to myself, so I keep my voice low.

"Get off my stationery. I have several letters to pen this morning."

Araminta raises her arms in a sleepy stretch and blinks her parchment lashes. "Morning already? I wanted to sleep in longer. I've never been so tired in my life."

An echo of the worry I felt earlier returns. She's normally bright-eyed and ready to annoy me first thing every workday. "Why are you so fatigued? What did you do all weekend?"

She smirks up at me. "Wouldn't you like to know. Let's just say David is a very patient lover with the stamina of a kelpie."

"Ew. I don't need to know that."

"Perhaps if you *did* know—from personal experience—you wouldn't struggle with your sexy art so much."

I lift my chin. "I'll have you know I finished my sketch to perfection."

Her eyes go wide as she sits up straighter. "You did? How? Did you find a husband or murder birds, or whatever it is you were planning on doing?"

"I'll tell you all about it if you get off my damn stationery."

ARAMINTA EATS up my every word as I describe my bargain with Monty. I leave out certain details of our first modeling session, particularly the part where I took off my shirt and forgot about it. My stomach churns as she flies off to study my sketch for herself, but when she returns she only says, "Not bad."

That's quite the endorsement as far as Araminta goes.

"So when is your first sex lesson?" she asks, lying on her

belly at the edge of my desk and kicking her legs against its polished mahogany surface.

Alarm ripples through my chest at her words, nearly causing my pen to slip from my fingers. I cast a glance at my nearest coworkers, but no one seems to have heard her.

"Courtship lesson," I whisper, dipping the golden nib of my pen into my pot of rich black ink. Writing may not be as fulfilling as painting, but I still treat the act with reverence. I return to the sentence I was in the midst of writing, a response to a promising query Fletcher-Wilson received a few weeks back. "Courtship. Not sex."

"But you could use the sex, couldn't you? How long has it been, anyway?"

I purse my lips, refusing to answer. While I enjoy sexual pleasure, and it has been quite some time since I've had a partner, I've yet to find someone I actually *want* to have sex with. Someone who makes me feel desire for *them* and not just the fantastic sensations this seelie body is capable of generating.

"I see you're ignoring my question," Araminta says. "Fine, I'll return to my previous one. When is your first *courtship* lesson?"

I finish penning my sentence. "This Saturday. We're demonstrating what Monty considers his most important principle, which is attending social functions where I can meet marriage material."

"That's hardly novel," Araminta says. "Though for you, I suppose socializing is a shocking concept. Where will you go?"

"He hasn't told me yet." My insides writhe with nerves. "I hate not knowing. I hate even more that I don't know who I'll meet or how I'll meet them. I wish we could orchestrate a chance meeting with a potential partner ahead of time."

Araminta snorts a laugh. "Do you even hear yourself? You

can't orchestrate a *chance encounter*. It's either chance or it's orchestrated."

"I know that," I mutter, lowering my head to finish my correspondence.

"How have you met previous lovers?"

"Work, mostly," I say with a shrug.

Araminta taps her chin with a tiny forefinger, a conspiratorial look on her face. "On second thought, I like your idea."

"What idea?"

She rises to her feet and tiptoes across the edge of my desk, balancing along the woodgrain like it's a tightrope. "Here's the thing. I need to get some of David's attention off of me. He's *so* clingy."

"Didn't you praise his skills as an expert lover?"

"He may be an expert lover but he is far too obsessed with me. He wants me to meet his friends this weekend as if I don't have a plethora of other things I'd rather do."

I arch a brow. "Like what?"

She turns to me with an innocent look. "Like spending time with you, bestie. So, what do you say we help each other? Once you know where your lesson will be held, tell me and I'll orchestrate this meeting with David's friends at the same place. You can practice your courtship lesson with one of these friends so that I don't have to pretend to be interested."

"So devious," I say with a shake of my head. Her proposal doesn't benefit me much, considering I'll still be meeting a stranger. Multiple strangers, if David intends on introducing Araminta to multiple friends. Yet I do feel some comfort in the predictability of our plan. I'll have one less surprise to worry about. I'll have some strategy to ponder ahead of time to ensure I'm armed with relevant small talk.

"What do you say? Is it a great idea?"

"Fine," I say with a sigh. "We'll...help each other."

"Great! How about another favor? Can I live at your place? Now that I know how amazing money is, I need a job and a place to live—"

"No."

Her lips pull into a pout as she sinks down onto my desk, shoulders hunched. "Will you pay me as your assistant, then? We can do a fifty-fifty split of your earnings."

I eye her with a stern look. "If you want a job at Fletcher-Wilson, you'll apply like everyone else and probably start off as an intern."

She wrinkles her nose in distaste. "I think I'd prefer something more glamorous." With that, she flutters off, leaving me to finish my work in peace.

CHAPTER TWELVE

DAPHNE

On Saturday, I arrive at a popular park on the outskirts of town. The vast grassy field is edged with trees before a picturesque backdrop of rolling hills and towering mountains, which makes it an attractive destination for picnicking couples. Today, however, the verdant field has been transformed into something else. Colorful tents have been erected across the lawn. Scents of food stalls and strains of music fill the air.

I hover outside the park's entrance, shoulders hunched, as I watch guests filter onto the grounds. My pulse rackets at the sight of so many people. The sounds. The scents. Monty's letter had informed me that our experiment would take place at the park and that the park would play host to a carnival all weekend, but I can only prepare myself so far. Experiencing a social event is always far more overwhelming than I expect.

At least the spring weather is mild, despite the sun

shining high overhead. A gentle breeze carries fresh mountain air while fluffy white clouds offer abundant shade. That's one consolation to make up for the sweat that prickles my brow, courtesy of my growing anxiety.

I nibble my bottom lip and shift my feet. Do I look strange standing here alone? Is there a better place to wait for Monty? I keep my eyes on the ground, not wanting to stare at everyone who walks past, yet unsure how else I'll know when Monty arrives—

"You wore a dress." I latch onto the sound of his voice, lifting my gaze to find him strolling toward me from the long line of coach traffic on the street. He's dressed in a full suit today, his hands adorned in gloves. His cravat is only loosely tied, but I suppose he wouldn't be Monty if some part of his attire wasn't askew. His pale hair is as roguish and dashing as ever with its messy waves.

My nerves settle with every step he draws closer to me. "Of course I wore a dress. It was your idea, wasn't it? You said to wear the finest day dress I own with fashionable shoes and lace gloves, so I have."

I flick my gloved wrist toward my ensemble. Since I rarely go out aside from work, most of my wardrobe consists of comfortable slacks, billowy blouses, form-fitting waistcoats, and the occasional skirt. Though I do have a dress or two, including the pink day dress I'm wearing now. It's on the plain side, merely linen and lace with pearl buttons down the sleeves and back, but it's appropriate for today's mostly human crowd. I still don't fully grasp human fashion, and my tastes tend to be either too comfortable or too bold with nothing in between. Hence my one purposefully in-between dress.

"I don't recall agreeing to take fashion advice from you in our bargain," I say.

He stops before me, lips quirked in a sideways smile. "Yet you obeyed my every suggestion. Such a good girl."

My stomach takes an unexpected tumble at his teasing praise.

"Count fashion as part of our case study from now on," he says, then holds out his elbow. "You know how to properly walk with a man in public, do you not, Daffy Dear?"

I glower at him but place my hand in the crook of his arm. "It may shock you to hear this, but I once studied etiquette. So, yes, I know how to walk with a man. Though one would think simply walking wouldn't require so much forethought."

"Yes, well, walking is never *just* walking in human society. Especially not for a lady seeking courtship."

"Right," I say with a sigh as Monty guides me into the fray of guests and onto the park grounds. I tense as the bodies around us grow denser and the scents and music grow stronger.

"When did you study etiquette?" Monty asks. It's not a question I want to answer, but at least it distracts me from the sea of stimuli assaulting me. His voice is like a tether to calm, the focal point in a chaotic painting. Something to let my attention rest on in a sea of clashing colors.

"I, uh, attempted to debut in high society ten years ago. It didn't go well."

Monty stares down at me with a furrowed brow, and I can tell he wants to know more.

Before he can ask, I say, "What did you do last night? It was Friday, so did you fight at the club? You didn't damage my merchandise again, did you?" I say the last part with a poke to his arm.

He rolls his eyes. "I fought. I lost. Your *merchandise* is a little worse for wear, but I doubt that will get in the way of our next modeling session."

"Our next session is in color. How can I accurately depict Alexander's skin tone if you're covered in purple splotches? Is that perhaps the real reason you're dressed so nicely, gloves and all?"

"I lost in the first round, so damage was minimal."

I notice he avoided answering my question in full, but as we reach the first carnival attraction, my attention shifts from him to our surroundings—my new focal point in this cacophony. Outside a brightly colored tent stands a towering fae, their skin made of rough bark, their fingers twining branches. Their face is merely a collection of vines that form a lipless mouth and sockets filled with glossy black eyes. Their hair is a mass of moss and leaves.

"Step inside and witness the marvels of fate," the fae says. "Mistress Maythorn can read the lines on your palm as if they were words in a book. Will you be lucky in love? Make a magnitude of money?"

I tighten my grip on Monty's arm, worried the tree fae might scoop me up and usher me inside the tent against my will, but they do no such thing, they only call out to the next cluster of guests. As we proceed, I notice several more tree fae up ahead, either standing outside tents or pushing confection carts. Some are tall and very much treelike as the first fae was, while others are slender and youthful with humanoid bodies and leafy hair. Others are somewhere in between with ancient visages of weathered bark but still somewhat humanoid.

My anxiety fizzles away, shifting into fascination. I glance at Monty. "It's a dryad carnival?"

"Indeed it is. The Wandering Trees Carnival is a famous attraction, and a blessing to any court it travels through. This park and the surrounding vegetation will be lusher than ever after this weekend."

I daresay he's right. Dryads are tree spirits and are known

for encouraging the growth and health of plant life. According to my landlady, my apartment's former tenant was a dryad, which explains the tree growing in the middle of my parlor.

"I've never been to a carnival," I say, "much less a dryad one."

"I thought you'd like it, despite the noise and crowds." He turns a dimpled grin my way. "Even if we fail to introduce you to any romantic prospects, we could at least have fun."

My stomach takes another strange tumble. I didn't expect him to have anything other than his case study in mind when he chose the first location for our lesson. Does he mean to say he chose the carnival for entertainment purposes too? Entertainment to enjoy *with* me?

"Socializing may be the first courtship principle I present in my book," Monty says, "but meeting one's future partner isn't something I can help my readers with. Even when I play matchmaker, I don't set up strangers. I merely notice a spark between two people that they don't notice themselves."

"You're not a matchmaker at all, then," I say with a wry grin. "You're more of a…match-noticer? Spark-finder?"

He gives a good-natured roll of his eyes. "Call it whatever you want. The point is you can't force the spark. Sometimes it can grow from nothing, but you still must test and observe before you can nurture it."

"So that's what we'll be doing today? Mingling with others and seeing if you notice a spark between me and anyone?" I'm reminded of the plan I made with Araminta. We orchestrated a meeting with David's friends; we didn't assess compatibility or this so-called spark.

"No, Daph. The purpose of this principle is to teach my readers to socialize for the sake of joy, not romance. Romance is the goal, yes, but it can't be forced. Socializing is the key to meeting prospective mates, but enjoying it is what makes the process less miserable."

I frown at him. "I feel like I've been tricked. You brought me here not to try and meet prospective partners but to... have fun?" On one hand, that's such a relief. No pressure. No need to force myself to talk to strangers or cultivate a relationship I only want for logical purposes. On the other hand, I don't have an abundance of time to secure a husband. Not if I want guaranteed freedom from the handfasting I'm desperate to get out of.

"Yes, because you represent many of my readers," Monty says. "Working class women who don't utilize the societal freedoms they have, yet wonder how they're supposed to find love. In many ways, they have more freedom than the upper class. They aren't relegated to their family's parlor, waiting for visitors to call upon them, only going out for extravagant social functions or careful outings with a chaperone. That, of course, makes it both more and less difficult to meet a prospective partner. With more social and sexual freedom comes more ambiguity. It isn't always clear whether a suitor has courtship, marriage, or sex in mind, because these topics remain taboo to speak so directly about. Which is where I come in. I know the signs that set a gentleman apart from a rake. But meeting said gentleman or rake is up to chance or destiny or...who knows. It can take time. Which is why it's important to simply enjoy yourself."

With a grumble, I cast my gaze around the colorful tents and stalls. Despite the ever-rising noise and bustle of guests around us, my nerves have settled to a steady hum in my gut, a mild hitch in my lungs. Probably thanks to Monty's familiar presence. Maybe he's right about enjoying myself. This could be fun, like the boxing club ended up being. Maybe I've missed out on similar enjoyment simply out of fear.

"I suppose I can have fun," I mutter.

Monty chuckles and gives the hand I have nestled in the crook of his elbow a consoling pat. "I assure you, socializing for the sake of fun is not as terrible as you think. Besides, there's still a chance you'll meet someone you like today. We'll have plenty of opportunities to mingle with prospective partners."

Just like that, my comfort unravels and anxiety takes its place, writhing like a nest of snakes in my belly. But I have a solution for that. "Do you think there's a carousel?" I say in a rush. "I absolutely must find the carousel."

Monty's eyes narrow the slightest bit, but he escorts me through the crowds until tinny mechanical music reaches my ears, along with the sight of a rotating circular platform set with dozens of intricately carved fae creatures—dragons, puca, kitsune, selkies—painted in pastel colors. The creatures serve as seats for the ride's occupants, bobbing up and down as the platform turns. Mirrors and faceted jewels decorate everything from the central pillar to the pitched roof, making the whole ride glitter beneath the afternoon sunlight. One of the towering types of dryads works a large crank that operates the ride. Off to the side, I glimpse a figure adorned in a plenitude of black ruffles, easy to spot amongst the neutral tones worn by the carnival guests or the bright hues of the rides and tents.

I release a feigned gasp. "Isn't that…Araminta? Oh, let us pay our respects." I make a beeline for her, tugging Monty along with me.

My tall, lilac-haired friend bounces on the balls of her feet as she waves profusely. This is the second time I'm seeing her in seelie form, and she has on an entirely different mourning ensemble. I'd like to ask which deceased widow she stole from this time, but I've already rehearsed what I say next.

"Araminta, how lovely to see you."

"And I you, my dearest best friend," she replies, her tone a tad too benevolent. "Coincidences are such a funny thing, are they not?"

"Funny indeed. Oh, but I see you are with company." I glance briefly at the two human males behind her. One I recognize as David from the boxing club while the other looks to be his same age with dark hair and thick lashes. Both are dressed more casually than Monty—slacks, suspenders, open waistcoats, and tweed caps—and neither appears aware of our ruse. I'm quite relieved to find only one friend with them after all.

"I am with company," Araminta says, "but I would be honored if the two of you would join us. I would love to introduce you. Particularly to David's unattached friend." She gives me a rather inconspicuous wink.

I turn an innocent smile to Monty. "What luck! A male has appeared in the wild and he seems unmarried. Shall we use him for our lesson?"

He faces me fully and speaks in a whisper. "What are you doing? Did you plan this?"

"Maybe I did."

"We're not ready for introductions," he says, pulling me a few steps away from the trio. "There are other topics we need to discuss first."

"Like what?"

"Like…is he even your type? Are you comfortable with his age? He can't be more than two-and-twenty."

I scoff. "You speak like you're so much older than him. What are you, five-and-twenty?"

"Eight-and-twenty."

"You're practically the same age when I'm three centuries older."

"Still…" He glances at Araminta and the two men, a tic

pulsing at the corners of his jaw. Why is he so flustered? Surely this is what he wanted. He lives for matchmaking. He should be pleased we've found a potential specimen to assess my possible *spark* with so soon. "Lesson One was supposed to demonstrate socializing for the sake of fun and that meeting a lover can take time. Instead, you staged a setup."

I arch a brow. "If meeting a mate can take so much time, how were you ever planning on finishing your case study before our bargain expires? You know I need a husband before Lughnasadh."

"I would have introduced you to people I've personally vetted." Monty's eyes dart briefly at the unnamed man beside David, his expression darkening. "*He* is not who I had in mind for you. I would have selected someone better than your…your wicked little co-conspirator has chosen."

Wait.

Could it be…

Is he jealous that Araminta stole his role as matchmaker?

There's something satisfying about the prospect of making him jealous. Not that he's jealous over *me,* only his favorite hobby.

"Does this not still suit Lesson One?" I say. "I never would have agreed to meet Araminta were it not for this specific lesson. Your readers could relate and find encouragement in what I'm doing. Isn't saying yes to outings with friends essential to socializing for the sake of fun? It's not like you need to mention in your book that this meeting was contrived for courtship practice."

He heaves a ragged sigh. "I suppose, but—"

"You wanted to coach me, right?" I hold his gaze and infuse my tone with a hint of taunting. "So coach me. We can move on to your next principle. I'll demonstrate as many as you see fit."

His eyes narrow, that tic still pulsing at his jaw. Cursing

under his breath, he breaks my gaze. "Fine. But remember, this still only counts as one lesson where our bargain is concerned. Each of our lessons or sessions lasts for as long as a day, so you won't get more modeling from me by coercing me into teaching you more than one principle at a time."

"Understood." I purse my lips to hide the satisfied grin that tugs at them. "What's our next lesson, teacher?"

CHAPTER THIRTEEN

MONTY

Hearing Daphne refer to me as *teacher* does something strange to my belly. Strange but pleasant. If only it was pleasant enough to erase how pissed I am at this turn of events. Though why I'm pissed is beyond me. I should be thrilled to have company. I should be celebrating the ease with which we encountered a practice specimen, no matter how contrived it was.

Yet this derails my plans. I was supposed to teach Daphne how to enjoy herself. To ease her into socializing so she can realize there's more to life in seelie society than work. She wants to be an illustrator so badly that she's willing to enter a quick marriage just to cut ties with her home village.

The reminder that she's engaged to a goddamned honey badger—and will be forced to live with him in her hometown if she doesn't find a husband in less than three months—makes me even more pissed. It also gives me the fuel I need to go along with her ruse.

"Lesson Two," I say, keeping my voice low. "Do not chase or waste time on uninterested parties. We'll allow Araminta to make introductions, and I'll maintain my distance to give that boy the opportunity to demonstrate his interest. If he doesn't take it, we extricate ourselves from their party and continue our lesson my way. Agreed?"

"Agreed." Her smile widens, showing her relief in having swayed me to go along with her and Araminta's setup. That's perhaps what pisses me off the most. That Daphne didn't trust me. Maybe I don't deserve her trust after how cold I was to her after The Heartbeats Tour, but I still know her. I understand her. In many ways, she's the same shy yet snarky little creature she was in her unseelie form. In other ways, she's new and bold and different, and not just based on appearances. Doesn't she know that I *see* her? That I would never put her in an uncomfortable position for the sake of my case study?

Then again, maybe I'm the only one who's noticed how easily our friendship has rekindled, despite the lapse of time and the pain I caused.

"Anything else?" she asks, and I realize I'm staring at her. "Or can we join them now?"

My jaw shifts side to side. "If he does show interest, we move on to Lesson Three: a first meeting is merely an interview. Act with curiosity. Listen and assess. Share about yourself for the sake of connection, but don't give everything away. And continue to keep Lesson Two in mind. If he disrespects you, repulses you, or loses interest, we move on. Give him a chance, but only so far as he deserves. We do not waste time on unsuitable options."

"Agreed," she says again, and her studious expression tells me she's truly taking my words to heart.

I force my mouth into a false grin. "Let's go meet this fucking boy-child, shall we?"

My lips threaten to shift into a snarl as we return to the three interlopers. Araminta makes our formal introductions, first between me, Daphne, and David, the man from the boxing club whom I technically was not introduced to at the time.

"It's so lovely to officially meet Ari's parents," he says with a formal bow.

"Not my parents," Araminta snaps.

His face is flushed as he straightens. He leans close to Araminta and whispers, "Who are your parents then?"

"I don't know," she says with a shrug. "They're worms."

Next, she introduces David's friend, Conrad, who pales as I tighten my hand around his during our handshake. Of course his name is Conrad. What an insufferable name. Though I can't say I've ever disliked the name until now.

Daphne greets him with a polite yet casual curtsy, and I'm reminded of what she said earlier about having studied etiquette when she debuted in high society. That's a story I'm desperate to hear, yet the look on her face relayed what a sensitive subject it is.

That sparks a protective fire inside me as I assess Daphne and Conrad's first verbal exchanges. She asks a few rehearsed-sounding questions, which he answers with a lopsided grin. Her posture is tense, her fingers tightly knit at her waist, cheeks burning crimson. My annoyance flares at seeing her blush for Conrad. Why the hell should she blush for him? He should be the one blushing—well, he too is getting a bit pink in the cheeks, especially when he addresses her by her first name.

My gloved fingers curl into fists at the sound of *Daphne* on this stranger's tongue. I make a mental note to convince her to take a surname before our next lesson, just so fuckers like Conrad don't think they're special in being allowed to address her so casually.

The man's gaze suddenly flicks to me. "How are the two of you acquainted? Are you…"

That's when I realize I'm hovering a little too closely for someone who is supposed to give the impression Daphne is unattached.

Daphne pulls her chin back. "Us? You mean me and Monty?"

Conrad's expression flickers with disappointment, probably at hearing her refer to me as Monty and not Mr. Phillips. I'd be lying if I said I wasn't feeling smug about that. Yet I can't let my pride interfere with our lesson.

"We're merely colleagues," I say, forcing a disinterested drawl into my voice. "I'm a columnist at the *Cedar Hills Gazette* while Daphne works at Fletcher-Wilson Publishing. We're currently working on separate projects in a similar field."

"Are you writing an article on the carnival?"

I give him a mirthless grin. "Something like that."

He turns his gaze back to Daphne. "And you? What kind of work brings you to the Wandering Trees Carnival today?"

"I, uh…" Her cheeks flush all over again and she tucks a strand of her dark hair behind a pointed ear. "I'm an editorial assistant. And sometimes I illustrate book covers. With bodies on them. There are so many…bodies around us, aren't there?"

Conrad's grin turns a bit perplexed. He opens his mouth, but Araminta speaks first.

"Shall we play some games?" she says, her arm linked through David's. "I read all about the carnival in the *Gazette* yesterday when I was browsing obituaries, and apparently games are *fun*." She says it with the enthusiasm of someone who doesn't realize most of us already know what carnival games and fun are.

Daphne wrings her gloved hands, the only other person

not acquainted with the subject matter. "I've never played a carnival game."

Conrad's eyes brighten. "Oh, we simply must play."

We.

He said *we*.

That paired with the hope in his eyes as he stares at Daphne tells me one thing.

He's interested.

Fuck.

"Yes," I say, extricating a cigarillo and lighting it. "Let us play."

CONRAD IS absolute shit at carnival games. Either that or he's using his ineptitude to draw Daphne closer. She's maintained a polite distance from him while I've done my best to edge as far from the couple as I dare. Whenever I stray too far, Daphne reels me closer with a panicked glare. So I must stay close enough to appease Daph yet distant enough to allow Conrad to flirt with her. Which means I have to hear every inane word that comes out of his mouth.

"How do you think I should position this?" he asks Daphne. He holds a mock rifle in his hand, one made from thin twining vines. It's a toy modeled after a hunting rifle, and it's tethered to the stall's counter. Behind the stall stand several rows of tall panels, one before each shooting station. Each panel is covered in moss interspersed with bulging green bubbles of varying sizes. The objective of the game is to pop the bubbles with the burst of air that shoots from the toy rifle. The bubbles are so dense that only a direct hit at the center will pop them. For every bubble that pops, a green vine grows vertically from the counter beside the rifle. The smaller targets are worth more and grow the vine faster. It's a group game, and whoever grows their vine to the stall's brightly colored awning first wins.

There is still a minute or so before the game begins, so the players are still settling in. I hover at the far end of the stall, near a pair of open seats, not intending to play.

"Should my hands be here?" Conrad asks. "Or perhaps here?"

I clench my teeth. He's asking her how he should grip his fucking gun. If I had even the slightest inkling the innuendo was intentional, I'd haul him behind the stall and punch him in the dick, but I honestly think he's just that stupid.

Daphne shrugs from the seat beside him. "Maybe like everyone else is doing."

Bless Daffy Dear for her complete ignorance of his poor attempts at flirting. To be fair, up until now, she's been brilliant at discovering the trick to most of the carnival games we've played. Or *they've* played, I should say. I've merely watched Conrad fumble balls, rings, and darts while restraining my desire to show him up. Even David and Araminta are better than he is.

"I've never held a gun before," Conrad says with a boyish grin. "It's rather intimidating."

I roll my eyes and take a long drag of my cigarillo. Of course he hasn't held a fucking gun before. While guns are generally forbidden on the isle, hunting rifles are permitted for temporary use under strict guidelines, and only during scheduled hunts on approved grounds that don't put unseelie fae creatures at risk. It's rare to see even a toy rifle, which gives credence to his lack of familiarity with the weapon.

"Aren't you going to get ready to play?" He casts a questioning glance at the rifle she's yet to pick up.

Daphne wrinkles her nose. "I'll just watch."

"If you're just going to watch, we should team up. Here,

you hold the barrel while I pull the trigger. That way you don't have to do it alone. I know it's strange holding such a large weapon for the first time, but it will be fun if we do it together."

I bristle at his words. First he asks her how he should grip his rifle. Now he's asking her to hold his *large weapon* for him. I flex my fingers, my eyes boring into the side of Conrad's head. *Not one more insidious reference, you cunty bastard.*

With a grumble, Daphne moves closer to Conrad.

"You can sit in my lap if you want—"

And that's the last fucking straw.

I clamp my cigarillo between my lips, reach for the rifle at the empty shooting station before me, swivel, aim, and fire.

The smallest bubble on the mossy panel bursts with a loud pop.

The other players turn startled gazes toward me.

"It's not that fucking hard," I snipe at Conrad.

"You!" shouts the dryad at the far end of the stall. She's one of the youthful types with a humanoid figure and long strands of willowy green hair. With a dark glower, she turns a crank under the counter and a new bubble grows to replace the one I popped. The vine that had begun to grow beside the rifle shrinks down to a bud. "I didn't say you could start yet. Take your seat."

I'm about to tell her I've no intention of playing when Daphne bounds over to me, eyes bright as she stares down at the weapon in my hands. "That actually looks fun!"

"To your stations!" the dryad shouts, signaling the game is about to begin.

With an excited squeal, Daphne scrambles into the open seat next to me and takes up the rifle at her station. I meet Conrad's disappointed stare and grin back at him. I hold his gaze without falter as I finish my cigarillo and extinguish the butt beneath the heel of my shoe. Then I take my seat beside Daphne and lean toward her. "How about a game between just the two of us? Whichever of us loses owes the other a favor."

A vicious boldness curves her lips. "You're on."

The dryad shouts for us to begin just as a jangling, mechanical tune begins to play behind the counter. I swear this carnival utilizes the most ear-shattering music to disrupt players' concentration. Yet I manage to hit three out of my first five targets.

"How are you so good at this?" Daphne says, her voice rich with laughter as it carries over rifle shots and music.

"I've gone hunting before," I say, lining up my next shot and popping one of the larger bubbles. My vine has grown elbow-high already. "It's an aristocratic pastime."

"I've gone hunting before too." She shoots off several rounds, only hitting one target. "I've probably killed more prey than you."

"Yes, well, I've hunted with a rifle."

"This can't be much different. I just need to find my prey's weakness." She shoots again. Again. Her next shot pops another bubble. She lets out a proud squeal. "I get it now! The problem is the looky thing."

"The sight," I amend.

"Whatever it's called, it's inaccurate. I have to aim to the right of where it shows."

I'm sure she's correct. Knowing carnival games are almost always rigged, I haven't bothered using the sight at all. I give her a teasing smirk before I pop my next target. "You may have figured out the trick, but I have a head start."

She ignores me, taking aim with precision and popping her next six targets. Her vine is as high as her shoulder while mine is maybe only a foot taller. She's catching up to me.

Yet I remain calm and pop my next target.

Daphne releases a frustrated growl, then half rises from her seat to prop her knee upon it, elbows on the counter. When her next shot misses, she growls again.

I chuckle at her annoyance, popping another target with ease. "Don't be too hard on yourself when you lose, Daffy Dear. I'll make sure the favor I ask of you isn't too humiliating."

She huffs a laugh. "Don't get too confident. I haven't lost yet." With that, she rises further from her seat, props her foot on it, and hikes the hem of her skirt clear up to her thigh.

Just the sight of her gartered stocking in my periphery is enough to make me miss my next shot.

Meanwhile, she props her elbow on her now-exposed knee, supports the butt of the rifle on her other shoulder, and blasts six small bubbles in a row. Her vine is now equally as tall as mine.

I swallow hard and force my eyes fully on my panel of targets. I successfully pop my next bubble. "That's quite improper, Daph."

"Oh, come on," she says, striking her next two targets. "You've seen my legs before."

"That may be true," I say, keeping my breaths steady as I pop just enough bubbles to keep her vine from outgrowing mine. Only a foot remains until one of us will reach the top. Half my mind remains tangled in what she said. How I've seen her legs before. She's referring to the sexy yellow dress she wore to the gala during The Heartbeats Tour. The one embroidered with pink flowers and a scandalously short hem. That was the first time I saw her in seelie form and nearly died of shock when I first laid eyes on her stockinged legs. "But that was at a gala where half the crowd was dressed as boldly. This is a public carnival in the middle of the day. People are looking."

"I don't think they are," she says, popping three more

targets while I manage to hit only one. "I think you're the only one looking. Are you really so flustered, Monty? Even after I almost showed you my breasts?"

My next shot misses spectacularly, thanks to the hitch in my chest. She lets out an unrestrained cackle. I cut a glare at her. "Daph! We're in fucking public. You can't talk about that."

"Worried about my reputation?" She gives me a mock pout. "Worry about your own after you lose to me."

I can do nothing but stare as she shifts her gaze back to her target, a wicked grin on her lips that's so wide, it shows the dainty points of her canines. I've never noticed them before. Then my eyes sweep over the length of her white stockings, the hiked-up hem of her pink day dress, the soft golden flesh on display around her garter. Her shooting posture is far from ladylike, as is the unrestrained squeal she utters as she hits her next target. It's the strangest combination of feminine and feral I've ever seen.

Blazing hell...Daphne is goddamn gorgeous.

My breath hitches yet again, and my pulse rackets. Daphne is so close to winning, and I'm almost of a mind to forfeit. Almost. Yet I've never backed down from a challenge. Never forfeited a game unless I was losing on purpose.

And now that Daphne has flustered me so, I'm determined to get revenge.

I take a calming breath and face my target. Lift my rifle. Aim.

"Hey, Daph," I say as I pop one of the bubbles.

"What?"

"Remember at the club last weekend when you sucked candy floss off my fingertips."

She yelps, and it isn't a sound of triumph. At the same time, her rifle fires without popping any bubbles. She bares her teeth at me, cheeks flushed pink.

It's my turn to grin wickedly. "It got me thinking."

"About what?" she says, voice tight as she carefully aims her next shot and misses.

"About that skilled tongue of yours."

She pauses, her only movement the heavy rise and fall of her chest.

I pop six more targets, then glance briefly at her with a wink. "And how it might feel on my cock."

Her mouth falls open, cheeks burning crimson.

I pop four more bubbles, and a celebratory mechanical melody erupts over my station, announcing me and my towering vine as the winner.

CHAPTER FOURTEEN

DAPHNE

I don't know how I manage to snap out of my stupor in the wake of Monty's words, but as soon as I do, I take aim with a vengeance and pop enough bubbles to secure second place amongst the rest of the contestants. Not that I was in much danger of losing to anyone else. The rest of the players are still struggling to grow their vines past shoulder height.

But the private game between me and Monty…

I march up to him, my cheeks burning hotter than ever. He stands just outside the stall, and when he catches my furious glare, he smirks. "Ah, sweet victory. How does it feel to lose?"

Now I regret facing him because I can hardly look him in the eye as his taunting words echo through my mind all over again. My stomach flips with a strange medley of sensations. Embarrassment. Amusement. And…was there a part of me that maybe *liked* his vulgar teasing? Why are my lips curling into a grin?

"You played dirty," I say, throwing a harmless punch at his arm. My eyes refuse to lift higher than his chin.

He catches my wrist before my punch can land, then lowers his face into my line of sight. His voice is rich with mirth. "You played dirty first."

I avert my gaze slightly, still not daring to look at him. "I was stating facts," I mutter. "You were teasing."

"Was I?" He leans into view again until I finally meet his eyes. "Or was I merely stating facts too, dear?"

My stomach flips all over again. Not only because he just called me dear—not Daffy Dear, not Daph—but because I've never been on the receiving end of his flirtatious mocking. I've only seen him tease others like this, like when he'd rile up Edwina and William during his matchmaking game. But he's never teased *me* this way, not with such sexually charged subject matter, and I can't pretend his actions are for the sake of matchmaking. If he wanted to tease me to make my suitor jealous, he'd wait until Conrad was paying attention. But he's still playing the shooting game.

The feel of Monty's fingers around my wrist absorbs all my attention, as do the scant few inches that separate us. My breaths grow heavier in my chest, and Monty's mirth begins to fade into something more serious. Something like the intensity he showed during our painting session.

This would be a great opportunity to tease him back. I shattered his composure during the game. I could do it again. But even though my mouth opens, my words don't come, and I find myself drawn deeper into silence. Deeper into his gaze. It's strange because I don't normally love prolonged eye contact, but with Monty…I don't hate it. Moreover, I can't keep myself from studying the particular shade of gray in his eyes. Like a storm cloud. A shade so beautiful I'm suddenly desperate to paint—

A drop of moisture lands on my lashes, forcing me to blink. Then another falls on my cheek. I tilt my face back and find an overcast sky overhead. The clouds must have overtaken the blue while we were playing our game, and now rain has begun. In a matter of seconds, the light sprinkle turns into a deluge.

A burst of laughter escapes my lips. I close my eyes and lift my chin higher, luxuriating in the feel of the cold drops dancing over my face and hair. Soaking my arms. Then a tug on my wrist reminds me Monty is still holding onto it.

"Come on." He gently guides me back under the stall's awning, where the now-finished players and several other carnival guests crowd in close to the counter. I grin at the sight of the grass becoming soaked, at the stalls filled with people desperate to wait out the shower. Meanwhile, it takes all my restraint not to run back onto the grass and pounce from puddle to puddle.

I love the rain.

Yet that love is not one I can heed, the proof being the aghast looks I catch from those in the stall across from us. One woman whispers into another's ear, their eyes on me. As both break into laughter, I'm thrown back to my debut season as the source of mockery and gossip.

Did you see her tear into that steak with her hands?

Did you hear her growl when I merely bumped into her?

I shake the memories from my head, burying the part of me that yearns for rain, and remind myself that being soaked through is not admirable in society. Instead of fantasizing about frolicking through puddles, I should be fretting over my hair like all the other ladies are doing.

"You're drenched." A panicked male voice draws my attention to the side, where Conrad shuffles between bodies to reach me and Monty. Araminta and David follow in his wake. "Are you all right? Why were you just standing there?"

My mood sours. I'd forgotten about Conrad during the shooting game. His incompetence was wearing on my nerves, so playing with Monty was a much-needed break. Is that what Araminta meant when she talked about being annoyed by David's obsession with her? Because I was certainly annoyed.

"Why were you staring at the rain?" Araminta asks, genuine concern in her eyes.

"I like the rain," I confess, but no one hears me over the rhythmic beat of droplets that pound the awning overhead.

Araminta arches a brow at Monty. "And why were you just staring at *her*?"

My breath catches. I swivel my face toward Monty but he's pointedly ignoring our group. And Araminta's question. Did he even hear what she said? Is it true? Was Monty… staring at me while I was basking in the splendor of the rain? I recall his expression before the downpour began. The intensity that swept over his expression. I shudder to think he continued to watch me like that, even after I turned my face to the sky.

Yet the shudder I feel…

It isn't at all unpleasant.

Conrad steps in closer. He lifts his hand to the sodden ends of my short hair, and I habitually flinch away. Thankfully he pulls his hand back. His expression turns sheepish as he tucks his palms in his trouser pockets and rocks back on his heels. "After the rain lets up, would you care to join me for tea in the concessions pavilion?"

I open my mouth to refuse him, but I'm not sure how to best go about it. Or if I even should. Is accepting his offer essential to continuing Monty's courtship lesson?

When I don't answer, he speaks again. "We could warm up and dry off—"

"We're leaving." Monty's voice silences him, and something warm and heavy falls over my shoulders. It's Monty's jacket, and a glance at him shows he's doffed his gloves and rolled up his shirtsleeves, his cravat now hanging loose. I'm surprised it's taken him this long to dress down. Then his words register in my mind, and the next thing I know, his fingers lace through mine. He gives me a wicked grin.

And then tugs me out into the rain.

The breath leaves my lungs in exhilarated surprise as we dart over the wet grass, our shoes making squelching sounds that are almost as loud as the downpour.

"What are we doing?" I shout at him, my words strangled with laughter.

"We're running."

"I can see that." I can also see more disapproving faces staring out at us from under the safety of the tents, but I find it hard to care this time. This is heaven for me. But for Monty...he's not normally playful like this. His play tends more toward words and jests. I don't think I've ever seen him so much as canter. "We could wait it out."

"We could, but you wanted to run, didn't you?" His curls have uncoiled into damp strands that cling to his face as he turns a wild smile to me. "You love the rain."

My pulse kicks up, and I can't take my eyes off his face as he continues to pull me on. I'm so moved I could cry. He knows I love the rain. He heard me say so when no one else did. He could tell I wanted to frolic and play.

I utter a yelp as my foot slips in the slick grass, but my shout quickly dissolves into another strain of laughter. "We might fall."

"We might," he says. "That's why I'm holding on to you. I can take you down with me."

"So we can fall together."

"Something like that."

We're nearing the park's entrance now, where a line of coaches await. Soon our jog will be at an end, and I wish with all my heart it would last.

I'M STILL breathless as our hansom cab pulls up outside my apartment building, and my fingers are chilled to the bone. The rain has only let up slightly and the temperature has dropped. That's Earthen Court spring for you.

A giddy smile curves my mouth as we dart from the cab through a light sheet of rain. We race up the steps to my building's entrance and catch our breath all over again.

"That was probably the most fun I've had in this body," I say, facing Monty on the top step.

I expect some quip about how I clearly need to do more interesting things with my body, but it doesn't come. Instead, Monty gives a shaky nod. "I'm glad," he says through mildly chattering teeth.

I frown, taking in his pallor contrasting the pink in his cheeks and nose. "Are you all right? You're pale but your cheeks are flushed." I lift a hand to his cheek. His eyes widen at my touch, but he doesn't pull away. "You're burning up."

"I'm a little sensitive to rain."

"You're sensitive to rain?" I echo with a scolding look. "To *rain*? The stuff we just ran through and soaked ourselves with? And why the hell are you sensitive to it?" A ripple of panic moves through me. I've heard some humans with weak constitutions are prone to suffer during rain and cold weather, but Monty has never seemed anything but fit.

"I'll be fine." He tries to give me a reassuring grin, but its effect is negated by the hunch of his shoulders and the way he crosses his bare forearms over his chest in an attempt to warm up.

"And you gave me your jacket! Monty, you fool. Come on. I don't care if you were already planning on coming up or not, because you are now."

"I really will be fine, Daph. I was merely walking you to your door like a gentleman, but I'll be on my way."

My heart clenches at how much weaker his voice sounds than usual. I glance out at the street where the hansom cab has already departed. "No, you're coming inside." When he opens his mouth to argue, I say, "Come inside or I'll bite you. I'm incapable of lying, which means I must follow through. Now do what I say, or I *will* bite you. Hard."

A corner of his mouth quirks up. "That's just a recipe for a good time."

"There he is," I say with a roll of my eyes.

I open the door to my building and am gratified when he follows me inside. I wince with every step we take upstairs, knowing we're leaving soggy footprints and probably mud behind us. I'll make it up to my landlady later and clean the stairs myself.

Once inside my apartment, I close the door behind us and order, "Clothes off. Now."

"Daph—"

"Don't argue. Just do it. We already made enough of a mess on the stairs. I won't have my rugs soaked out of misplaced modesty."

With a resigned grumble, he turns away and begins to strip. I tug off my shoes and stockings, then reach for the tiny pearl buttons at the back of my dress. With them so slick and my fingers so cold, I can hardly gain purchase on a single button. My landlady employs a maid in the building for times like this, but I'd rather not ring for her and draw her attention to the soaked stairs. Instead, I turn my back to Monty.

"Will you loosen my buttons?"

His only answer is a sharp intake of breath.

I glance at him over my shoulder, but now it's my turn to inhale. He's dressed down to his underpants, his musculature coated in a sheen of moisture, his hair dripping rivulets over his face. I've seen him shirtless twice now, but never out of his trousers. Fresh bruises mar his ribs, proof of his most recent fight at the club. It never occurred to me to go last night, but now I wish I had, just to know how he got each contusion. I'm struck with a sudden realization of how much of his life I'm not a part of. It's been so easy to fall back into a friendship. To converse like no time at all has passed. Like he didn't hurt me with his dismissive goodbye all those months ago. But now I'm aware that time *has* passed and Monty has a life outside of work and our arrangement. He has a past I know very little about. He has hobbies I was only vaguely aware of before. He has a sensitivity to rain that I've only discovered today. What else is there to know about him?

Hunger fills me, a yearning to know everything.

I face forward again. "Please," I say, my voice coming out softer than I intend.

His footsteps approach.

Then his fingers fall on my top button. It occurs to me now he may not be in any better shape than I am to unbutton my dress, but the thought is barely out of my head before I feel the first button loosen. Then the next.

Leave it to Monty to maintain expert skills at undressing a woman, even when he's unwell.

Although…

Now that I think about it, despite all his previous talk about being a womanizer and a rake, I've never seen him with a lover. Not once. Not a single dalliance during The

Heartbeats Tour. Not a single concrete anecdote about past or present paramours.

Only salacious teasing and a reputation for rejecting advances from the ladies at work.

The next button comes loose, and his fingertips skim my back, just above my bralette. I suck in a gasp as his fingers flinch away.

"Sorry," he whispers.

"It's all right," I say with a chuckle, my attempt at lightening the mood. Yet somehow it only gets tenser. A heavy, vibrating, fluttering energy settles in my chest, tightening my lungs. At the same time, I feel safe. Comfortable. Trusting. What a curious contrast. It takes all my effort to keep my voice nonchalant. "I could hardly expect you to unbutton me without making contact with my skin."

He says nothing, only loosens the next button. I could probably undo the rest on my own, or at least shrug out of my dress now, but I can't find the will to tell him that. I look at him over my shoulder again. That intensity has returned to his face, and the next time his fingertips skim my back, over my silk bralette this time, he doesn't flinch away.

A strange sensation burns low in my belly. It's something I haven't felt before, not when another person is touching me, at least. It's the way I feel when I read sexy scenes in books or look at romantic artwork. It's how I feel when I'm posing before the mirror, preparing to sketch—

My breath hitches again as I understand what this might be.

Is this...arousal? But what could be arousing me? The feeling of someone touching me, or...

Or *Monty* touching me?

"There," he says, voice soft as he steps back. All my buttons are loose now. He turns around to give me privacy—not that I care for it, considering my confusion over the double standards regarding human nudity—and I let my dress drop to the ground. I rush to my linen closet for towels and a blanket, wrapping one of the towels around my torso before handing the rest of the bundle to Monty.

"Get comfortable on the settee," I say and set about lighting my stove and hanging our clothes on the drying line. Slowly, my apartment gets a little warmer. I'm already feeling warm enough, which may be partially due to the flush of heat I felt when I was aroused, but I worry about Monty.

By the time I return to him, he looks worse than ever. He's slumped on my settee, body trembling beneath the blanket I gave him. How the hell did he unbutton my dress in this state? I thought he was feeling better after we got inside my apartment. I crouch down, still dressed in only my underclothes and the towel, and press my hand to his forehead. It's even hotter than it was before.

I glance at his still-soaked hair. "You didn't even properly dry yourself."

"Sorry," he says with a sheepish smile.

"What are you apologizing for?" Taking up one of the barely used towels, I perch on the arm of the settee, just behind his head, and begin drying his tresses.

"For taking advantage of your hospitality." His words are slightly slurred.

"You're not taking advantage of anything. I'm the one who ordered you in here on threat of biting. But if it assuages your guilt, we can count this as the favor I owe you for winning the game."

"Ah, right." He releases a weak chuckle. "You had fun, then?"

A grin curves my lips as I squeeze the towel around his hair. "I did. But you really shouldn't have run in the rain with me if you're so sensitive to it."

"I'll always run in the rain with you."

I frown down at him and his uncharacteristically sentimental tone. "You truly are a mess right now, aren't you?"

He makes a noncommittal sound followed by another "Sorry."

"Who knew Monty Phillips was a master of apology when he's sick." I remove the towel from his hair and lean over him. His eyes are closed, his expression pinched. He continues to shiver even though my apartment has warmed significantly.

I descend from the arm of the settee and tuck the blankets tighter around him. My gaze settles on the steady rise and fall of his chest, and an idea comes to mind. Dropping my towel to the floor, I close my eyes and turn my attention inward, focusing on the second side of me. The small, soft creature. The hunter. The part of me that loves frolicking through rain even more than my seelie self does. I connect with that version of me and feel a hum of magic radiate up and down my limbs, infusing my blood and bones. A shudder racks my body from my head and down my spine. Once it reaches my toes, I land on four soft paws.

From the ground, I stare up at the settee. Monty looks larger now that I'm in my pine marten form, yet it's a view I easily recall. In a single leap, I hop onto his chest and settle my small body at its center, letting my warmth radiate through the blanket to infuse him.

I did this once before, during The Heartbeats Tour. After a late night out, he returned to the place we were staying at, seeming a little worse for wear. Now I wonder if he'd joined an amateur boxing match in the city we were visiting. He settled into a chair, complaining that he was cold, and I offered to curl up on his chest until he was warm. That resulted in both of us falling asleep. When I awoke the next morning, I was mortified, bemoaning my humiliation over having *slept* with him. I'm embarrassed to recall how naive I was then, and the situation was only made worse when Monty teased me.

...I have a type. Four legs and furry isn't it.

I still don't know why it hurt me so much when he said that. Why would I expect a human to see an animal fae as anything else? Of course it meant nothing to him that a fae creature slept on his chest. It truly wasn't a big deal.

Yet it still hurt that he felt that way.

I study his face from where I lie, and I remind myself that he could hurt me all over again. He could say something cruel or cutting. He could push my friendship away like he did before. My yearning to understand more about him, to learn the hidden sides of him I'm only just starting to suspect are there, could lead to pain.

The kind of pain that made me drunk and reckless once before, so desperate for a lasting connection after Monty rejected me that I got myself handfasted to someone I had no intention of marrying.

My friendship with Monty could lead me back down that sharp and agonizing path. It might be better to keep my distance—to tuck tail and run from him—as soon as our bargain is fulfilled. Run. Hide. Isn't that what I do when I'm afraid?

As I close my eyes and lower my head, lulled by the sound of his heartbeat, I remember that Monty is the one who ran *with* me today.

CHAPTER FIFTEEN

MONTY

I wake to complete warmth. It radiates all around me, a soothing heat that nearly lulls me back to the depths of slumber until my mind sharpens just enough to tell me none of this is familiar. Not the firm cushion against my back or beneath my side. Not the scent of the blanket covering me. Not the feel of the arms wrapped around my torso. Not the soft body flush against mine. Not the feel of the silk beneath my palms.

I open my eyes and find a dark apartment, lit only by the moonlight streaming through the windows, but it isn't the dingy single-room unit I downsized to two years ago. No, this is Daphne's apartment, as evidenced by the ceiling of twining branches, extending from the tree trunk at the center of the parlor. I'm lying on my side on her settee, covered in a blanket. My clothes are strung on a line over the parlor stove.

Which means I'm fucking naked.

And the woman in my arms…

I look down, but she's hidden beneath the blanket, nestled against my chest. My awareness sharpens to every part of me she touches. The feel of her breath against my skin. Her arm slung over my waist. One of her legs tangled with mine. Then my focus shifts to my own body. The arm that dangles off the settee, her head propped upon my bicep. My heart that pounds against her cheek. My hand splayed over… something.

I move my fingers slightly, feeling only flimsy silk. The curvature beneath it doesn't make it hard to guess I'm palming Daphne's ass. A rather ample, perfect ass, I must say.

—If I were an asshole. I would only say that *if* I were a complete and utter asshole, which I'm determined not to be with her.

She makes a soft sound in her sleep, then wriggles against me, drawing new awareness to the pair of breasts pressed to my torso. Damn it all, the way my cock stiffens—or stiffens *more* because apparently I'm already hard—does nothing to support my *I'm not an asshole* bit. My pulse races, my blood rushing through my ears. I lift my hand from Daphne's ass and tug the blanket down, finally revealing the sleeping face of my friend. The sight of her parted lips and the squish of her cheek against my chest does something painful to my heart, but I don't let myself linger on it. Not when I haven't a fucking clue what's going on or how we got like this.

I shift to the side and extricate my arm from under her head. Her eyes flutter open as I pull myself up partway. Our legs are still tangled, as is the blanket we're covered in. The latter slips down her body as she arches in a tired stretch, revealing that lacy bralette I was introduced to last weekend. I avert my gaze as she props herself up on her forearms.

She makes another sleepy moan that turns into a yawn. "You're awake."

"Daph..." I swallow the strain in my throat. "What did we do?"

"What did we..." Her echoed words are languid and end in another yawn. Then she looks down at herself with a surprised smile. "Oh, right. I must have shifted in my sleep."

"Shifted."

"I laid on your chest in my unseelie form. You were shivering so I thought it might help you warm up."

Her explanation conjures memories. Running in the rain. Her smile. Her laughter.

Me feeling unwell on our ride home.

Daphne forcing me to come inside.

Us undressing.

My fingers undoing the buttons on the back of her dress.

Me feeling feverish and lying on the settee.

That's the last thing I remember.

"We slept together," I say, a nervous edge to my voice. "Naked."

She gives me a withering look. "That's what you're worried about? Monty, I'm not going to make it weird this time. I get it now. Sleeping together isn't the same as *sleeping* together."

It takes several moments for me to understand what she's referring to. Then I remember. She once napped on my chest when she was a pine marten. She was so humiliated in the morning, as if I'd stolen her virtue. In return, I was cold and dismissive of her feelings. Because those feelings frightened me. They meant she saw me differently than I'd thought. She saw me as someone who *could* sleep with her in the carnal sense. Someone she could feel self-conscious around.

Someone she could have feelings for.

Which I don't deserve. I don't deserve anyone's fucking feelings, nor am I capable of providing what any kind of lasting lover needs.

So I panicked.

I did what I always do.

I carved distance between us with sharp words and cold behavior.

Something I've since promised myself I wouldn't do with her again.

I take several steadying breaths before that same panic can convince me to say something I don't mean. There's no reason to. I've already placed a much kinder boundary between us. I'm serving as her matchmaker. I'm helping her find a husband by Lughnasadh.

A bolt of anger shoots through me, but before it can grow, Daphne draws my attention back to her.

She sits up straighter and gives a consoling pat to my shoulder. "We did nothing that counts, all right? It meant nothing." Her words sting despite her placating tone and the gentle smile on her lips. She's parroting exactly what I said to her when this happened during the tour. Yet I don't get the feeling she's being facetious.

I suppose I should take some solace in her not holding a grudge against me, but...ouch. We didn't do anything that counts? It meant nothing? She warmed me up and held me close when I was feeling ill. That fucking meant something.

"I'll make us some tea." She rises from the settee, the blanket falling the rest of the way down her torso, her hips, her legs. Now I see the silky undershorts I palmed in my sleep.

I force my gaze above her shoulders and reach for her wrist before she can walk away.

Her eyes widen as she whirls back to face me.

For a moment of pure madness, I imagine tugging her toward me until she's straddling my hips, then cradling the back of her head, guiding her face to mine until our lips meet in a tender kiss. A kiss that grows heated as my hands rove her bare skin, cup her breasts, and tug those silky shorts down—

I shake the vision from my head. What the fuck is wrong with me? That's not why I touched her.

She frowns down at the wrist my fingers encircle, as if wondering why the hell I *did* reach for her.

"Thank you," I say in a rush, "for taking care of me."

Her expression softens. "It's what friends do."

My mouth mirrors her grin, and I relinquish my hold on her wrist. Tension uncoils from my chest. "I suppose you're right."

She takes a step back only to halt at once, her expression shifting back to a frown. Before I know what's happening, she stands before me, plants one knee on the settee beside my blanketed thigh, and leans down. Then her hands find my hair, her fingers running through my tresses.

My fevered imaginings return all over again, and I picture pulling her into my lap once more. Is that what she's about to do? Is this happening? And do I...stop her? Why the fuck would I stop her?

Her fingers rake through another section of my hair, and I have to bite back a moan that nearly escapes. Blazing hell, what is she doing to me? I close my eyes and ball my fingers into fists at my sides, refusing to touch her until I know for sure—

"It's still damp. Sorry, I did a terrible job drying your hair." With a chuckle, she ruffles my tresses until they fall into my eyes and then saunters toward the kitchen.

My chest pulses as I struggle to catch my breath. For my mind to catch up with what just happened. She was... checking my hair to test if it was dry, not running her hands through it for pleasure's sake.

What is wrong with me? These things I keep imagining doing with her. The way my body responds to her. I run a hand up my forehead, slicking back the hair Daphne disrupted.

I'm aroused, that's all. I haven't bedded a lover in at least two years. That normally isn't a problem, because my sex drive isn't normally so out of control. All I've needed before is a quick wank, a cold bath, and a reminder that taking lovers brings too much risk. Hearts to break when they want too much from me, even after I've stated what I can and can't give. Pain when I start to crave more than I can give. Secrets that could be discovered.

This time, the reminder does very little to calm the erection that has raged in my lap since I woke up with Daphne in my arms.

Her voice calls out from the kitchen. "Do you want to have tea on the roof?"

I should say no. I should get the fuck out of here.

But that's just the panic talking. I know what I must do. I know how to calm this madness and keep my friendship from derailing beneath my lust.

"Sure," I call back as I leave the settee to take my clothes from the line. "I'm going to use your washroom first."

Where I can beat my unruly cock into submission.

CHAPTER SIXTEEN

DAPHNE

I'm glad to see Monty is doing much better. I didn't consider his earlier condition when I asked him to climb the tree in my living room so we could make our way to the roof. But he didn't even argue. In fact, he seemed rather energetic as he followed me up the notches in the tree trunk and then obeyed my instructions to gently stroke the bases of the lowest branches. That's all it takes to convince my tree to spread its tangled limbs and allow the small opening that serves as my way out to the open sky.

Now we recline on a blanket, porcelain cups in hand, a teapot between us.

The rain has stopped and the air is refreshing without being cold. Just the right temperature to keep me comfortable in my silk robe. I donned the garment after Monty left my washroom and informed me I was still in my undergarments. He'd already gotten dressed in his shirt and trousers, and I scurried to my bedroom to wrap myself in my favorite teal robe.

The city is quiet around us, barely a sound to be heard. A rustle of my tree's leaves. The hoot of an owl here. The pitter-patter of a raccoon there. According to the clock in my kitchen, we slept until three in the morning, so there are very few people awake in this part of town.

As silence stretches between us, I realize I'm not entirely sure why I invited him out here. Aside from how hot I was starting to feel in my apartment, of course. My whole body warmed when I touched his hair. It was an innocent gesture on my part, as I wanted to ensure he was dry and wouldn't suffer whatever ailed him during the rainstorm.

Then came a moment when his lashes fluttered shut and he leaned slightly into my touch. I was struck with the most overwhelming heat between my legs, one so strong I was tempted to claw my fingers tighter into his hair, maybe tug his head back and lower my lips to his. For the second time in a span of hours, I realized the truth.

I'm attracted to him.

To Monty.

Not just aesthetically, but sexually. I've never experienced sexual desire for a specific person before. I've felt aroused. I've enjoyed pleasure. I've even taken pleasure with other people, but I've never experienced desire so deeply entwined with another person.

After that, my body flooded with warmth. I could only think to get some air.

Why I asked Monty to join me, I don't know. He could have left. Could have gone home.

Yet here we are, sipping tea in silence under the starlight.

I refill my empty teacup, my gaze snagging on Monty as I set the pot back down between us. He's hardly more than a silhouette of shadows with how dark the early morning is, but I find it hard to look away. My eyes trace the curve of his throat, the arch of his Adam's apple, the shape of his lips wrapped around the cigarillo he's smoking. He's fixed his hair, and by that I mean he's mussed it in the way it normally is, not the comical nest of curls it only halfway dried in while we were sleeping.

My chest tightens.

Was he always this damn beautiful?

I'm not sure whether to be startled or elated at my newfound awareness of him.

On one hand, it's good, isn't it? If I can feel desire for Monty, something that's only grown as I've become more comfortable with him and gotten to know him better, surely I can hope the same might happen between me and my future husband.

On the other hand…this is bad. Because the desire I feel is for Monty, and he's made it clear he doesn't see me that way. Made it clear he is not interested in settling down or getting married. And I need someone who will settle down, and quickly at that. If I don't marry by Lughnasadh, I risk being stuck in Cypress Hollow with Clyde the honey badger as my mate. I risk giving up my dream to be an illustrator. I suppose both options include marrying without love, but only one will allow me to follow my artistic dream. That is what matters the most.

I force the worries from my head. Desire is just desire, even if it's attached to a specific person. If I can feel it for Monty, I can feel it for someone else. I'll take this as a good sign and enjoy all the strange flutters in my chest and between my legs. I can use it as fuel for my art.

For the love of the All of All, I might truly understand what it *feels* like to be close to someone, to touch them and feel them touching me, to look at them and be filled with an ache so strong I yearn to sate it with the object of my attraction. For the first time, I understand my art on an emotional level, not just the intellectual level I understood it before.

As for a physical level…

I pull my gaze from Monty's profile and heave a sigh. I'm starting to regret inviting Monty out here, for if I was alone, I could satisfy this heat right here and now. Tug open my robe and slip my hand beneath my undershorts and coax myself to climax, with only the moon and stars as my witness.

Good grief, what is happening in my mind? I've never been so preoccupied with sex.

I squeeze my thighs together and down a heavy gulp of tea. Part of me wishes it was liquor but that might make things worse.

"So…how did I do today?" I ask, breaking the silence just to give me something rational to focus on. I keep my voice low so as not to carry beyond the rooftop. "For our courtship lesson?"

Monty takes a long drag of his cigarillo, then removes it from between his lips. A breath of floral smoke fills the air. "You did well. You had fun, which was our primary lesson. Furthermore, you didn't overexert yourself to gain your romantic subject's interest, which was Lesson Two."

"I think I failed at Lesson Three," I say with a grimace. "You told me to act with curiosity, but I wasn't at all curious about him."

"He wasn't your type?"

I ponder that for a moment. "I think I have to get to know someone well to understand if they're my type. So maybe I didn't give him enough of a chance."

"No," he says with a decisive shake of his head, "you made the right judgment. He was a fucking idiot."

I snort a laugh. "I suppose that's what I get for interfering with your lesson and conspiring with Araminta. I was under the impression there'd be more than one romantic subject to choose from."

"You're telling me you were going to subject me to the company of multiple Conrads?"

"That sounds like a nightmare," I say, wrinkling my nose.

Monty takes another drag from his cigarillo while I sip my tea. He speaks again. "If it takes time and familiarity for you to determine if you're attracted to someone, how are you going to find the right partner by Lughnasadh?"

I shrug. "I wasn't planning on a love match. Only someone who will serve my purposes."

He shifts on the blanket until he's facing me on his side, propped up on one elbow, his cigarillo in his free hand. "You made that clear when I first asked you what you wanted in a husband. All your answers revolved around your modeling needs and getting out of your handfasting."

"I suppose I've always viewed relationships from a rational perspective," I say. "Pine martens mate out of instinct and they don't stay with their partners or their children after their kits reach maturity. I was raised that way. It wasn't until after the war, when the territory lines of all the courts changed and the Earthen Court was relocated in the south, that I witnessed a different perspective. When I migrated south, I got my first glimpses of human cities on the way. I saw communal lifestyles. By the time I settled in the court's new unseelie forest, I was too curious about all I'd seen to return to solitude. Too entranced by the art I'd glimpsed. Instead of settling in a quiet tree burrow, I took up residence in Cypress Hollow. It's an unseelie village that caters to fae creatures while giving them a taste of society. They live in houses, cook, work, and marry. It was quite strange to get used to."

Monty nods his understanding. "I imagine so, after three centuries on your own."

"It was even stranger when I took the next step and debuted in human society. Now there were rules about what I could and couldn't do, and my every aim was to secure a husband. There were numerous qualifications for who my partner should be and none of them included love, sex, or attraction."

Monty's posture visibly perks. "Back up a moment. How did you go from living in an unseelie village to debuting in high society?"

Of course he wants the full story. He was intrigued the minute I briefly mentioned it when we arrived at the carnival. It isn't my favorite story, but I suppose I can oblige his curiosity.

I lie back on the blanket and fold my hands over my belly. The sight of the stars and the crescent moon peeking behind the swaying branches of my rooftop tree sets my nerves at ease, even as I summon the words to explain one of my least favorite memories.

"One of the most respected figures in Cypress Hollow decided to take seelie form one year. She left for the nearest human city and came back not only a married woman but a pillar of high society. She wanted to give a selection of us the same chance she'd had and sponsor our debuts in society. I'd recently learned to shift into my seelie form by then, and I was still haunted by the memory of all the art I'd glimpsed when I snuck into the human cities during migration. I craved another look at the paintings I saw, another chance to study the impossibly intricate sculptures I'd seen. When I discovered a societal debut would include art lessons, I was sold. Obsessed, more like. It was the perfect opportunity, and I took it. I had to learn etiquette too, of course, and the steps to a few dances that I was too afraid to perform. But above all else, I learned to draw."

"So that's how you honed your craft," Monty says with a

warm smile. "It all makes sense now. Though I don't suppose you were drawing scantily clad ladies back then."

A blush heats my cheeks. "Oh, I was, and I was scolded for it, especially since mine were self-studies and not recreations of the acceptable classics. So I learned landscapes and portraits too."

He shifts slightly at my mention of self-studies, but his expression soon turns serious. "You said at the carnival that your debut season didn't end well. What happened?"

"I did all the right things. At least I tried to. But there were certain aspects I never understood. There were rules to polite conversation, which I memorized and thought I excelled at until I noticed some of the girls would say things that defied my comprehension. They would state the most mundane of phrases and then laugh as if they'd told some joke. I'd always laugh along with them, but later—often weeks after the fact—something would click into place and I'd realize I'd been made fun of, right to my face."

Monty's eyes turn down at the corners. "The elite have a way with words, don't they?"

"It was humiliating. There was one fellow debutante who was particularly cruel yet so clever and loved by everyone around her. She took a strong dislike to me, which she masked as friendship. When I realized what she was doing—that everything she said in front of me, to me, and to others in my presence was meant to cut me down—I lost it. I lost my patience for the entire charade, for her, for society, for those who laughed at me, and my inner hunter took over. We got into a very public confrontation, which ended when I…"

I purse my lips, realizing what I was about to admit. I've never told anyone what happened next.

"What did you do, Daph?" There's no disapproval in his tone, no wariness. Only genuine curiosity.

I cover my mouth with my hands and mutter the truth beneath my palm.

Monty chuckles and leans across the blanket. With his cigarillo perched between his lips, he pries my hand off my mouth. "I didn't hear that, dear. What did you do to that wretched harpy?"

I meet his eyes with a guilty look. "I bit off the top of her ear." A beat of silence. Then my next confession. "And I ate it."

He throws his head back with a hoot of laughter. When his eyes return to mine, his are glittering with mirth. "That's my fucking girl."

My heart flutters at those words, doubly so when I realize he's still holding my hand. To my disappointment, he releases my palm and settles back on the other side of the teapot, still chuckling to himself.

I clear my throat and push myself up to sitting. "Now you know why I'm anxious around strangers," I say as I pour a fresh cup of tea. My hand still tingles from where he touched it. "That's enough about my humiliating past. You asked about my type, and now you know why I don't have one. So, what about you? What's your type?"

He furrows his brow. "My type?"

"Yes, your type." I cut him a good-humored glare. "I know it isn't four legs and furry."

As his face falls, I realize I've said the wrong thing.

I flap my hand at him. "I'm not mad—"

"I'm so sorry." The emotion strangling his voice silences me. "I never should have said that to you that morning on tour. I didn't mean it."

A lump rises in my throat. The last thing I was seeking was an apology. I was more trying to lighten the mood. I force a smile and try a different angle. "Oh, so you *are* into bestiality. Noted."

The soft smile that breaks through his somber look tells me he has at least somewhat taken my bait. "No, I am not sexually attracted to fae creatures in their animal forms," he says with a roll of his eyes. "But...you know what I mean. I'm sorry."

I sip my tea. "I know. I'm not mad about it, honestly. I've learned a lot these last couple of years."

Monty sits up and props his arm on one knee. He finishes his cigarillo only to extract a new one, which he flips over his fingers, unlit. "You say you're not mad, but you had every right to be. To still be. I know how I am with people. How I... push them away. It's what I've always done. There are reasons I can't get too close to another person, so when I'm afraid that's happening, I act cold."

My breaths go shallow. I'm too afraid to move. Too afraid to make a single sound, for fear that he'll end this unexpected candor.

"When I'm not pushing others away on purpose, I'm hurting them unwittingly because I'm a fucking asshole, born and raised."

"Why would you say that?" It's not the first time he's been so self-deprecating. During the tour, he'd remind Edwina how he's a heartless rake and not a hero, always with the kind of smile that made me wonder if he was being serious. The way he says it now, there's no doubt. He truly doesn't hold himself in high regard.

Several long beats of silence pass.

"I had a furry little friend once," he finally says. "A fox. I was quite young and spent much of my time playing outdoors on our country estate. Every time I went outside, my fox would come to visit. She was a curious creature. A fennec, more often found in courts with warmer climates like Fire, Summer, or Solar. I'd drag her around like a house cat, climb trees with her, dress her in my sister's baby clothes. Then one day, my fox spoke. What a magical moment, to discover one's animal companion can talk. A dream come true, for most children."

Despite his hopeful words, his voice holds no joy.

"Then she said, 'Monty, I'm sorry but I can't be your pet anymore. I'm leaving.' That's all she had to say before she ran into the forest, never to return." He shakes his head, his eyes brimming with remorse. "I made a friend of a fae creature and I treated her like a pet."

My heart aches at the pain in his expression. "You didn't know she was fae."

He gives me a sad smile. "Should I have been so unruly with a wild creature, even if she wasn't fae? Should I have dressed her in bonnets and carried her in a basket?"

"You were just a child."

"Yet I didn't learn, did I? You said yourself that I treated you like a pet." His voice holds no criticism for my accusation, only regret and self-loathing for himself. Twice I've insinuated that he treated me like a pet. First, after I woke up on his chest during the tour. Next, when we parted the day he got fired.

I shake my head. "I don't feel like you were treating me that way. Not anymore."

His still-sad grin turns wry. "Don't make excuses for me. You're not the only one I've hurt. Not the only woman I've treated like shit."

I want to reiterate that he didn't treat me as badly as he's determined to believe, but I'm curious what he means regarding other women.

"I was particularly cruel to my first love."

My heart slams against my ribs. He's never mentioned any former lovers. I swallow hard. "What did you do?"

"We were together since we were young. We planned on getting married. Then, as we grew older, things…happened.

I was dealing with anger and personal issues. I couldn't be honest with her, and she could tell I was hiding something. She left me for someone else. When that relationship didn't work, she returned, begged me to take her back. I hated her for having left me and that made me unfeeling toward her. I…did things I'm not proud of. Used her obsession with me for my own selfish pleasure without ever fulfilling her hopes that we'd get back together. We carried on a sexual relationship for years without forming a true connection. It was a terrible thing to do with an aristocratic woman whose virtue is everything. She treated me like something disposable one time, yet I treated her like rubbish for years."

Despite his self-condemnation, the spike of anger that pierces my chest isn't directed at him but this first love of his. She's the one who left him, and during what sounds like a difficult time in his past. Then again…

"What were you hiding from her? What couldn't you be honest about?"

"There are things I simply can't share about myself. Family issues that aren't mine to admit. Secrets I literally can't speak of." He rubs his fingers over his lips in an anxious gesture as if he regrets having said what he did. His eyes meet mine, and there's a haunted look in them. "I will not say more than that. I know that means I can never truly be a worthy friend, but I hope you can accept the pieces of me I can give."

My heart cracks for whatever pain he's hiding. "You don't have to tell someone everything to be a worthy friend. At least not for me."

His expression unravels, smoothing with relief. "You think so?"

"I do. There are plenty of things I don't admit to you, Edwina, or Araminta."

Like the urges I've started to feel for a certain someone. I plan on keeping that to myself.

He holds my gaze for a few more beats, then gives me a dimpled grin. "That means a lot. That I can still be your friend, regardless of secrets."

I finish my tea and lean back on my forearms. The faintest blush of sunrise begins to peek over the mountains in the distance. "Are you ever going to answer my question about your type?"

He lights the cigarillo he'd been playing with, takes a drag, and heaves a smoke-filled sigh. "I don't have a type anymore, and I don't take lovers. It's better to be alone than to hurt someone like I always do."

He doesn't take lovers? He isn't a womanizer after all?

"That leads us to Lesson Four," he says. "A man's actions must align with his words and vice versa. If he says one thing but does another, don't waste your time, even if he makes you feel like he has the potential to give you exactly what you want. For example, if a potential partner states he is not seeking marriage, only sex, but you *feel* like he's falling for you, do not give him your heart. Do not try to fix him. You'll both only get hurt in the end."

The edge in his tone makes it clear he has personal experience with this lesson. After what he said about his past, it makes me wonder...who exactly is this first love he hurt? What's the full story? Was he truly so cruel to her? And who else did he hurt?

But as I recall the haunted look I glimpsed in his eyes, I think the real question is who hurt *him*?

CHAPTER SEVENTEEN

MONTY

Monday mornings are poorly regarded by members of the working class, but they're my personal favorite. Not only am I well rested after the weekend and far more optimistic than I am by Friday, but Mondays are also when I get to read my newest *Ask Gladys* mail. Since all the lead columnists at the *Cedar Hills Gazette* write under pseudonyms and those who write to us do so anonymously, the best time to turn in questions is over the weekend when the office is closed and our drop box is open. Monday means ample entertainment, sometimes even terror, over the queries I receive.

Yet there is one thing I've come to dislike about Mondays lately.

How far away they are from my next weekend session with Daphne.

I force this sentiment from my mind as I arrive at the *Gazette* for my workday. Such mental meanderings can only lead to more meanderings, and soon I'll be recalling the feel of her sleeping form against my chest and the curvature of her ass under my palm—

Swine.

That's what Daphne would call me if she knew how often that memory has looped through my head.

I settle in at my desk, my newest stack of *Ask Gladys* mail in my hand. A bustle of activity is already underway outside my closed office door and its frosted glass window. As one of the lead columnists, I'm afforded a small private office attached to the main newsroom. The room features exposed brick walls decorated with paintings of kittens, piglets, and cherubs. An enormous floral arrangement crowds the doily-laden side table beside my coat stand, filling the room with the fresh fragrance of roses and daisies. One might assume the feminine touches were already in place when I inherited the *Ask Gladys* column and took over for the previous Gladys, but that would be false. I added the hideous doilies and painfully sweet paintings because the décor helps me get into character. Otherwise it would only be me, my wide oak desk, and clouds of lavender-scented smoke.

I light a cigarillo and open my mail one piece at a time. From there I read each letter and separate my papers into different piles. One for fan mail, which I'll reply to. Another for letters with the potential for a feature. And another for letters I have no intention of answering via my column. Finally, I read a query so amusing it doesn't go into any pile. Instead, I lay it open on my desk, extract a fresh sheet of paper, and refill the ink reservoir of my fountain pen. I rewrite the letter in the proper format for publication in the column, editing out any extraneous information.

Dear Gladys,

I've recently taken a new lover, a sea serpent. Our sex life is rather fantastic, but there is one thing I'm not confident about. You see, my lover has two penises, and I never quite know what to do with the second one when we have intercourse. I've used my hands, but often the angle is all wrong, or I end up focusing so much on performing that I forget to enjoy myself. If I ignore the second member, I fear I'm neglecting his pleasure. Can you help?

Sincerely,
Perplexed by Plural Penises

My grin stretches wide and I take a drag of my cigarillo. I read my edited letter a few times over and deem it publication-ready. Then I pen my reply.

Dear Perplexed by Plural Penises,

My darling, I can do more than help. I can open a whole new world of pleasure for you both. It is time you discovered the joy of ass play. Yes, I understand the concept is shocking for the faint of heart, but I promise you will thank me later. I am not suggesting you take an anus full of sea snake cock in one go, dearest reader. I'm implying you simply learn to play with your ass. Start with a finger and go from there. Never work with a dry canvas and always communicate your comfort and safety needs with your lover. Enjoy!

Forever yours,

Gladys

I fucking love my job.

I finish my cigarillo and my perusal of my mail, selecting four more letters to feature in upcoming issues of the *Gazette*. None inspired quite the same level of excitement to immediately answer, but I have plenty of time to ponder how to reply. For now, I can work on penning out the details of my case study with Daphne thus far.

From inside one of my desk drawers, I extract my copy of my manuscript. I flip through it to determine where I should insert the first anecdote regarding the study. Certainly somewhere in the chapter about Lesson One. On a fresh sheet of paper, I begin to scribble out some of the details about Daphne's lesson. To keep her identity anonymous, I refer to her as Miss D. I drum my fingers over my manuscript, considering the best way to spin Daphne's ploy with Araminta so that it sounds encouraging to readers, something they can replicate on their own. I scrawl out my idea.

One of the key components to socializing and fun is accepting invitations. Miss D, who normally opted to remain home and refuse all offers of social engagements, finally agreed to an outing with a friend. She had no inkling that the potential for romance awaited her on the other side, yet lo and behold—

A knock sounds at my door. I halt my sentence, noting I'd begun to dig the nib of my pen a little too hard into the paper as I was preparing to summarize Daphne's meeting with Conrad. Fucking Conrad. He doesn't even deserve to grace the pages of my book.

"Come in," I call out, and the door swings open.

One of the *Gazette's* secretaries enters, a fae female named Sally with a mousy voice and round gray ears instead of the pointed ones you more commonly find on seelie fae. "You have a visitor."

I frown. I never get visitors. Neither at work nor at home. "Who is it?" A potential option occurs to me, and I rush to stand, my chest warming and my pulse quickening. "Does she have short black hair?"

Sally's eyes widen at my burst of excitement. "No, her hair is light brown and quite curly. Even curlier than yours. I assume you're related? She says she's a Miss Phillips."

My mind goes blank. Sally can only mean one person, but I'm surprised my sister would come to my work. "Where is she now?"

"In the lobby. Shall I send her away with a message, or would you like her to come up?"

I probably shouldn't take personal meetings at work, but I haven't seen my sister in months, and I'm concerned over what could have brought her here. "Please send her up. Thank you."

As soon as Sally closes the door behind her, I scramble about my office, putting away all evidence of *Ask Gladys*. Not only are columnists tasked with keeping the identities behind our pseudonyms private, but the last thing I want is for my little sister to catch snippets of sentences like *Perplexed by Plural Penises* and *ass play*. Angela may be twenty years of age, but she'll always be my baby sister.

I manage to hide all damning evidence—save for the décor belonging to a geriatric female, of course—by the time Sally returns with Angela. My sister is barely through the door before she leaps at me, a wide smile on her lips as she crushes me in a hug.

"It's been so long," she says. I nod at Sally over my sister's head, and the secretary closes the door. I return Angela's embrace before she breaks away to look me up and down. Then at my office. "What's with the décor?"

"Good question," I say, and thankfully she just frowns instead of asking me to elaborate.

"I'm glad to see you're hale and whole," she says.

"I am, and I'm glad to see you are as well."

Her cheeks have a healthy flush and her state of dress is neat and fashionable like always. She wears a tartan skirt and matching jacket, her light-brown curls pinned beneath a dainty maroon hat.

She lifts her chin. "If you're so well and good, then why haven't you been writing to me every week?" As she says the last part, she swats me with her beaded purse.

I grin at her fiery confidence. She was always such a shy and reserved girl, even more so when she was at boarding school, where she was shunned by her peers due to her perfect grades and well-known affluence. Maybe being named our father's heir in my place has been a boon to her self-image. If so, I'm glad. It's part of the reason I got myself disowned by our family.

"I'm sorry I haven't written enough, Angie. I have missed you."

"I've missed you too. It isn't the same at home without you. Not that I'm there much now that I'm in college." Her expression falls and she worries her bottom lip. "I still don't understand what happened between you and Father. He won't say a thing. Was he truly so angry that your engagement to the princess fell through? You can't be blamed for that—"

"Angie." My tone comes out sharper than I intend. "It's fine. I'm fine."

"Then why don't I ever hear from you? Why did I have to find out where you work from Thorne?"

"Thorne told you where I work?" I'm surprised she found out through my best friend and not Father. Even though I go through great pains not to communicate with the asshole who sired me, I know he keeps track of my movements. Where I live. Where I work. He probably thinks he does it out of love, and even if that's true, it's a twisted, controlling love. I've considered leaving Jasper and the Earthen Court altogether just to place distance between us, but I stay close for several reasons. Sheer stubbornness. Proof that we may live in the same city, but my life is my own. And Angela.

If I ever catch even the slightest whiff that he's pulling the same bullshit with her that he pulled with me, I will end him. His reputation, his position in the government. I'll end all of it with the secrets I keep.

But ruining my father means ruining the whole Phillips name, Angela included.

Which is why I chose to leave the family yet remain close by. To stay quiet. To bear this burden alone.

"Thorne is the reason I had to hunt you down," Angela says. She removes a letter from her purse and hands it to me. "He wanted to ensure you received this in person, so I offered to deliver it."

I open the envelope and pull out the letter inside. The script is messy and slanted in expression of my friend's displeasure.

Greetings fucker,

Why haven't you RSVPed to my goddamned wedding yet, you prick? Oh, I know. It's because your answer is so obvious you've decided a response would be superfluous, right? Right. You're my best man, you asshole. Get your pathetic ass to the Cyllene Hotel by Friday afternoon next week or my soon-to-be wife will haunt your nightmares, and I'll bake you into a pie.

I'm serious.

I will kill you.

Best,

Thorne

I glance back up at Angela. "You didn't read this did you?"

"No, why would I? It's quite rude to read one's personal correspondence."

"Good. Thorny boy uses quite a lot of expletives when dealing with me."

She rolls her eyes. "I'm in college now, dear brother. You wouldn't believe the colorful language I hear on the daily. You don't have to be so protective."

I read the letter over again, guilt sinking my gut. To be honest, I forgot about the wedding invitation I received several months back. Between establishing myself at a new job and fretting over loan payments, I left my best friend's wedding in the back of my mind. I didn't realize the time had already come. Now that it has, I'm not sure what to do. If I'm expected at the Cyllene Hotel by next Friday, I'll have to leave the day before. I'll have to miss one of the fixed matches and, in turn, my weekly payment. Furthermore, if the wedding is on Saturday, I'll be gone all weekend. I won't have any case study lessons or modeling sessions with Daphne.

"So," Angela says, "are you going to go? You can't refuse."

I give her a scolding look. "You said you didn't read it."

"I didn't, but I know what it's about. I'm going to the wedding, after all."

Of course she's going. She's always considered Thorne Blackwood a second brother, and most of the time she seems closer to him than she is to me.

She wrings her gloved hands. "Well, in truth, I can only go to the wedding if you're going. Father won't allow me to travel so far unless I have a proper escort."

"I doubt Father considers me a proper escort," I say under my breath.

"He said so himself. If you agree to act as my chaperone, he'll give me permission. He's just outside if you want to confirm—"

"He's here?" My lungs tighten, my eyes darting to the closed door to my office. The blood leaves my face with every panicked pulse of my heart. I can't stand the thought of seeing his face. Hearing his voice.

"He's at the café across the street," Angela says, her expression pinched with worry.

I heave a breath and take a cigarillo from my silver case. My igniter trembles between my fingers as I light it. After a deep inhale of the herbal smoke, my nerves begin to calm. I return my attention to my sister and find her eyes on me.

"What happened between you?" she says, her voice soft. "What happened to our family? What are you and Father and Mother not telling me?"

I take another drag while I consider what to say. I hate keeping such a secret from her, but she can't know the truth.

She can't know because Father has ensured I can't tell a soul. It's his fault I can never get close to anyone. His fault I bear life-altering secrets bound in a bargain of silence. His fault my sister considers my best friend more of a brother than me.

Yet that's the way it must stay.

I blow out another breath and force a wide grin. "It's nothing to be concerned about, Angie. I'll consider my attendance at the wedding, and I'll write to you by next Monday if I decide to go."

She studies my face for several quiet moments before she gives me a sad smile. "Very well. I hope you choose to go. Not just for my sake but for Thorne and Briony's. They want you at their wedding."

My chest warms at her words. She's right. Thorne wouldn't have used quite so many expletives if he didn't. It fills me with equal parts gratification and guilt. There were several years when my relationship with Thorne was tense. I'd pushed him so far away that he almost stopped considering me a friend. I've managed to mend our relationship somewhat in the last few years, enough that he truly wants me at his wedding. Yet going to his wedding means missing a loan payment. Which means my lender will move my loan's due date another week forward. Another week sooner that my family's secret is set to be revealed. Do I risk it?

I reiterate my promise to consider the invitation and give my sister a parting hug. After I'm left alone in my office, I simply sit and smoke and stare and think. No answers come to me, and when I gather the will to return to my work, not even my love for Mondays can replenish my mood.

CHAPTER EIGHTEEN

DAPHNE

There's a half-naked man and a sobbing girl in my parlor. This is not the Saturday I was looking forward to all week, having anticipated only one of these aspects. But when Araminta arrived unannounced at my apartment door this morning with puffy eyes, I couldn't turn her away. Now she lies face down on my settee in seelie form and her usual mourning attire.

Monty, who only recently arrived, stands at my bureau in the same position I had him in during our sketching session. Like before, he grips the pillow in place of the heroine on my canvas. With a furrow of his brow, he flicks his gaze toward my settee. "Are you sure she's all right?"

"This has been going on for two hours now," I say, squeezing a dollop of cadmium red onto my palette. My canvas is propped on my easel, and the sight of it fills me with the medley of dread and excitement that always strikes when starting the painting stage. I've already finished the underpainting as well as some of the background. Now it's time to paint the hero. "Pay her no mind."

"What's wrong with her?"

"She ended things with David."

Araminta bolts upright on the settee in a swish of her voluminous black skirts. "*He* ended things with *me*."

I roll my eyes, blending the cadmium red with yellow ochre and white. "I thought you were growing tired of him anyway."

She sniffles. "Yes, well, I wanted to be the one to end things with *him*."

I angle my body toward the settee. "Does it matter?"

"Oh, it does," Monty says, drawing my attention back to him. "This is quite common, actually. One person will tolerate a courtship with indifference, if not downright dislike, only to fall apart and question their entire self-worth when the other person breaks things off with them. It's the internalized perception that someone they didn't even like had the audacity to like them less."

"That's exactly what this is," Araminta says with an exuberant nod. "How dare he break up with me? I'm a prize. I'm incredibly cute." The last word ends on a wail, her face crumpling.

My chest squeezes. As ridiculous as I think she's being, I do feel for her. I may not have been driven to such unending tears, but I've been struck with emotional agony before. With a resigned sigh, I set down my palette and head for the kitchen, retrieving the one thing that always cheers me up when I'm feeling down.

I bend down, extending a plate before her. "Want some bacon?"

With a sniffle, she lifts her tear-stained face from her hands, looking from the plate to me. "Bacon? Why would I want bacon? More importantly, why do you have an entire plate of bacon at the ready in your kitchen?"

I pull the plate back. "It's my favorite snack."

She arches a brow. "Don't you have chocolate? Wine? Something more comforting than snack bacon?"

"If you don't appreciate it, you don't have to have any." I turn my nose up at her and take a bite of bacon out of spite.

On my way back to the kitchen, Monty stops me with his words. "I'll have some bacon."

"Don't you dare move," I say, just as he's about to remove his hands from the pillow.

He tilts his head in an annoyingly coy look. "Please, Daffy Dear. Unlike little Ari here, I appreciate a good snack bacon."

How can I say no to that? Anyone who appreciates delectable meat as much as I do deserves to be rewarded. I release a grumble and bring the plate to the bureau. "Don't move anything but your mouth."

"If you insist."

I lift a piece of bacon to his lips, watching as they part. His tongue draws the thick cut of meat into his mouth, making my breath hitch. I'm drawn back to the memory of me licking candy floss from his fingers. And—more recently—when he teased me about the feel of my tongue. He holds my eyes as he reaches the end of the bacon. I'm about to pull my hand away when he closes his lips around my fingertips. I freeze, a jolt tearing through me at the swipe of his tongue followed by the pressure of a brief suckle.

"There," he says with a wink as he pulls his lips away. "Now we're even."

I blink at him a few times. He said we're even, but was that an act of revenge? Or benevolence? Because I can't say I hated it.

"If you've got a food kink to explore," Araminta says, making me jump in place, "I can leave."

"Stay," I bite out and rush back to the kitchen as fast as my legs can carry me. I set down my plate and slap my cheeks, willing the heat in them to cool. Once I think I've gathered my composure, I return to my easel, pouring all my attention into my palette. My traitorous fingers still tingle with warmth from where Monty's mouth—

No. Art. My mind is only meant for art.

"I'm curious," Monty says, and I'm relieved to find his attention is on Araminta. "Why did David end things with you? He seemed infatuated at the carnival."

"He broke things off because I got a job." Her eyes light up as if she's been waiting for an opportunity to talk about it. "Can you believe it? He said I didn't care about him if I was going to leave in the middle of a date for a random job offer."

"When was this?" Monty asks.

"At the end of the carnival. First, I blame a certain traitorous friend of mine for abandoning me when our whole plan was created to provide me a little freedom from David's full attention."

I refuse to meet her condemning gaze and instead compare the peach-tan shade on my palette to Monty's skin tone. I add a little more yellow ochre.

"After the two of you left and the rain let up," Araminta says, "I was approached by a talent scout who offered me a paid job. It had to be done that afternoon, and I had to leave with him at once. So of course I accepted! Otherwise, I would have had to hear more about how smitten Conrad was with Daphne or David's anecdotes about his school days. The All of All have mercy on my soul if I ever have to be subjected to that again."

"What kind of job did you get?" I ask, now mixing hues for the highlights and shadows. I'm relieved that my voice comes out even. Not a hint of lingering agitation from the bacon incident.

"Didn't I tell you?"

"Between your mysterious absence from Fletcher-Wilson all week and bouts of sobbing on my settee? No."

She flips her lilac braid over her shoulder and bats her lashes. "I'm a model."

I stare at her with disbelieving eyes. "You, a model? For what?"

She rises from my settee and moves to the narrow table in my entryway, where she rifles through the broadsheets upon it. "Aha!" With a skip in her step, she bounds over to me, pointing to a spread of advertisements in one of this week's earlier issues. "There I am."

I pause mixing my colors and squint at what she's pointing to. It's a black-and-white photograph of Araminta outfitted in a chemise and corset, bent over in a pose that is one part provocative, one part coy. She has her palm to her mouth, a look of playful surprise on her face as she glances back at her own rear. It looks more like something one would find in a pin-up magazine, not the *Cedar Hills Gazette*. I frown, studying the photograph closer. What kind of disreputable company can afford advanced Star Court technology like photography, yet needed Araminta as their last-minute model in such a pose? Then I notice the image of a vial that partially overlaps the photograph and the typography that goes along with it.

I give Araminta a withering look. "Harvey Blandwell's Hemorrhoid Potion?"

Monty snorts a laugh.

Araminta's pride isn't at all dimmed by our reactions. "The model they'd originally scheduled canceled once she learned which product she was supposed to model for, but I don't have such qualms. I'll take money no matter what."

"Do you even know what a hemorrhoid is?" I ask.

"Nope." She skips over to the settee and settles onto the cushions with her paper. "Oh, obituaries! I love shopping."

I exchange an amused look with Monty and return to mixing my paint.

I'm awarded a long stretch of peace and quiet, and ample progress on my painting. I lose myself to the flow of my art, my eyes darting between Monty and my canvas, the muscles of his arms and chest that I contour with the values of my paint. I pay extra attention to his fingers, the shadows between each digit, the highlights on each joint, the dimples they make in the heroine's hips. His expression requires a little more imagination, for I can't ask him to replicate that lustful expression while Araminta's here. Not when it took me standing shirtless before him just to spark it for a moment.

A wave of heat barrels through me at the memory. I can't even imagine what kind of impact seeing that expression would have on me now that I'm aware of my attraction to Monty. Or...maybe I *can* imagine it and rather *shouldn't*. Despite my best efforts, the memory surges through me as I paint the creases next to Monty's eyes, recalling the intensity of his stare when his hand fell on mine, just before I was about to bare myself to him. Then there was last weekend when his lashes fluttered at the feel of my fingers raking through his damp hair.

Another wave of heat sparks right between my legs, and I release a soft breath that almost sounds like a moan.

My eyes fly to Monty's profile. For the love of the All of All, did he hear that? His expression shifts the slightest bit, and his eyes slide to mine. The corner of his mouth quirks. Not in a teasing way, but in a friendly smile. My muscles relax, and I return the grin. No, he hasn't a clue about my naughty thoughts—

A wailing sob shatters the moment. Araminta's quavering

voice follows. "Do you think David would have stayed with me if I'd put a finger in his butt?"

I whirl to my friend. "I beg your pardon?"

"Ah," Monty says. "That must be Wednesday's issue."

I lean toward Araminta and glance at the page she's crying over. It's the *Ask Gladys* column. I briefly scan the words *ass play* and arch a brow at Gladys himself. "Really, Monty?"

His grin turns sheepish.

I give Araminta a scolding look as I return to my canvas. "Ari, stop fretting over David. You didn't even like him."

"That's not true. I did like him...when I felt like being around him. It was his attention and constant presence I disliked, and he could tell. He said I acted indifferent toward him. What if it was my fault? What if I didn't do enough to prove I wanted to maintain our relationship?"

"Is that something I have to worry about in courtship?" My lips curl into a grimace. "Do I have to proactively prove I'm interested to keep a lover's attention?" I've never had to worry about this because I've never been attracted enough to another person to want something long-term. But what if securing a husband isn't as simple as finding a compatible specimen with marriage in mind? When I was a debutante, it seemed like there was an abundance of men seeking wives, and it wasn't a matter of love or interest, but an alignment of needs to be met. Sometimes it was family connections or an attractive dowry. Other times it was a need to procreate or establish a lady of one's household. Not that I'd know this from personal experience; my debut season didn't last long enough for me to meet suitors.

"Do not bear that responsibility in any relationship," Monty says, tone firm. "Neither of you. Otherwise, you'll be plagued with questions like: *Why hasn't he written or called upon me, even if he said he liked spending time with me and wanted to see me again? Does he not realize I like him? Did I need to encourage him more by proving my interest?"*

"That's what's going through my head right now," Araminta says.

"What's Lesson Four, Daph?" Monty asks.

I perk up at his attention, excited that I know the answer. "A man's actions should align with his words and vice versa."

"Exactly. If a man likes you, he won't care if you like him back. He'll pursue you to an annoying degree."

I wrinkle my nose as I sweep my paintbrush over the canvas in delicate lines to form the hero's hair. "I can attest to that. Conrad won't stop sending love letters to my workplace. Thank the All of All he doesn't know where I live."

Araminta heaves another sob. "David pursued me like that. He liked me deeply and relentlessly. Did I ruin it? Was I wrong to act so cold to him? Why did I want space from such a good man?"

"Only you can answer that," Monty says. "However, ask yourself if you wanted space out of fear of intimacy or from true discomfort and incompatibility. It's normal to second-guess yourself when a relationship ends, but is it out of fear that you made a mistake or true regret? There's a subtle difference, and only you can be the judge."

Araminta chokes back her tears. After a hiccup, she says, "You sure are wise for someone who has no relationship to show for it."

Monty chuckles. "I have plenty of relationships to show for it. Just none of my own."

"Why not?" Araminta rises from the settee to assess Monty with a perplexed look. "Why don't you just marry Daphne yourself to kill a bunch of birds with rocks, or whatever it is she says?"

My paintbrush slips out of my fingertips and falls to the floor with a clatter.

Araminta continues, oblivious to the daggers I'm shooting at her with my eyes. "Won't that solve your case study and Daphne's drinking problem? You're already using a pseudonym, so why not write about yourself as one of your subjects? You can prove your lessons work by pretending Daphne expertly utilized them to win your heart. And she'll have the husband she needs to break off her engagement."

Fire floods my face and neck. How can she bring up such a forward subject, suggesting Monty and I…

I shake the thought from my head. My pulse races. Why did I have to go and tell Araminta about what happened last Lughnasadh and my arrangement with Monty? "Ari, that's—"

"I can't marry anyone." Monty's voice is edged with something I can't quite name. Is it remorse? Anger? Annoyance?

"Why not?" Araminta's question brims with innocence, and as much as I want this conversation to end and save me from embarrassment, I find myself desperate to hear how he'll answer.

His throat bobs, and for a moment, I doubt he'll reply. Then he speaks, each word careful yet still infused with that same edge I sensed before. "I refuse to further my father's legacy or give him any reason to bring me back into the family. He disinherited me because I vowed never to marry. To never be the son he wants me to be. If I so much as court someone publicly, I am duty-bound to return home and take my place as his heir. Which will make me and my potential partner miserable."

That's different from the reason he gave me for not taking lovers when we talked on my rooftop. He said he avoided romance so that he won't hurt anyone again. But his eyes hold the same haunted look I glimpsed then, which tells me this might be another layer of truth.

"Why do you hate your father so much?" Yet another

innocent question from Ari. Another one I crave an answer to.

His eyes remain distant for a few more beats of my racing heart. Then the look is gone, like it was never there to begin with. His lips curve in a crooked grin. "A rake like me can't be tied down to the tedium of high society. I like it better where I am."

He winks at Araminta, which seems to satisfy her curiosity enough to return her attention to her broadsheets, but I'm not at all convinced.

I pick up my paintbrush, clean it, and return to my art, more desperate than ever to know the parts of Monty he keeps hidden.

CHAPTER NINETEEN

MONTY

That was fucking close. I can't believe how much I just gave away. I had no intention of voicing my hatred for my father, even though my confession barely scratched the surface, but I couldn't help it. When Araminta asked why I couldn't marry Daphne, and I saw the flush of Daph's cheeks, the way the question flustered her, the brief hope in her eyes, I wanted Daphne to know. That if I ever push her away, if she ever wonders why our friendship can't be more, it's not because of her. It could never be because of her.

It's me. It's my family. It's a mess I'd never wish upon her or anyone.

Though now that Daphne has resumed painting and my nerves have settled, I question why I didn't take the opportunity to reiterate the boundary between us. I could have said I can never marry Daphne because we're just friends. Or I could never feel that way about her. I'm shocked I took the harder path—the path of truth—instead of falling back on my usual patterns.

How curious…

Night has fallen by the time Daphne deems our painting session complete.

"Thank fuck." I release a grateful groan, shaking out my arms and legs. Most of my limbs have lost feeling, even after the intermittent breaks Daphne allowed me. I roll my head from side to side, resulting in several audible cracks.

"I'm glad I'm not that kind of model," Araminta mutters.

"When is our next courtship lesson?" Daphne says as she cleans her brushes. "Tomorrow? Next weekend?"

I don my shirt and start doing up the buttons. My stomach drops at her question. "I might be out of town next weekend."

"Where are you going?"

"My best friend is getting married," I say, putting on my waistcoat and leaving it open. I seek out my small silver case and remove a cigarillo from inside. "Though I haven't decided if I'll attend."

Daphne sets down her brushes and approaches me. "Your best friend…you mean the baker? I remember you mentioning him on the tour."

"Yes, the baker. He and his fiancée are the match I'm proudest of making. I'm supposed to be his best man and escort my sister so she can attend as well."

"Best man is an important role, isn't it? You must go. Where is the wedding?"

"The Cyllene Hotel in the Star Court."

Daphne's mouth falls open. "Are you serious? The *Cyllene Hotel*? As in the Cyllene Hotel with the ballroom that has the domed ceiling that perfectly replicates a meteor shower without any magic, only a human painter's mortal talents?"

Ah, I can understand her awe now. "That's the one."

She stares at me with an irked expression. "I...I'm so jealous. I'm experiencing such vast envy I sort of want to punch you."

"Punch him!" Araminta says in support, clapping her hands together.

Daphne takes a step closer. "You have an opportunity to not only serve as your best friend's best man but to witness one of the greatest artistic marvels on the isle?"

"I have my reasons—"

"Take me."

I blink at her. Before I can reply, she speaks again, eyes wide with fervor.

"Take me with you, Monty, I'm begging you. It's not just that I'm desperate to see the ballroom with my own eyes, but the location is the perfect background for my next cover. I've envisioned my piece being set in a ballroom, but the ones here in Jasper don't evoke the right atmosphere. I need to paint the Cyllene Ballroom. To sketch it, at the very least. Please take me with you."

"Sorry," Araminta says in a lazy tone, "I can't go. I have another modeling job next weekend."

"No one invited you," Daphne snaps. "When are you going home, anyway?"

Araminta stretches out on the settee, her legs hooked over one of the arms. "I don't have a home yet, and I'm tired of sleeping at the office now that I've grown accustomed to this seelie lifestyle. Just let me stay the night. Please? I'll get my own place soon."

"Fine," Daphne grumbles, then returns her attention to me. She wrings her hands, wincing. "I guess I shouldn't scold Ari for inviting herself to places when I'm doing the same thing. But can I *please* invite myself, Monty? Please, please, please?"

Did she always sound so cute when saying my name?

Blazing hell, when she looks at me like that, I find it impossible to care about the repercussions.

If I leave town over the weekend, I'll miss another payment and incur another penalty; my lender will move the due date for my loan up another week. But I'm fucked regardless if I can't get another loan to pay this one off, and I can't get a legitimate loan without that signing bonus as collateral and proof of long-term employment. Which means my book—my case study—takes priority.

And my case study depends on Daphne.

I flip my unlit cigarillo over my fingers. "If I take you with me, we'll need to hold our next courtship lesson over the weekend. And since I'm supposed to arrive Friday and the train ride there is a long fucking haul, we'll have to leave early Thursday evening and miss work on Friday. Probably Monday too."

"Friday is my illustration day," she says, unable to keep the excitement out of her voice, "and Mr. Fletcher often lets me do illustration work from home. Missing work Monday shouldn't be a problem either. I rarely take time off."

"Then I guess…" I pause to watch her squirm a little, to watch her eyes grow rounder with pleading and her smile grow sweeter. "I guess you can come with me."

Daphne collides with me, her arms encircling my waist in a crushing hug. She's surprisingly strong for a woman so small in stature. She hops in place while hugging me, her cheek crushed to my chest and making my whole torso shake from the force of her excitement. Then she tilts her head back and meets my gaze, her eyes crinkled with joy. "Thank you."

My breath catches, my pulse quickening. I'm struck dumb looking at her, at her adorable expression, the coral flush in her cheeks, the mussed strands of her hair from where she squished her cheek against my chest. Her body is soft against me, yet her arms continue to hold tight around my waist. My hands are still loose at my sides, but I'm suddenly aware of them, curious about how it would feel to return her hug—

She steps back, releasing me, and brings her fists under her chin in a bashful gesture while her grin remains wide. "Sorry. I got too excited."

"It's fine," I say, mortified at how soft and choked my voice sounds.

"Don't I get to pick the next lesson topic?" she asks, unaware of the effect her spontaneous hug had on me. "You said we could alternate who chooses our topic if I wanted."

I do my best to recover my senses and arch a brow at the manuscript, still on the table where I left it the last time I was here. "Have you read my book yet?"

The guilt shows all over her face. "No, but I will. I'll read it this week."

"Then if you have any requests, you can make them. Meanwhile, I'll draft out a lesson plan I believe would be most effective for our circumstances."

She gives an exuberant nod.

I see myself out, but only after Daphne thanks me a thousand times more.

Once outside, I heave a sigh and light my cigarillo. I find I don't need the herbal blend's calming effects. Even though I'm wary about leaving next weekend and attending a damn wedding, I'm relaxed too.

As I proceed down the sidewalk, I absently rub my palm over the middle of my chest. I know I'm only imagining things, but my shirt still feels warm where Daphne crushed herself against me. Or maybe it's my chest that's warm. Or my heart? Whatever the case, I must be a madman for agreeing to take a woman to a wedding with me. Daphne doesn't know what a big deal society places on gestures like taking a date to a wedding, though even if she did, she knows it's not like that with us. Besides, I'm escorting my sister to the wedding too. I'm only taking Daphne so she can work on her illustration and so that I can help her make progress in finding a husband.

My jaw tenses at the thought, bringing a flash of anger along with it. I hate the idea of setting Daphne up with another idiot like Conrad. Or maybe I hate the idea of setting her up with anyone. I don't know a soul who's good enough for her. Not that I make a habit of knowing many people these days.

Still, I must try. I must do more than enjoy our time together. I must do more than focus on my case study. Her needs are just as great as mine, and if she doesn't marry by Lughnasadh, she'll be bound to someone worse than Conrad. At least I assume Clyde the fucking honey badger is worse because he participated in a handfasting ritual with a drunk person. Not only that, but she'll have to stay in her hometown.

And I'll never see her again.

The thought makes my stomach roil.

I take a long drag from my cigarillo and breathe my worries away. Shifting all my stressors aside, I'm left with a prospect equal parts terrifying and exciting: I'm going to spend an entire weekend with Daphne.

CHAPTER TWENTY

DAPHNE

The last time I boarded a train was during The Heartbeats Tour. Traveling on one now fills me with nostalgia for that month of my life when we rode from city to city, staying in a new place every few days. I didn't appreciate it much at the time and found the whole ordeal quite a bother. The crowded train cars grated on my nerves, as did the busy events Monty and I were responsible for managing. Even though I didn't socialize after hours with the new friends I'd made, I began to enjoy myself more.

Now I can say with certainty that I miss those days.

"This almost feels like before, doesn't it?" I grin at Monty across the small table between us, set with tea and cookies. We're seated in the public car on a pair of velvet-cushioned seats that line the wood-paneled interior. Emerald-green drapes flank windows that glow with late afternoon sunlight, a view of the Earthen Court countryside speeding past on a palette of every shade of green. Our accommodations aren't as comfortable as the private compartments we traveled in during the tour, but our travels aren't funded by a company budget this time. We'll be here for the entire eighteen-hour ride. Thankfully, the public car isn't too crowded and our fellow passengers keep to themselves, their conversations too hushed to carry.

"Yes," Monty says, "except you're not sleeping on the luggage rack."

My grin widens. That was how I preferred to pass my time during train rides back then. I'd doze away from the rest of the group, always keeping one ear open to rejoin my party only when I found a conversation topic of interest. I was so shy back then. So anxious I might say the wrong thing or forget myself and go against social norms. It was only last year that I confessed this to Edwina, and she'd had no idea. She thought I came across as clever and confident. She thought I took time to myself or stayed quiet because I preferred my own company over socializing. While that is somewhat true, it doesn't represent how I feel inside. My yearning to fit in versus my dislike of loud places and tedious conversations. My love for my friends and my desire to spend time with them versus my protection over my comfort levels.

Yet a couple of times now, Monty has helped me find balance between the sides at war within me. Like when he brought me the noise-softening candy floss. Or our shooting game during the carnival. Or running through the rain afterward.

I never told Monty what I told Edwina.

Somehow he already knew.

"Is my presence not a significant difference as well?" asks the human woman beside me. Monty's sister smiles wide over the teacup she holds in her hand, her gaze volleying between us. "I'd love to hear about the tour you managed together. I only read about it from that interview you did in the *Gazette* all those months ago."

Monty chokes on his own sip of tea, his cheeks going crimson. "You read that?"

"Of course I did. It sounds like the tour was rather lively." Angela Phillips gives a proud nod, not an ounce of teasing on her face. Then she angles herself toward me. "I hope he wasn't too much of a pest. He can be a lot to deal with."

My pulse spikes as it always does when I'm getting used to conversing with someone I don't yet know. Especially someone like Angela, who is as well-dressed as she is well-spoken. She's outfitted in a gown of navy taffeta and a matching hat, her light-brown curls styled expertly beneath it. Meanwhile, I'm dressed in my usual work attire—trousers, blouse, waistcoat—and hardly bothered to do more with my hair than tuck the ends behind my ears.

But the sight of Monty across the table steadies my nerves. He's dressed as casually as I am, not a hint of his aristocratic upbringing on display.

My lips curl into a taunting smirk. "Pest is certainly a word for Monty, though I can think of several more apt terms."

His nostrils flare and he gives my foot a playful kick under the table.

Before Angela joined us at the station today, he asked me not to bring up any inappropriate topics in front of his sister that involve him. "She knows I'm a careless rake," he said, "but she doesn't need to know to what extent. Particularly about my *Ask Gladys* column."

While I'm bound to keep my promise and am charmed by how protective he is of her, I can still make him squirm a little.

"Will you be able to see your friends while we're in the

Star Court?" Angela asks. "The author and the actor? They live in Lumenas, don't they?"

I beam at Monty, eagerly anticipating his answer. Edwina and William recently purchased an apartment in downtown Lumenas, which is in the same court we'll be in. However, their city is in the far north while we'll be in the south, so the chances that we can meet with them over the busy weekend are slim.

"Unfortunately," Monty says, crushing my hopes at once, "neither is home. William is currently touring the isle in support of his new stage play and Edwina is traveling with him while she pens her newest book. I sent them a telegram just to be sure."

My shoulders sink. "The four of us should make plans to reunite. We haven't been together in the same room even once since you were an—" I clear my throat before I can say *asshole*. "Since you were a *pest* to me."

Angela's mouth falls open. "Did the two of you have a falling-out? I swear, my brother cannot maintain friendships for the life of him. Did you know Thorne Blackwood is the only person who's been able to tolerate Monty long-term? Aside from me, of course. Thorne and Monty have been friends since they were children. Father was always encouraging Monty to make friends, but my brother didn't give anyone the time of day until he met Thorne. Good thing Papa went into business with Thorne's father or the boys never would have met."

I train my expression into a look of casual interest, though I'm more curious about the complete lack of vitriol in her voice when she mentions their father. Monty has made his disdain clear, but Angela doesn't seem to share his feelings.

She continues. "But even Thorne kept his distance from Monty for a time. They seem much closer now, but my brother went through this moody phase where he lost all his friends. Even Cosette—"

"Please, do not bring up Cosette." Monty's tone is firm. It's the first time I've heard him use such a voice with Angela thus far.

She lowers her teacup, her posture dejected. "You never told me what happened with her."

"She hasn't tried to correspond with you, has she?"

"No," Angela says with a pout.

"Good. You have better friends than her now. Pay her no heed, even in memory."

Tension radiates off Monty, and I can't help wondering if Cosette is the first love he told me about. He never mentioned she was once friends with his sister, only that he had known her a long time.

Angela heaves a sigh. "Very well. I won't speak of *her*, but I am glad you at least made up with Thorne. Who would have guessed you'd become better friends after he fell in love with your fiancée?"

"Fiancée," I echo. "We're going to the wedding of your former fiancée?" My mind reels over this information. If this woman named Cosette isn't his first love, then could the bride be? He told me she left him for someone else. Could she have left him for his *best friend*? Anger and annoyance writhe within me, though I'm not sure who I'm angrier at—Monty for not explaining this beforehand or the bride I'm going to meet.

"Did he not tell you?" Angela asks. "It was quite a big deal. His engagement to the princess was supposed to make the Phillipses part of the royal family. That's why Father was so angry when Monty refused to marry her and she ended up falling in love with Thorne instead."

"A princess?" I blink at her, trying to paint more comprehension onto an already messy canvas. I cut a glare across the table. "You're taking me to a royal wedding? What the fuck, Monty? Why didn't you tell me that before?"

Several pairs of eyes shoot our way from nearby tables, but I'm too flustered to care.

Monty holds out his hands in a placating gesture. "She's not a princess anymore. She left her royal family—who are no longer royals, by the way—as did Thorne."

I don't think my eyes can go any wider. "Your best friend comes from a royal family too?"

"Sort of, but not really. It's a long story."

"I thought you said he was a baker."

"He is. Well, he's a baker and the owner of one of the most popular bakery chains in Faerwyvae. And the lord of Blackwood Estate."

I sink against my seat cushion, mind still whirling. There is one question that hounds my mind more than any other. I hold his gaze and speak through my teeth. "Is she the one? Your first love—"

"No, Briony Rose and I never had any love between us. Our engagement was arranged by our parents but neither of us wanted it. That's why I encouraged her and Thorne's attachment when I sensed the spark between them."

My anger cools. His explanation cuts my theory in two. So the bride is not the woman who hurt him—and whom he hurt in return. She's merely a former fiancée from a loveless engagement who fell for his friend. It sounds rather awkward, but it's a better situation than the one I was imagining a moment before. If I forget about the whole former princess part.

"First love," Angela says, brow furrowed. "Brother, you've never been in love before, have you?" When he doesn't answer, she adds, "You know, I wouldn't call what you did for Thorne and Briony encouragement. You *tormented* them. You were so annoying."

The tension finally leaves Monty's expression. His lips curl into a grin. "I was incredibly annoying to them. Briony won't likely have the best things to relay about me." He says the last part to me. Then I feel something soft against my ankle. It's the tip of his shoe gently grazing me from ankle to shin, the gesture apologetic. Well, he should be sorry for not preparing me sooner for what's in store, but at least I know now.

Angela gives me a somber nod. "I can only imagine the anecdotes Briony could share. You should have heard the idiocy leaving my dear brother's lips back then. He was all *let's turn our engagement into a game* and *let's see how well my bride can ride,* and he was absolutely speaking in innuendo."

Monty pinches his brow. "Good God, Angie, please don't repeat the horrible things I do or say."

"Then I'd be struck mute when trying to talk about you, wouldn't I?" Angela immediately breaks into tittering laughter, pleased with her own insult.

I can't help smiling too. Despite how much Monty coddles his sister and treats her like an innocent girl, it's clear she's clever. She may have a heavy dose of the naiveté that's characteristic of highborn young women, due to the propriety she was raised with, but she doesn't seem fragile.

"Just wait until you see how he acts around Thorne and Briony," she says. "He's like a completely different person."

I arch a brow at Monty as I lift my teacup from its saucer and take a sip. "A different person, hmm?"

He says nothing, only holds my gaze as he sips from his own cup.

Perhaps I'll get my wish about seeing the secret sides of Monty after all.

Lesson Three

LUST
AND THE ADVANTAGES OF A FULL-LENGTH MIRROR

CHAPTER TWENTY-ONE

MONTY

We arrive at the Cyllene Hotel by noon the next day. It's a towering building of pale marble that looks more like a palace than a hotel, with several floors lined with long balconies and ending in towering turrets. Surrounded by trees and rolling hills, with only a massive garden in between, it's just as private as a palace too. At first, I'm confused about how such a widely renowned hotel could be located in a small countryside town like Antilia Falls, with hardly more than a modest market square to its name. Where do guests find entertainment? Recreation? Where do they dine? Buy clothing?

It all makes sense as soon as we step through the front doors. We halt in place and take it all in.

Daphne gasps in awe from beside me, as does my sister. I don't blame them. The hotel's interior is a sight to behold. It feels more like we've stepped into a new world.

The walls are stucco and marble in warm pastel tones, the

high ceiling enchanted to mimic the perfect sunny outdoor sky. The floors above are tiered, each boasting a façade of arched windows and faux crenelated rooftops to give the impression of a town built on a hillside, with walkways interspersed to connect opposite sides. A canal filled with crystal-clear aquamarine water weaves through the first floor of the hotel, with arched bridges that cross it and storefronts that line it featuring everything from cafés to galleries. No wonder the hotel is so successful despite its remote location. Everything one could want while on holiday is here in one building.

Glittering sprites and tiny birds flutter overhead, landing on balconies or the multitude of potted plants. The atmosphere reminds me so much of the Solar Court that I can't help wondering if this was, in fact, a palace at one time, long before the war ended. Back then, all the fae courts were relegated to the north. The land we stand on now may belong to the Star Court, but three decades ago, it was Solar.

This wouldn't be the first time one of the abandoned palaces of old was turned into a hotel. Smart business, honestly.

"I'd give anything to paint this," Daphne says, clasping her hands at her heart as her eyes flit from one impressive sight to the next.

With my hands tucked in my trouser pockets, I lean in close to her ear. "We've hardly stepped inside. I'm sure there's more to admire. Besides, haven't you grown immune to such impressive locations after The Heartbeats Tour?"

She shakes her head. "I could never grow immune to art. Especially in this body. Beautiful things look different through these eyes. They *feel* different, here." She rubs her chest and swivels her face to mine, eyes still wide with wonder. "Everything feels different."

My breath catches. Now that we're face to face, I realize

how near I'm standing, how close I've leaned, with her lips a breath away from mine. The impassioned expression on her face is an echo of the one I've glimpsed in the sketches she's shown me. Sketches I know she models for.

I can't stop my eyes from dropping to her mouth, parted in awe, the tips of those adorable canines peeking out. A sharp yearning seizes me, and I'm desperate to know how her veneration tastes. How does it feel against my tongue? How does that body of hers—the body she claims feels things so differently, so much more acutely than her unseelie form —feel against mine? How can I inspire this look on her face?

Her brow furrows slightly, as if she's reading my thoughts.

Thoughts she really shouldn't read.

Fuck. What's wrong with me?

Not only is this forbidden territory my mind is wandering down, but my sister is standing on the other side of Daphne.

Shame, you fucking pervert. Get your act together!

I suck in a breath and straighten to my full height. I can't recall the last word either of us said, and heat has already begun to crawl up my neck, so I march away like an idiot and make a beeline for the reception desk. That gives me a solid few minutes to clear my head as I check us in. The receptionist directs us to where we can meet the bride and groom, and I return to Daphne and Angela with a mask of indifference.

"Come along," I say and angle my head toward the main avenue that runs through the center of the hotel. I keep my hands in my pockets so as not to be tempted to escort Daphne. My sister is the one I should be escorting, but she doesn't mind. Instead, she links her arm through Daphne's. Daph stiffens, and I realize my carelessness at once. She doesn't like being touched by people she doesn't know, and I doubt our twenty-hour train ride was enough to make them friends.

Then, to my surprise, Daphne's posture relaxes and she returns to admiring the wonders of the hotel's interior, her grin as bright as Angela's as they walk side by side.

My lips curve too. There's something sweet and satisfying about seeing Daphne at ease with my sister. The member of my family I care about the most.

We make our way down the avenue, along one side of the canal, until we reach a florist's shop. Scents of lilies and roses fill the air, the walls and floor space crowded with overstuffed bouquets. There, at the counter, stand the figures I'm looking for.

A tall male with rounded ears, shoulder-length dark hair, and spectacles grins at the woman beside him. She's rather tall herself with pointed ears, long golden-blond hair, and a curvy figure. The man is dressed in casual attire, his shirtsleeves rolled up to reveal the coiled snake-like patterns tattooed on his forearms while the woman is outfitted in a white day dress. Beside her stands a young fae girl, no older than seven or eight in appearance, with white bunny ears and pale hair arranged in two braids.

I take a deep breath, prepared to greet my best friend. To be the version of myself that I must be with him. "Thorny boy!" I say with a crooked grin.

Thorne Blackwood stiffens, then rounds on me with a glare. "About time."

When it comes to our relationship, that's Thorne's way of giving me a warm greeting.

I pat him on the back then meet his soon-to-be wife, Briony Rose, in a loose hug. "And there's my lovely former fiancée. Congrats on your upcoming nuptials. Second time's the charm, isn't it?"

She scoffs as we separate. "Yes, particularly because you

lacked charm entirely. Perhaps you still do." The fact that she had to add *perhaps* to the last part tells me my charm has at least somewhat grown on her. While Thorne is half fae—a demon, to be exact—and capable of lying, Briony is a pure-blood succubus and can only speak the truth. *Perhaps* is a common modifier fae use to deceive without lying.

Thorne's expression turns warm as he shines a smile upon my sister. "Angie, I'm so glad you could make it."

Angela throws herself into Thorne's arms, then Briony's, radiating excitement as she congratulates them.

Daphne edges closer to me, the back of her hand brushing mine. I can almost feel the anxiety pulsing through her, so I step in close and link a finger around hers, our hands hidden between us behind the folds of her pink day dress—the same she wore to the carnival. Her shoulders drop as she squeezes my fingers, just in time to brace herself for Thorne and Briony's attention.

Daphne, however, isn't the only one who appears nervous. The fae child next to Briony stares at us with wide blue eyes, the whiskers beside her pink little nose twitching as she clings to Briony's sleeve. I'm unacquainted with this child, but courtesy requires I introduce Daphne before I ask about the rabbit fae.

I clear my throat, my fingers still linked with Daphne's. "Thorne, Briony, this is my friend, Daphne. Daph, meet Thorne Blackwood and Briony Rose. Soon to be Briony Blackwood."

Daphne finally releases my fingers to dip into a brief curtsy.

"I had no idea," Thorne says to me.

I frown. "That I was bringing a plus one? I sent a telegram—"

"No, I had no idea you had friends." He turns his gaze to

Daphne. "Do you consider him a friend or is he paying you to pretend to tolerate him?"

She stiffens all over again, but this time I get the sense it isn't out of anxiety but irritation. Could Daph be taking offense on my behalf?

I chuckle to convey that this sort of banter is how Thorne and I express our affection. Not entirely unlike how Daphne insults me.

Her eyes flash to my face and she relaxes. "I may consider him a friend," she says, tone dry, "but I need not mention whether I tolerate him."

Thorne and Briony chuckle, and another wave of sweet satisfaction washes over me. Just like that, Daphne has won over my best friend and his fiancée. I'm not sure why it's so important to me that those I care about like Daphne...but it is.

Briony puts her arm around the fae child and hugs her close to her side. "I'd like to introduce our daughter, Tilly."

Angela gives a delighted squeal. "I'm so happy to finally meet you, Tilly."

Meanwhile, I feel like I've been punched in the heart. "Daughter?"

Thorne gives Tilly's head an affectionate pet, eliciting a warm smile from the girl. "The adoption was made official last month. We're thrilled we got to bring her home from the convent in time for the wedding."

My heart volleys between pain and joy. Joy for obvious reasons. My best friend has a daughter now. They must have adopted her from the same convent Briony was raised in, the Celesta Convent School for Girls, located not too far from here. Yet the pain remains because...

Because my best friend has a daughter.

And I had no clue.

Did he not tell me because he thought I'd be uninterested?

If that's the case, I can hardly blame him. That's part of the act I put on. The distance I create between us.

My sister was right when she told Daphne about the *moody period* I had where I lost all my friends. Thorne was the hardest to lose, yet he was the hardest to keep, which was why I pushed him the farthest away. I simply couldn't bear his company. Not because I disliked it but rather because I liked it too well. He was my best friend. And if anyone could understand what I was going through, could understand the weight of the secret I'd recently uncovered, it would be Thorne.

Thorne, who had a secret lineage. Raised by two humans, one of whom was unrelated to him by blood.

Thorne, whose secret I uncovered all on my own, but never spoke about.

While I had to remain silent about my own. Never confessing that I was just like him.

Son of an aristocratic father.

And a mother who claimed me as her own despite the lack of any blood relation.

Both he and I are bastard born.

But while Thorne's lineage wasn't a secret of infidelity, merely complicated family history, mine was. Mine was a secret that could shatter the Phillips name. My family's reputation. My father's place in government. My sister's prospects.

I couldn't tell Thorne.

And I still can't tell him. Can't tell anyone.

My throat constricts, my lungs tight—

"Pleasure to meet you." Tilly's small voice snaps me out of my thoughts, as do the fingers that squeeze mine. It takes me a moment to realize the latter belong to Daphne. Just like I did with her, she's stepped in close, hiding our hands to link our fingers together.

Some of the pressure eases from my chest. I manage to speak with only the faintest tremble in my voice. "An honor to meet you as well, Tilly."

Briony and Thorne exchange a look of shock at my kind greeting. Or maybe it's the sheen I can't seem to blink from my eyes.

Oh…fucking hell. I'm going to cry. I never would have guessed meeting my best friend's daughter for the first time would move me so, but I'm on the verge of tears. It's not like I'm ashamed of emotion, but this is a side of me I can't show Thorne. I…I'm just not ready, I—

Before a single tear can fall, two palms frame my face. Daphne wrenches my gaze to hers, locks our eyes, and slaps my cheeks.

The force isn't violent, but it's just hard enough to distract me. I'm so shocked, so delighted by the momentary sting of her palms, that my eyes dry up. She holds my gaze a beat longer, then steps back, removing her hands.

I blink at her, unsure of what just happened. Though, come to think of it, I've caught her slapping her own cheeks a time or two, normally after I've flustered her. Did Daffy Dear just rescue me in her own strange way?

My heart, no longer strangled with pain, thuds with warmth.

But as she and I return our attention to our companions, we find only confused glances locked on us.

I open my mouth to utter some kind of explanation, but Daphne speaks first, taking another step away from me as she points an accusing thumb my way. "He touched my butt."

All at once Thorne, Briony, and Angela shake their heads or roll their eyes, fully unsurprised by Daphne's words.

I, however, am very surprised. Daphne can't lie—

Well, I suppose I *have* touched her butt, when I woke up

with her in my arms at her apartment. It may not have been just now, but it's technically true.

Yet that means Daphne was aware of it.

My pulse rackets.

"Really, Monty?" Briony says. "Can you not be lecherous for one weekend?"

Daphne puts her hands on her hips, nodding along with Briony's words, a note of taunting in her eyes. She's clearly enjoying this.

Thorne claps me on the shoulder. "I suppose this is a good time to take Monty away and allow you ladies some peace. He is my best man, after all, and I have a stag party for him to organize. It's tonight, so you have…six hours."

"Six hours?"

"If you wanted more time, then maybe you should have arrived earlier. Or, I don't know…replied to my fucking—pardon." He winces, giving an apologetic look at Tilly. "My *darn* letters."

Good God, daddy Thorne is adorable.

"I suppose I can plan a party in six hours," I say with a sigh. "I was once a tour manager, after all."

"Don't get too carried away," Briony says. "I want him coherent tomorrow."

"What about your hen party?" Angela asks. "Is that tonight as well?"

"It is." Briony turns to Daphne. "You're more than welcome to come. We'll take a tour of the hotel, stopping for dinner, dessert, and drinks followed by—"

"Please, no," Daphne says in a rush, then grimaces at her own words. "I'm so sorry, that sounded rude, didn't it? What I mean is…" She shifts from foot to foot.

"What Daffy Dear means," I say, lifting a hand to the side of her face only to realize I haven't a clue what the fuck I was about to do. Tuck her hair behind her ears? Touch her cheek?

I correct course and give a playful tug to a lock of black hair, a gesture to which she responds by biting at my fingers. "—is that she prefers to settle in at the hotel by much quieter means tonight."

"In that case," Briony says, "I'll take her to the ballroom."

Daphne presses a hand to her chest. "I get to see the ballroom now?"

Briony gives her an indulgent grin. "Monty sent a telegram informing me of your desire to sketch it. So I arranged for you to have access anytime today, as it's not in use."

Excitement glitters in Daphne's eyes, all traces of the anxiety she showed upon meeting Briony and Thorne gone. I suppose art and poking fun at me are two ways to soothe her nerves. She looks to me, either for reassurance or comfort or maybe just to share her joy.

I wink. "Have fun."

"Lesson One," she says with a nod, and I'm reminded that we're supposed to use this weekend for my case study.

My stomach sinks.

"You, on the other hand, don't have too much fun." She pokes me in the chest with her forefinger. She does it again, grinning as if enjoying the firmness of my pectoral.

Before she can poke me a third time, I capture her finger and link it with my own. "Worried about me, Daffy Dear?"

She lifts her chin and slides her finger from mine. "More like worried you might be a bad influence on a soon-to-be married man."

I give her a coy look. "When have I ever been a bad influence?"

Angela speaks up. "Didn't you bring your two authors from The Heartbeats Tour to an orgy?"

"Why does everyone bring that up? I had nothing to do with the voyeurism room. I was high on the roof all night."

"Nope." Briony covers Tilly's long bunny ears and speaks in a furious whisper. "No talk of getting high or going to orgies. You will drink, gamble, and talk shit like sensible gentlemen. Got that?"

"On my honor," I say, giving Briony a somber bow. She rolls her eyes.

Thorne kisses Tilly on the head and Briony on the lips before his fiancée leads the ladies out of the flower shop. I watch Daphne until she's out of sight. Then I heave a sigh.

"Interesting reaction there, Monty boy." Thorne's voice draws my attention to him. His gaze is locked on the hand I have pressed to my chest. The place where Daphne poked.

I force my hands to my sides. "What's so interesting about it?"

Thorne shrugs. "It's just interesting, that's all."

"I haven't a clue what you fucking mean," I mutter, stalking out of the shop before he can catch the heat in my cheeks.

CHAPTER TWENTY-TWO

DAPHNE

The Cyllene Ballroom is even more beautiful in person than any of the pictures I've seen. It's a circular room with a domed ceiling painted in the most exquisite hues from the darkest blue to vibrant pink, purple, aqua, and gold. I haven't seen anything more breathtaking. It's a meteor shower brought to life with paint and paint alone. No enchantment like the ceiling in the main part of the hotel. No tricks of light.

"Your reaction isn't much unlike my own when I first saw this," Briony says.

I realize I'm gawking, but at least I'm not the only one. Angela and Tilly look equally as impressed. I draw my gaze to the rest of the room. Tables and chairs have been set up around the perimeter behind the row of intricately carved columns that separate the dining area from the dance floor. The room is half set up for an event—for Briony's wedding, I assume—with ribbons tied around the columns and half the tables set with silk cloth and empty vases, the rest bare.

"May I practice my dances, Mama?" Tilly asks, grinning wide to reveal adorable buck teeth.

Briony strokes her daughter's hair. "Of course, love."

Angela leans down slightly and speaks in a gentle tone. "May I dance with you?"

Tilly's cheeks turn pink, but she gives a bashful nod. The two scurry to the center of the dance floor.

"The porter will bring your art supplies as soon as your luggage arrives from the station," Briony says. "I'll wait with you until then."

"You don't have to," I rush to say. "None of us brought much, so it won't be long."

"Well, I can hardly interrupt their fun now, can I?" Briony nods toward Tilly and Angela, who've begun dancing a reel. "How about we take a turn about the room?"

My pulse quickens. I haven't been asked to *take a turn about the room* since my debutante days. It was always an opportunity to sneak in gossip or make some clever quip that was meant to be overheard by the room at large. Never for me, of course. I never understood the veiled humor or the subtext beneath my companions' beautiful words. When I spoke, I spoke plainly, and I expected the same in return. We were taught to be polite and demure, after all. Polite and demure ended up being nothing more than a mask for some of the girls. And I was their easy target. I was the prey that used to be the hunter.

"We can simply walk and talk," Briony says as if reading the tension in my posture. She clasps her hands behind her back, not making any move to touch me or pull me close to whisper salacious gossip in my ear.

My stomach uncoils. Right. Briony isn't like the debutantes who teased me to my face. And I'm not the same girl I was then. I'm now familiar with the scent of dishonest assholes. Briony isn't one of them.

We take a leisurely stroll around the perimeter of the dance floor while Angela and Tilly continue to practice the reel. Angela appears to be a skilled dancer, but I'm surprised that Tilly is as well. From what little about Briony I managed to learn from Monty, I know she loves to dance and teaches lessons to the girls at the convent school where she was raised. Turns out the former princess thing really is a long story. Something about a sleeping spell and family curses.

"I hope Monty doesn't get Thorne into too much trouble tonight," Briony grumbles.

"There isn't a boxing arena here, is there?"

"No, I don't believe so. But there is ample liquor. Thorne will probably end up spending his whole evening sobering up Monty like usual." She says the last part with a chuckle.

I frown. "Monty doesn't drink, though."

Her face whips toward mine. "He doesn't? Since when?"

"He hasn't since I've known him. I believe he quit shortly before we set off on the tour we managed. So a couple years, perhaps."

She tilts her head to the side. "I had no idea. How unexpectedly responsible of him."

As her eyes grow distant, I wonder if I've given away some secret of Monty's. He did nothing to hide his sobriety from us on tour, though he didn't make a big deal out of it either. He only stated he no longer imbibed because he was a working man now and needed to be responsible. Maybe he just never found it pertinent to mention to Briony and Thorne.

"Equally as unexpected," Briony says, recovering from her momentary shock, "is that he brought you. I never thought Monty would bring a date to my wedding."

I shrink down a little. "Oh, is that offensive? Since he's your former fiancé?"

She barks a laugh. "Stars, no, that's not what I meant at all. It's more...I haven't seen him court anyone."

"We're not courting," I say, waving my hands. "We're former colleagues, but now we're just...friends."

"*Just* friends?"

Why is my heart pounding so hard? "We had a falling out, but we've recently reconnected. But yes, we're...friends. Furthermore, he's helping me find a husband."

Briony rolls her eyes. "Monty and his matchmaking. The gall of that man taking credit for people's relationships when he hardly has a hand in it. That's not matchmaking. That's just...observation and interference."

I give her a wry grin. Now that I've seen Briony, Thorne, and Monty interact, I understand how much of their affection for each other is layered with insults. It made me bristle at first, but now I know it's a product of their brutally honest friendship. I admit, though, I am a little jealous. Briony must know Monty a thousand times better than I do. She's known him much longer.

That does make me wonder...

"So, you've really never seen him court anyone?" I ask, keeping my voice level and my steps measured. Just a casual question. No reason to act too interested in the answer.

"Not unless I count Cosette Dervins, but I'd hardly call that courtship." Her expression sours.

My pulse leaps at the name. "You know Cosette?"

She halts in place and whirls to me with wide eyes. "I'm more surprised you do. Please tell me she isn't stalking him again."

I pause too, pulling my head back. "I only heard about her on the train yesterday when Angela mentioned her. She was his stalker? Not his first love?"

"Oh, she was his first love, as far as Thorne has told me."

We resume our stroll and Briony waves at Tilly. She and Angela link arms and skip in a circle, then switch arms and repeat the move in the opposite direction.

"Monty says he was terrible to her," I say. "Is that true?"

"I mean, he wasn't pleasant to her, but she was one of the least pleasant people I've ever met." She lowers her voice to a whisper. "She befriended Angela just to get close to Monty. Angie doesn't know, and no one—including me—wants to tell her. Back then, Angie was bullied by her schoolmates, and Cosette was her only friend. As soon as Monty made it clear to Cosette, once and for all, that he was never going to be with her, she stopped talking to Angie completely. Thankfully Angie has a bevy of good friends now."

My heart aches for Angela. No wonder Monty was so furtive yet sharp when his sister mentioned Cosette on the train.

Briony speaks again. "Even if not for how she was using Angela, I disliked her on principle alone. She had the audacity to try to interfere with my engagement to Monty, trying to seduce him right before my eyes. I didn't exactly mind, since I so vehemently disliked him, but she disrespected me regardless. Thorne's last words to her were something along the lines of *fuck off*, and that's a sentiment neither of us are keen on revoking anytime soon." She gives me a conspiratorial grin.

I return the smile, then ask, "Do you still dislike Monty?"

"No, I like him well enough now. The more I get to know him, the more I feel like we don't know him at all. That he keeps his heart hidden. Yet I can tell he loves Thorne and Angie. I saw the emotion in his eyes when he met Tilly."

My chest tightens at the memory. I sensed it before I saw it, my inner hunter alerting me to vulnerable prey. He radiated with a need to hide, to pretend, to camouflage with his surroundings like a mouse in the underbrush. That's when I did the one thing I could think to do. I slapped his cheeks.

"I wonder if there's a reason he keeps people at a distance," Briony says, expression thoughtful. Then she shakes the look from her face and gives me another wicked grin. "I think the worst thing about him is that he hates dancing. Who could ever hate dancing?"

"Does he?" I arch my brows. That's the first time I'm hearing of this. "I suppose that explains why he was so bad at it."

Briony halts in place again. "He danced with you?"

I nod. "During the tour we managed. There was a gala and I danced in public for the first time. He claims one of my partners had wandering hands, and he stepped in."

Briony's gaze turns assessing. "Is that so?"

"I had no idea he hated dancing. There's so much about him I don't know."

"On the contrary," she says, her clever grin lifting her lips once more, "I think you might know him better than any of us."

Several hours later, I'm lost in the pleasure of my art. I'm alone now, Briony, Angela, and Tilly having left long ago, and only have my sketchbook and canvas for company. I didn't bring my easel, so my canvas lies over a spare tablecloth on the floor. Several sheets of paper are strewn around me, featuring every angle I've sketched the ballroom from. Once I settled on an angle I liked best, I began a clean sketch on the canvas. Now I glance from the sketch to the room, dreaming up what colors I might use once I begin the painting stage back home. Cerulean blue here. Cobalt violet there. Titanium white mixed with yellow ochre to highlight the glow of the—

"I thought I might find you here." Monty's voice has me leaping in place. I didn't hear him enter the room or notice when he leaned against the nearby column.

I set down my graphite and shift on my knees to face him, smoothing my wrinkled skirt to no avail. I probably should have changed from my day dress into my casual attire, but I was too excited to get started after my art supplies arrived. After that, I forgot what I was wearing entirely and hiked my skirt to my knees, smearing graphite along the way. Yet there's no reason to be self-conscious around Monty. Especially since he's equally as unkempt as I am right now.

My gaze sweeps over him. His hair is even more mussed than usual, his cravat absent, his waistcoat unbuttoned, and his shirt half tucked and open at the collar. His cheeks are flushed and his eyelids are heavy. He looks very much like someone who just rolled out of his lover's bed. Wait...did he? Was Thorne's stag party of an indecent nature after all?

A strange sensation tightens in my chest, followed by a pinch of fiery hot rage.

He straightens, pushing off the column as his brow knits into a furrow. "What's that angry little look for? Are you upset I didn't come sooner?"

I blink, smoothing my expression as best I can. I hadn't realized I'd worn my emotions so plainly on my face. "Look? What look?"

He saunters over to me. "I came as soon as the party ended. What a fucking chore. I had no idea being dubbed best man meant I had to do everything Thorne said. I was practically his waiter and jester. Can you believe he made me dance shirtless on a table? It wouldn't be the first time I've done it, which is why Thorne insisted, but it was certainly the first time I've done it sober."

My rage melts out of me. That's why he's in such a disorderly state? Because he had to strip for his friend? A grin curves my lips. "Wish I'd seen that."

"I bet you do. You'd have laughed or savored every second to draw later. Probably both."

"You didn't *have* to do it, though, did you? You could have refused. I don't think *best man* comes with a binding bargain, even if your friend is half fae."

He rubs the back of his neck. "Perhaps, but it was his stag party, and this is his wedding weekend. The least I can do is make a fool of myself and dance like an idiot."

I'm reminded of what Briony told me. I keep my voice nonchalant as I ask, "But don't you hate dancing?"

"Not particularly. Though this wasn't exactly dancing, it was merely me shaking my ass and—ooooh." He nods, a glint of realization in his eyes. "Briony told you, didn't she?"

I give him a sheepish smile.

"Of course I told her I hated dancing when we were engaged. She loves it, and I needed her to hate me thoroughly."

"So you don't hate dancing? Because you danced with me one time, and I'd feel bad if you'd hated it all along—"

He steps forward and thrusts his hand toward me. "Come on."

I stare at his open palm. "What?"

"Just take it. Let me show you how much I hate dancing."

I frown, then reluctantly place my palm in his. All at once, he pulls me up. As soon as I'm on my feet, he places his other hand at the center of my back and begins skipping to the side. A burst of laughter leaves my lips as I stumble to mirror his movements. We skip and turn onto the empty dance floor, our steps echoing through the room.

"What are we doing?" I ask, my voice strangled with mirth.

"The gallopade."

"Yes, but why?"

"To show you how much I hate dancing."

"This doesn't feel like hate."

"That's because it isn't. You see, I *like* dancing. With you." Our eyes lock as he speaks. My heart takes a tumble, and my feet nearly do too before he shouts, "The waltz!"

He leads me into a slower tempo, allowing me to catch my breath. We step and turn in a circle, light on our feet, and I realize this is the dance we shared at the gala so many months ago.

"We were clumsy last time," I say, recalling how often I stepped on his feet.

"We were. I think we laughed the entire song."

"We're laughing now."

His eyes crinkle at the corners. "True, but look how much more graceful we are. Especially you. Have you been practicing?"

Every inch of my skin flushes at his praise. I shrug. "I think I'm merely more comfortable in this body. I did learn the steps long ago."

"Right. During your debut season."

"My season ended before the first ball."

"Shame on everyone else for missing out on your company. If only your enemies could see you now, a goddess of grace."

I scoff. "Goddess?"

"The polka."

A squeal leaves my lips as he increases our tempo and transitions us into another skipping dance. This time, he leads us off the dance floor and straight for the perimeter, which is crowded with tables and chairs. I gasp as we skip along, Monty expertly leading every twist and hop around the furnishings. Then he does the last thing I'm prepared for.

He leaps onto one of the chairs. Before I can collide with it, he reaches for my waist, hefts me up, and plants me on the chair next to him. From there, he steps onto the table and pulls me up after him, where we seamlessly continue our polka. Thankfully, this portion of the room hasn't been set up for the wedding yet, so the tabletops are bare and free from items we could damage or trip over.

My heart slams against my ribs, both from my surprise and the pace of our dance. After we skip across the table, Monty leads me down the chairs, to the floor, then onto the next table over. His shoes slide on the surface, but he manages to keep his balance.

"This is dangerous," I say, my cheeks aching from how much I'm laughing.

"But so much fun." His grin is as wide as mine, taking years off his visage. "I see the way you leap on your furnishings at home. It feels a lot like how you move when you're a pine marten, doesn't it? That's why you do it."

My cheeks grow hot. "You noticed?"

He nods, his dimples deeper than ever. "It's cute."

Cute. I may have been offended at being called cute when I was a pine marten, but now...

Now it makes me feel seen in a way I never have before. He's seen and known both sides of me. The little fae creature. The woman who isn't quite at home in her body. He's witnessed those sides collide when I'm in the comfort of my home...and thinks it's cute.

Something warm and bright spreads through my chest, my limbs.

"The waltz," Monty says, and we return to our previous dance, shifting and swaying upon the table. With our foot space now limited, I step in closer to Monty, the fronts of our bodies only inches apart. His hand moves lower down my back, making my breath hitch. I'm suddenly aware of the heat of his palm, the firmness of his shoulder beneath my hand, the feel of the two hands we hold clasped together.

I can't tear my gaze from his face, from the intensity in his gray eyes, the laugh lines around his eyes and mouth, the bob of his throat, the nearness of his lips. I'm struck by the urge to taste them, to run my tongue over his bottom lip and drag my teeth over it. To press our mouths together and breathe in the scent of him—

He lowers his head and heaves a sigh, our dance slowing to stillness. "It's late." His words come out rough, and it takes him an extra moment to release my hand. The palm at my back is the last to come away as he takes a slow step back. Though the mirth hasn't left his face, there is something like fatigue in his eyes. Fatigue or…regret, perhaps? "We should retire to our rooms. It's past midnight."

"It is?" I blink at the ballroom with fresh eyes. I hadn't realized I'd been drawing so long.

He hops down from the table and offers his hand to me. I take it, and he helps me down, even though I don't really need his aid.

"I'll come see you tomorrow, after I've fulfilled more best man duties," he says as we return to my canvas. "We can go over our lesson plan."

My mind is slow to process his words. "Oh, right. The case study."

"The case study," he echoes, a distant quality to his voice. This time I know for certain there's regret in his tone, but he shakes the mood away as I gather up my supplies. "Speaking of, do you have any requests for the lessons you'd like to demonstrate?"

I grimace.

"You still haven't read my book?"

"I will."

"You said that last week, and you, Daffy Dear, aren't supposed to lie."

"It wasn't a lie at the time," I say as I carefully tuck my sketches back into my book. "I had every intention to read it. I simply…didn't."

"Why not? Are you worried I'm a terrible writer?"

"Maybe I am. Maybe I'm worried it will be full of perversion and lecherousy."

He huffs. "Lecherousy. Is that even a word? If you're worried about tainting your angelic perception of me, then do avoid Chapter Eight."

I hug my sketchbook to my chest and heft my canvas under my arm. "What's in Chapter Eight?"

"I said don't read it, didn't I? Just read the first seven chapters. That's all we need to focus on for now."

I smirk, knowing I most certainly am going to read Chapter Eight, just to see what he doesn't want me to read. We leave the ballroom, our shoulders nearly brushing as we stroll down the main hall toward the staircase that leads to the suites. Every now and then he glances over at me, just as I'm glancing at him. We look away each time, grinning to ourselves, and I can't help but wonder if he feels the same way I do: regret that our playful dance had to end.

CHAPTER TWENTY-THREE

MONTY

I never knew being someone's best man involved so much work. It isn't even six in the morning when Thorne sends over a list, delivered straight to my door by a bellhop, of chores I need to accomplish by noon. Floral arrangements to count by hand to ensure there are exactly one hundred and twelve, Thorne's suit to pick up from the hotel's tailor, breakfast to deliver to the bride and groom in their separate rooms. I'm convinced the bulk of these chores are merely for the fun of it, petty revenge for all my years of being an annoying best friend. And I can't say I mind it.

Still, I'm glad to be done when noon rolls around, and I head straight for Daphne's room. We have a lesson plan to discuss. I'd intended to do so last night, but after the exhausting evening I had entertaining an inebriated Thorne and his other friends attending his stag party, all I wanted was to let loose a little with Daph.

I hesitate as I stop outside her door, the memory of our

dance sending a ripple of shy awareness through me. Blazing hell, she was so cute last night. The way she smiled, the way she laughed unrestrained as we skipped across the tables. I loved seeing her like that, in her most playful element, dancing in a pink day dress covered in graphite smudges. Toward the end, during our last waltz, I was struck with the most intense yearning to kiss her.

Then I remembered myself.

Remembered my case study.

Our lessons.

Her need for a husband.

My inability to marry.

The secrets I can never tell her.

It's not even a choice. I physically can't tell her my family secret, just like I physically can't marry.

I'm *bound* not to.

That sobers me from my boyish glee, and I force my posture into something casual, ruffle my hair, and loosen my already loosened cravat. Then I knock.

At first, there's no answer, so I knock again.

Finally, just as I'm about to knock for a third time, the door slowly swings open. Daphne is dressed in loose trousers and an untucked blouse, the collar open to reveal the dips of her collarbones. She doesn't even look at me, her eyes affixed to the piece of paper in her hands. Her cheeks are flushed, her lips parted. Her breaths are short and sharp, yet I don't see any signs of distress. Only…

Good God, is she aroused?

She finally deigns to look up at me, a dreamy look on her face. "Oh, it's you."

"Who were you expecting?" I wince at the accusing tone in my voice but try to make up for it with a teasing grin.

"I wasn't paying much attention at all," she says as she abruptly hides the paper behind her back. "I was just…"

"Just...reading, perhaps? Pray tell, what is your reading material of choice? Did Edwina send you her newest manuscript?"

"Hmm? Reading? Manuscript?"

Now I must know. I step through her doorway and she steps back, careful to keep the paper behind her. I close the door behind us and lunge to the side, reaching for the paper. She whirls away with a half yelp, half laugh, and I pursue her, reaching for the paper again and again as she continues to keep it just out of my reach. The next time she spins away, her eyes go wide as she finds her back against the wall beside the door. I close in on her, caging her with my hands on the wall beside her head. Holding her gaze, I lean my face close to hers. "What filth were you reading, dear? Come on, don't be greedy. You're not the only one in this room who likes smut."

Her chest pulses with the tempo of her breaths, her hands still behind her. Then, with a sheepish grin, she pulls the paper from behind her back and slowly lifts it between us, obscuring the bottom of her face while she makes innocent little doe eyes at me.

I release her gaze to read the page.

My breath catches.

It isn't one of Edwina's manuscripts but mine. Just like she promised last night, she's reading my book. But not just any part of my book. It's the chapter titled *How to Have Better Sex*.

My eyes fly back to hers. "Chapter Eight? I told you not to read it."

Her gaze wanders over my head, to the side, to the paper, anywhere but at me. "I was curious and found it...rather informative."

"Informative." My mind goes wild at that word. At the certainty that I've aroused her with my written instruction on having better sex. Then a spike of irritation pierces my chest. I clear my throat and push off the wall, increasing the space between us. "You won't need to worry about Chapter Eight this weekend if you interact with honorable specimens. Which I will ensure you do."

She steps away from the wall and lifts her chin. "I wasn't reading that chapter with this weekend in mind. It was for future reference. You should be ashamed of yourself for trying to hide this kind of intel from me." With that, she marches toward the sitting area.

I follow her with my gaze, taking a few steadying breaths to gather my composure. Daphne's hotel room is a mirror to my own, an open space with a sitting area, a marble hearth, and a bed. The windows are tall, inviting in streams of glittering sunlight through the partially drawn curtains. The walls are papered in ivory-and-gold damask, the floor covered in plush floral-patterned rugs. It's a modest yet beautiful space, much larger than my cramped apartment back home and ten times as fine.

Daphne lowers herself into one of the wingback chairs beside the unlit hearth, and I belatedly follow to claim the chair beside her, on the other side of a small tea table between us. Upon the table rests a stack of papers that I recognize as the rest of my manuscript. She sets the single page on top of it and then sprawls in the chair, her legs tucked up on the seat cushion.

"So," I say, propping my chin on my hand and my elbow on the armrest. I give her a taunting smirk. "Did you only read Chapter Eight, or did you peruse the rest of my book?"

"I perused it. Some of it. Then I went back and read Chapter Eight all over again."

I snort a laugh. "You really wanted to disobey me, didn't you?"

Her cheeks flush deeper. "I told you, I found it informative. It…it's really good. Your book. What I read of it, I mean."

My pulse quickens, my heart fluttering. I had no idea how much her feedback meant to me until now. How desperate I was for her to approve of my writing. "I'm glad to hear that."

She worries her bottom lip, meeting my eyes for only a beat before looking away again. When she speaks, her tone is hesitant. "Can I really do what you wrote about?"

My elbow nearly slips off the armrest. "Pardon?"

"The part where you mention asking for what I want in bed. Can I really do that?"

Fucking hell, why did she have to ask me that? I swallow hard and force my voice to remain level. "You have as much of a right to pleasure as your partner. Of course you can ask for what you want." Does she hear it? The tremor in my voice?

"It's just…my partners have never seemed amenable to suggestions, but perhaps I just don't know the polite way to ask."

I bite the inside of my cheek, relishing the pain as I force my brain to assess her question from a grounded perspective. From Gladys' perspective. "Any decent partner would be eager to know what you want. Some will ask and be happy for your honest answer. Others will need direct guidance."

"What kind of guidance?"

Fuck. I'm going to lose my mind. "Well, for starters, say your partner is touching you. Maybe you'll…move his hand. Adjust the placement of his fingers to where it feels best for you. Or you can state your requests, asking him to slow down or go faster—" My words dissolve in a cough.

Her eyes are glued to me now, and she nods along eagerly as if memorizing my every word.

My gaze falls to her lips to give me some anchor to focus on, something to steady me while I describe the next part.

"Other lovers will be more intuitive. They'll read your wants in the motion of your body, the sounds you emit, the quickening of your breaths. They'll adjust their speed, their touch, based on the way you respond to them."

"I want that," she says in a rush. "How do I find one of those?"

I shift in my seat, aware of the way my cock hardens in my lap. "It's not something you can know by looking at someone. You'll have to experience it together, and any couple can learn to be more intuitive about each other. An awkward first time doesn't have to be telling of the entirety of the relationship."

Daphne deflates a little. "Perhaps I've been too harsh of a judge."

My fingers curl into fists. Why are we still talking about this? And why can't I stop myself from asking what's on the tip of my—

"Have you never had good sex, Daffy Dear?"

"Not with a partner. On my own it's great."

On her own it's great, she says. Is she trying to fucking kill me? "Has a partner never made you come?"

She shakes her head. "The only time I was close, I bit down on my partner's shoulder just as I was about to climax. He was repulsed that I'd bitten him and ended things right there."

The word *climax* echoes through my head. Or perhaps that's just the blood rushing through my ears and toward my cock. I focus on what else she said. "Repulsed? What for?" Doesn't he know how lucky he was to have been bitten by Daphne? How pleasurable pain can be?

She winces. "I did draw a little blood."

Blood. She drew blood while in the throes of pleasure. That's so goddamn hot, my head feels light.

She speaks again. "Then my last partner didn't even get

me close. He barely kissed me more than a few times before he went for insertion."

That clears my head somewhat, and I focus on my ire. "No foreplay? Nothing to warm you up? Get you—" Another cough. "Get you…ready?"

"Nothing. I thought he'd at least touch my breasts." She absently squeezes her upper chest as she says the last part.

My fingers curl even harder, my nails digging into my palms. What kind of monster wastes his chance with a gorgeous spitfire like Daphne and doesn't grope a single tit? Doesn't work her sex with adequate foreplay before settling inside her? Maniacal rage ripples through me, and I'm glad I don't know of whom she speaks, because I'd have to murder the asshole. Whether for touching her or not touching her enough, I know not. No, I hate him for touching her. I hate everyone who's ever touched her before me.

Before me?

What am I thinking?

It's not like I've touched her in that way either. Or ever will.

I can't…

We can't…

I run a hand over my face and blurt out, "Let's move on to our lesson plan."

CHAPTER TWENTY-FOUR

DAPHNE

A pout curves my lips. I was enjoying our discussion on Chapter Eight and still have so many more questions. Now that I know it's possible to have better sex just by asking my lover to make minor changes or engage in the activities Monty outlined as *foreplay* in his book, I'm determined to learn more. I know I can't be too particular when it comes to choosing a husband. He already needs to be model material, encouraging of my career, and ready to marry by Lughnasadh. I can't demand he be an intuitive lover as well. At least Monty assured me it's a skill that can be learned in any relationship.

He clears his throat a little too loudly, then taps the stack of papers on the tea table. "Since you've only read Chapter Eight—"

"I skimmed some other parts."

He narrows his eyes. "Since I doubt you have any lesson requests due to your preoccupation with Chapter Eight, I'll make the lesson plan for the weekend, which will revolve around courting at formal events. It's rather simple. We'll revisit all the lessons we've already practiced while adapting them to this specific environment."

"How do we adapt them?"

"During formal events, it's important to demonstrate the behaviors expected from guests, regardless of your social station. Tonight is not only a wedding ceremony but a formal ball."

"So I can't dance on tables," I say with a wry smile.

He mirrors my grin. "And you can't lift your skirt to shoot guns."

"And here I thought balls were supposed to be fun."

"They can be, if you work them right," he says with a wink.

Laughter bursts from my lips.

His cheeks flush at my reaction. "Sorry," he says with a shy grin.

Since when does Monty apologize for his dirty humor? Then again...since when do I laugh at it? Normally I'd snarl, roll my eyes, or call him swine. Yet it's a little late in our friendship for me to pretend I don't find him funny. I've always been amused by him. Lately, it's been easier to show it.

Monty averts his gaze, expression still bashful. "Why don't you demonstrate your formal curtsy? You'll be meeting potential suitors who wish to dance with you."

A rush of panic moves through me, but it disappears just as quickly. I'll have to meet strangers tonight, but at least Monty will be there. If he's with me, I can manage.

I rise from my chair and dip into a curtsy. It's clumsy and more on the casual side.

"Slower," Monty says. "Keep your eyes down just a second longer."

I repeat the motion, recalling what I learned as a debutante ten years ago. With as much grace as I can manage, I dip down, keeping my eyes lowered until the last moment.

"Much better," Monty says with an approving smile. He rises from his chair and stands before me. "Now, let's practice introductions."

With one arm held gracefully behind his back, he lifts his other. My pulse quickens, unsure what I'm supposed to do. Then he nods at his proffered elbow. Right. If we're practicing introductions, and he's the one escorting me, I'll need to walk with him like a lady. I place my hand in the crook of his elbow, just below his rolled-up sleeve. A shudder runs through me at the warmth of skin touching skin. Tonight, I'll be wearing gloves and he'll be in a proper suit, but right now we have no such barriers between us.

He guides me a few steps away, then dips his chin in a polite bow. "Mr. So-and-so," he says to an invisible figure, "how lovely to see you. May I introduce Miss—" He faces me, dropping the act. "You know, I think it's time you chose a surname."

"You think so?"

"The upper class values surnames, and it helps place a proper barrier between you and your suitors."

I know he's right. "A surname. Well...I choose Heartcleaver, then."

"Heartcleaver?" He barks a laugh. "Daph, that sounds more like a name you'd hear at the boxing club."

"That's why I like it."

He gives me a withering look. "I cannot introduce you as Miss Heartcleaver without scaring half your potential suitors away. How about Hartford?"

I pull my lips into a pout. It's boring, but I suppose it will do. "Fine."

He straightens and returns to the act. "Allow me to introduce Miss Daphne Hartford." He swivels to stand before me in the pretend-suitor's place and offers a bow. "A pleasure, Miss Hartford," he says in a ridiculously haughty voice.

I stifle my giggle and breathe deeply, seeking the mask I must wear. My body tingles with discomfort, but I know how I'm expected to act amongst high society. Just like I know I could never measure up to those born with status. Still, I keep my motions slow and controlled as I dip into my curtsy. Then I speak in a higher, softer voice than normal, modulating the way I've heard others do. "The pleasure is mine." When I meet Monty's eyes, I'm startled to find such a sad expression on his face. I must have done something wrong. "Should I try again? Sorry, I—"

He places a hand on my shoulder to stop me. "Daph..." His throat bobs before he manages to speak again. "I hope you know you don't have to pretend to be anyone you're not. You deserve to be loved for exactly who you are."

My chest tightens. "What lesson is that?" I ask, my voice coming out a whisper.

He shakes his head. "It should be a lesson."

I don't know what to say to that, so I simply stand there, trapped beneath his gaze.

He coughs into his hand—a very fake-sounding cough if you ask me—and takes a step back. "Let's move on to fashion. What are you wearing tonight?"

"You want me to show you?"

"Yes, I told you to bring your three best dresses, didn't I? We've already agreed that fashion is now part of our lessons, which means I get the final say. So, go on."

I brought three dresses, just as he'd requested, but one of them is now covered in graphite until I can have it washed. Of the two remaining, only one is even remotely formal. I suppose that makes my first choice easy. I scurry over to the gilded wardrobe beside the bed and throw open the door.

Just as I'm about to slide the dress from the hanger, I dart a glance at Monty. "Should I step into the washroom to change? It's a rather small space in there."

His face flushes and he whirls around impressively fast. "I didn't realize you're changing now. The ceremony isn't until six."

My shirt is already off when I pause. "I thought that's what you wanted. To judge my choice of dress."

"Yes, but—it's fine."

I watch his back, noting the stiffness in his posture. For someone who makes crude jokes and acts so far removed from social modesty, he sure gets flustered by my lack of reserve. I smirk at the back of his head and finish shimmying out of my clothing. I'm about to step into the dress when I recall the low square cut of the bodice. That means I can't wear my bralette, and I don't even own a corset. So I strip out of the undergarment and don the dress. I reach behind me to secure the lowest clasps, not bothering with the rest. If the wedding ceremony isn't until six, I'll be taking the gown off as soon as I get Monty's approval anyway.

"I'm dressed," I say. Monty slowly turns around, and now it's my turn to feel apprehensive. This ensemble is so different from the modest day dresses I wear and even more so from the shirts and trousers I prefer. Yet it remains my favorite article of clothing. Does he recognize it?

He sucks in a breath, which tells me maybe he does. "You're wearing that?"

There's no condemnation in his tone. Only…surprise, perhaps?

My shoulders climb to my ears and I fidget with the short hem. It's the dress I wore to the gala, the first time he ever saw me in seelie form. It's a confection of golden-yellow silk patterned with pink-and-white chrysanthemums. The top boasts a simple square neckline and cap sleeves while the skirt begins just below my bust and flares out over multiple layers of cream lace. The hem lands just above my knees, showing off far more leg than is appropriate in seelie society. It was a gamble bringing this dress with me, but I figured a fae wedding might be the right place to wear it. The fae are far less particular about propriety in fashion, and Briony and Thorne seem like the opposite of uptight.

I nibble my bottom lip as I tug my hem again. Monty still hasn't said a word.

"Is it…all right?" I ask.

His gaze sweeps up and down my form, some strange combination of agony and awe on his face. "It's beautiful."

Heat floods my cheeks, and I whirl toward the full-length mirror beside the wardrobe before he can catch sight of my blush. I admire my reflection and will my cheeks to cool. Yet I'm hardly given a chance before Monty's face appears just behind mine.

"You didn't secure the clasps," he says, voice thick as he draws nearer.

"I'm only going to take it off again in a few moments."

He freezes and meets my reflection's gaze. "Why?"

My breaths are halting. Shallow. That toe-curling intensity has filled his eyes, even more potent than the first time I glimpsed it during his first modeling session. It takes no small effort to find my voice. "I'm not going to lounge around in this dress until six in the evening."

"Ah, right." He heaves a sigh, but that only washes away half his intensity. He takes another step closer, then I feel his fingertips alight upon my spine, just above the first open clasp. Molten heat pools in my core. The tops of my breasts pulse above my bodice. His eyes narrow to that part of my reflection, his fingers trembling against my skin. His breath skates over the back of my shoulder as he speaks in a whisper. "I could secure them the rest of the way. Just for now. Until I leave."

Leave? I don't want him to leave. The heat that grows between my thighs spreads hotter and hotter. This isn't even the first time today. My repeated reading of Chapter Eight had me so tightly wound I was ready to tend to my release just before he got here. Our conversation didn't dampen it much, only stirred my curiosity more. But more than anything, more than his written words or erotic topics, it's his presence that brings my desire to a peak. His expression. His nearness. Him. Just *him*.

This kind of attraction is so new to me. So powerful it makes me dizzy. I want to explore it. *Need* to explore it.

I gather in a deep breath and finally reply. "Or you could undo them the rest of the way."

CHAPTER TWENTY-FIVE

DAPHNE

His eyes flick to mine in the mirror, his pupils blown wide. "Why would I undo your clasps? Do you…require my aid?"

My entire body trembles with restraint. With want. "Well, you see…it's about the pose I'm working on. For the couple on the ballroom cover."

"Yes?" He holds my gaze so fiercely, his fingers still pressed against my spine.

"I haven't been able to get it right." Not a lie from these lips. I spent my morning sketching ideas for the couple's pose but nothing felt inspired. Nothing felt sexy enough to evoke the passion in Edwina's book. That's when I discarded my sketches in favor of reading Monty's book. And there my inspiration was sparked.

Now, as I watch us in the mirror, I realize this is it. This is the tenuous passion I wanted to capture. This is the tension I wanted to evoke, to express the push and pull between the characters.

For the love of the All of All, I feel so connected to my art like never before.

That paired with the need that continues to build inside my core emboldens me.

"Can you help me?" I ask.

"You want me to pose for you? Now?" His voice is soft yet heavy.

"Not a long session," I say. "I just want to see it."

His head moves in the slightest shake to the left, and I fear he's going to deny me. Then a breath leaves his lungs, and with it comes the word "Yes."

"Undo the rest of my clasps."

He arches a brow, making no move to obey.

"The heroine's dress should slouch off her shoulders just so." My voice sounds so unlike my own. So breathless. So quiet.

A wicked glint fills his eyes, and his lips quirk at one corner. Finally, he fulfills my request, loosening the bottom clasps. My bodice slides down, baring an inch more of my cleavage. He drops his hands, but I reach for one, guiding it to the hem of my skirt.

"The hero's hand should be here, lifting her hem to her thigh."

He clutches the fabric between his fingers and lets me guide his hand up my leg, baring it almost to my hip crease and the lacy hem of my undershorts. I watch his reflection, a thrill running through me at the sight of him biting his lower lip.

"His other hand," I say, guiding the other to my shoulder, sliding off the cap sleeve and making my bodice dip even farther on that side, "here."

He stiffens behind me, and I feel the firmness of his erection, even through the layers of my skirt.

"Daph," he whispers, eyelids heavy with want.

"Or maybe..." I release the hand that lifts my hem. His fingers stay curled around the folds of my skirt, arms trembling with restraint. I tug my bodice beneath the hand he lays upon my shoulder. Once. Twice. It slides down several more inches until it finally bares my breast. His eyes widen at the sight of it, at my firm nipple. Then, with slow moves, I guide his hand from my shoulder until he's cupping me fully.

A groan escapes his lips and he pulls me tight against him, rolling his hips against my ass as his face falls to the crook of my neck. I lean into the hand that cups my breast, aching for friction. But he doesn't move again. Instead, he goes still, save for the tremors that rack through him, the pulse of his lungs as his chest heaves against my back.

"What are we doing?" His words are hardly more than a breath on my neck.

"Chapter Eight," I say, pressing my thighs together to sate the burning heat that continues to pool.

He lifts his lips to my ear. I watch in the mirror as he grazes his teeth against my lobe. The sight and feel combined send a violent shudder through me. "Chapter Eight isn't a lesson. It's supplementary information."

"It's information I want," I say, rolling my backside into his straining length. "Information I'm unfamiliar with. Which makes it a lesson."

Another groan reverberates through him. "You're supposed to perform these lessons with a suitor."

"I thought you said I wouldn't be doing Chapter Eight material with a suitor this weekend. Should I, then? Should I practice on a test subject instead?"

He bares his teeth and glares at the side of my face. "No."

"Then teach me. It doesn't have to mean anything more than that. I...want this. I want to know what it's like to experience pleasure with a partner. I want to learn how to ask for what I want. I'm comfortable with you. I'm not afraid to try things with you. So I'm asking. Will you teach me?"

His hand tightens on my breast but he says nothing.

A ripple of apprehension dampens some of my desire. Am I coming on too strong? Am I doing that thing I do when I misread the mood of a room? Misread a person? My posture stiffens. "If you don't want to—"

"I want to." He brings his face back to my neck, resting his forehead there as he gathers a few breaths. "I want to, but..."

My heart falls and I brace myself for rejection.

"We can't kiss," he says, and there's remorse in his tone.

I angle my head toward him. "We can't?"

He lifts his eyes to mine. "If we do this, we do it for the sake of sex and pleasure."

"Isn't kissing part of sex and pleasure?"

"It's more intimate than that. To me at least. If we kiss, it's real. If we don't, it's just...sex."

I ponder his words. I never considered kissing to be more intimate than sex, but I think I understand what he means. One can separate sex and pleasure from emotion. I've done it before, especially when I was a pine marten and mated out of instinct. Every sexual encounter I've had with a partner in seelie form has been devoid of emotion. So I suppose he's right. It is more intimate in a way. Furthermore, it's more vulnerable on a practical level. When two people bring their faces so close, they put themselves at risk. I glance down at where his pulse tics at his throat. All it would take is a small movement from me and I could rip out his jugular with my teeth. I doubt that's exactly what he meant, but it helps me understand.

"Fine," I say. "No kissing."

His eyes widen as if he's surprised I've agreed. He tightens his grip on my breast again, then drags his hand over its outer curve, then higher, over my collarbone and up the length of my neck. "We're only doing foreplay."

I nod aggressively.

His lips curve into a wicked smile. His fingers glide along my jaw, then to the side of my chin. "We're in agreement then," he says, his lips just an inch from mine. He holds my gaze a moment longer, then tugs my chin, pulling my gaze to our reflection. "Watch carefully or this lesson will go to waste."

He removes his fingers from my chin and brings them to his lips. I watch his every move with hungry fascination as he rolls his tongue over his fore and middle fingers, depositing saliva onto them. Then he brings those digits down to my breast, over my nipple, and rolls his slick fingers over it. I gasp, my knees buckling. I would have fallen if his other hand hadn't caught me, now under my skirt and braced over my lower belly.

"You like that?" he asks. "Does that make up for that asshole who didn't fucking touch you right?

"Yes." But not enough. I arch my back, willing my bodice to slide down. Finally, my other breast crests the top.

"You want me to pay attention to the other one now? Good girl. I can read you like a book." He licks his fingers again and plays with my other nipple, eliciting the sharpest, most delectable pleasure. I only wish it was his tongue instead of his fingers. My lashes flutter closed until he gives my nipple a little pinch. "Keep your eyes open."

I do as he says and watch as his fingers round one curve of my breast, then the other.

"Fuck, look at you." His eyelids are as heavy as mine. "You're so goddamned beautiful."

His words have my knees buckling again, but there's so much more I want from him. I slide my hand under my skirt until it rests over his. Then, trying—and failing—not to rush,

I push his hand down, guiding it beneath the waistband of my undershorts to the mound of curls there.

"You're ready for me to touch you here?"

"Please." The word comes out half gasp, half cry. I've never been more ready. More desperate.

His hand leaves my breast to join the other beneath my skirt. Then he lowers my silk undershorts, shimmying them over my hips, my thighs, until they fall to my feet. I step out of them and kick them to the side. I nearly weep with relief as he brings his hand back where I want it. Then slowly—so slowly—he slides his fingers down until they meet my sex.

A whimper escapes my throat as his digit skates over my slick center.

"Fuck, Daph," he says with a groan. "You're dripping wet for me."

He slides his fingers over my folds, and my legs give out completely. This time, instead of holding me up, he helps me down to my knees, seating himself behind me, and letting me rest against him.

His palm goes still over my sex and our eyes lock in the mirror. "Do you want to watch what I do?"

I nod.

"Lift your hem."

With trembling fingers, I drag my hem up over my thighs, tucking my voluminous skirts away to get a full look at Monty's hand. With his other, he gently guides my knees wider. I watch as my center parts, watch as Monty's fingers begin moving again.

"Look at that," he says, dragging two fingers along opposite sides of my center before circling my aching clitoris. I moan and throw my head back against him but manage to keep my eyes open as I witness every tantalizingly slow movement. His other hand returns to my breast where he does the same motion to my nipple. My entire torso is bare now, my dress hardly more than a puddle of silk around my middle. I watch with rapt fascination, equally turned on by the pleasure of his touch and the arousal of witnessing it happening.

I've never imagined anything so erotic. So all-encompassing.

My desire builds, craving more. I arch my back and roll my sex against his hand. He obeys my silent command and slides his fingers down.

"You're doing such a good job," he says against my ear as his fingers tease just outside my glistening opening. "Such a good girl."

"I'm hardly doing anything," I manage to say, even though his praise sends a renewed jolt of pleasure through me.

"You are. The way you move speaks volumes. Every roll of your hips, every gasp. I hear you, Daph. Feel you. I know what you want now." With that, he plunges his finger inside me. He pumps it in and out of me, then adds another.

I reach behind me, gripping the back of his neck as he lowers his lips to the side of my throat. A thrill runs through me at the thought that he might kiss me. Who would have thought I'd be so shocked by a kiss after what we're already doing? But he doesn't. He merely drags his mouth over my skin, then bares his teeth, as if it takes all his restraint *not* to kiss me. Does it even count if it's not on the mouth?

He thrusts his fingers deeper. I rock against him as he picks up his pace, riding his palm as it rubs over my clit. My pleasure builds hotter, my release welling up like a raging tide against a dam. He lifts his eyes, mouth still pressed against my throat, and they lock on his hand in the mirror.

"God, that's fucking art," he says. "Do you see that? Do you see how beautiful that is?"

"Yes," I say, but I'm looking at his face. At the want in his eyes. At the strain in his jaw, the pulse in his temples, the pleasure in the curve of his mouth. Somehow, even though I'm the one being stroked and sated, he's enjoying this too. His cock continues to dig into my backside with every rock of my hips. "You feel so good around my fingers. Look so good grinding against my hand."

My arm remains angled behind me, palming the back of his neck. I drag my fingers to the base of his nape and claw them into his scalp. His eyes flutter shut and he emits a low groan. That's what does it for me. That's what drives me over the edge. I tighten my grip on his hair as my walls pulse around his fingers. My moan barrels through me in time with my release. Monty's hand dances with my orgasm, cresting with it, then guiding it down, down, until we both go still.

He hugs me against him with one arm as he slides his fingers out of me. I drink in his reflection as he watches me, an awed smile on his face. He heaves a sigh and falls onto his back, chest pulsing. I collapse on top of him, boneless in the wake of my pleasure. We fall into a symphony of panted breaths as we regain our composure. Once I manage to gather some semblance of strength, I push myself to sitting, my dress still pooled around my middle.

He meets my eyes, his lips still tilted in a grin. For a moment I'm not sure what to say. What if this changes things between us? What if this places a strain on our friendship? Then his smile widens, and I remind myself we're still us. Nothing has changed.

"That was amazing," I say to him as nonchalantly as possible. "You're...a wizard or something."

A laugh rumbles through him. "We live in a world where magic and fae exist, and you call me a wizard."

"Fae and magic are real. Wizards aren't. And you are some mystical being with how you worked my clit."

He throws his arm over his eyes, his grin widening. "For

the love of the All of All, she just called me a sex wizard," he mutters through his laughter.

My eyes leave his face and rove over his body down to his—

"Shit, Monty."

He lifts his forearm from over his eyes, alarm written over his face.

I gesture at his rather obvious erection. "You're still hard! I'm so sorry, I didn't tend to you at all." Should I...touch him? Straddle him? I was so fixated on my own pleasure that I didn't spare a thought for his. I only delighted in how pleased he looked touching me. But of course he couldn't be satisfied with that. I flutter my hands, unsure of what to do with them—

He sits upright and catches one of my wrists, stilling me. "Daph," he says, tone gentle, "this wasn't about me. This was for you."

"Yes, but...isn't that selfish?"

He shifts my wrist until my palm is in his. With soft motions, he strokes his thumb over the back of my hand. "Lesson Number...I don't fucking know. Sex doesn't always have to be a transactional exchange. You don't owe me anything for what I did just now. Sometimes one's pleasure is found in pleasuring someone else. You deserve to enjoy an orgasm, end of story. You deserve to be spoiled with them."

"But what about you? I don't need fifteen steps for fantastic fellatio. I can—"

He silences me with a finger to my lips. The finger he had inside me. I nearly melt at the realization. "Take this lesson, Daffy Dear, and stop feeling like you have to do more. Let yourself be the one to take pleasure for once."

I give a reluctant nod, resisting the urge to pout. The truth is, I want to do more. I want to make Monty feel the way he made me feel. I want to see what kinds of expressions

I can coax, what kinds of sounds. I want to know how he feels when he comes. Just as badly, I want to feel him against me. On top of me. Inside me. I want more of him.

He studies my face for a few beats more, then removes his finger from over my mouth. His eyes, however, linger and he doesn't fully pull his hand away. Instead, he shifts it until it cradles the side of my face, then runs his thumb over my lower lip.

If I didn't know better, I'd think he was about to kiss me.

But he won't. He can't.

Because if we kiss, it's real. That's what he said.

And this isn't real.

It isn't.

Yet, as he finally drops his hand and fixes my dress, I can't deny that part of me wishes it were.

CHAPTER TWENTY-SIX

MONTY

Thorne is going to kill me, I'm sure of it, after I answer yet another question with *hmm?* I've been a shit best man all evening, ever since I arrived at his suite to help him prepare for his ceremony with my mind elsewhere. All I could think about was Daphne. All I could do was steal glances at my hands, marveling at how they'd coaxed her to climax and drew out the sweetest of moans and whimpers just hours before. I was harboring half a hard-on as I tried to pretend I was present with Thorne and his other groomsmen, and now I can't pretend at all.

Because there she is.

I stand on a rounded dais at the far end of the hotel's main avenue, where the glittering indoor canal ends in a large pool. The dais is set upon a wide terrace, flanked by intricately carved marble walls adorned with faux windows and a massive array of floral arrangements. A string quartet plays from a nearby balcony, filling the air with their sweet melody. The back wall is enchanted to replicate the sunset, and before it stands an arched trellis woven with climbing jasmine. Briony's bridesmaids—Angela included—stand on one side of the dais while Thorne, his groomsmen, and I stand on the other.

But my eyes take in none of this. Instead, they're locked on Daphne.

She sits in one of the gondolas that glide through the pool toward the terrace, beside figures neither of us know. Her shoulders are slightly hunched, her hands in her lap. I hate that I couldn't escort her, for everyone she's even mildly acquainted with is in the wedding party. Still, she assured me she'd be fine before I left her hotel room. Before I forced myself away from her when all I wanted to do was kiss her, take her to bed, and make love to her for the rest of the day.

I should win an award for my restraint.

Or perhaps I should be punished.

Her gondola arrives at the dock, and she and the other passengers disembark. My eyes remain on her as she climbs the steps onto the terrace. As soon as she reaches the aisle, her gaze finds mine. My chest tightens. My mind goes blank.

Fucking hell.

I *am* being punished.

Because there she is in that same yellow dress I made her come in just hours ago. Her legs are covered in white stockings, her hair no longer mussed from the pleasure I gave her, but every inch of my body remembers how she looked, how she felt, how she smelled. How hot and slick she was around my fingers. How soft and languid she was against me.

"Are you going to answer my fucking question?" Thorne's whispered words have my spine going rigid. He stands facing the growing audience with his head angled toward me.

"Hmm?" I blink at him.

"I asked if you're all right. You've been absentminded all goddamned evening."

I shake the lust and...and the warmer feeling from my head. "I'm great. Besides, I should be asking you that. You're the one about to be married."

Thorne heaves a sigh that seems to relax his entire being. "I'm better than great. I just can't wait to see her." He meets my eyes, and I find tears in his as he gives me a shaky smile. "She's going to be my fucking wife."

I bite the inside of my cheek to keep from tearing up myself. I've never seen Thorne like this, and I've known him almost my whole life.

He faces forward again, and my eyes dart back to the aisle just as Daphne reaches her row and takes a seat. Our eyes connect again, and she gives me a warm smile and the smallest of waves.

I'm glad everything is still normal between us. Comfortable.

"Who's the girl in yellow?" I bristle at the voice that comes from the groomsman on my other side. I met him during Thorne's stag party and again earlier this evening as we helped the groom prepare for his ceremony. He's one of Thorne's newest friends, and they've already grown close enough that he's a fucking groomsman.

I may have a slight jealousy issue when it comes to my friends making new friends, but that's neither here nor there. Not when he's asking about Daphne.

It's all I can do not to snarl at him as I arch a brow his way. What is his name? Paul? Paolo? No, it was Patrick. Patrick Wright.

He meets my eyes without falter. "Do you know her?"

"Yes," I bite out.

Thorne angles his head toward us. "She's Monty's newest victim in his so-called matchmaking," he whispers.

Patrick's eyes widen. "Matchmaking?"

"He's helping her find a husband."

I turn a perplexed look to Thorne. How the fuck does he know that?

"Briony told me," he says, answering my silent question.

My chest tightens. Daphne must have told Briony, then. It's true; I am helping her find a husband. So why does it make me so uncomfortable that Patrick knows? So irritable? Why does it make me feel like I'm going to crawl out of my skin?

"Can you introduce me?" Patrick asks.

I pointedly ignore him. Thankfully, I'm given the perfect excuse.

The music shifts to a new song. The last of the guests have arrived and a single gondola floats toward this end of the pool.

Thorne sucks in a breath and stands up straighter. The boat's occupants are hidden behind an enormous lace parasol, but as the gondola arrives at the dock, the parasol lowers to reveal Briony and Tilly. Hand in hand, they disembark the boat and climb the steps to the aisle. Briony is dressed in a curve-hugging gown of white silk, her golden hair spilling over one shoulder, adorned in pearls and white roses. Tilly wears a ruffly lace dress, a crown of pink and white roses nestled on her pale hair around her bunny ears. As they proceed down the aisle, Thorne wipes a hand over his jaw, and I hear the telltale shudder of his breath. He's trying not to cry.

Finally, the bride and child reach the dais and stop before Thorne. The three link hands and stand before the trellis, where a human minister awaits. What follows is a ceremony that somehow blends human wedding traditions with a heavy dose of fae influence. They exchange rings, speaking vows that are personal to their relationship. I shiver at the sound of their promised words. With Thorne being half fae and Briony pureblood, their vows are binding. Not just legally but magically.

Just like the bargain I made to never marry.

A vow I physically cannot break.

And the bargain I made before that, to never tell a soul about my lineage. I can't even write it down or try to relay the truth without words, for part of my bargain included not *letting* anyone find out. The only reason I didn't suffer the harmful consequences of breaking my bargain when my goblin lender read my secret with his magic was because I had no say in what he did. No intention to convey my secret. I've never been brave enough to test it any further. Not when breaking bargains means death, and the circulation of the secret I carry means the ruination of my family name.

My lungs tighten, but I narrow my attention on the bride and groom. On their love for each other. Their eyes sparkle as they hold each other's gaze, repeating words that bind their love. Then the minister directs them to face Tilly. The young girl looks surprised, even more so when Briony slips a ring off the tip of her pinky finger and hands it to Thorne. He places the ring on Tilly's index finger, and her wide blue eyes well with tears.

"Do you, Tilly Blackwood, take Thorne and Briony to be your beloved parents?"

Oh fuck.

My chest lurches, my throat constricting. Tears glaze my eyes and this time, there's nothing to stop them. Especially as the girl sobs, nodding her head. Then even more so as Thorne, my stoic best fucking friend, states his vows to be her father.

Tears stream down my cheeks, and there's no hiding them.

For the love of the All of All, I've taken pleasure in pain

before but this is on a whole new level. This erases my soul from the face of the earth and builds it back up. Purifies me. Tears me to shreds and then stitches me back together.

This is love.

This is family.

This is what I've always yearned to see, in all my half-jested attempts at matchmaking. I've always been desperate to prove love is real. That it looks different from how it looked during my childhood. That it's warmer than the loveless marriage my father had with his wife—the woman who pretended to be my mother yet never fully loved me, despite her warmest efforts, despite never having received such love from my father aside from their mutual fondness for Angela. I wanted to see that it looked different from the mother who left me without hardly a backward glance. That it looked different from Cosette, who chose someone else only to beg to have me back, without any true adoration for me. Only desperation.

This is it. This is what it's supposed to look like.

I glance at Daphne. She watches the couple, head tilted curiously to the side, as if she too is realizing the same thing. That this is what a wedding should be. This is what she deserves, not a rushed pairing just to get out of her handfasting.

Her gaze slowly slides to mine and my heart stutters. Can she see the truth on my face? How badly I want this for her?

No…

It's not just that.

I want this for her…yet I don't.

I want her to be freed from her handfasting. I desperately do. She can't be stuck in her hometown when she wants to be an illustrator. She can't be chained to a goddamned honey badger who doesn't share her vision for the future. She needs a husband to sever that tie. Yet I don't want to think of her up here with anyone. No one.

No one except for...

I swallow the thought as if banishing the lump in my throat might keep my feelings at bay. Feelings that are growing harder to ignore.

Daphne's expression turns soft. She must see the tears on my cheeks. Her own eyes glaze with a sheen of moisture and she gives me a subtle nod. A silent assurance that it's all right.

It's all right to be moved.

To feel.

But is it truly all right to feel? When the one thing I'm starting to feel the strongest about is something I can never have?

CHAPTER TWENTY-SEVEN

DAPHNE

I never knew a wedding could be so beautiful. I've heard of lovely weddings. Of the extravagant ceremonies that have become popular amongst humans and seelie fae. But this is my first time witnessing one. It's so different from how I imagined it could be. When I entered seelie society, all I knew of marriage was its practical aspects. The importance of making a fine match based on certain statistics. Even amongst the working class, most of my peers marry quickly, especially those who favor human values of chastity and propriety, the whole of their relationships formed in view of chaperones and friends. It's what I resigned myself to when I decided a husband would be the surest way to get out of my handfasting.

It was enough for me. I hadn't experienced sexual attraction to a specific person before, so what did it matter how I found my husband? I figured I'd enjoy him well enough, so long as he fulfilled my purposes. So long as I could continue to paint.

But now I have experienced attraction. Desire. And, more recently, bone-deep pleasure and satisfaction at the hands of a lover.

I can't help wondering…will I miss out on something greater, a love of the heart, if I settle on a marriage of necessity?

After the ceremony, I make my way to the ballroom with the other guests. I do my best to keep my breathing steady amongst so many strangers, so much chatter. The wedding party left the ceremony separately, which means I am without anyone I know. For now. Monty promised he'd come find me as soon as he could.

My chest tightens at the thought of him. Of the unfettered emotion on his face during the ceremony. For how often he acts flippant and careless, there's a deep well of empathy and kindness inside him. And a deep well of pain, too. Pain I don't fully understand.

Once inside the ballroom, an usher guides me to a table where I find my name on a place card. My heart leaps with relief when I find Monty's and Angela's cards at the same table. Other than me, the table is empty, and I'm not sure whether to feel anxious or relieved about that. I've done my best to prepare myself for the inevitable—talking to strangers—but I can't help dreading it. I sit on my hands to keep from fidgeting and mentally rehearse polite small talk.

Finally, once everyone is settled at their tables, the bride, groom, and their wedding party enter the ballroom to soft applause. The string quartet plays a lovely melody as the group makes their way across the dance floor to the empty tables. Monty gives me a wink as soon as our eyes meet, and I feel every muscle in my body relax.

He, Angela, and two others from the wedding party settle in at the table. I smile at Monty as he takes his seat beside me. He leans in close and I find myself leaning in as well, as if magnetized to his presence. "Did you like the ceremony?" he whispers.

"I did," I say, my voice a little breathless as my eyes drop to his mouth.

Then my breath catches.

Because that's when I notice the warm hand on my stockinged thigh, just beneath the hem of my skirt. The touch isn't groping or belligerent. It's...comforting. The way Monty placed it there felt as natural as breathing. It's only my mind that realizes this isn't the kind of touch one generally does in public. Not that anyone can see us, hidden as we are beneath the table skirt.

Monty stiffens, realizing what I already have. His ears burn crimson and he drags his hand away, straightening his posture. I'm grateful he doesn't apologize. Instead, he gives me a shy smile.

"Mr. Phillips," says a voice on my other side. My shoulders tighten as the stranger angles himself toward us. He's a male with rounded ears—human, or perhaps half human like Thorne; it truly is impossible to tell with most hybrids—and expertly styled brown hair. He glances from Monty to me and back again. "Are you going to introduce me to your lovely companion?"

I curl my fingers at my sides, bracing myself for the small talk I've dreaded. When Monty doesn't speak, I look his way, finding his jaw tight. Then, with a smile that doesn't reach his eyes and a tone that lacks all warmth, he says, "Mr. Wright, allow me to introduce Miss Daphne Hartford."

I startle at the sound of my newly acquired surname. I'd almost forgotten about choosing it, what with the mind-blowing pleasure that followed shortly after its conception.

"Miss Hartford," Monty says, "meet Patrick Wright."

"A pleasure," the man named Patrick says, offering his hand for me to shake. I'm surprised, as a handshake is considered an almost vulgar greeting between opposite sexes—a gender divide I've never been fond of. I suppose it earns him at least a smidge of my respect.

I place my gloved hand in his and remind myself of my purpose during tonight's ball. My courtship lesson. I train my voice into something soft and feminine and reply with the expected greeting. "The pleasure is mine."

DURING DINNER, Mr. Wright seeks my attention again and again, asking casual questions about me, my work, and my hobbies. To my surprise, he doesn't so much as blanch when I mention the covers I'm illustrating, nor does he belittle my choice of career. Unlike some men I've spoken to in the past, he doesn't talk about my workplace aspirations like they're something temporary, a passing fancy until I marry. Instead, he praises my work ethic and my involvement with the arts. He tells me about himself as well. He's the youngest son of a wealthy family and an attorney.

Despite coming across as a respectful and decent man, I'd rather be talking with Monty or even Angela. Still, I force myself to maintain conversation, to continue to modulate my voice, speak in a feminine tone, and keep eye contact at the right times. Tonight isn't about enjoying my time with Monty. It's about performing for his case study.

Aren't I doing this to find a husband too? a small voice inside me asks. It's almost mocking, as if it's aware of the doubts that have taken root inside me. But of course it's aware. That voice is mine, just like the doubts are. The doubts that question whether I truly want to secure a husband like this.

I must get out of my handfasting, I argue back to those doubts.

Do you?

Yes.

But do you truly need a husband to do so?

My mind goes blank at that. It won't be entirely necessary if I'm promoted during my performance review. If I can state, without an ounce of deception, that my career is so secure and so important to me that I must remain living in Jasper, Clyde and Elder Rhisha will free me from my vow. But that's only if I'm promoted to full-time illustrator. My position as an editorial assistant isn't enough. One short-term commission for four book covers isn't enough. I know that down to my bones, and belief is everything when it comes to speaking truth as a fae. Which means marriage is still the surest way. A legal bond that's stronger than my year-and-a-day engagement to Clyde.

Yet my doubts pierce my heart whenever I catch Monty watching me and Patrick. The tightness that never leaves the set of his jaw. The way his hand brushes my thigh now and then, his touch too lingering to be accidental. Though he does nothing to pull me from my conversation with Mr. Wright, I can sense how badly he wishes to.

Or perhaps I'm the one who wishes he would.

After dinner, Briony and Thorne take their places at the center of the dance floor. The string quartet plays a waltz, and the couple swishes and sways alone under the beautifully painted dome, their steps graceful. Then the air shimmers and the painting...moves.

No, it's not the painting but an enchantment that casts the room under an indigo haze, glittering with luminescent auroras that ripple overhead. My mouth falls open at the magic on display. Monty told me Briony is a succubus with powerful dream magic. She can pull subjects into dreams and can even conjure dreamscapes for others to see while awake.

"It's beautiful, isn't it?" Monty whispers. A shudder runs down my spine, doubling as his knuckles caress the back of my hand beneath the tablecloth.

Keeping my gaze on the elegant couple dancing beneath the dreamscape, I splay my fingers, gently catching his, and lace them together. His hand stills, and I wonder if my touch was too bold. Then he adjusts his palm so he's holding mine tighter. Firmer. He runs his thumb over my hand in the sweetest, softest caress. My lungs tighten, my heart fluttering, tumbling, like it might fall out of my chest.

"Daph," he whispers, quiet enough for only me to hear, "dance with me—"

"Miss Hartford." Patrick rises from his chair and extends a hand. "Will you do me the honor of your first dance?"

I blink at him, then at the dance floor. Only now do I notice other couples have joined the bride and groom. My heart falls as I realize Monty was about to ask me the same question. He'd just been too quiet for Patrick to hear, our linked hands hidden from view. Our connection invisible.

Yet how can he not see it anyway? How can he not feel the pulse in the air between me and Monty? The magnetic force that nearly has me leaning into the man I—

Monty's grip loosens and he rises from his chair.

Relief washes over me as I expect him to correct Patrick, to inform him he'd already been in the process of asking me.

But he doesn't.

"Excuse me," he says, voice tight, then walks away.

My hand feels cold where his palm had been.

"Miss Hartford?" Mr. Wright's smiling face wrinkles with a furrow. His hand remains extended toward me, awaiting my answer. "Is everything all right?"

"Yes," I say in a rush, my mind whirling to catch up with

what's happening. What needs to happen. Monty didn't leave because he's upset or jealous. He left to give me no qualms about accepting Mr. Wright's offer. Because that is what I'm supposed to do. That is the purpose of this weekend's lesson —demonstrating courtship during formal events.

I bite the inside of my cheek to fight the urge to run and hide. To refuse.

"I...yes, I will dance," I say with feigned warmth. I can't even bring myself to say *I'm honored* or *I'm happy to*. Because I can't lie.

We stand at the edge of the dance floor until the waltz comes to an end. Then we join the other dancers preparing for the quadrille. My pulse rackets. I may have grown more comfortable dancing in this body than I was at the gala two years ago, but in other ways, I'm more anxious. Maybe it's because Mr. Wright has made his interest in me so clear.

Or maybe it's because I wish I was dancing with Monty instead.

We begin our dance, circling each other to a jovial beat, then skipping to the side. Mr. Wright smiles all the while, his eyes on me even when we separate to weave through the other dancers. I'm grateful for the part of the dance when we momentarily trade partners, my lungs easing with every inch of space I'm awarded from him. Why the hell do I feel this way? This man has been nothing but respectful. He's handsome, and even though I'm not personally attracted to him at this moment, I've learned attraction can grow through a deeper acquaintance.

We return to each other, linking hands and skipping to the side again.

"You dance well," he says.

I don't know whether the compliment is genuine, and my first instinct is to make some wry jest about how he must say that to all the ladies. Then I recall that's not who I am tonight. Tonight, I'm a well-behaved woman seeking a suitor. Even though Monty told me not to pretend to be someone I'm not, I don't know how else to act with a man like this. Being myself feels worse than putting on a subtle act. So instead, I return his hollow praise. "As do you."

"I hope it's not too bold of me to secure your company in the next dance as well."

I nearly trip over my feet but somehow maintain my composure. "Two dances? In a row?" I know what two dances with the same gentleman means. It is undoubtedly a show of interest on his part. I remember this well from my days as a debutante. One dance is polite. Two dances are a demonstration of romantic intent. Three is scandalous.

"If you'll have me," he says.

We separate, circling the other dancers in the square, and giving me another break from Mr. Wright's attention. I nibble my bottom lip, my urge to flee stronger than ever. Then the most welcome sight comes into view—Monty at the edge of the dance floor, his eyes on me, stalking me like prey as I move between the dancers. Our eyes remain locked, even as I return to Mr. Wright and skip to the side with him. Monty watches me with undeniable hunger, and I'm suddenly taken back to the first time we danced, at the gala.

I hadn't donned seelie form in public since my debut several years prior. I was equal parts giddy and terrified as I danced with a partner for the first time. I was surprised by how quickly my dance card filled up and how eager my partners were to dance with someone as unskilled as I was. It was a charity event, after all, and a full dance card meant an ample donation from a benefactor. Then I saw Monty, circling the floor, watching my every move. Until one of my partners held me a little too tight, his hands roving a touch too low. That's when Monty charged up and cut in on the dance, but not before squeezing my partner's shoulder like he'd mangle it.

A tableau of the past plays out now, and my pulse quickens as I expect it to repeat in full. For Monty to stride over at any minute and cut in. Or, at the very least, claim my next dance before Mr. Wright can remind me of the question he left hanging between us.

Yet Monty doesn't. Instead, he hovers, watching us, running a hand through his hair, over his jaw, like it's taking all his restraint not to come over to me.

But I want him to. So badly I do, and not even just to rescue me from Patrick Wright. I don't need to be rescued this time. Mr. Wright is gentlemanly and kind. He's just…

He's not Monty.

Monty is the one I want to dance with. I want the ballroom empty save for just the two of us. I want to leap on tables and laugh while we waltz. I want to run through the rain and hold hands while mud soaks the hems of our clothes.

I want Monty.

I…more than want him.

The dance comes to an end, and Monty still hasn't interrupted us, though his shoulders are tense, his stare fierce.

I curtsy, thanking Mr. Wright for the dance. I already know what he's going to say before he asks the next question.

"About the next dance?"

My stomach plummets, even as I reply, "Of course."

Monty looks mutinous as we get into our places for the cotillion. The music starts. We exchange curtsies and bows, first with each other, then the other dancers. Mr. Wright takes my hand and we step from side to side, then do a skip and a hop, before joining hands with the others to skip in a circle.

"I'd like to call on you next Friday," Mr. Wright says as we stand side by side, waiting our turn to perform the next steps.

I glance at him with wide eyes. "Pardon?"

"I'll be in Jasper next weekend for work. I'd like to call on you then, if you don't mind."

My words stick in my throat. This is all moving so fast. I only met him an hour ago. Now he wants to call on me? There's no convincing myself it isn't out of romantic interest. This is how I always expected a courtship to go. I was taught they move fast. It's why I thought my marriage solution was such a feasible one.

I open my mouth but I still don't know what to say. Monty and I never got this far in our lessons. I only expected to engage in Lesson Three tonight, if anything. Though I suppose this is where Lesson Four comes in—waiting to see if his words align with his actions. Even if I allow him to call on me, there's no guarantee he'll follow through with it.

It's our turn to skip forward and dance in a circle, which is when I catch sight of Monty again. Thorne is at his side, but Monty doesn't seem to notice. His eyes watch only me.

Why doesn't he move?

Move, Monty.

Don't leave me to answer Mr. Wright's question on my own. Not that he can hear our conversation. Not that he knows what's running through my head. The wish that's begun to burn in my heart.

Finally...he moves, taking a step onto the dance floor.

But Thorne stills him with a hand on his shoulder. Whispers something in his ear, expression serious.

Monty freezes.

His shoulders fall.

He watches me for a few beats longer, then marches out of sight.

CHAPTER TWENTY-EIGHT

MONTY

I don't stop walking until I exit the lobby doors, filling my lungs with crisp night air. There's nothing but quiet all around me, nothing but the sleeping countryside surrounding the hotel, and the music from the ballroom too distant to hear. No guests funnel through the lobby doors and no coaches circle the courtyard, as most of the hotel's guests are either sleeping, dining, or attending the wedding.

Yet not even the silence and solitude set me at ease. With tense fingers, I extract a cigarillo from the case in my jacket pocket and place it between my lips. It takes me three tries to light it with my igniter, with how my hands shake, but soon floral smoke fills my mouth. The scent, the taste, the routine, all serve to calm my racing pulse.

After another soothing drag of my herbal remedy, I drop myself onto a bench at the edge of the cobblestone courtyard. I flick the ash from the end of my cigarillo, wondering what the hell is wrong with me.

Why did I so badly want to stop Daphne from dancing with Patrick Wright? Why did it enrage me to see them settling in for another dance? Patrick's interest in her shouldn't come as a surprise. He asked me to introduce him. He talked to her throughout dinner like she was the only person at the table. But that's not what has me riled, is it?

No, it's what Thorne said to me just as I was about to cut in.

He's looking for a wife, not a fling. He's exactly the kind of person you'd want to match her with. A good man. He won't hurt her.

He won't hurt her.

Unlike me.

I know that's not what Thorne meant. He meant I had no reason to fear the man had foul intentions with Daph. Even if Thorne had meant it the other way, could I blame him? I've never given him any reason to believe I'm anything but a careless rake. In fact, I encouraged him to think that way about me. It was the mask I wore, to keep him from fully respecting me. From caring too much.

He's exactly the kind of person you'd want to match her with.

Thorne was right, and this was always the goal from the beginning. Daphne needs a husband. I need a case study. Patrick's show of interest is not something either of us should discourage. If they form a relationship, both Daphne's and my problems are solved. I'll have the perfect ending to my case study. Daphne will have incontrovertible proof that she can't become Clyde's mate. Yet there's one key component that's missing; there was no spark between them. I sensed not a single flicker. Not when they danced. Not when they spoke.

The only spark…

The only spark I sense…

Panic seizes my chest, tightening it in a vise. I take another deep drag of my cigarillo, willing the ache to leave, but it doesn't. Not fully. Maybe it's been there all day. Or perhaps it's been weeks. I wish I could blame the emotionally charged ceremony, as it left my emotions raw, but I've felt this way before. This terrifying flame burning in my lungs.

I remember the last time.

It was on a night much like this, during The Heartbeats Tour. The gala. The first time I saw Daphne in seelie form. I recall the shock that tore through me, followed by a fierce protectiveness when I watched her dance. I'd already been protective of Daphne throughout the tour. She was the smallest of us, and while she was armed with a fierce bite, I still wanted to look out for her. That instinct grew when I saw her in that beautiful dress, dancing awkwardly with one partner and then the next. Then came the partner with the roving hands, and I stepped in.

But that wasn't where my panic ignited. It was later that night, after the gala had ended. Our lust-addled authors had decided to make the kitchen in our shared suite their personal fuck nest, so Daph and I got the hell out of there. We found an empty balcony and there we spent the next couple of hours. She drank her favorite berry cordial while I smoked. We didn't even talk much; we simply enjoyed the quiet night. Then Daphne climbed onto the balcony rail. My heart lurched into my throat, but she kept her balance with ease, just like she did in unseelie form. She extended a hand into the dark, grasping at something I couldn't see.

Then I realized what she was after. Cherry blossoms were raining down from the night sky. Or—more accurately—our hotel. The gala took place in an enormous living tree. Everything from the walls to the furnishings to the balcony was composed of this tree. I'd come to take such marvels for granted, for we'd been traveling across the isle, staying in a multitude of marvelous places. I'd grown used to whimsy. But then, as I watched Daphne snatching cherry blossoms from the air, her black hair limned blue in the starlight, her feet balanced on a twining, living balustrade, I felt like I was experiencing whimsy, beauty, and magic for the first time.

She finally caught one of the blossoms.

And turned to me with a joyous smile.

I'd never seen her smile before. Not in seelie form. It was so similar to how she bared her teeth to express her happiness as a pine marten, yet new. Different. Stunning.

That was when I felt like my heart had caught fire. When my lungs pinched tight.

The spark.

It was a pleasant flame at first, but my stomach sank, taking all my beautiful, burning awe with it.

Because I knew then, as I watched her so wild and free, so beautiful and innocent, that she was too good for me.

She was someone I could hurt.

I left her on that balcony shortly after, feigning fatigue, and I kept my distance in the following days, weeks, months, until I severed our friendship the day I got fired.

The memories cloud my heart, doubling my panic. How did I get myself in the same position I was in then? How did I let things go so far?

I take another drag, tipping my head back to exhale a lavender-scented cloud.

She's still someone I could hurt.

...someone who could hurt me.

I frown. No, that's not it. I live a dangerous life. I'm racked with debt. I could hurt her.

She could hurt me.

No, I hurt everyone around me.

Everyone I've loved has hurt me.

I shake the small voice from my mind. I'm truly losing it, aren't I? I'm the one who hurts people. I hurt my sister and all my friends when I sank into my dark mood after I found out about my mother.

And not a single friend noticed the pain you were hiding.

I hurt Briony and Thorne in my matchmaking attempts, partially to keep Briony from liking me and to encourage her affections to grow for Thorne, but partially because I liked causing trouble. I enjoyed the discord I stirred.

Briony disliked me the moment she laid eyes on me. Before I'd said or done a single cruel thing.

I hurt my first love, Cosette—

I didn't think my engagement would upset you, Monty. This time it isn't my own voice speaking to me but a memory from the past. *It's not like you and I were ever serious.*

I…I hurt my fox—

I can't be your pet anymore. I'm leaving.

I even hurt my father, in all my disobedience—

Why did you keep me from my mother?

Because you're male and I needed an heir.

I close my eyes tight against the memories and rub my chest as if it will rid me of this invisible ache.

"Monty?"

My eyes fly open at Daphne's voice. The sight of her standing beside me is so unexpected that my cigarillo nearly slides from my lips before I catch it. My eyes lock on hers, and every dark emotion that clouded my chest disappears. The tightness leaves my shoulders. My lungs expand. She hasn't said more than my name. Hasn't done a thing more than simply stand there. Yet her presence is enough. It's enough.

"What are you doing out here?" I ask, a rasp in my voice. I try to smile, but I know it doesn't reach my eyes.

"I came to find you."

"How did you know I was here?"

Her gaze slides down to my cigarillo, and her mouth quirks at a corner. "Lucky guess."

I clear my throat and control my tone to keep it steady. "You've had enough dancing for the night?"

She heaves a sigh. "I'm tired. It's exhausting trying to be well-mannered and demure. I know tonight was supposed to be a chance to perform for your case study, but I've done my part. You've clearly done yours as well, considering you're out here."

I sit up straighter, surprised by the bite in her tone. "You're angry with me?"

"You said we'd do this together. That you wouldn't leave me to do this by myself."

She's right. And yet…

"I can't be there for every step of the way. There are certain…lessons you can only advance on your own with your suitor."

"Yes, well, I've gotten as far as I can with Mr. Wright." She crosses her arms over her chest. "He's asked to call on me next weekend, which means we're on Lesson Four. Waiting to see if his actions align with his words."

I clench my teeth. "Is that why you came to find me? To update me on my case study's success?" I can't help the ire that infuses my tone.

"No, I came to find you because…because I wanted to be with you. I wanted to dance with you tonight, not Mr. Wright. Yet you left." She stomps as close to me as she can, arms still crossed, until she's standing between my legs. Her glare is furious as she stares down at me. "You left me all alone with him."

I want to argue that she wasn't alone, she was in a room full of people, but that's not what she means, is it? She wanted to enjoy the night with me, just like I wanted to enjoy it with her. The case study was a mere excuse for her to attend the ceremony and ball.

The truth is, I wanted her here. With *me*. No one else.

I stare up at her furious face, beautiful in her anger.

With every fiber of my being, I want her all to myself. I want every inch of her. I want to drag my hands under her skirt, up her thighs, and pull her onto my lap. I want to kiss her until she's dizzy. I want to bury myself inside her, show her just how badly I want her too. I want to fuck her here on this bench, make her come in this dress all over again. My body radiates with need. With desire. With an unquenchable thirst for her.

Holding her gaze, I extinguish my cigarillo and toss the butt to the ground. Then, slowly, I reach for her knees. She shudders at my touch, the anger on her face shifting to surprise. My fingers skate higher, over the smooth silk of her stockings. Then higher, where the top of her stockings give way to soft flesh. When my hands frame her hips, I give them a squeeze, then pull her onto my lap.

She utters a small yelp as she lands on my thighs, straddling me, her hands braced on my shoulders. I lean back slightly, bearing my weight on one arm while the other hand reaches for her jaw, her cheek, tracing the angled tip of her ear before my fingers slide around to her nape. Her breasts pulse above her neckline, her breaths sharp. My cock hardens as her lips part. I claw my fingers into the ends of her hair, ready to pull her face to mine. To taste her lips for the first time.

If we kiss, it's real.

I freeze, and my mind catches up with what my body is doing.

She senses my sudden trepidation, her hands tensing on my shoulders, her eyes volleying between mine as a furrow forms on her brow.

Fucking hell, I want to kiss that furrow away. I want to show her how I feel. But what I feel is more than the lust that courses through me. It's more than want. More than this aching need.

It's bigger. Softer.

It's love.

I fucking love her.

And I will not use her for pleasure when I can't be what she needs. If we can't be what I desperately wish we could be. Because I'll only end up hurting her.

She'll only end up hurting me.

I banish the voice from my head and slide my hands out from under her dress, wrapping them around her waist instead. With a quavering sigh, I drop my forehead to her shoulder and squeeze her tighter, wishing I never had to let her go.

CHAPTER TWENTY-NINE

DAPHNE

What I wouldn't give to freeze a moment in time. To bottle it up and return to it at will. If I could, I'd go back to the moment Monty pulled me onto his lap beneath a starlit sky, his lips an inch away from my own, unmasked desire written over his face. I'd stay there, balanced on the knife's edge between hope and disappointment, in the single, beautiful second when I was certain he was going to kiss me. To make what's been growing between us real.

Even after the pleasure he gave me, the boundary we crossed when he touched me in front of my hotel mirror, I wanted that kiss more than anything. That deeper intimacy.

Now it's all I can think about, even a day and a half later as Monty, Angela, and I journey our last few hours home by train. Our extended weekend is over, our goodbyes to the bride, groom, and little Tilly have been said, and I fear everything that happened at the hotel will stay there.

Despite Monty's strange mood during the ball, he's back to his usual self. It's hard to believe he hugged me so tightly—a memory I cherish almost as much as my hope for the kiss that never came—with so much sorrow in his posture, so much desperation in the arms that clutched me. For endless minutes, we stayed like that. I caressed his hair, his back, while he buried his face in my shoulder and simply held me. After he finally pulled away and gently lifted me from his lap, there was still grief on his face, but he hid it behind a smile. We parted after that, with me retiring to my room and him insisting he needed to remain at the ball until the end so he could help clean up after. I was too tired to even consider going back with him, drained after my conversation with Mr. Wright. By the next morning, it was time to depart.

Even though Monty's sorrow appears to have passed, I can't help noticing the downward tilt of his eyes. The smile that slips when he thinks no one's looking.

I assess him now, grinning as he sets several plates on the table before us. We're in the dining car of the train, our destination still hours away, and Monty offered to procure our snacks. He settles into the empty chair and passes one plate to Angela, the other to me. The third he keeps and pours himself a fresh cup of tea. On each of our plates are several round, doughy treats dusted in sugar.

Angela utters a delighted gasp. "Are these Lumies?"

Monty winks. "Star Court's specialty confection. These are extra special, as they're stuffed with different fillings. I got them at the hotel yesterday morning but forgot about them until today. They should still be fresh though."

Angela bites into one of hers, eyes going wide. "Strawberry! My favorite."

Monty's gaze slides to me, and my heart flips in my chest. It's been like that every time he's looked my way, the air between us vibrating with some invisible intensity. Maybe it's just my imagination, but his breathing seems shallower whenever our eyes meet. "Are you going to try yours, Daffy Dear?" Even his voice sounds strained when he speaks to me.

I shake my head to clear it, blinking away from Monty's storm-gray irises to assess my plate. I heard about Lumies during The Heartbeats Tour, when we were in the Star Court city of Lumenas—where Edwina and William now live. One of the friends we made during the tour, Zane, raved about Lumies and insisted we try them while we were in town. I never did.

Lowering my head slightly, I sniff my plate. Scents of sugar, cream, and something rich and savory flood my nostrils. I take up one of the dough balls and bite into it, noting how the lightly crisped fried exterior gives way to an airy interior. My second bite includes some of the filling. Now it's my turn to utter my delight. "Is this bacon?"

Monty sips his tea, holding my gaze. "Candied bacon and maple cream."

Angela wipes sugar from her lips as she chuckles. "Candied bacon and cream? Why did you choose such a strange combination for Daphne?"

I open my mouth to spout my love for bacon, but Monty speaks first, his eyes still locked on mine. "Bacon is Daffy's favorite."

My heart flips all over again. Perhaps it's silly to feel so moved over bacon, but I am. My cheeks flush, and I hide my satisfied grin by popping an entire Lumie into my mouth at once. Monty's lips quirk at one corner as he watches me chew my mouthful in what I know is a rather unladylike manner.

"You've changed a lot, brother." Angela sips her tea, then studies him with a curious expression. "You're quite thoughtful lately, and you weren't at all annoying at the wedding like I thought you would be."

She's right. I didn't see the side of Monty she'd mentioned on our initial journey. Yet I did get my wish about seeing a deeper side of him. I witnessed an emotional rawness, an openness, a vulnerability he hadn't shown before. I watched tears trail down his cheeks during the ceremony. I felt his arms wrap around me in the kind of embrace I've never shared with anyone. I got to laugh and dance and climb upon tables with him. And then, of course, there was the mirror foreplay...

My cheeks heat, so I swallow the rest of the bite down with a gulp of tea, then fan myself as if the liquid was too hot.

"You were a respectable gentleman all weekend," Angela says. "It was almost unsettling. You didn't flirt with anyone, nor did you dance. Though I know how you feel about dancing." She says the last part with a wry glance at me, as if I too know of his disdain for it. But I don't. I've only experienced the opposite.

I like dancing. With you.

Angela continues. "I daresay there were several disappointed ladies who'd been trying to catch your eye all night. Yet you didn't so much as offer them a conciliatory glance. I thought perhaps you were too distracted looking out for our dear Daphne here, but even after she departed the ball, you didn't relax or flirt with a single soul."

Monty's gaze finally leaves mine as he shifts uncomfortably in his seat.

I, however, radiate with smug satisfaction. It never occurred to me that he might take a lover for the night after I left, but hearing how aloof he was during my absence gives me far more pleasure than I could have imagined. Even if nothing untoward happened, I know what a flirt he can be. Was he merely trapped in his sorrowful mood? Or...

That spark of hope lights in my chest again, and I try not to let myself consider what it means. How badly I want to be the reason for his restraint. But perhaps he was trying not to be an asshole at his best friend's wedding, simple as that.

"I wasn't in a flirtatious mood," Monty says, his tone light. "Being someone's best man is a serious job."

"I suppose your work ethic has grown strong, considering you're an employed man now. I'm proud of you."

"My dear sister is proud of me for not causing a scandal or acting like a lecherous swine. I think I've earned the pinnacle of respect."

She rolls her eyes at his dry tone, then faces me. "How did you enjoy the wedding? Did you manage to finish your illustration?"

"I made great progress," I say, swelling with pride. After I left the ball, my mind was too active for sleep. So I stayed up and worked on my sketch of the figures. When I told Monty I needed his help finding the right pose before the mirror, I meant it wholeheartedly. Even though our activities turned to pleasure, the sight of us together is forever emblazoned upon my mind's eye. I took that memory and sketched it. Not the part where I was a boneless mess, half reclined upon him while he worked my sex, but before that, when I first guided his hands, one lifting my hem, the other alighted upon my shoulder, his head angled to the side as he looked at me. My inspiration was stronger than ever before, and by the end of the night, I had the clean sketch perfected on my canvas, along with the background I'd sketched of the ballroom.

"I'm glad to hear it," Angela says. "I'd love to see it! Or any of your illustrations."

I nearly choke on my sip of tea. The last thing I want is to show Angela a sketch that was inspired by her brother in such a suggestive pose. I'm not sure either of us told her what kinds of illustrations I do.

"Sorry, Angie," Monty says, coming to my rescue with a lie. "Daph is under contract. She can't show off designs for the covers she's working on."

Her lips pull into a pout. "That's a shame."

"A true shame," Monty agrees. Then his eyes lock on mine, a wicked gleam in them. "Especially since I'd like to hang her latest work-in-progress in my bedroom."

I purse my lips to hide my smile. There's that shameless flirt I know and love, all signs of his strange mood from the other night erased.

My heart stutters as my mind reverses, lingers.

Know and...love.

I echo the sentiment again and again, my chest tightening. Then loosening as I realize, without a doubt, that it's true.

AFTER WE FINISH OUR SNACKS, it's time to return to the passenger car. Angela goes on ahead while Monty heads to the smoking car. I, meanwhile, use the lavatory. Once I exit the lavatory compartment, my gaze snags on the passing scenery, a blur of green, gold, and blue. We've already entered the Earthen Court and will soon pull into Jasper City Station. As beautiful as the Star Court was—as well as the many other courts I've visited—I've always loved the Earthen Court the most. I love the lush fields, the evergreen mountains, the freshness of the air, the spring rainstorms and mild summers. I linger in the corridor and prop my arms on the windowsill, admiring the landscape.

"You're still here." I startle at Monty's voice. I don't know how long I've been standing here, but it must have been long enough for Monty to have returned from the smoking car.

He strides down the corridor and stops beside me. "Watching the view?"

I nod. "I must have lost track of time."

"Shall we return together? We'll be arriving—"

The train's momentum shifts, slowing as it rounds a bend and causing the car to jolt. I stumble, my feet losing purchase beneath me. Monty's hands come around my waist, even as he too loses his footing. We shift to the side just as the train's motion levels out again, and Monty catches us against the wall beside the window. One hand remains braced at my lower back while the other clutches the windowsill. My back presses against the wall, his front flush with mine.

It takes me a few seconds to gather my bearings, but when I do, I notice the placement of my hands. One is pressed over Monty's chest, splayed over the pounding drum of his heart hidden beneath his unbuttoned waistcoat. The other is clenched around his open collar. Neither of us has moved, and once again, our lips are merely an inch apart.

Our breaths mingle as our gazes tangle, neither daring to break away. The tempo of his heart increases, slamming against my palm.

How easy it would be to lift my chin and claim his lips. Why should I wait for him to do it? Why should I let him take the lead in declaring what we are, what we can be? I'm well beyond the realm of denial. Even though I told him our sexual pleasure didn't have to mean anything—and it's true; it didn't *have* to—he'd already begun to mean a lot to me before that moment. It's just that now I'm starting to understand the word that goes along with these feelings. With this desire.

I suck in a breath, gathering the nerve to press my mouth to his...

Then doubt plagues my heart. He could have kissed me

last night, but he didn't. Why didn't he? I know he desires me. I felt the proof digging into my backside during our foreplay session.

And yet...

He didn't act on that desire.

Is it because he doesn't want to? We could have done so much more in my hotel room. I offered to, and he refused. I didn't feel rejected at the time, but what if that's exactly what that was? What if I make a move and he rejects me again?

I imagine leaning in, only to have him pull away. I don't know if I can bear that pain. I hardly managed to recover from him rejecting my invitation to catch up over a meal the day he got fired. How could I handle him refusing a kiss?

It conjures a memory I haven't thought of in a while. A ring of girls, staring down at me with terror and disgust while I wipe fresh blood from my lips. Blood from a girl who cowers, covering her ruined ear as she calls me a monster—

Monty clears his throat and slowly steps away. Whether I shattered the moment with my hesitation or it was never there to begin with, my chance has passed. He runs a hand through his hair, tousling his pale curls. "Shall we?" A sweet smile curves his lips, tinged with shyness. Maybe I didn't imagine that moment after all.

Maybe this...*thing* that's growing between us, this emotion that's already taken root, means to him what it means to me. Maybe he feels what I do. Maybe I just need a moment to tell him. To ask. Maybe I don't need to brace myself for rejection.

You're a monster. You may look like a lady, but you're nothing more than a beast.

...Or maybe I'm just getting ahead of myself.

No sooner than we return to Angela does the train arrive at the station. As we gather our belongings, I steal a few glances at Monty. He returns them with that same shy smile he gave me in the corridor. Tenuous hope blooms in my chest. It grows as we exit the train car, and he holds my hand to help me down the steps, giving it a squeeze as I land on the platform beside him. He leans in close and whispers in my ear, "I really do want to hang your newest piece in my bedroom."

A shudder runs through me. Why is he saying this now, when we're in public, surrounded by passengers who flood the platform? Why couldn't he have said this when his body was pressed against mine in the empty corridor? It could have given me the courage to kiss him like I wanted.

At least it serves to embolden me now.

"Why have just a painting when you could have the real thing?"

His eyes darken. Then a corner of his mouth quirks in a thrillingly seductive grin. "No, the real thing is too pretty for my shabby apartment."

I arch a teasing brow. "So you're saying my art is less pretty?"

"Not at all. I've seen your…art. I know how magnificent it is."

Heat pools in my core. I don't know if he intended to speak in innuendo, but my mind fills with the words he said to me before the mirror.

God, that's fucking art.

Do you see that? Do you see how beautiful that is?

"Maybe I can paint something special for you," I whisper back. There's no denying what this is. We're flirting. Seducing each other with our words. Words that would sound benign to anyone who overheard us but mean so much more to us. Just us. "I'd need you to pose with me again. I do have a full-length mirror at home."

"I think I can accommodate you," he whispers, then steps

back. Angela descends the stairs and strides past us, oblivious to the secret smile we exchange behind her back.

It's yet another beautiful moment I wish I could keep.

Another divide between hope and despair.

Before the moment is shattered with Angela's excited squeal. "Father!"

CHAPTER THIRTY

DAPHNE

Monty's reaction to seeing his father is immediate. He sucks in a breath, face going pale, shoulders tensing.

I turn to watch Angela bound over to a middle-aged man. He's tall and lean with sharp features, dark hair, and a smile that doesn't meet his eyes. Just behind him stand two human figures, who I assume must be servants. A maid and butler perhaps. I see only a small resemblance between father and son, which makes me wonder if Monty takes more after his and Angela's mother. All I know for sure is Monty is not pleased to see him.

"What the fuck is he doing here?" Monty mutters under his breath.

It occurs to me now how strange it is that Monty continues to reside in the same city as his father when he despises the man. Does he remain close for Angela's sake? Or sheer stubbornness?

Lord Phillips greets his daughter, who speaks to him with animated gestures. Monty hasn't taken his glare off the man, not even when Angela hurries back to us.

"Father came to fetch me from the station," she says, still showing no sign of the disdain Monty has. Though she does lower her head slightly at the sight of Monty's clear unease. "I'm sorry. I had no idea he'd come. I know you don't like to see him—"

"Angela," Lord Phillips says, taking a step our way. Monty's glare darkens. "Go get settled in the coach. Mr. Jones will gather your luggage."

She gives another apologetic look to Monty. "Thank you for chaperoning me. It truly was a lovely weekend." She turns to me next. "And it was so wonderful meeting you and getting to know you. I hope we can see more of each other in the future."

I don't get a chance to reply before she joins the servants, and the maid escorts her away. I'm glad for the missed opportunity to speak, for I haven't a clue what to say or how to act in front of Lord Phillips. And Monty clearly has no desire to linger.

"Let's go," Monty says under his breath while his father waves at Angela.

Before we can take a step away, Lord Phillips stops Monty with a hand to his arm. "I'll have a word."

"You won't," Monty says with an air of lazy annoyance, his countenance shifting into the version of him I used to know best. Casual, flippant, arrogant. "We were just leaving."

"I'll have a word," his father repeats, tone stern, his hand still clutching Monty's forearm.

I expect Monty to shake the man off. Lord Phillips doesn't appear to be particularly strong, and Monty doesn't seem afraid of him. Yet instead of arguing, Monty slouches, eyes wandering around the crowded platform as if he'd rather be anywhere else. "Make it quick. I have things to do."

Lord Phillips ushers Monty to where he stood when we disembarked. My pulse quickens as I find myself standing alone, unsure if I'm meant to follow them. I'm annoyed by Monty's lack of attention, but perhaps it's intentional. An act. He hasn't so much as spared me a glance since his father spoke to him.

I shift awkwardly from foot to foot as I stare at the hem of my skirt. I know I shouldn't care what Monty's father thinks of me, but I'm suddenly grateful I wore my spare dress —the one *not* covered in smears of graphite—instead of my workday attire.

"Why are you here?" Monty asks in a lazy drawl that barely carries over the din of the crowd. His voice would be lost to me completely were it not for my keen fae hearing.

"When Angela said you were bringing a friend to the wedding, I wanted to see her for myself," Lord Phillips says.

My cheeks blaze hot, and I consider forcing my focus away, tuning out of my hunter's senses so as not to eavesdrop. But when he speaks again, I can't resist listening.

"So, you're courting someone after all. You remember your bargain?"

I frown. What bargain is he referring to? Does he somehow know about mine and Monty's? But no, that's not what this feels like. This feels like something I don't have enough context for.

"Yes, I remember my fucking bargain." Monty has lost his indifferent air now, revealing his true annoyance. "This has nothing to do with that."

"That's not what it looks like. Who is she?"

"She's no one," he says through his teeth. "She means nothing to me, so don't get your hopes up."

His words drive a spear through my heart. I know there's

a reason for what he says. He told me and Araminta how he refuses to further his father's legacy. How he convinced his father he'd never marry and that courting someone would bring Lord Phillips' unwanted attention right back to him. Not only to him, but his lover too.

"Is she from a decent family?" Lord Phillips says. "What does her father do? Is her mother a respectable woman?"

I bristle. It doesn't take much to imagine how horrified he'd be to discover my father's occupation is *cowering after copulation* and my mother is respected but not at all respectable, as far as his definition would go.

"Like you have a right to ask about one's mother." Monty's tone darkens, though I don't know what he means by that.

"At least she's fae," his father says, and I can feel Lord Phillips' gaze on me.

Every instinct begs me to meet his eyes and bare my teeth. To snarl at him, like I did the boxer who fought Monty at the club. But I don't.

Lord Phillips speaks again. "A fae bride is perfect. Well done—"

"Did you not listen to a goddamn word I said? We aren't courting. There is nothing between us. *Nothing.* And there never will be. So stop praising me like I've done a damn thing worth your admiration."

Lord Phillips releases a heavy sigh. "You disappoint me."

My eyes flick toward the pair in time to see Monty give his father a humorless grin. "That's your fault for expecting anything more."

They're silent for a long stretch. Then Lord Phillips says, "If anything changes and you get over your rebellious stage, I expect you to take your proper place as my heir—"

"It's Angela's proper place. *Her* place, not mine, and we both know it."

Lord Phillips gives a disappointed shake of his head. "Take care, Son." he says without warmth, then strides away.

Monty stands there, jaw tight, for several seconds before I force my legs to move and join him. He doesn't look at me. Doesn't acknowledge the hand I place on his shoulder.

"Are you all right?"

"Let's go," is all he says as he marches toward the luggage car.

He's quiet on the cab ride home, his posture tense, his gaze fixed out the window. I stare down at the hand he has curled on his thigh, tempted to place my palm over it, to give it a reassuring squeeze. We've given each other comforting touches before, but this is a new side of Monty. He feels like he's a million miles away, so much colder than the version of him who held me tight outside the hotel. Still, I want him to know I'm here for him.

It takes me several minutes to gather the courage to finally speak. "I'm sorry about your father. It must have been hard seeing him so unexpectedly."

He sucks in a breath, the only sign that he heard me, but makes no reply.

I stare at his hand again, his knuckles white from how tightly he clenches it. Then, slowly, I reach for him. He startles as I place my hand on his. "Are you all right, Monty?"

He turns to me for the first time since we entered the hansom cab. He blinks at me a few times, as if puzzled by my presence, then dons a mask of wry amusement. "I'm fine," he says, turning his hand over to squeeze mine back.

Then he releases it. Drops it. Shifts so that we're no longer touching.

His every move is casual. Easy. Yet his distance feels intentional.

"It was good, actually," he says. His lips curl in a half smile, but there's a strain in his eyes. A current of grim resignation beneath his nonchalant tone. "It served as a reminder."

"Of what?" I ask, folding both hands in my lap to keep from touching him again.

He heaves a sigh and tilts his head against the backrest. "To not get carried away."

"What did you get carried away with?"

Silence. Then he waves a dismissive hand. "Oh, this and that."

"If you want to talk about it—"

"You have a date this week, don't you?" He angles himself toward me, extracting a cigarillo from his case and flipping it between his fingers. His buoyant mood is such a stark contrast to the cold, brooding figure who sat silently beside me for the first half of our ride. I can't tell whether he's trying to distract me from my line of questioning or simply feels guilty for having neglected me and is now trying to make up for it.

Regardless, his change of topic sours my stomach. "A date?"

"Patrick Wright asked to call on you this coming weekend, didn't he? We never did discuss our plans for your next lesson demonstration, but alas it's your turn. You owe me big time."

"I owe you? For what?"

"For our impromptu modeling session at the hotel." He says it without so much as a blush, which delays my understanding.

Then I realize what he's referring to. Our mirror foreplay.

While it's true I proposed our activities as a brief modeling session, and it certainly aided my art, hearing him speak about what we did so casually, so devoid of the flirtatious innuendo he spoke with earlier, has my heart falling.

He speaks again. "That means I modeled for you twice in a row—at your apartment the weekend before the wedding, then in your hotel room—to your single courtship lesson this past weekend."

My cheeks blaze but I force my voice to come out even. "Wouldn't you say what we did in my hotel room was also a lesson demonstration? Chapter Eight, remember?"

"Ah, that's where you're wrong, Daffy Dear. Our bargain states our sessions can last for up to a full day. Your courtship lesson was reserved for Saturday."

He's right. We'd planned for our lesson to take place the day of the wedding. Which was the same day we...

Irritation ripples through me. Maybe it's wrong of me, but I hoped he'd treat what we did together as separate from our arrangement, even though *I'm* the one who said it didn't have to mean anything.

But...it meant something.

To me, at least.

Did it mean nothing to him?

"Our bargain also states," Monty says, oblivious to my ire, to the lump that rises in my throat, "that you must perform a courtship lesson for every session I pose for. Which means it's your turn. Unfortunately, I won't be able to be with you for this one, but you're ready. After all, he isn't a stranger anymore."

I bite the inside of my cheek to keep the unexpected tears at bay. What happened to the overprotective male who stared daggers at Patrick every time he spoke to me? What happened to the man who held me so tightly, as if he yearned to merge me with his soul?

"You feel it too, don't you?" His easy smile remains etched on his lips, but there's a wild quality to his eyes that reminds me of cornered prey. A creature resigned to death yet desperate for an impossible rescue. One that will never come. "This is the grand finale. The happy ending to my case study, and the solution to both of our problems."

How is this a happy ending? I want to shout it at him, but I don't trust myself to speak.

"I never did tell you the reason I need to secure the publishing contract, did I?"

My pulse quickens and hope sparks inside me. Is he going to divulge something? I remember the desperation he showed the night we made our bargain. I recall thinking he had more reasons for needing our arrangement than he'd let on. But I never pried. Never asked for more than what he gave.

He flips his cigarillo around and around. "I'm in debt. Massive, massive debt. When I was first disinherited, I took out a loan for living expenses and spent it immediately. Clothes, food, entertainment, and a year-long lease in a luxury apartment. This wouldn't have been too life-altering had I secured a loan from a regular lender. But I hadn't, because trustworthy banks wouldn't work with me. Instead, I went into debt with a shady loan shark who charges interest at illegal rates. Interest so high I stopped being able to afford my luxury lease as soon as the first year was up, which is why I've lived in a shithole apartment the last two years. And now the interest is so high, I can't afford my weekly loan payments. So I pay by fighting in fixed matches. You remember the club? That fight you witnessed was meant to be a fixed match. Bare-knuckle boxing used to be fun for me, but now it's a hobby I participate in out of necessity. I get beaten out of necessity. I beat people out of necessity. Pain is akin to pleasure for me, but bloody hell, I miss when it was fun. I want that back."

"Why are you telling me this?"

"So you understand my priorities. My life is a mess. I'm a mess. My family is a mess. But if I get this publishing deal, I receive a long-term contract to continue writing as Gladys at the *Gazette,* along with a signing bonus from my boss. I'll have a chance to secure a legitimate loan to pay off my lender. Finishing this case study the way we always intended is the most important thing to me right now."

The most important thing.

Not me.

Not us.

Not taking a chance on what this might be.

Shouldn't that be my priority too? I need to get out of my handfasting, or I'll have no future in Jasper. I'll be mated to a honey badger who will never agree to leave Cypress Hollow, a town inhabited by unseelie creatures, not humanoid artists with a love for illustration and a deep respect for opposable thumbs. To sever that bond, I need a husband.

Don't I?

But what if…

"Be a good girl and give Patrick a chance, all right?" His smile falters the slightest bit, a crack rending his voice. "Just stay true to the two most important lessons. Lesson Two: don't waste your time on suitors who don't put in effort to pursue you. If he likes you, he'll prove it. He'll move heaven and earth to secure your affections. If he doesn't pursue you, it means he's uninterested, not that he needs encouragement from you. Remember?"

I nod, averting my gaze out the window so he can't see my expression fall. I know what he's doing. I know what he's trying to convey. This isn't about Patrick. It's about him. I don't need to tell him how I feel or make the first move. He already knows. And he's reminding me that he's not pursuing me.

"What's Lesson Four?" His voice is soft now. Painfully so.

I swallow hard before answering. "A man's actions must align with his words."

Monty says nothing, and he doesn't need to. Because I remember what he said the night he first relayed this lesson, as we sat upon my roof and he told me about his first love.

If he says one thing but he does another, don't waste your time... Do not try to fix him. You'll both only get hurt in the end.

I'd been so focused on what this lesson meant regarding his past, I hadn't taken it for the warning it was meant to be.

...if a potential partner states he is not seeking marriage, only sex, but you feel *like he's falling for you, do not give him your heart.*

Monty made it plain from the beginning. He is not seeking marriage. He can't, because of whatever is going on with his family. The secrets he won't tell me.

I, on the other hand, *am* seeking marriage. We've both known it all along.

I watch the city streets of Jasper roll past the window of our cab, the sounds of horse hooves on cobblestones drowning out the crash of my sinking, crumbling heart. The heart that didn't heed Monty's warning.

The heart I already gave to him, whether he wants it or not.

CHAPTER THIRTY-ONE

DAPHNE

My heart hurts but bacon makes it better. It makes everything better.

I slouch at one of the tables in Fletcher-Wilson's break room, a strip of bacon in one hand and a telegram in the other. The plate of bacon is one of six batches I cooked up earlier this week to take to work with me, while the telegram is from Patrick Wright and was delivered to my desk this morning. It seems he's planning on making good on his intentions to call on me this weekend and has even set a time and place for us to go on a date. That, of course, only reminds me of my last conversation with Monty. The pain of his subtle rejection.

I crumple the telegram in my fist and shift my attention to Araminta's non-stop chatter. She leans against the long break room counter in seelie form, her lilac hair hidden beneath a silk scarf. Her eyes are obscured by spectacles with tinted lenses while her figure is adorned in her signature ruffly black mourning wear. "You really missed out on so much," she says, catching her breath after a lengthy run-on sentence. "You should be honored I took the time out of my busy schedule to come visit you at work."

"So honored," I say in a monotone, then shove another strip of bacon in my mouth. I may not show it, but I truly am glad Ari is here. When I returned home after my extended weekend, I expected her to have wreaked havoc in my apartment the entire time I was gone, but there was no sign of her. It wasn't until today, Wednesday, that I finally saw her. Apparently, she really did have a busy weekend. Her modeling career has gotten off to such a successful start that she's managed to secure her own apartment in town. She also relayed that she's gotten back together and broken up with David about four times. One would think I was gone a month, not a handful of days.

"Hey, aren't you eating a little too much bacon?" she asks.

I bristle, teeth bared to warn her away in case she's considering taking my plate from me. "There's no such thing."

"Are you sure? Because that's a lot of bacon. It looks more like a whole pig."

I defiantly shove a whole strip in my mouth, delighting in the crunchy richness that melts over my tongue. "Are you bacon-shaming me?"

She shrugs. "I suppose I have no reason to. You're not the one who has to watch her figure, unlike me. I'm practically famous, you know. This body belongs to several respected brands." She says the last part a touch too loud, her eyes darting around to the break room's other occupants. None of the three figures glance our way, as two are locked in jovial conversation and the third has just finished up her meal and exits without a backward glance. With a huff, she removes the scarf from her hair and the spectacles from her face. She settles into one of the chairs at my table and pushes a paper across the surface to me.

My heart pinches when I see it's the *Cedar Hills Gazette*. Monty's paper.

She doesn't allow me to dwell on that, flipping the pages before me to the advertisements. "Look at my newest advert," she says, tapping a black-and-white photograph. I immediately recognize her, though she's dressed down to her undergarments. When my eyes reach the text that overlays the photograph, I nearly choke on my bacon.

When pussy wants to play, use Intrepid.

I slam my chest to free my airways, then take a heavy swallow of tea.

Ari tilts her head in question.

"That's some, uh, interesting choice of words," I say.

"Why?"

I lean in close and lower my voice. "It says *pussy*, right there on the ad."

She gives me an innocent grin. "Yes, and I'm holding a kitten."

I drop my face in my hands. For the love of the All of All, does she have any clue about the brands she models for? I lift my head and whisper, "Intrepid is a contraceptive and reproductive health tonic."

She gives an excited nod. "I know! It tastes like cherries."

So she does know what Intrepid is.

I take another piece of bacon off my plate. "I prefer the blackberry flavor."

Araminta's eyes go wide. "You use the tonic too? But... why? Your sex life is soooo boring."

Once again, I nearly choke on bacon. My eyes dart to the two other figures in the room, but they're two tables away and still very much engaged in conversation. "Could you not say things like that so loud?"

She shrugs. "But it's true. I, on the other hand, had quite the weekend. Can you believe I had my very first threesome? It was actually quite awkward. I got bored quickly so David and Conrad just had sex with each other while I watched and ate chocolate, but it was still an experience. What about you, Daph?" She gives me a taunting grin. "When is the last time you let pussy out to play?"

My cheeks flood with heat, both from her scandalous words and because...because it has no longer been quite so long.

She must read the truth on my face. Her expression turns to shock and her voice takes on a serious edge. "Wait, when was the last time? When's the last time pussy came out to play, Daphne?"

I speak in a furious whisper. "Lower your damn voice." When she repeats the question in a true whisper, I say, "She, uh, came out to play over the weekend."

She bounces in her seat and claps her gloved hands. "Wow! With whom?"

I try to keep the disappointment off my face when I answer, but I can't help the quaver in my voice. "Monty."

Her lips pull into a grimace. "That bad, eh?"

"No, it's not that. It's just..." I force away memories of our conversation in the cab, of the strange sorrow that fell over him when he hugged me outside the hotel, of the way my heart cracked open wide when we danced on tables. If I just focus on the non-emotional aspects, if I merely convince myself that what I said before the mirror remains true...

It doesn't have to mean anything...

Right. It was just foreplay. Monty is just my friend who offered some pleasure. I may have gotten carried away, and perhaps he did too, but I won't anymore. Not ever again.

Because I would rather be safe than risk everything. I would rather secure a husband than trust I'll get the promotion I'll need to get out of my handfasting otherwise. I would rather be paired with a sensible match who fulfills all my needs and requirements on a practical level than be hurt by someone I have feelings for.

It's better to be safe than to be rejected.

You're a monster. You may look like a lady, but you're nothing more than a beast.

I take a deep breath and mask all my hidden emotions behind a smile. "It was incredible."

Araminta hangs on to my every word as I relay what we did. As if it was nothing more than fleeting fun. As if it meant nothing. Then I show her Patrick Wright's telegram and recite all the ways he's right for me. All the reasons it makes sense for me to go on a date with him on Friday.

My heart crumples inside.

But at least it's safe in my chest.

Where the words I never said to Monty can burn to ash.

CHAPTER THIRTY-TWO

MONTY

Every day without Daphne feels like a punch to the chest.

It's not like we've gone much longer than normal this week without seeing each other. In fact, ever since we reunited, we only saw each other on weekends. Maybe it's that I know I won't see her this weekend that makes me count each day like a prison sentence.

But I don't dare see her. Not until she's given Patrick a chance.

He deserves a chance. I fucking know he does. I trust Thorne was right about him, and when I take myself out of the equation, I can see that he is perfect for Daph. Maybe there's no spark between them, but she wasn't looking for one anyway. And my case study isn't about uncovering some mystical connection no one else can see. It's about following the rules of courtship to find an ideal match. Which Patrick is.

Unlike me.

I don't deserve her.

I could never deserve her.

I'll only hurt her, like I hurt everyone else.

I repeat this throughout the week, every time my unruly heart begs me to seek her out. To tell her I didn't mean what I said, what I hinted at.

But that would be a lie.

I did mean it.

I can't pursue her. I won't pursue her. I won't drag her into this disastrous life of mine and this disastrous family. I won't play with her heart when I can't give her what she needs. If I get in the way, we could both lose. If she chooses me over a safe bet like Patrick, we could both get hurt. If she has nothing but her career to rely on to end her handfasting, and it ends up not being enough, I'll be to blame. Then she'll be stuck in her hometown, and I'll be without her.

At least this way we can stay friends. She can continue to live in Jasper, and I can keep her in my life.

Even if she belongs to someone else.

The thought has my pen nib digging too deep into the paper I'd been writing on, sending a splotch of ink over the surface. Shaking my head, I lean back in my chair and crumple the sheet upon my desk. I haven't managed to write a single decent article this week. Thankfully, I have a few older drafts I've kept handy for weeks when my readers provide little in the way of entertaining content.

Today is Friday and Daphne is going on a date with Patrick.

I know this because I sent a series of telegrams to Thorne, none of which did well to hide my desperation. He didn't tease me about my line of questions, only answered them briefly. The latest of which confirmed Patrick will be taking Daphne out to dinner tonight.

I push back from my desk and pace the perimeter of my office. My lungs feel like they're going to burst from my chest along with my heart. It's all I can do to keep from running out of here to find Daphne, to tell her not to go.

I can't do that.

I can't be selfish.

By the end of my workday, I've done more pacing than writing and far more fretting than anything that even resembles work. I'm not even remotely pleased with the article I turned in for Monday's issue, as I didn't have the heart to make a single dirty joke, but at least something will go to press. Maybe by next week I'll have my wits about me. Maybe by then Daphne will see I was right.

She'll have given Patrick a chance and realized I was only getting in the way.

Then maybe it will be safe for us to see each other again.

My shoulders slump as I leave my office and make my way across the newsroom, papers fluttering overhead on enchanted winds as the staff hurry to finish their tasks for the weekend.

As soon as I'm outside, I extract a cigarillo and my igniter, lighting it at once. The botanical smoke only calms the sharpest edges of my nerves. Everything else simmers in my chest, too close to boiling over. The sun sinks toward the horizon, painting the business district in hazy blue, pink, and orange. The sidewalks are crowded with figures ending their workweek, eager for the respite the weekend will bring.

I wish I felt the same.

I make my way toward the edge of the business district where it meets the industrial district. This is where my apartment is located. Only when I'm a block away do I notice the rhythmic footsteps following behind me. Muttering under my breath, I whirl around and extinguish my cigarillo under my heel. There stand the two nameless thugs I have the displeasure of seeing every Friday.

"You missed last week's payment," says Cane, his fist gripped tight around the top of his lacquered walking stick. "Boss isn't pleased."

"I had to go out of town," I say with an air of indifference. These assholes have never scared me, as they're nothing more than their boss' cronies. And their goblin boss deals in secrets and fixed matches, not excessive violence in public spaces. Still, I'm not looking forward to what I know they're going to say next.

"Due date's moved up," says Meathands. Were I in a better mood, I'd chortle at his newest scarf—a pastel pink atrocity with a pattern of puppies and kittens. "Another payment missed means your little secret's coming out another week earlier. Boss didn't appreciate you skipping town without a word, though, so it's two weeks earlier this time."

The blood leaves my face. Two weeks earlier? I do the math in my head. The date already moved up from August 6th to July 30th after I botched my fight with Grave Danger. If it has moved up two weeks more, that places it on July 16th now. Good God, that's only a month and a half away. I open my mouth to argue, but what can I say? I already knew my moneylender was a shady bastard. He can change the terms of our loan without consequence because his business model allows him to get away with it. If I go to the authorities and try to shine a light on his bad practices, I'll be in breach of my loan contract, and he'll reveal my secret at once without having to wait until my due date. The only way out is to pay off this debt.

And I'm running out of time. I need that contract at the

Gazette. I need proof of long-term employment so I can pay off my moneylender with a legitimate loan. Otherwise, the secret about my birth mother comes out and my family—my human family whose reputation relies on human virtues like fidelity and honesty—falls to ruin.

I don't care about my father. But Angela...

I can't let her get swept up in this. Not when this is my fault. I never should have taken out this loan. I never should have spent it so fast and frivolously, digging myself into a grave of debt.

"Fine," I say, doing all I can to hide the anxiety burrowing in my gut. "In the meantime, I'll work off my fucking payment tonight, same as always."

Cane smirks. "Same as always, yes, but tonight we have special instructions. Tonight, you're going to lose, but not until the final round. You're going to stay in the ring until the end, and you're not going to put up a fight. Keep your defense minimal."

I clench my jaw. Of course. Tonight isn't just about paying interest, it's about paying for skipping town last weekend and robbing their boss of his fixed match.

To be honest, this works well enough for me.

Because I'm in the mood to be punished.

Lesson Four

LOVE AND REASONABLE ACTS OF VIOLENCE

CHAPTER THIRTY-THREE

DAPHNE

There's one thing I hate more than raw broccoli, and that is salad. Whoever thought drizzling oily sauces over cold leaves was a good idea should be arrested. I push the soggy leaves across my plate with my fork, eyes downcast while I try to act more demure than disgusted. Thank the All of All dainty bites are considered polite. And that there's bread.

My date and I sit across from each other at a small table in a dimly lit restaurant called The Golden Stone. The walls are dark slate interspersed with trickling water features that evoke the feeling you're inside a cave. The occasional lightbulb hangs from climbing ivy while green fire sprites flutter overhead. The restaurant is in the fashionable part of town, a portion of the city that serves very little interest to me. For fashionable places mean crowds, and this restaurant is no exception. Each table is occupied by a well-dressed party, most of whom wear evening dresses or suits with frock coats. No one is outfitted in workday attire like me.

I came directly after work, choosing a leisurely walk over hurrying back to my apartment to change. At least I wore my nicest waistcoat, one of mauve brocade, and my slacks are wide-legged and flowing, almost giving the impression of a skirt. Then there's my date. Patrick Wright is outfitted in a gray suit, though upon seeing my attire, he removed his jacket. I expected him to question my choice of clothing, but he merely greeted me and thanked me for meeting him after work.

All in all, he's a kind, polite human male.

Nothing to complain about.

Aside from him ordering me salad.

"How is your latest illustration, Miss Hartford?" he asks, taking a sip of wine. His salad plate is empty, and our entrées should arrive soon.

I take the opportunity to set down my fork and feign interest. "It went well," I say, modulating my voice the way I know I should, pitching it slightly higher, softer. I'm reminded of what Monty said to me when we practiced formal introductions.

...you don't have to pretend to be anyone you're not. You deserve to be loved for exactly who you are.

I force the memory away and continue. "My first two covers are officially finished, and I turned the latest one in for the art director's approval today. She loved it."

He gives me a warm smile. "Congratulations. I'm truly impressed by you."

I wish my heart fluttered at his words. Or his face. Aesthetically speaking, he's perfect. Too perfect. His hair is styled so neatly it looks like a painting, not a strand falling out of place when he moves. His brown eyes are kind, his nose is straight, and his jaw and cheekbones are sharp enough to cut the metaphorical corset strings on any blushing heroine's undergarments. It's like he stepped straight off the pages of one of Edwina's books. And that makes him the ideal specimen to serve as my model.

My heart grows heavy as I reflect on what my supervisor said when she approved my painting today. "There's so much emotion here. So much tension. I feel like I'm looking at a true moment in time, witnessing something meant to stay behind closed doors. Perfectly provocative."

She was right. My latest painting—the one I based on my mirror activities with Monty—was a true moment in time. I finished it quicker than any other, not even needing a reference for the hues, tints, and shadows. Everything remains clear in my mind. Not just about what we did in my hotel room, but every moment from that weekend.

Including what Monty said on the ride home from the train station.

Be a good girl and give Patrick a chance, all right?

That's exactly what I'm doing. I pull myself out of my head and turn my attention over to my date. To his gentle gaze, his strong hands, his handsome visage. Try as I might, I can't stir an ounce of sexual attraction, but I can't let that sway me. I simply need to get to know him better, and that takes time. And I do still have some time before I need to secure a husband—

The word *husband* conjures images of a laughing face, of shoes skidding across muddy grass, of leaping onto tables, of my own expression glowering at bad jokes, of fingers that wind through mine when my panic rises, of my hand running through pale wet curls, of thoughtful gestures and keen attention that sees deeper into me than anyone ever has.

"Are you all right?" Patrick has leaned forward, his head tilted to the side. His expression is kind—so *annoyingly* kind.

Why does it irritate me so? Why does his perfection grate so aggressively on my nerves?

Before I can answer, a waiter comes to take our salad plates and replace them with our next course. It's a hearty stew, which thankfully has meat in it this time. Even so, my appetite is weak as I stare down at my bowl.

A palm falls over the back of my hand, and it takes all my self-control not to flinch away. "Miss Hartford, are you—"

"Why did you ask me out to dinner?" The words leave my lips, devoid of my prior efforts to sound ladylike.

His brow creases and he slowly pulls his hand from mine. He drums his fingertips on the table as if giving my question ample thought. "As you may have surmised, I'm seeking a wife. I enjoyed meeting you at Mr. Blackwood's wedding and wanted to get to know you better."

"Yes, but why me? Was it merely convenient proximity? Is there something about me that makes you think I'd pair well with you?"

He gives an easy chuckle. "I'm not going to insult you by pretending we had some dazzling connection or that I fell for you during our conversation and subsequent dance. I simply found myself attracted to you and wanted to see if there was compatibility between us."

"You were intrigued by my looks? That's all? You're attempting to secure a wife based on visual appeal?"

"I have other criteria, but physical attraction is what draws me to a potential spouse. That may come across as superficial, but I don't mean to be. I come from a family that has always approached matrimony this way. When a man is ready to find a wife, he chooses someone who suits him and his needs—or our family's needs—during a predetermined timeline. Love comes later. I have more freedoms than my older brothers and a career that generates personal wealth, so I don't need to marry for prestige. I'm ready to settle down, simple as that. I'm a touch too pragmatic to wait for the whimsies of love to carry me away before I choose a bride. I apologize if that is unromantic."

I shake my head. "No, it's…it's relatable." If we'd had this conversation a month ago, we'd have been on the same page. This was exactly how I'd intended to find a husband. Not only did I not have the luxury of time to let my heart guide me, but a logical match felt safe. If I married before someone could see the rougher sides of me, I'd be at less risk of being alone. Less risk of being discovered as the untamed creature I really am—and rejected for it.

You're a monster.

But that changed after this weekend. I saw what marriage looks like for a true love match. I've witnessed vows from the heart. Ever since, a yearning for that has taken root, and it isn't even about matrimony. It's about that connection. That kind of relationship. That true knowing between two people. Being seen and accepted.

You love the rain.

Even though I've acknowledged this new yearning, I don't know what to do about it. Ever since I first glimpsed the first human city and fell in love with art, I've battled the opposing sides of my heart. The one that seeks comfort. That runs and hides when I'm scared or feels rejected. That avoids crowds and friendships unless they're forced upon me. That participated in a drunken handfasting out of a temptation to bind myself to someone who will never leave or hurt me.

Then there's the other side. The one that snuck back to the first human city I saw, to covertly visit galleries, lurking in corners in terrified fascination. The one that took the opportunity to learn to draw, even if it meant donning uncomfortable dresses, mingling with young women I didn't know, and learning etiquette too. The one that returned to society, even after I'd experienced so much pain the first time. That picked up a paintbrush all over again and bled my heart onto canvas. That took the terrifying step and guided Monty's hands on my body and asked for what I wanted.

It pulls me even now, one side begging me to accept this kind, straightforward man's advances, the other telling me to run, to find Monty and tell him what's in my heart.

My throat constricts at the thought.

No, he already rejected me.

Patrick releases a soft sigh. "Miss Hartford, I know you aren't interested in me the way I want you to be."

My pulse quickens. I open my mouth but it's not like I can lie. Besides, do I even want to?

"I had an inkling even during our dances," he says. "Your affections were—and likely still are—engaged elsewhere."

I sink against the back of my chair, shoulders falling as I lose all remaining motivation to keep up my cultivated guise.

He chuckles. "It's selfish of me, I know. I'm burdening you with having to reject me. Regardless, I'm prepared."

"You knew..." I shift uncomfortably in my chair. "You knew I wasn't interested, yet you pursued me anyway?"

"I knew, but I didn't *know* know. Until you outright state your disinterest, I can't be sure. Though before you can reject me, I suppose I must first state my intent. I wasn't prepared to do this tonight, but you are far more direct than I expected you to be. So here it is. I am seeking a wife and am interested in courting you. Will you accept?"

"Why?" My voice trembles. "Why ask if you think you know my answer? Isn't it going to hurt if I reject you?"

He shrugs. "It might, but it might hurt just as badly to never know if I'd had a chance. Furthermore, don't you deserve to know how I feel? Or at least my intentions with you? It must feel gratifying to know you're desired, even for superficial reasons."

I suppose he's right. His attention is flattering, and were

my heart not so tangled up with Monty's, I might be more than flattered. I might be elated. Especially now that I've dropped my guard, and he hasn't shown an ounce of disappointment in me. I arrived at our fancy date dressed in casual attire. I slumped in my seat and ceased trying to speak softly. And he's still waiting for me to reject him.

I've never seen myself this way. As someone who could do the rejecting.

Maybe that's because I've hidden myself away as much as I could, all to avoid being rejected. Scorned. Disappointing people—*repulsing* people—when they realize I'll always be a wild fae creature at heart.

Maybe I hold more power than I've ever given myself credit for.

"Now, come on," Patrick says, his voice full of resignation despite the easy grin on his face. "I'm ready if you are."

I blink at him. He really expects me to state it out loud? But it's so obvious. Wouldn't he rather keep his pride?

His earlier words return to me.

Until you outright state your disinterest, I can't be sure.

It might hurt just as badly to never know...

My mind catches on that, replaying his words until something clicks into place.

Until you outright state your disinterest...

I rise from the chair so fast that the feet scrape against the stone floor. The hum of quiet conversation cuts off from our neighboring diners as they stare at me with curious looks. I pay them no heed, my eyes unfocused. "He didn't reject me," I say under my breath. "He hinted at it, but he didn't state his disinterest outright. It hurts just as badly to never know."

Patrick tilts his head. "Miss Hartford?"

I lift my gaze to his, and my lips curl into a sympathetic smile. "I'm so sorry, Mr. Wright. I'm not actually quiet and demure. I'm quiet, but it's because I'm shy around strangers and socially awkward. It takes all my energy to pretend otherwise. One time, I bit a girl's ear off when I realized I'd been the butt of several ongoing jokes. Tonight, I didn't want salad or soup or whatever main course you ordered for us. I wanted steak, and I wanted it rare. I wanted to eat it with my hands. These are things you probably would have eventually learned about me, if I gave you a chance. I think I could come to like you. I think you could be the perfect model for my paintings. Probably the perfect husband too. But...there's someone else."

His expression falls, and I realize how painful it is to be the one doing the rejecting. But I can't lead him on, just like I can't shield myself from emotional pain. "There's someone else," I repeat, voice trembling. "He's not perfect, but he already knows me the way I want to be known. I need him in my life, whether we're friends or lovers. He deserves to know how I feel, because it's like you said. It must feel good to be wanted, right? I want to tell him all of that, even if it hurts me in the end."

Patrick blows out a soft breath, then gives me a small grin. "Thank you for telling me."

"I'm sorry," I say, stepping away from the table. That's when I remember the attention I drew when I stood. Attention that is very much fixed on me still. Heat crawls up my neck, and I dip into a clumsy curtsy, then grimace at the tables around me. "Sorry. I...I'm going to...go."

Patrick rises, maybe to offer me a parting bow, maybe to try and walk me out. I don't know because I don't look back. Instead, I run out the door and down the street, my heart racing. For once, I'm not running from fear or pain. I'm running toward it.

CHAPTER THIRTY-FOUR

DAPHNE

It's Friday night, so I know exactly where to find Monty. The evening sky is overcast, and soon a drizzle begins. As much as I'd love to luxuriate in the gentle rainfall, I'm on the opposite end of town from where the industrial district is. It makes more sense to hail a hansom. Everything inside me buzzes—with hope, with terror—and I can hardly sit still in the cab. I want to shout at the coachman to drive faster, to reach outside the window and slap the horse's flank and prod him into a gallop myself, but I settle for sitting on my hands.

Finally, the cab enters the industrial district, and I ask him to drop me off. The abandoned textile building isn't yet in sight, but I'm not sure I should direct public attention to the club's location. The rain has let up to an even softer drizzle, coating me in mist as I run the rest of the way. I don't hesitate when I reach the fence; I dart through the gap and race toward the door. There's no line this time, as the fights have likely already begun.

I knock at the heavy door, politely at first, and then slam on it with my fist. The kangaroo fae who served as doorman and referee appears through a slim crack in the door, eying me with suspicion.

"I'm late," I say, my words breathless. "I'm here for the fights."

He assesses me through slitted lids. Then he opens his palm and extends it to me. "Six emerald chips."

I hand over the gemstone currency, and he begrudgingly lets me in. Before I stride toward the rush of noise that beckons from ahead, I face the kangaroo fae. "Have you seen Monty—" I snap my mouth shut, remembering that none of the fighters go by their real names. What was his stage name again? "Have you seen Lucky Lovesbane tonight?"

"Ah, right," he says, his countenance softening. "I remember you. His special guest from a few weeks back. Yeah, he's in the ring right now."

My heart leaps into my throat. "Thank you!" I rush the rest of the way into the main portion of the building, swarmed with an onslaught of scents and sounds. My insides scream at me to cover my ears, to shrink down, to leave this chaotic, busy place, but I tamp down my fear. I can't see the ring from here, with so many tall figures crammed around it, but I glimpse a flash of motion from up ahead, illuminated by the spotlight formed by the cluster of yellow fire sprites that fill the enormous glass orb overhead.

With a deep breath, I start forward, pushing my way between bodies and offering muttered apologies. I exhale a cry of relief when the ring comes into view. Just a few more bodies stand between me and the stage, so I push my way through, all the way to the front, until my view is clear.

First I recognize Gabby Stabbington, the broad-shouldered butcher who fought in the first match I watched. She's dressed in the same ensemble as before, including her blood-splattered apron. She shuffles on her feet, back facing me. Then she steps to the side, and I'm granted my first glimpse of Monty.

My chest tightens at the sight of him. One of his eyebrows is split, blood running down the side of his face, mingling with the sweat that coats his skin. Bruises bloom over his bare torso, and his heavy movements make it clear he's exhausted. Their match must have been going on for quite some time.

They circle each other, and Gabby lands a punch to his sternum. He doesn't so much as raise his arms to block it, and instead heaves in on himself and stumbles to the side.

His name leaves my lips with a sharp cry. "Monty."

His gaze shoots to mine, and his eyes widen with surprise. I don't hear what he says next, but I can make out the shape of his lips. "Daph?"

Just then, Gabby Stabbington sends a vicious right hook into his jaw and sends him toppling to the floor.

Monty doesn't get knocked unconscious this time, but he does stay down long enough to mark his defeat. My guts writhe with anxiety. Monty mentioned how his fights are fixed, allowing him to work off his weekly loan payments. I was hurting too much when he told me about this, so I didn't dwell on what I heard, but now I can't help wondering if he was meant to lose tonight. If not, did my presence distract him at a critical moment? Was it a mistake coming here?

My feet beg me to flee, but I don't. I root myself in place, determined to face this head-on, no matter what.

Gabby and Monty meet at the middle of the ring in a friendly handshake. Monty descends from the platform, and as soon as his feet hit the concrete, I'm there. Our eyes meet, and I don't know what to say, what to do. Monty's expression is impossible to read, obscured by blood, sweat, and bruises. For several shallow breaths we simply stare at each other as if trying to make sense of a sudden apparition. Then he heaves a sigh, drops his gaze, and gathers his belongings from the base of the stage. He toes on his shoes, retrieves his shirt, and pulls it over his head, not bothering to secure the top buttons. Once both arms are through, his fingers come around my wrist and he drags me away from the stage.

His grip is gentle, but his manner is curt. I follow him through the swarm of bodies and out the door. He pulls me across the vacant lot and onto the quiet night streets of the industrial district. The sky continues to drizzle a soft mist of rain.

"Where are you taking me?" I ask.

He walks ahead of me, picking up his pace whenever I try to catch up with him. "I'm getting you in a cab back home."

"Monty, stop, it's raining."

"Good. I need a fucking shower."

"But you're sensitive to rain. Why don't you have an umbrella? Shouldn't you carry one with you?"

He halts, releasing my wrist and whirling to face me. "Why are you fretting over me? You're supposed to be on a date."

I pull my head back. "How did you know about my date?"

He averts his gaze, jaw tight. He says nothing as he stares off into the dark streets and alleyways around us. The overcast sky leaves us with little light, save for the occasional streetlamp or the subtle illumination coming from a few surrounding factories that run overnight. But my vision works well in the dark. I can see the still-open cut on his brow, the way the mist coats his skin and sends trails of blood down his face, soaking his open collar. He hasn't done up his shirt yet, and his trousers are still rolled up to his calves from the fight.

My eyes lift back to his face, taking in the bruises Gabby left there, the largest being the most recent from her final right hook. I step closer and lift a hand to his jaw. "You're hurt."

He intercepts my hand before I can touch his face, clasping my fingers. "I heal quickly."

My pulse quickens at the feel of his hand around mine. It isn't a warm touch, but it isn't harsh either. And he hasn't released me. "Even in the rain? You're the one who told me you're sensitive to it."

He opens his mouth, but before he can argue, the sky opens up, turning the rainfall from mist to a deluge in a matter of seconds. It feels incredible after the stuffy, smoky club, but I don't imagine Monty feels the same. He bites out a curse, but I can barely hear it over the downpour.

I shift the hand he holds until I'm the one grasping his fingers, and I tug him down the slick streets. With my keen nocturnal eyesight, I can find us an alcove in which to wait out the storm, or perhaps to leave him while I find a cab. He follows me without question, turning down the next street where a large warehouse looms on the corner. I recognize it from my much slower, much more curious trip to find the club with Araminta. The warehouse consists of two towering brick buildings with a system of bridges and walkways that connect them and their many floors.

I pull him into the alley between the buildings. The ground is mostly dry, and only a trickle of rain falls through the gaps between the crisscrossing walkways overhead. As soon as we pull to a halt, a green glow emanates from one of the walls. I startle at the sudden light, but it's only a bioluminescent mushroom growing from the brick. It's as wide as a dinner plate with a shelflike shape. No sooner than it brightens to an emerald glow does another illuminate, then another, as if set off by the previous mushroom's glow. Soon the entire wall is alight with mushrooms, and each one's color changes, from green closest to the mouth of the alley, to blue, then purple, to pink at the far end. Whether the mushrooms were encouraged to grow here intentionally to brighten the space during late-night work hours or the fungi simply chose this place to grow of their own accord, I know not. Either way, it's stunning.

Forcing myself out of my awe, I turn to Monty and find him catching his breath, his gaze on the mushrooms. His hair is soaked, and he's slicked it back, revealing a forehead that's normally covered with his messy waves. The rain has washed away some of the blood on his face, but the cut on his brow remains open.

"Why did you come here?" he says through panting breaths as he slides his fingers from mine. "I didn't want you to have to see…I didn't want you at tonight's fight."

He meant for the latter words to sting, but it's too late. I heard what he was about to say. He didn't want me to see tonight's fight, probably because he knew he was going to lose. "Your defeat was predetermined, wasn't it?"

He curls his fingers into fists, battling with himself not to answer. Then he heaves a resigned sigh. "Yes, it was predetermined, and it was meant to hurt as punishment for having missed last weekend's payment. I was directed to stay on my feet until the final round, taking as many punches as I could without being defeated too early."

My chest tightens. "That's what happens when you don't pay? Isn't there another way? Can't you refuse to fight?"

"If I refuse to fight, I have to pay in currency, and the interest has made my weekly payments outrageous. I can't afford them. I can't refuse to pay altogether, for every time I miss a payment, the due date for my debt moves up a week."

"When is your current due date? And how much do you owe?"

"The sixteenth of July. My remaining sum is just over twenty thousand emerald rounds."

My eyes nearly bulge from my head. "You have to pay twenty thousand emerald rounds in a month and a half?"

He gives me a cold, humorless grin. "I told you my life is a mess, Daph. Now do you believe me?"

I realize that's the only reason he's answering my questions honestly. He wants to show me what a mess he is. "What happens if you don't pay off your loan by then?"

He hesitates again, eyes narrowing. His face is awash in the blue-green glow from the nearest mushrooms. "My lender deals in secrets," he says, voice low. "If I don't pay, he reveals my secret publicly. He'll sell it to every prominent gossip columnist on the isle. Only the most trusted ones with reputations for being correct about the gossip they share."

"What is your secret?"

"I can't tell you," he bites out. When I arch a brow, he adds, "I *physically* can't tell you, even if I wanted to. The only reason my lender knows about it is because his magic allowed him to extract my most closely guarded secret with a single glance. If it gets out, my family is ruined."

I puzzle over his words. There's only one explanation for what he's saying. "You made a bargain."

He throws his head back, drops of rainwater falling from the ends of his hair. "If only you knew the weight of the bargains I'm buried under."

So there's more than one, and I have a feeling ours isn't one of the bargains he's referring to.

I take a step closer to him. "Like the one you made with your father?"

His posture stiffens. Slowly, he lowers his head to meet my gaze, eyes narrowed.

"I overheard your conversation on the train platform," I explain. I hadn't been certain then, but I am now. His reaction makes it clear.

His expression flashes with apprehension before he speaks. "After my engagement to Briony ended, I assured my father I would never marry. I convinced him I would mess it up again and again. That I couldn't be his heir. He was at his wits' end and made the only good choice he's ever made—disinheriting me and naming Angela his heir. But not before I made a bargain that I would return to my place if I ever settled down. In precise terms, I would return to the family if I courted someone. I would reclaim my role as heir if I married."

I reflect on his words, replaying them, stacking them up against everything else he's said. He really meant it when he said he couldn't marry. He'd made a bargain not to. Yet this can't be the big secret he unwittingly sold to his moneylender. He said he physically can't tell anyone that secret. Which means this marriage bargain is only secondary to whatever he's hiding. Yet how did he make these bargains in the first place?

Keeping my voice even, I ask, "You used a bargain broker, then? To conduct the bargain between you and your father?"

A bargain broker is necessary for bargains forged between humans. Or even between fae, if a formal record is desired to make the bargain both legally and magically binding.

Monty stills at the question, shoulders tense. His eyes go wide.

Like cornered prey.

The remaining pieces click together in my mind.

I heal quickly.

I'm a little sensitive to rain.

My eyes rove over his rounded ears, then the bruises marring his skin. It only occurs to me now that while I've seen him beaten up and noticed scabs on his knuckles, his wounds have never been there long. Why would a human consider himself a fast healer? Why would he be sensitive to one of the elements?

My heart clenches tight in my chest, the answer spilling from my lips. "You're half fae."

CHAPTER THIRTY-FIVE

DAPHNE

He steps back so suddenly, he looks as if I've punched him in the chest. "You can't know," he blurts out. His hand flies to his chest, his breaths turning sharp. His face contorts with pain. "I can't tell anyone. I can't let anyone find out. I can't..."

Alarm rushes through me as I realize what's happening. Everyone knows breaking a bargain is deadly, but one of the first repercussions of breaking a bargain—or coming close to it—is physical pain. I close the distance between us, my mind whirling to find a solution. I place a palm on his jaw, opposite where Gabby punched him. "You didn't *let* me, Monty. Do you hear me? You didn't tell me and you didn't let me find out. I found out all on my own with no help from you, just like your lender."

His breaths remain sharp for a few agonizing moments, then finally start to calm. Thank the All of All. With fae magic, intent and personal belief is everything. So long as

Monty acknowledges that he didn't do anything to compromise his bargain, he'll recover.

Once his breathing returns to normal, he steps back until he comes up against the alleyway wall. The mushrooms on the opposite wall continue to glow, while curious dust-sized fire sprites in the same colors as the fungi flutter around us, descending from the mushrooms they'd been nesting on. Monty keeps his eyes closed, head thrown back, the drum of raindrops pounding relentlessly outside our refuge.

I stand before him, studying his face under a new light. Monty is half fae. That's the big secret he harbors. The one he couldn't tell his friends and loved ones. Not even Angela seems to know, nor do Briony and Thorne.

When Monty finally opens his eyes, they're full of pain. "No one can know."

"I won't tell anyone." I bite the inside of my cheek, gathering the courage to pose a potentially dangerous question. I lower my voice to a whisper. "Which of your parents is fae?"

He says nothing, but the answer is obvious. If both Lord and Lady Phillips are well-known human figures, then one of them was guilty of infidelity. And the parent he despises…

"Your father had an affair. Your mother was fae."

He sucks in a breath, but again no answer.

I study him, the rain slicking his skin, the shivers racking his shoulders. He's sensitive to rain but not necessarily water. It's being drenched in *cold* water that makes him unwell. "She's some kind of fire fae, isn't she?"

His eyes turn down at the corners, his posture sinking with something like relief. He's probably never had a soul to talk about this with. He rubs his chest, as if checking for any sign of pain, any sign that he's compromising his bargain. But if his terms only required that he not tell anyone or intentionally let anyone find out he's half fae, then the danger has passed. I already know the secret, just not the details. He gives me a sharp nod.

"Did you never meet her?

"I knew her for a time," he says, voice weak, "but I never learned her name and I had no idea she was my mother. I couldn't have known. I was raised to believe Angela and I had the same mother, yet Lady Phillips is the reason I found out the truth. She was overly fond of drink and made an inebriated comment about how I was just like my mother, and it was a shame she couldn't watch me grow up. When I confronted Father about it, he tried to play it off, but I refused to give in. Finally, he explained the truth. That my mother was a courtesan, and he coerced her into giving me up upon my birth, convincing her I'd have a better life as a respected human couple's son than the bastard of a fae prostitute. By the time he told me this, I was fifteen and my mother was long gone."

"I don't understand. You said you knew her for a time."

His throat bobs. "She used to sneak onto my family's property in unseelie form. She left because...because I treated her like a pet."

Understanding crushes my chest. "Your mother was your animal friend. The fennec fox." It makes sense now. Fennecs are desert creatures, and I imagine most fae ones are native to the Fire Court, where the dunes are located.

"My family's reputation is built on lies. A lie Father made me bargain never to reveal, threatening me with how badly my little sister would suffer if this all came out. And he's right. If the public finds out my father had an affair with a fae, that he kept his son's fae lineage a secret and passed himself off as a man with perfect human values, the Phillips family will be ruined."

I frown. "This shouldn't be your secret to bear. It's his. And if it gets out, he only has himself to blame."

"That may be so, but he won't be the only one to suffer. My sister will. Even Mother—Angela's mother—will be hurt by it. Father is our court's Human Representative. He's supposed to represent the pinnacle of human propriety. If they found out he birthed a bastard and hid the truth, the Phillips name would be tainted."

"Those are his actions, not yours. I understand you want to protect Angela from such awful repercussions, but you don't need to bear that responsibility."

"I do though," he says, pushing off the wall and straightening. "I'm to blame for the position I'm in. Me. I made the idiotic mistake of taking out a loan that deals in secrets. I thought I'd have a choice of what secret to share, but I should have known better. Angela deserves to be heir. She can reshape our family name under her guidance. I want that future for her, as the head of all of Father's business dealings. She's already thriving in that role. If this secret gets out, it will be my fault. Her future will be ruined because of me."

Irritation ripples through me. I understand his reasoning, yet it still enrages me. "Does your father know about the loan? Surely he'd pay it if he knew."

He gives a mirthless laugh. "Oh, he'd pay it. Then he'd use it as leverage to bring me back into the family."

I furrow my brow. "Then refuse."

His mouth falls open, eyes locked on mine. There's something like terror etched on his face, but I don't understand the source. "It's not as simple as that," he whispers.

"How is it not simple? He's already disinherited you. You're bound to a bargain never to tell a soul his secret and never to marry, but you don't have to obey him in any other aspect of your life. Offer him the chance to save himself by paying off your loan, and then cut ties with him on *your* terms, not his. Let him clean up his own mess."

The terror in his face grows. "But Angela—"

"You can still see Angela even if you refuse contact with your father. When he asks to speak with you, you can say no." Protective anger flares when I remember how Lord Phillips demanded a word with Monty at the train station, and how Monty obeyed. He put on a flippant act, but he obeyed nonetheless. How does Monty not see how much he caters to a man he professes to hate? Why didn't he leave the family of his own accord, instead of waiting until he'd vexed his father enough to convince him to disinherit him? Why agree to a bargain that he'd return to the family if he ever married?

Could it be...

Could he want to keep their bond intact, even as toxic as it is? Is he somehow afraid to lose his father completely? He pushed him away just enough without severing the relationship entirely. And Lord Phillips isn't the only one he's done that with. He did the same with his first love, Cosette, carrying on a sexual relationship when he could have refused.

Why is he afraid to lose the people who've hurt him?

Monty's expression turns hard. "I can't explain it to you, and you already know more than you should. You should go back to your date."

I prop my hands on my hips and burn him with a glare. "I didn't want to go on that date in the first place. I came to where I wanted to be."

He rolls his eyes. "I told you not to chase after uninterested parties."

"Am I chasing you, Monty? Or am I simply giving a shit about my friend? Whether you have romantic feelings for me or not, we *are* friends, and I'm not going to let you push me away. I want to care about you. As for your interest or lack thereof, you haven't stated a damn word to convince me one way or another."

"That's not what I taught you. There's no lesson in my book about getting verbal confirmation about whether someone likes you. You're supposed to assess, judge, and react—"

"I don't care what you taught me. Maybe you think a lady should sit back and wait for a suitor to prove himself to her, and I understand the value in not fawning over lovers who won't give you what you need. But this isn't about your case study. This is about you and me. And you can do fucking better than that pathetic subtle rejection in the cab. If you don't want me in a romantic way, say so. If you want to stay platonic friends, say so, but then treat me like a true friend. Don't push me away. Don't make decisions for me. Don't be an asshole."

He opens and closes his palms, his expression flashing between his icy mask and the vulnerability beneath it. The latter wins out, and he averts his face. "Why would you expect me to do better after everything I've told you about myself? I told you about my dangerous lifestyle. My crippling debt. I told you what I did to Cosette, how I used her—"

"Don't you dare bring her up as an excuse. You've learned from your mistake. You feel guilty for how you treated her, and I haven't seen you treat anyone else that way, aside from the occasional flirtatious jest."

"Even when we were together, I didn't treat her well enough. That's why she left me for someone else."

I step in closer, leaning into his line of sight. "Cosette was an asshole, Monty. It was her choice to leave you. Whether you believe you deserved it or not, her rejection blindsided you. It hurt you."

He swivels his face to mine, leaning close and speaks through his teeth. "Yes, she hurt me, but I hurt her right back. Because that's what I do. I hurt people. Whether it's through the silence of keeping my secrets or simply because I'm cruel,

I hurt them. And I…" His expression crumples. "I'll hurt you, Daph. I'll hurt you and I can't fucking bear that."

The pain in his voice spears my heart. I lift a hand and rest it on the side of his face, keeping his eyes locked on mine. "Monty, don't you see what you've done? You've already hurt me by trying *not* to hurt me."

He gives a subtle shake of his head, but he doesn't pull away from my hand. "I'll hurt you worse."

"Why do you think that? Why do you believe you're so bad and broken? Who have you *truly* hurt just by being you? And don't bring up Cosette again." I say the last part with a snarl.

His eyes turn down at the corners, and when he speaks, his voice quavers. "I treated my…my mother like a fucking pet."

I can only imagine how much that pains him. How all those happy memories of playing with the creature he thought was his fox friend—who he only later found out had been fae all along—were tainted the minute he learned who his birth mother was. I brush a damp curl off his forehead. "She wouldn't have come back again and again if she didn't like the time she spent with you. She knew you couldn't know who she was. She just wanted to see you."

"Then why did she leave?"

"I don't know."

He closes his eyes. "Don't tell me you don't know. I'd rather know I'm at fault than to be stuck with uncertainty."

And that right there explains everything. The conflict in his heart, constantly at war between pushing people away and keeping them within arm's reach. The way he acts, positioning himself as the reason why his relationships crumble. "You're scared. That's why you act the way you do in relationships."

"Yes," he says, opening his eyes. "I'm afraid I'm going to

hurt you. I'm no good. I'm involved in fixed fucking boxing matches. I'm drowning in debt."

I exhale a heavy sigh. "No, that's not it at all. You've never been worried you're going to hurt me. You're worried *I'm* going to hurt *you*. You're worried I'm going to leave you and you won't know the cause."

His eyes widen, and all that's left of his protective mask shatters.

I speak again. "You reject people before they can reject you. I know what that's like. We may do it in different ways, but we're just rejecting ourselves."

He makes a strangled sound and lowers his head to my shoulder. I wrap one arm behind him, caressing his sodden back while the other smooths his hair. "How do you see so deep inside me?" he mutters against my shoulder. "All my flaws? How can you look at me so tenderly when you know how broken I am?"

"I like imperfect things. I like messes and rain and mud. I like eating with my hands. I like my steak rare. I like watching boxing matches and salivating when they get extra violent. I like climbing on furniture and taking off my clothes when I feel like it. I like the taste of small rodents' blood in my mouth and the feel of their tiny bones cracking between my teeth." I stop myself from saying more, afraid that the last bit was a little too intense. Then I swallow hard and relay the most raw and dangerous confession of all. "And I like...I love you."

He stiffens in my arms. Silence stretches between us, save for the pound of rain on cobblestones outside the mouth of the alley. Panic laces through my throat but I resist the urge to change the subject. To take his silence as rejection. Finally, he lifts his face and meets my eyes. "I can't marry you."

"I never asked you to."

"But your handfasting..."

"My career is enough. My life here is enough."

And if it isn't, I'll do whatever it takes to make it so. Even if I must destroy every connection I made in my hometown. Even if I must break hearts and hurt the people I love. Understanding Monty has made me realize I'm not the only one who led others on. I'm not the only one who ran away from relationships or let them remain ambiguous instead of severing them completely. But I need to sever the ties in Cypress Hollow that no longer serve me.

I take a bracing breath, gathering my resolve to finish my confession. "You're enough, Monty. Even if you don't love me back, you're enough as my friend, and I want to keep you in any form."

His lips quirk at the corner, the first sign of a smile I've seen all evening.

I encourage it to grow. "I may want to fuck your brains out, but we'll get through that, won't we?"

He snorts a laugh, and all the tension leaves his body. Slowly, he stands taller and wraps his arms around me. "What have you done to me, Daffy Dear?" He leans down, and my heart leaps. I try not to get my hopes up. Try not to expect too much, even as his lips inch closer—

"Isn't this fucking sweet," drawls a male voice.

Monty and I startle, whirling to face the mouth of the alley as two figures saunter toward us.

CHAPTER THIRTY-SIX

MONTY

Of all the inconvenient and unwelcome distractions. The woman I love just confessed her affection for me. The last faces I want to see interrupting our moment are those of Cane and Meathands. Yet here they are, gracing us with their unwanted presence.

Meathands smirks, his face illuminated by the green glow of the mushrooms nearest the mouth of the alley. I can't make out the pattern on today's scarf, but I'm a bit envious of how snug and dry he must be between that and his bowler hat.

Already I can feel the cold seeping into my bones while the cloudy feeling that precedes a fever is settling in. As a fire fae, heat can stave off my opposing element's ill effects, and not just physical heat. It can be the heat of anger or passion. The latter of which I was just starting to tap into when these blokes ruined everything.

Cane scrunches his nose, eying me with what he probably

thinks is a threatening glare. "Almost lost your scent in the rain, you slimy prick."

"Who are they?" Daphne asks, panic flashing over her face.

"Assholes," I mutter back. "Harmless, mostly, but incredibly annoying." I shift to the side, placing myself between them and Daphne. To Cane and Meathands, I say, "What the fuck do you want? I did my part tonight. I lost like I was supposed to. I put up as little defense as I could."

"There were two minutes left," Cane says. "You got knocked out too early."

"I got knocked out in the final round, just like I agreed."

"We said to stay until the end," says Meathands.

"I didn't agree to wait until the last possible second."

Meathands and Cane exchange a look. Cane takes a step forward, swinging his walking stick up to prop it on his shoulder. "Still, it's a bit unfair you escaped the full extent of your punishment, so we're here to amend that. We'll finish the round between us gents."

"Plus," Meathands says, "we got a few emerald rounds from Grave Danger in exchange for roughing you up a bit."

"Grave Danger," Daphne echoes from behind me. She witnessed my fight with that scaly fae bastard, so of course she recognizes the name.

The thugs' eyes flash to her, so I take another step toward them to reclaim their attention. "What's Grave Danger's grudge?"

"He's a bit miffed the two o' ya never got a fair fight," Cane says.

My mouth falls open. "A fair fight? He's the one who goaded me into getting disqualified. He would have won if he hadn't gotten himself disqualified too. And now he's paying the two of you to rough me up? How unhinged can he be?"

"He's a bored little snakey with too much of daddy's money," says Meathands with a roll of his eyes.

"If you're so keen to accept his daddy's money," I say, "then you must be more strapped for cash than I thought. I suppose that's what happens when you work for a goblin who gets off on outing his client's secrets rather than collecting their loan sums. How's your side business going, by the way? Sell any scarves lately?"

With a sneer, he steps closer and unwraps his scarf from around his neck with surprisingly tender motions. The mushrooms illuminate the pattern—little yellow ducks on a pale blue background. If he wasn't such a prick, I'd be impressed with his handiwork. He folds it with care and sets it on a dry patch of ground, away from the drops of rain that continue to sprinkle between the gaps from the overhead walkways. Then he slams a fist into his palm. "Let's finish yer round."

"Shit," I say under my breath. While it's true what I said to Daphne about these assholes being mostly harmless, I'm not in the best condition to fight them, what with the rain and chilly air weakening my strength. At least my anger serves to keep me on my feet.

"Two minutes on the clock," Cane says, sauntering closer, twirling the cane still propped on his shoulder, "then we'll let you go. Since this ain't boss' orders, we've got no rules to follow."

"No rules?" I say. "Then I can fight back."

Daphne clings to the back of my shirt. "You're not really going to fight them, are you?" she says in a furious whisper.

"It's all right," I say. "It will be over quickly. They're unskilled fighters. Sloppy."

It's true. They've done their darndest to rough me up before, which might as well have been a tickle to the ribs.

Pleasant, even. Of course, that was under the boss' rules, meant more to scare than to injure. Now...

Well, it's not like I have much of a choice. The alley ends in solid brick where the two buildings are connected. Cane and Meathands will intercept me if I run forward. Besides, I've never run from a fight. Two minutes will be easy, so I'm not worried about myself.

There's only one person on my mind.

"Shift," I say, stepping back as the two cronies slowly close in. "Shift into unseelie form and either climb or dart away. They won't go after you. I'll come find you as soon as this is over."

"I'm not leaving," she bites out.

"You can fight back," Cane says as he halts, legs spread wide. One hand is tucked in his pocket while the other gives his cane another twirl on his shoulder. Then his grip tightens, knuckles going white. "But it won't be much of a fight with two on one."

Meathands chuckles, flexing his fingers as he takes up a fighting stance.

I pivot my feet, a slight bend to my knees, and raise my arms. My muscles scream in protest, fatigued after the lengthy bout in the ring paired with the additional strain caused by the rain. "Shift, Daph," I say, voice low. "I'll come find—"

"Just one?" she says, striding up beside me with her hands on her hips. "Two on *one*? Am I invisible?"

"What are you doing?" I mutter, not daring to take my eyes off my opponents.

Daphne ignores me, and Cane and Meathands exchange an amused glance.

Meathands waves a dismissive hand. "Don't worry your pretty head, sweetheart. This has nothin' to do with you."

Rage sparks in my blood, a welcome sensation to clear

my mind. I've never had much of an opinion about Meathands. He's just a dummy doing his job like the rest of us, but hearing him call her sweetheart…

I'd like to rip his tongue from his mouth.

She emits a low growl. "I think it does."

Cane laughs. Actually *laughs* at my feral little love. "Fine, it'll be one on one, then." He nods to his companion. "Hold her back. She can watch her loverboy bleed."

With that, the two charge forward, so much faster than I expect. In a flash, Cane is before me, swinging his weapon straight for my face. My mind is on Daphne's safety, but all I can do is react to my first threat. I dodge to the side and intercept the strike of the cane with my palm. Pain radiates across my hand, through my wrist, and up my arm. My vision nearly goes black, but I focus on my anger, gritting my teeth as I close my fingers around the lacquered wood and pull with all my might.

My reaction catches Cane off guard, and his weapon slips from his fingers. I shift it to my non-dominant hand—the one that isn't obliterated with pain—and swing it into the side of his stunned face. His head whips to the side as it makes contact, and he falls to his back at once. I pivot to the side, my eyes seeking Meathands.

He looks just as shocked as Cane was, but I spare him only a meager glance. My attention shifts to Daphne, whom he clutches to his chest. One arm is pressed across her shoulders while the other covers her mouth. She squirms in his grip, snarling against his palm.

I lift the cane and point it at him. "Get your fucking hands off her."

His expression flashes with uncertainty, then darkens as I hear Cane rise clumsily to his feet behind me. "Our two minutes ain't over," Meathands says.

"Bastard," Cane mutters under his breath. He stumbles

into my periphery, cradling the side of his face. "That's gonna leave a bruise."

"Let her go, you cunty prick," I growl through my teeth, "or I'll ram this through your eye socket."

Meathands snorts a laugh. "Such big words, but I'm bigger. Let's see how you fare against me. You take the girl." He thrusts Daphne to the side toward Cane, his gaze locked on me.

Cane extends a hand, ready to pull her to him...

But Daphne clings to Meathands' palm.

With both fists encircling his wide wrist, she opens her mouth...

And clamps down hard below his thumb.

Meathands cries out as she sinks her teeth into his palm, then makes a strangled sound as she tears her mouth away, ripping a chunk of flesh with it. Cane goes still, his beady eyes bulging at Daphne as she darts away with graceful ease. Meathands' mouth gapes wider as he stares down at his ruined hand.

"She bit me," he says, voice panicked. "She bit my fucking hand off. She...she really bit me."

My muscles are coiled like a spring, my fist tightening around the cane as I anticipate Meathands' retaliation. One move and I'll shove this stick straight through his—

With a sob, he falls to his knees, weeping as he cradles his hand.

I'm so shocked, my mind goes blank. All I can do is stare as his tough demeanor shrinks.

"No, no, no. Not my hand." He stares up at us with tear-filled eyes. "I have two hundred snowman scarves to knit by winter solstice. Two hundred. This was supposed to be my big break!"

Daphne spits a chunk of mangled flesh at the ground before him. "You're fae," she says, her voice firm. "You'll heal. Maybe stop beating people in alleyways in the meantime."

"I was following orders."

"No," Daphne says, "you were following spare change, from what it sounds like."

"You didn't have to bite my hand. I was going to be gentle with him. Just a few punches, is all."

She shrugs. "You said there were no rules. Now stop taking odd jobs and leave Monty the fuck alone."

Cane takes a step to the side, but at Daphne's growl, he freezes. Slowly, he holds up his hands and tilts his head to something nearby. She gives him a nod, and he retrieves Meathands' scarf. Then, crouching beside him, he gives a gentle pat to his comrade's shoulder and hands over the scarf. "For your wound."

Meathands cries even harder as he presses the scarf to his palm. "Not the duckies. This one was my favorite."

"Come on, big boy," Cane says, helping his friend to his feet. To us he says, "Uh, our two minutes are up. We'll take our leave."

"Wait," Daphne says, halting their retreat. "Are we good here? You're not going to do this again, are you?"

"No, we'll stick to our jobs," Cane says and Meathands gives a rapid nod in agreement.

"Promise me," Daphne demands, and they utter promises —binding ones, since they're both fae—that they'll keep all further contact with Monty non-violent. All the while, they take backwards steps toward the mouth of the alley, eager to flee.

My stupefied mind sharpens, pulling me from my shock at seeing Meathands' pathetic reaction. I clear my throat and take a step forward. "Wait."

They freeze as I close the distance between us. Cane pales as I make a beeline for him, his eyes darting from my face to his walking stick and back again. "P-please," he stammers, "I meant my promise—"

I hold the cane out for him. "Here."

"You're giving it back?" He hesitates before inching his hand toward the stick. As soon as his fingers close around it, I give it a tug, pulling him a step closer.

"To remember our dance by," I say with a wink, my free hand coming to the side of his face where I struck him. I give his cheek a gentle slap, eliciting a wince, and then release the cane.

The two fae take off at once.

I stare after them, catching my breath. My pulse beats at a rapid pace, vertigo tearing through my head at my relief.

Fuck, that could have gone terribly. But it didn't. They're gone, and neither Daphne nor I sustained any injury, save for the hand I caught the cane in. I whirl to Daph and find her staring at nothing, eyes unfocused, as if she too is reflecting on the events we just lived through.

My mind fills with a vision of her biting Meathands' palm, then spitting his flesh back at him, snarling down at him like she isn't half his size.

Blazing hell, she...

She's even more incredible than I ever knew.

So fierce and terrifying in the best kind of way.

The most stunning creature alive.

My relief and adoration merge into one, culminating in a rupture of sound that bursts from my chest. The bark of laughter echoes through the alley, and another strain escapes my lips before I manage to pull myself together. My eyes meet Daphne's and I expect to find her laughing with me.

But she isn't laughing at all.

CHAPTER THIRTY-SEVEN

DAPHNE

Monty's laughter shatters whatever spell I was under, my cold confidence thawing and leaving only cracks in its wake. As soon as I sensed we were in danger, my inner hunter took over. Now that the threat is over, she's retreated, and I'm left to come to terms with everything I said and did.

A coppery tang fills my mouth, and I recall the rage that tore through me when I ripped flesh from the fae's hand. It's a rage I've felt before, and it throws me back ten years in the past, when I tackled a girl to the ground and bit off her ear. The crowd had been cheering before, egging us on as we exchanged arguments. But as soon as I took it a step too far, they went silent.

And then, as shame caught up with me and I was forced to reassess what I'd done, I knew I'd made a mistake. Blood dripped down my chin—just like it does now—and drenched the other girl's previously pristine white dress. She stared at me in horror, clutching her ear with a shaking hand. The mirth that had brimmed in our spectators' expressions was gone, replaced with disgust. One person laughed. A dark and strangled sound. "She's an animal," she said, her amusement fading to revulsion.

And then my victim shouted up at me with tears spilling down her cheeks. "You're a monster. You may look like a lady, but you're nothing more than a beast."

Then all the young women joined in, jeering—

Monty takes a step closer, and I flinch, whirling away from him. My mind shifts back to the present but my heart is still in the past. For the love of the All of All, I can't bring myself to look at him. How will I manage it if he looks at me the same way those girls did?

He wouldn't, says a calm part of my heart, but this frantic, panicked side is so much louder. It's the side that's protected me all this time, ensuring I remember my manners, say the right things, make eye contact at the right moments, modulate my voice, smile when I'm supposed to. Be what society expects. Fit in. Don't get cast out. Retreat to the quiet solitude of my apartment to recover from the exhaustion that comes with pretending.

You've never, ever had to do that with Monty, that calm part reminds me.

I sense him before I see him, then he's standing before me, gentle hands framing my shoulders. I keep my eyes down, the blood on my chin out of his sight.

"What's wrong, dear?" His voice is a caress, but I bristle at it.

"Don't look at me," I bite out.

"Why not?" he asks, undeterred by the iron in my tone. "Why rob me the pleasure of looking when I like the view so much?"

His fingertip comes to my chin, and he lifts it. I could

fight him. I could nip at his fingers or yank my head to the side. But I allow him to angle my face, bracing myself for whatever his expression holds. Tears glaze my vision as our eyes lock. I'm tempted to keep the sight of his face obscured, but I should know the truth. Can he really accept me like this? I blink, and his face clears.

His lips are curved in a sideways grin, eyelids heavy.

That isn't disgust on his face.

No, it's...

Desire?

"Tell me what you said before we were interrupted," he says.

My mind goes blank. He...he doesn't hate me. He doesn't think I'm a monster.

"Not the part about fucking my brains out, though we'll revisit that shortly. Tell me what you said before that. Remind me how you feel about me."

I'm stunned. My heart softens, yet it's still prickly. Still raw. Still unsure if he simply hasn't seen the blood on my lips. The two halves of my heart collide, and I avert my gaze. "I said I love you, you idiot," I mutter.

He presses his palm to my cheek and tilts my face again, forcing my eyes back to his. His grin is wider now, deepening his dimples. "I like what you added this time. Say it again. Call me an idiot with blood running down your lips. I want to watch."

He does see the blood. And he isn't at all put off by my surly demeanor. My heart slams against my ribs, its riotous rhythm filling my ears and clearing the clouds of the past. I swallow the lump rising in my throat, then croak out, "Idiot."

Tears glaze his eyes, as if I just uttered the most heart-warming phrase. He runs his thumb along my jaw, over my bloodstained chin, then across my bottom lip. "Fucking beautiful."

My lips part at the hunger in his eyes, but before I can marvel at the sight, he lowers his mouth to mine.

The kiss is so sudden, so startling, so desired and needed and desperately craved, I forget to react. I freeze in place, my eyes open, his face filling every inch of my vision. His kiss is hard and claiming, sending a jolt to my heart.

How I wanted this kiss so badly.

If we kiss, it's real.

How I imagined it time and again, but never in a damp alleyway illuminated by mushrooms, with bruises marring his skin and someone else's blood filling my mouth.

But *this* untamed kiss is ours. This is us.

Finally, my mind settles and sharpens, allowing me to sink deeper into this moment, close my eyes, and kiss him back. As soon as I yield against him, his lips part, and he sweeps his tongue into my mouth, sharing the taste of copper between us.

I can't imagine Monty has ever tasted another person's or creature's blood. Not intentionally. As far as I've surmised, he's never gotten to live in his unseelie form—if he knows how to shift at all. He's never hunted prey or eaten raw flesh. Yet as his tongue continues to move against mine, as his arms wrap around my waist to pull me flush against him, as he tastes me as if he can't get enough, I realize there's a hunter inside him too. A beast that doesn't shy away from that same part of me.

I throw my arms around his neck and arch against him, desperate to be closer. His hands move to my thighs, and he hefts me up, lifting me until my legs wrap around his waist. My fingers wind into his hair, still damp from the rain. He sucks my bottom lip between his teeth before moving his mouth to my chin. There he drags his tongue over the very place I know is smeared with blood. I don't shy away this time, instead letting him cleanse away my shame as he sees fit, luxuriating in the attention, the vulgarity of what he's doing.

Then he pulls back and holds my gaze. I stare down at him, perfectly secure in his arms. I caress his hair back from his forehead, plant a kiss above the cut on his brow. When my gaze returns to his, he smiles.

"Do you know what this means?" When I don't answer, he softly brushes his lips against mine.

I know what he's telling me. This kiss wasn't just a flight of fancy or an accidental stumble into temptation.

"If we kiss, it's real," he says. "And this is real."

"It's real?" The question comes out with a quaver of emotion.

"I love you," he says, and my heart races even faster. "With blood running down your lips and a man crying at your feet. In a yellow dress and clumsy dance steps. With your skirt pulled up to your thigh and a rifle in your hands. With four paws and a cute little face. I love you, Daphne Heartcleaver."

He loves me. It isn't one-sided. It isn't my imagination. He loves me back. Then his latter words send a ripple of amusement through me. "Heartcleaver? I thought you said my surname should be Hartford."

"I changed my mind. Hartford doesn't suit you at all."

"But Heartcleaver does?"

"Yes, my vicious little love, it does."

He hefts me higher, and I frame his face with my hands, lowering my mouth to his. I've never felt so seen, so accepted, so torn between wanting to cry and wanting to make love and everything in between. I want to taste every inch of him. I want to learn every expression his beautiful face can make. But before I can get too carried away, I separate my lips from his and study his bruised visage. I run a hand along his jaw, where Gabby struck her victorious blow. Then through his damp curls.

"We need to get you warm and dry," I say, unable to hide the disappointment in my voice. The last thing I want is for him to put me down. To have to maintain even an inch of distance as we return to the main streets. Perhaps even part ways for the night, if it's too soon for us to take this tenuous, precious thing between us further. "After everything that happened, you must be exhausted. I can't imagine that's good for your wounds. You may heal faster than a human, but half fae don't heal nearly as fast as pureblood. And with the rain—"

"Daph," he says, his lips curling in a wicked smirk, "you don't need to worry too much about me. It's true heat is most healing for a fire fae, but there are other ways to generate it."

His words spark heat of my own, simmering in my lower belly. Mischief infuses my tone as I rake my fingertips against his scalp. "Is that so?"

He nods. "We can go home if you prefer. Light the stove. Undress each other. Sleep in a nice warm bed. Or we can give in to what I think we both want."

I know exactly what I want. Based on the rock-hard length just beneath my ass, I think he feels the same. But I want to hear him say it. "What is it you want?" My voice comes out breathless, and I lower myself slightly, rocking my hips, wishing to the All of All that I'd worn a damn dress tonight, something I could lift with ease.

He bites his lip, tightening his grip around me. "I want you right here, Daphne, right now. In this musty alley that's flecked with rain and blood, where anyone could see us if they chose to walk by. I want you against that wall, propped on one of those weird fucking mushrooms. I want the danger of getting caught. I want us just like this, filthy, sweaty, and burning for each other. And I want to make love to you until I'm on fire."

A spark of desire surges through me. I lower my mouth to his. "Yes," I breathe against his lips.

Our kisses reignite, fiercer than before, a dance of tongues and teeth. I lick up the side of his face, tasting sweat and blood. He smells like rain and pungent ale from the air at the club, but beneath it all, he smells like *him*. Smoky Moon-petal and lavender, drifting on a current of lust.

I pull back just enough to undo my waistcoat and blouse, tearing the articles from my body and throwing them to the ground. I don't know how he's managed to hold me up this long without so much as a twitch of fatigue in his muscles, but maybe what he said about heat is true. Passion blazes between us, igniting our hearts, warming the rapid pulse of our shared breaths, and pooling between my thighs. I roll my hips against him, biting my lip at the agonizing distance my trousers create. Then I feel my back press against a rough, cold wall, and a wide shelf of blue-green fungi brightens above my head. Our personal spotlight.

He releases my legs and gently sets me down, and my fingers fly to the bottom of his shirt. Together we pull it overhead, baring his chest. I take in the sight of it, my palm roving wherever my eyes do. He winces as my hand grazes his ribs, which tells me he must have sustained injuries from his fight there, but there's no sign of bruising. Already he must be healing.

His lips return to mine, and this time he's the one exploring my torso, smoothing over my belly and my waist, then over my bralette. I arch into his touch, and he slides his hand beneath the silk, palming my breast. He spreads his fingers, rolling my nipple between them, and I breathe out a whimper. As he pulls his hand from beneath my bralette, I tug the entire undergarment over my head, tossing it aside. Then I work my trousers, undoing the top closure. Monty doesn't aid my efforts, instead bracing his hands against the wall on either side of my head and staring down at my body, my hands, watching as I slide my trousers down my hips, then my undershorts.

He sucks in a breath at the sight of me bare before him, and I realize this is the first time he's seen me naked. The last time we engaged in this sort of activity, I kept my dress around my middle. There was something erotic about that, yet this—being completely bared to him—is a whole new layer of vulnerability.

"Blazing hell, you're so fucking beautiful," he says, gaze sweeping up and down my form. I'm about to pull him against me, to reach for his trousers next, but before I can, he kneels on the ground before me.

I suck in a breath as one hand moves to my calf, urging me to part my legs and lift one.

"What are you doing?" I ask, bracing my hands on the two nearest mushrooms beside me. Thankfully, they're strong and don't give way beneath the pressure. I turn the rest of my weight over to the wall behind my back and let Monty guide my leg over his shoulder.

"Getting on my knees for you and groveling," he says looking up at me. Then he lowers his lips to the apex of my thighs and presses a kiss there. Still holding my gaze, he says, "I'm sorry I was too afraid. You were right about me."

I make some unintelligible sound that turns into a moan as he parts his lips and drags his tongue over the center of me. If not for the way he braces my hips, the way my leg is cradled over his shoulder, the sturdy wall beneath my back, I would collapse from the shock of pleasure that tears through me. The stroke of his tongue is so different from how his fingers felt. A sensation that's entirely new to me.

He licks me again, his gaze unwavering. "I love you, and I'm not going to run. I'm not going to push you away again." With that, he buries his face between my legs, licking, sucking. Eliciting sensations that send stars to my eyes. I roll my hips against his mouth, and he moves one of his hands from my hip to tease my entrance, painting it with the shared medium of his saliva and my arousal. Then he thrusts the finger inside me, all the while flicking his tongue over my swollen clit.

It's the most delicious thing I've ever felt, and soon I'm riding his mouth, his fingers, cresting the wave of my release. I throw my head back, crying out as the wave barrels through me. His tongue swirls over me, dancing with the pulse of my orgasm, until my hips cease rocking.

Slowly, he slides his fingers out of me, then plants a kiss to my inner thigh. He trails a line of gentle kisses up my body until our lips meet. I breathe in the heady scent of my own sex, then taste it as he slides his tongue over mine. Every move is slow and soft, and I'm filled with the dreadful thought that this is over. That, like he did in my hotel room, he's only going to deliver my pleasure.

Before he can consider such a ludicrous thought, I hook my fingers around his waistband and tug him closer. "More," I manage to say through my panting breaths. "I need more."

He quirks a brow, his smile cruel and taunting. "What did I tell you, Daffy Dear? Sex isn't always transactional."

"Grovel more for me, then," I say, holding his eyes as I undo the closures of his fly. With trembling hands, I shove his trousers down, then his undershorts too. Then I grip his length, solid and ready beneath my palm, and give it a squeeze. "Grovel with your cock. Fuck me against this wall like you said you would."

His eyes darken, and that's all it takes to end his teasing. He steps between my legs and kisses me hard, then drags his tongue down my neck, across my collarbone. Lowering his head to my breast, he flicks his tongue over my nipple and takes it into his mouth. I gasp, once again learning just how incredible his tongue feels on my most sensitive places. With a final graze of his teeth, he releases my nipple and brings his mouth back to mine. I spread my legs wider, and he hooks one around his hip, angling me. The head of his cock meets my entrance, and I'm already wet for him, eager to feel this next new sensation between us.

"You want this?" he asks, guiding his cock more firmly in place. I stare down at where our bodies meet, and I realize just how big he is. I may not have ample sexual experience with humans, but I'm still shocked at his girth, how huge he looks as he runs the head over my slit.

I lift my gaze back to his and nod. "Yes."

He pushes into me then, and I cry out as I feel my walls open around him, resisting at first, but taking him in one inch at a time as he pulls out and slides back in. Then, with a final thrust, he's seated to the hilt. I bite back a whine, and he kisses the tip of my arched ear. "You all right?"

"More than all right," I whisper back.

"Can I fuck you hard?"

I whimper. "Please."

He pulls out and thrusts back in, but this time he doesn't stop, doesn't slow down. My shoulders scrape against the wall, but I like how it feels, such a contrast to the pleasure building between my legs.

"Oh my God, Daphne, you feel so good," he says, voice tight. "I can't believe we're doing this. I can't believe you're mine."

"I'm yours," I say with a gasp, and he quickens his pace. Already I can feel another climax building, sparking hotter and hotter as every thrust reaches deeper inside me, hitting a place I've never felt before. Stars fill my vision, and I lower my mouth to his shoulder, my teeth grazing his salty flesh. Then I open my mouth wider, settle my teeth just a little firmer—

"Don't..."

He halts his thrusting, and terror runs through me as I realize what I was about to do. I've bitten a lover during sex before and it shattered the mood—and our relationship—at once.

Before panic can fully drain my lust, Monty speaks again, his voice strangled and breathless as he whispers in my ear. "Don't bite down all the way until you're ready for me to come. Because I won't be able to hold back."

Euphoria surges through my blood.

He isn't disgusted by my yearning to bite him.

He's turned on. So much so that the feel of my teeth will drive him over the edge.

If I wasn't already building to another climax, I am now. He resumes his motions, slamming into me again with renewed vigor. I keep my mouth on his shoulder, tasting every quiver of his muscles, every ounce of restraint he's utilizing to keep this going. My fingers weave into the hair at the base of his neck. He slides a hand between us, working my clit as he drives harder, faster. Just when I'm starting to unravel, I bite down on his shoulder. Not hard enough to draw blood, but hard enough to hurt.

He moans, his pace stuttering. "Oh, fuck, Daphne. Where can I come?"

"Inside me," I gasp. I'm already on the tonic and I'll be damned if he robs me of the experience of him filling me up in every way.

His thrusts regain their steady rhythm as his fingertips continue to circle my clit. I whimper against his shoulder and bite down harder, marveling at the taste of his skin, the scrape of the wall against my ass, the fullness of him inside me. At his next deep thrust, my vision blurs, and I pulse around him, my release melting around his cock. I cry out his name, muffled against the skin I'm still biting. He comes next, filling me with a wet warmth that draws out my orgasm so long, it feels like it might never end. Our rhythm slows with his final pulsating thrusts. As we go still, our bodies quivering in an echo of our shared climax, I lick the place I bit and cover it with a kiss. He aids me down the wall, sliding out of me and setting my feet on the ground. There we press our foreheads together until we catch our breath, shuddering and sweat-slicked.

I don't know how much time passes. Seconds. Minutes. Hours.

Then Monty slants his mouth against mine, and I feel him smiling against my lips. As he pulls away, his eyes dance with mirth. I'm shocked to see no sign of the bruising on his jaw. The cut over his brow has closed too, leaving only dried blood where it had been.

He steps back, slicks his hands through his messy hair, and heaves a joyful sigh. "Blazing hell, Daph, that was fucking incredible."

I can't agree with him more. Maybe not everyone would fancy their first time with the man they adore taking place in an alleyway, but I love everything we just did. Everything that we are together. Everything we might be. A scared part of my heart continues to shy away, reminding me our worries aren't over yet. I still have a handfasting to sever, and Monty has a loan to pay, not to mention a familial relationship that holds him back. But those are worries for another day.

Monty must feel it too. He returns his eyes to mine, his smile softer now, but still genuine. "Let's go home."

"Home?" I echo.

His expression turns bashful. "It's time I showed you my place."

CHAPTER THIRTY-EIGHT

MONTY

The rain has stopped by the time we make our way out of the alley, our clothing haphazardly replaced. I reach for Daphne's hand, and we walk side by side down the dark streets. It doesn't take long for us to reach where the industrial district meets the business district, separated by a few streets of housing. My apartment is located amidst identical brick row houses. It's nothing like Daphne's street with its elegant streetlamps and sidewalks lined with well-kept shrubbery. Here the architecture is practical and utilitarian, catering primarily to those who work in the factories. No charming gables, no bright paint, no lovely window treatments. At least it's quiet. Most of my neighbors who drink their workweek sorrows away do so on Rook Street, where the nearest pub is located. And they won't be coming home until closing time.

We reach my building and quietly make our way up the

front steps to the main door. I'm too anxious to see Daphne's reaction, to note if she's apprehensive about my unfashionable building. In my heart of hearts, I know she won't judge. Still, she's the first person I've ever brought here. I never had any intention of showing her my place, but I'm done hiding from her. I'm ready for her to see all of me.

We enter the building and climb the staircase past the closed doors of the other units until we reach the third floor. Like Daphne, I live on the top floor. I don't have access to the roof, or a balcony, or really anything interesting, and my living space is about a quarter of the size of hers—

I shake my head, realizing I've frozen outside my door, key in hand. Daphne looks up at me with an encouraging smile. I heave a sigh and return the grin, though mine probably looks only somewhat convincing. Then I unlock the door and welcome the woman I love into my home.

I tug a dangling chain just inside the doorway and several hanging bulbs illuminate, one at a time, until the meager space glows under full light. Daphne steps ahead of me, and I watch her, bracing myself for her reaction. Her eyes are wide and curious as they flick from one thing to the next. Easy to do when everything I own and use is in a single room.

I pull my gaze away from her and try to see my apartment through her eyes. The walls are rich oak, and the ceiling is crossed with exposed beams from which the lightbulbs hang. The nearest piece of furniture is a narrow settee, and beside it is a small table built straight from the wall with two chairs. Beside that is a countertop that comprises my kitchen as well as a sink and stove. The far wall boasts a pair of sliding doors. One opens to reveal the narrow washroom while the other hides my closet. Above that is the loft where my bed resides, accessible via a wooden ladder. The wall opposite the kitchen is covered entirely with bookshelves burdened with more books than can possibly fit. Edwina Danforth has several shelves dedicated to her. I own multiple copies of her books, many of which are out of print until Fletcher-Wilson publishes the new editions with Daphne's covers. There are also books from every other author I worked with during my time at Fletcher-Wilson, as well as an abundance of titles for recreational reading.

It's cluttered. It's incredibly small. But it's also…

"It's lovely," Daphne says, her voice rich with awe.

I shift from foot to foot. "You don't think it's too cramped?"

She gives me a withering look. "Too cramped? I spent the first couple hundred years of my life living in a tree burrow. This is incredible. Don't you feel comforted being able to see every wall of your home from one place? It's like a den."

When she puts it like that, I suppose it does feel comforting. I know my shame over my small apartment is a matter of ego. I was raised in grand residences, both a country estate and a city manor. I was waited on by servants and had dozens of rooms at my disposal, each bearing a different purpose yet never utilized all at once. There was so much empty space. Towering walls papered in elegant damask. Halls upon halls adorned with strategically spaced portraits bearing gilded frames.

But now, reflecting back, everything did feel too large. I often felt too alone. Especially after I discovered the truth about my mother. I never quite fit in, always fighting an itch to run and play in the fields instead of attending my studies, and after I learned of my heritage, it made sense. The understanding festered into bitterness when I discovered my father only took me from my mother—convinced her it was for the best—because I was male. Not because he loved me.

After that, I resented luxury. Resented my unearned privilege.

Yet what did I do the moment I gained freedom from my family? I took out a shady loan, paid a year's rent for a luxury apartment, and spent a small fortune on my wardrobe. I lost job after job that first year and used up all the funds I'd borrowed. By the time I finally gained stable employment at Fletcher-Wilson, I could no longer afford my lifestyle. That was when I really learned what it meant to be surrounded in luxury I hadn't earned.

I'd been overconfident in my ability to make an impressive wage despite having no experience in the workforce. It was a humbling lesson, and my ego took quite the hit. I thought my ego had died back then, but I was wrong.

I huff a laugh. "I've been a fool for so long."

Daphne pulls her gaze away from my rafters—probably wishing she could shift into unseelie form and climb them, like she used to do whenever she discovered a nice set of beams to scale during The Heartbeats Tour—and gives me a curious look.

"I was so ashamed of this place," I say. "So embarrassed to admit just how much I'd had to downsize after I gave up my apartment downtown. I didn't realize I'd come to like it here. That I chose this place. Out of necessity, yes, but also out of comfort. My inner fennec fox...likes this den." Tension rolls off my shoulders to admit it. That this suits me. That I'm not ashamed and have no reason to be.

Daphne gives me a consoling pat on the shoulder. "You may be a fool, but you're my fool."

My heart flutters like I'm a fucking schoolboy. "I'm yours?"

She dips her chin in a proud nod, but her expression quickly falters. "Oh, wait. Can you be mine? I mean, I want you to be mine, and I want to be yours, but I know you can't publicly court—"

I silence her with a press of my lips. She softens against me, her anxiety melting away.

"Yes, you're fucking mine," I growl against her lips. That's all it takes to reignite our passion. Her tongue sweeps into my mouth and, goddamn, I want to devour her. To taste every inch of her a thousand times over. We undress each other with eager hands, and the only thing that stops us from fucking right there in the middle of my living room-kitchen-dining room floor is the sensible side of me that knows our still-damp clothes are going to smell like a whore's handbag by morning if we don't wash and hang them to dry now. And I am not sending my ladylove home tomorrow doing the walk of shame in cum-soaked undershorts and a blouse splattered with blood. So I do laundry with a raging hard-on, which is quite nice when the love of my life plants teasing kisses up my spine and gropes my ass like the lecherous little minx she is.

Once our clothes are hanging to dry over the warm stove, I turn to Daphne and waggle my brows. "Want to fuck me in my bunk bed?"

She snorts a laugh. "Never thought I'd hear that from a lover's lips."

"My accommodations aren't the most mature, I know, but I promise I'm of legal age."

"You know, I live in a treehouse, and I'm three centuries older than you." With that, she gives me a daring look and saunters toward my ladder. I'm hypnotized as she climbs, giving me the most tantalizing view of her rear. The sight of her bare ass shifting side to side before me nearly has me undone right then and there. I grip her hips before she can climb too far. She lets out a delighted squeak as I bury my tongue in her sex from behind while she grips the rungs of my ladder. By the time we finally manage to make it all the way up to my bed, we're a tangle of sweaty limbs all over again. She rides my cock, setting our pace, working all the places she likes, and teaching me more about what gets her off. I don't think I'll ever get tired of hearing her soft sounds, watching the expressions she makes when she's in the throes of pleasure. I want to memorize the feel of my fingers sinking into the soft flesh of her hips as I unravel inside her, her walls squeezing every last drop from my cock.

After we're spent once more, we recline in bed, her body nestled against mine.

"I've changed my mind about that painting," I say into her hair, breathing in the scent of her.

She looks up at me from where her cheek is propped on my chest, her eyelids as heavy as her voice. "What painting?"

"The one I said I wanted to hang in my bedroom. I said I'd rather have a painting than the real thing, because the real thing is too pretty for my shabby apartment. But I've changed my mind. You're too pretty for any space indeed, but I prefer you over a painting."

"What a charmer," she says with a smirk. She angles her body to lift herself slightly on my chest and props her chin on her hands. "Speaking of painting...is our bargain fulfilled?"

I narrow my eyes. "Why, Daffy Dear, are you asking if my case study has found its happy ending?"

"That was one of the possible conditions for its fulfillment. Two, actually. Either we completed your case study or I entered a committed partnership."

I wince. "I don't know if anyone would consider me a favorable match." I chuckle as she jabs a weak punch at my ribs. "But you're right. We've completed my case study. You've won my heart, and there's no giving it back. And you no longer have a model problem."

She gives me a coy grin. "Does that mean you're my permanent model? Even when I want you to do dirty stuff in front of the mirror?"

"Especially when you want me to do dirty stuff." I give her ass a squeeze. She squeals as my palm rounds its curve, and again when my fingers slide along the seam of her cheeks. "We have a lot of exploring to do."

Her eyes go wide, her expression a mixture of fascination and apprehension.

"Don't worry," I say, giving her ass a playful slap. "No exploring tonight. If we don't sleep soon, we won't at all. And you probably want the ability to walk this weekend."

She sinks back down on my chest. Her voice comes out with a little pout as she mutters, "I don't *have* to walk."

We fall into a comfortable silence. I trace patterns up and down her arm while she breathes softly against my chest. I think she might have fallen asleep until she shifts, staring up at me again.

"Can I ask why you stopped drinking?" At my puzzled look over her sudden question, she adds, "You don't have to tell me if you don't want to. I never thought much of it until Briony told me you used to drink quite a lot. She hadn't a clue you'd stopped."

My heart sinks. I'm not too proud of the man I used to be, but I've already resolved to let Daphne see all of me. "Not long after I found out about my lineage, I turned to liquor. Angie's mother was quite the lush, so there was always a bottle hidden somewhere. It was an escape. Harmless, mostly, save for the damage to my reputation. I was a sloppy obnoxious drunk. The life of every party. But every now and then, I would drink too much. And when that would happen, I'd get sad. A sadness that often shifted to anger."

Daphne's brow wrinkles with concern.

"I never hurt anyone," I say, putting her worries to rest.

"The problem with my anger wasn't my actions, it was...the result. I told you already there are certain emotions that generate heat for a fire fae. Anger is one of them. It strengthens my magic. Magic I haven't a clue how to utilize. Magic I was *forbidden* to utilize. Yet the one time I shifted into my unseelie form, I was drunk and angry. Thankfully, I was alone. Well, not entirely alone. Father found me and gave me a verbal lashing so strong, he startled me back to seelie form. I wish I could say that was when I stopped drinking, but that was hardly the end.

"I kept drinking, knowing the danger I posed to my father's reputation should I ever accidentally shift in public. I was too much of a coward to out his secret by shifting on purpose, mostly because I wasn't certain it would cause me to break the bargain I'd made—if it would constitute as *letting* someone find out. But I figured if I did it unintentionally, it wouldn't count.

"Part of me hoped I'd be freed from my burden that way, even if it meant taking the blame for my family's ruin. Then, shortly after I was disinherited, I visited Angie. I wanted to ensure Father was treating her well now that she'd taken my place as his heir. If he was acting even remotely awful to her, I wouldn't need to feel guilty about destroying our family. But that wasn't at all what she relayed. She was thriving in her new role. She'd gained confidence at home and school. She'd finally stopped getting bullied and made friends. True and genuine friends, not self-serving assholes like Cosette.

"I couldn't take that risk anymore. I couldn't be the cause of Angie's downfall. It's the same reason I smoke relaxing herbal substances—merely another form of mood control. When my anxiety builds into rage, smoking or boxing helps take the edge off."

Her eyes are full of sympathy as she traces the line of my

jaw with her forefinger. "You've really worked so hard to keep this secret."

"I have," I say, lifting her hand from my jaw and laying a kiss across her fingers. "But you were right. It's time I let it go and took this burden off my shoulders."

As Daphne rests against me once more, her hand pressed over my heart, I come to terms with what I must do.

CHAPTER THIRTY-NINE

DAPHNE

I can't believe I'm admitting this, but I can't wait until I see Araminta. I've never been more desperate for a friend. As I walk to work Monday morning with a skip in my step, a weekend of great sex and love confessions behind me, I know a friend is exactly what I need. This isn't the kind of thing I can discuss in a letter to Edwina or bottle up until we meet in person. No, I need to tell my annoying book sprite friend. Otherwise, it's only a matter of time before I blurt out *Guess how many orgasms I had last night?* to the next stranger who smiles at me.

If only I knew when or where I'd next see Ari. She didn't show up at my apartment over the weekend, though I did spend half of it at Monty's, and I don't know where her new place is located.

I arrive to work in a love-addled daze, shocked when I find the editorial floor bustling with so much activity. It appears I'm the last assistant to arrive. Having a skip in one's step must not equate to an increase in speed.

I pull open the drawer to extract my pen and ink pot, eager to get started like the rest of my colleagues. I bite back a yelp at the tiny body curled up on my stack of papers. The lights overhead illuminate her paper wings, and I realize I won't have to wait long at all to see Araminta.

"No," she says, wincing at the bright light, "just leave me in this dark hole to wither alone."

I arch a brow. "Did you and David break up again?"

"God, no," she says, pushing up to sit with lethargic moves. "We've been over for ages."

I wouldn't call last weekend ages ago, but to each their own. I'm still brimming with excitement over everything I want to tell her, but I doubt she'd give me the response I want if she's in such a somber mood. Besides, I may have admitted I was looking forward to seeing Ari, but that doesn't mean I have to act like it. "What's got you crawling into dark holes to die?"

She flutters out of my drawer, allowing me to extract my writing supplies. There's a missive on my desk, so I set it aside, organizing my blank sheets of paper, my pen and ink pot, and the queries I need to read today.

Ari plops herself on top of the missive, face down, wings splayed flat. Her voice comes out muffled as she says, "I got fired."

"Fired? From your modeling gig? Which one?"

She lifts her head, her parchment lashes heavy over drooping eyes. "All of them."

"What did you do?"

"It's not what *I* did," she says, tone defensive. "It's Spears Marketing's fault. That's the company I work for. They're in charge of the adverts for Harvey Blandwell's Hemorrhoid Potion and Intrepid Contraceptive Tonic, among others.

Apparently there was a little outrage over my kitten photograph."

"I doubt it was the photograph so much as the text."

"Either way, this is the end for me. All my dreams have crumbled, thanks to the Modesty Committee." She says the last part in a deep and mocking voice.

"What's the Modesty Committee?"

She gives me a perplexed look. "Didn't you see them outside the building? They had signs and everything. Why do you think I'm incognito today?"

I tilt my head, racking my brain. "Come to think of it, there was a group of women outside the building today, holding up signs on wooden stakes."

"Didn't they yell at you when you walked into the lobby?"

I think back and recall that maybe they did. I wasn't in the best state of mind to notice much of anything, what with me skipping, humming, and reliving the euphoria of my weekend. "I just smiled at them and came inside," I say with a shrug.

Ari stands up at once. "You…smiled at them? But you never smile at strangers. You hardly look at them. Why would you smile at my archenemy? Not just mine but your own." At my furrowed brow, she continues. "They don't just have it out for Spears Marketing. They're on a mission to outlaw so-called inappropriate media of every sort and have waged war against every publication in the city that features mature content. It rose to a peak this weekend, with them standing outside bookstores, libraries, and newsstands, shaming anyone who even thought of buying what the Committee considers filth. Didn't you hear them shouting *Keep smut out of our children's hands* and *Bare chests belong in the bedroom?*"

My pulse kicks up. This can't be good. I look around the editorial floor, at my colleagues scrambling from desk to desk or furiously writing. I was so caught up in my own happy bubble, I hadn't sensed the tense mood until now.

"It's all here," Ari says, tapping her foot on the missive she's standing on.

I pull it out from under her so fast, it sends her tumbling through the air. I scan the headline of the missive: *Changes in Production Schedule Effective Immediately.* It looks like a general notice sent to everyone at Fletcher-Wilson, which explains the mass panic. If we're forced to make changes to our production schedule due to the current outrage from the Modesty Committee, it will affect everyone.

"Miss Daphne," says a deep and stoic voice. I glance up to find Mr. Fletcher standing on the other side of my desk. "Please come to my office. I have unfortunate news."

CHAPTER FORTY

MONTY

Walnut Avenue is the most upscale street in downtown Jasper, home to gentlemen's clubs, high-end dining, a private ballroom, and an opera house. I spent many family outings of my youth on Walnut Street, amongst the affluent, snobbish, and incredibly boring patrons it caters to. I've made it my mission the last few years never to step foot on this side of town unless necessary for work, and I wouldn't be here today if I didn't have a reason.

The most important reason in my life.

I take a drag of my cigarillo, the floral smoke calming my frazzled nerves as I make my way past familiar buildings, brushing past aristocrats and wealthy businessmen in top hats and frock coats. My body recoils at how smothered a full suit makes me feel, but I needed to dress the part to prevent any delays in fulfilling my mission. My workday starts in an hour, so I don't have much time. I'm determined to do this today.

I stop outside an enormous brick building with white columns along the first floor and tall arched windows lining the second. Gold lettering spells out *The Magnolia* above an enormous pair of double doors with gold handles. My stomach tightens but I remind myself this is necessary.

Every Monday when my father is in town, he starts his day drinking tea and reading his broadsheets at The Magnolia, his favorite members-only club. It's been his ritual for as long as we lived at Sandalwood Manor, my family's city home. Which means, unless he's off on business, he's here now.

I take a deep breath and approach the butler at the door. I give him my name, and he disappears inside for only a handful of seconds before he returns to escort me inside. I'm not surprised at how quickly my visit was approved. Despite having disinherited me, Father likely kept me listed as family at the club, to make it easy should I ever want to come crawling back.

But I'm not crawling, nor am I coming back. I'm facing him head-on. I'm doing what I was always too afraid to do before.

The butler leads me into a wide room with mahogany walls and a white coffered ceiling. Dozens of tables paired with leather chairs are set throughout the room, most of which are filled with male—primarily human, as far as I can tell at a glance—occupants. I find Father at his usual table, his broadsheets out and a fat cigar between his lips. He doesn't look at me as I claim the empty leather chair across from him, as if my presence is no surprise.

"Are you here to tell me I was right?" he says, turning a page in his paper. "You and that fae girl are an item after all, aren't you?"

My fists curl on my armrests. Of course that's how he greets me. "Good morning to you too, Father."

"I looked into her," he says, finally deigning to set down his cigar and broadsheets. He gives me an exasperated look and lowers his voice to a whisper. "She's not a proper match. I know you need a fae wife so when your children are born..." He relays the rest with an arched brow, and I know exactly what he means. He's always been adamant I take a fae wife so that when I conceive heirs, any fae nature they exhibit will be easily explained. "You cannot come back to the family unless—"

"I'm not coming back to the family," I say, not lowering my voice as quietly as his. My heart slams against my ribs. I can't believe it's taken me so long to say it, but I can't ignore the truth any longer. Daphne was right about me. All my life I've been terrified of being hurt by those I love. Terrified of being abandoned without understanding why. I've hated the ones who've hurt me yet I'm equally frightened of losing them. Because without their awful, fickle love, who do I have? I hurt friends, family, and lovers to keep them at bay, so I always knew I was to blame for our separation. So it would always be their choice to leave me, but also their choice to take me back. It's been a sick and twisted dance of hate, hurt, and a need to be loved.

But I'm done with it.

I don't need to push people away anymore. I'm strong enough to survive if they leave.

And I don't need to keep those in my life that are undeserving of my love.

I can make the choice.

I can sever the bonds.

I've done it before, with Cosette, when I finally made it clear we were over.

I can do the same with my father.

His face flushes crimson, and he glances to the nearest tables. "We should speak in private back home—"

"No, we'll speak here. I'll make it quick." I extract a piece of paper from my waistcoat pocket and push it across the table.

He narrows his eyes at me before taking up the paper and reading what I've written there. "What the hell is this?"

"The balance I owe a certain lender."

He leans back in his chair, chuckling. "Ah, I see. You've found out just how hard it is to live on your own and had to take out a loan. Now your debt is catching up to you and you want me to bail you out. You know my terms for financial aid. Return to your proper place as my heir and take a proper wife—"

"No, we're not playing that game." I lean forward, my lips curling in a cold grin. "Here's the thing. That loan isn't an ordinary one. My lender deals in secrets."

His face pales, expression dipping into horror before he recovers, donning a haughty mask. He keeps his voice a low whisper. "You couldn't have said a word, or you'd have suffered the effects of our bargain."

"I didn't say a word." My grin widens, growing colder. Crueler. "I didn't have to utter a single syllable because my lender read my fucking mind. Now he knows everything. And if he doesn't receive this balance paid in full by July 16th, your secret is out."

His jaw tics, rage pulsing at his temples. I can tell just how much restraint he's exerting to keep from shouting at me. It's a satisfying sight that makes this public meeting worth it, just to witness how much effort it takes for him to pretend to be a decent human amongst his peers. He grinds his teeth. "Of all the idiotic—"

"Here's how this is going to go. You're going to let me out of my bargains. Both of them. You will no longer burden me with keeping your secret. I will continue to protect our family's reputation by not intentionally spreading the truth, but

I'm not going to keep it from those I love. Furthermore, I will no longer be bound by the condition that I'll return to the family if I marry. You have no right to intervene with my love life and future happiness. You have no sway over who I choose as a wife, and you will have no influence in my life going forward. Because I am done with you. However, if you honor my request and free me from the two bargains we made, I will give you the name of my lender and *allow* you to pay my debt and save your sorry reputation."

I sit back and let my words sink in, watching his eyes widen as he processes my offer and assesses the repercussions. He takes a silk cloth from his jacket pocket and mops his brow. His voice comes out with a tremor as he speaks. "I need some time to consider."

"No, you will make your decision now. Rescind our bargains before I walk out that door, or in a matter of weeks, everyone in this room and beyond will know you're a fucking fraud. A mockery of what they consider the pinnacle of human propriety. If you think you'll get reelected as Human Representative after the Alpha Council finds out—"

"Enough," he says, the word loud enough to draw the attention of multiple club patrons. He returns his voice to a whisper, but it quavers with fear. "Enough. You've made your point."

We stare at each other in silence for a few tense moments.

My father mops his brow again, then says, "If I free you from our bargains, I need at least a binding promise that you'll do your best to keep your lineage from leaking to the public."

I give a cold laugh. "Did I say I was open to negotiations? Rescind our bargains now, no conditions, no promises. Simply trust that I care enough about Angela to do my part. The rest is up to you, asshole."

He bares his teeth. "How dare you talk to me that way, you ungrateful—"

I rise from my chair and start to stride away.

"Wait." His shout once again draws the curious eyes of the other patrons. "My dear son," he says, softening his tone, "it's been too long. We still have more catching up to do."

With slow steps, I return to him, stopping next to his chair and staring down at him. "End it," I say through my teeth.

I've never seen him so pale, so frail, so cowed. His gaze flicks to the other tables before he stares down at the paper again. Then, in the quietest voice, he sets me free.

My relief is dizzying, thrilling, thrumming through every muscle in my body. I'm free. I'm fucking free. Part of me is stuck in disbelief, convinced it was all a trick. It's so simple to end a bargain, so devoid of fanfare. In cases where one party set the bargain's terms to impose on another, the first party must revoke the bargain by verbally stating it is null and void and all terms have been either fulfilled or dissolved. Father stated exactly that—in a whisper only I could hear—but he said it. Twice, specifying which bargain he was ending each time.

Just to be sure, I halt before the next stranger I pass, a lanky human man with a long gray mustache. I grab him by the lapels. "My mother is a fox."

I wait for pain, for a tightening in my lungs, but it doesn't come.

"I'm a fucking fennec. My father is a liar and a cheater and a whore."

"Good God," the man says with a huff, shaking me off and dusting his lapels with gloved hands. He scurries away as if he fears he might catch my madness.

It worked. It really worked. I'm nearly sick with joy. There are so many people I want to tell. Thorne, who will be enraged that I kept such a secret from him but will probably relate to me most. He's had to deal with his own family secrets, and he'll hate that I never let him be there for me. And Briony, who might forgive me just a little more for being so goddamn annoying when we were engaged. I had reasons for not wanting to marry her, for being desperate to give my father cause to disinherit me. Angie needs to know too. It's time I stopped keeping her in the dark and acknowledge she's stronger than I've given her credit for. She deserves the truth. Of course, Edwina and William will get a kick out of this too.

But most of all...

Daphne.

I must tell Daphne that there's nothing standing between us now. There's no need to keep our love hidden. No limits to where our relationship can go.

My rational side reminds me to check my pocket watch and see how much time I have left until my workday starts, but I can't pay the ticking hands much heed. I have to see her. Now.

I hail the first hansom cab I find, directing the coachman to Fletcher-Wilson headquarters in the business district. Traffic is slow on Verbena Street, so I get out a couple blocks early, pay the driver, then jog the rest of the way. That's when I see what's causing so much commotion. Figures crowd the sidewalk holding signs and chanting slogans. Something about smut and bare chests.

I stride for the front doors, but a woman intercepts me.

"Good sir, will you sign my petition to keep bare chests off book covers?"

"Fuck off," I say and brush past her. At her shocked gasp, I halt to face her with an apologetic smile. "I'm so sorry. That was rude to say to a lady. What I meant was *kindly* fuck off."

I don't bother stopping at reception and instead climb the stairs to the editorial floor. It's a flurry of commotion, making it impossible to spot Daphne. I stride between desks, overwhelmed by the chaos. I wonder if this is how Daphne feels in new or crowded places, assaulted by sound and confusion.

"What are you doing here?"

I whirl toward the familiar voice, but it takes me a moment to locate its source. Finally, I find a paper pixie lounging on her belly on an ink pot, a manuscript open on the desk before her. I haven't seen Araminta in her unseelie form since the day I reunited with Daphne outside the break room. But if she's here…

"Where's Daphne?"

With lazy motions, she flips the page of the manuscript to read the next. "She's probably at the train station by now."

"What do you mean she's at the station?"

"Her book covers were canceled and her promotion was postponed or something."

My heart slams down to my feet. "Why did she go to the station?"

"Mr. Fletcher gave her the rest of the day off, and she said something about catching the noon train."

"To where?"

"Beats me. I'm too depressed for cognition." She turns another page of the manuscript. "Why else do you think I'm reading bad queries?"

I run a hand over my face as dread settles into my chest.

There's only one place I can think she'd go after learning her career goals have imploded.

She's given up, taunts the dark side of my heart. *Without her career, she has nothing to free her from her handfasting. You were never enough. Of course she ran away.*

She left. She fucking left. Before I could tell her…

Everything inside me wants to shrivel.

You never should have confessed your heart to her. It's only going to hurt more to lose her.

But I don't have to lose her. Not anymore. I can be what she needs me to be.

You can never be what she needs. She was here for her illustration career, not you—

I shake the small, frightened voices from my mind, seeking my anger instead. Anger at whatever shitshow is going on outside the building. Anger over her covers being canceled. My inner fire rises, and I don't shy away from it. I let it burn me up from the inside, turning those dark thoughts to cinders. My anger joins hands with my passion, my fiery love for Daphne, my burning resolve to fight for what I want for once.

A spark I've seldom felt lights my chest. This is normally when I'd breathe in my calming herbal remedy and soothe my rage, but I don't this time. This time I encourage it to grow, to spread through my limbs, simmer in my blood. Violet covers my vision, something I've only seen once. It's the color of fae magic, linked to the spiritual realm that powers one's ability to shift. My body radiates with it. It's strange and new and slightly terrifying, but I turn myself over to it. A shiver crawls up my spine, and as it radiates back down, I feel myself shrinking.

Then I drop onto four paws and dart back in the direction I came.

Araminta's squeal is the last thing I hear before I reach the stairwell. "Ohmygod, you're sooo cute!"

Her squeals aren't the only ones I encounter. More erupt from the women crowding the sidewalk, but I dart past them, between legs and under skirts, maneuvering much easier and faster than I could on two legs with so much commotion blocking my way. And thank fuck too. I have a train to catch.

CHAPTER FORTY-ONE

DAPHNE

My heart is a strange blend of heavy and light. I'm crushed by the news I got today, but it's only a partial crushing. On the other side, there's hope. So much hope. And love too.

Yet there's something I can't put off any longer. It may not be Lughnasadh yet, but I'm not willing to wait until then. To wonder. I have an engagement to end.

I settle onto the hard bench in the public passenger car. These aren't the velvet-lined seats on most of the other trains I've been on, but those are for longer travel. This train only makes a few stops in the Earthen Court, the last of which is just outside the unseelie forest on the northern end of the court. In a matter of hours, I'll reach Cypress Hollow. By the time I return in the morning, it won't be my hometown anymore.

I bring a nail between my teeth, nibbling it. Even though I

know what must be done, it doesn't make it any easier. But I'm ready to move on. Monty has given me the motivation. He's faced the part of himself that struggled to let his past go. Based on hints he gave me over the weekend, I think he's planning on talking to his father this week. By the time we see each other next, we might both have good news.

"Get back here! Do you have a ticket?"

Startled gasps erupt from the front of the car as a porter rushes onboard as if chasing someone. But I don't see—

"Yes, I have a fucking ticket. You can see it once I find her."

My heart stutters at the familiar voice, yet I don't see Monty anywhere. All I see is the porter rushing down the aisle. Then a tiny creature with fawn fur, a short slender muzzle, and enormous ears scampers onto the back of one of the wooden benches. For the love of the All of All…that's a fennec fox. That's Monty. And he's so cute I could die.

The porter turns this way and that, having lost sight of the creature he was chasing.

What the hell is Monty doing here? And in unseelie form! Am I dreaming?

Monty's large vulpine eyes find mine, and he leaps from seat to seat, even onto one man's shoulder in his attempt to scramble over to me. The porter finally spots him and chases him down the aisle. Monty reaches my bench, landing on four paws in the empty space beside me. He loses his footing, but as soon as the porter stops beside my seat, Monty's humanoid form appears in a flash. His hair is mussed, his cravat crooked, and I realize he's dressed in a full suit. With his body swiveled toward me, gaze still locked on mine, he reaches into his jacket pocket and flourishes a ticket at the porter.

The man takes it from him. "Give me one reason why I shouldn't evict you from this train for causing such a scene."

Monty ignores him, facing me more fully.

My eyes volley between his. "Monty, what's going on?"

He loosens his cravat and collar, then gathers my hands in his. "Daphne, please get off the train and marry me."

My eyes nearly fall out of their sockets. "What are you..."

"Let's go. Get off this train and we'll elope right now. There's no reason to risk it. No reason to return to your hometown pleading that Clyde will sympathize with your needs. We'll give him no option. Be my wife."

His words launch butterflies in my stomach, and I can't help but be moved by them.

And yet...

I shake my head. "I don't want to get married out of convenience. Matrimony means too much to me now that I know what it's like to love and desire someone. Maybe I've grown selfish, but I want what Briony and Thorne have."

"We can have that. I want to marry you, Daffy Dear, and now I can. Father freed me from my bargains. He's going to pay off my debt and leave me alone for good. There's nothing holding us back now. Don't you understand? I'll do anything for you. I'll move heaven and earth to make you mine, and I'll destroy anyone and anything who stands in our way."

Happy tears spring to my eyes. I remember when he used that *heaven and earth* line to describe how fervently a man would pursue a woman he was interested in. The part about destroying people is a new twist, but the violent flair suits him.

The porter clears his throat, but when neither of us gives him our attention, he marches back down the aisle, muttering, "This is above my pay grade."

"Let's go, love," he says, voice tinged with desperation. "Let's elope, let's—"

I lean forward and silence him with a kiss.

"If we kiss, it's real," I say against his lips. "This is enough."

When he tries to interrupt, I say, "There's no need to elope. There's one last step I can take to get out of my handfasting. I don't have to rely on convincing Clyde and Elder Rhisha that I have too many ties in Jasper. I don't have to be at anyone's mercy but my own."

"What do you mean?"

My lungs tighten as I confess the rest. "If I relinquish my citizenship of Cypress Hollow, I'll no longer be bound to its rules."

His shoulders relax as understanding dawns.

"I refused to consider it before because it means letting go of the place I can always return to when I want to run away from society. It's been my comfort knowing I have a place to escape to if my life in Jasper ever ends as badly as my debut season."

His eyes turn down at the corners. "There's nothing wrong with holding on to that kind of comfort."

"I know, and I would love to keep that door open. But if it means subjecting myself to a life I don't want, I have to say goodbye. I have to let go of that safety net, and I'm not waiting until the last minute anymore. I am committed to making my life in Jasper work, to going after my dreams to become an illustrator. Even if I get scared, even if I end up making mistakes. It's the life I want."

"That's why you're going back," he says with a sigh. "You didn't give up. Of course you didn't give up. You simply got stronger."

The conductor calls "All aboard," signaling Monty's chance to disembark if he isn't planning on coming with me. I know he only got a ticket to try to get me *off* the train and into a chapel. What a reckless lover I have.

He shifts, facing forward and draping an arm over my shoulders to pull me close to his side. The train begins to roll forward. That's when I notice several curious faces fixated on us. I narrow my eyes at every gaze I meet, silently conveying that the show is over and they can mind their own damn business.

"I guess I'm missing work today," Monty says as the train picks up momentum.

"Monty!"

"Do you think I want to be there anyway with that Modesty Committee farce going on?"

I wince. "I can only imagine what that means for your column."

"Whatever happens, I'll face it. To be honest, I'm not sure I want to accept the *Ask Gladys* position long-term, even if my book does get published. Why should I? Who am I to teach women how to date? The person I love broke all the rules to win my heart."

My stomach flips. I'm still not used to hearing him say he loves me. "Your book had some good points though."

"Perhaps. I've been obsessed with other people's relationships because I never thought I could have one of my own. I wanted to witness love from afar, to study it and see if honest love existed in the world, without ever risking my heart to experience it myself."

"Until now," I say.

"Until now," he echoes.

"If you're not Gladys, what do you think you'll do next?"

His eyes go unfocused. "I don't know, which is frankly terrifying. I want to find something for myself. When I got fired from Fletcher-Wilson, I discovered I'd only gotten the job because my father pulled some strings. And when I was hired at the *Gazette*, it was only because Mr. Fletcher personally recommended me for the *Ask Gladys* position. I'd like to earn something of my own. Find a vocation I truly enjoy."

"Like boxing?" I ask, unable to hide the grimace on my face.

"What's that look for?"

"Well, it's just...if your father is going to pay your debt, you can return to fighting for fun, and..."

"And?"

"And I worry. I don't like seeing you hurt."

"Oh, love of mine," he says with a chuckle. "You have no idea, do you?"

I tilt my head. "No idea about what?"

"I only lose when I'm ordered to. When I'm at the club, I'm holding back. When I give it my all, I win."

His confidence sends a violent thrill through me. "I think I glimpsed some of that in the alley the other day."

"Yeah?" he whispers. "You mean when I was fucking you against the wall?"

I swallow a squeak and purse my lips to hide my smile. I tuck the ends of my hair behind my ears. "No," I whisper back. "When you nearly split a fae male's face open with his own cane."

"I think I saw a similar side of you."

I lift my chin. "Maybe I'll go into amateur boxing too."

"Don't you dare. You'll eat your opponents alive. Maybe literally."

I elbow him in the ribs, and he gives me a sweet smile. Too soon his expression falls, flashing with horror. "Oh, God, Daph. I can't believe I haven't said this yet, but I'm so sorry about your book covers."

I shrug. "At least now I'll have more time to work on them. Not that I needed it. My skills have improved a lot, thanks to this sexy body." I poke him in the side, and he catches my hand.

"What do you mean you'll have more time?"

"Edwina's new covers have been postponed until early

next year, after everything is settled with whatever bill the Modesty Committee is trying to pass. Mr. Fletcher assured me it won't affect us too much in the long run, and he has a solution even if their bill passes. We're going to proceed with my sexy covers, but we're going to print something called a dust jacket. It will not only protect my artwork from damage but will also hide the smut so only folks who want the good stuff can see it."

He runs a hand over his face. "I'm so relieved. Ari said the covers were canceled."

I roll my eyes. "Ari is depressed that she can't model for hemorrhoid potion in her undergarments until this mess dies down. She can't pay a lick of attention to anyone else right now, and it's her loss. I was going to relay our weekend sexcapades in graphic detail."

"Aww," he says with a coy look. "I'm so honored my cock is so brag-worthy."

A middle-aged man in a top hat whirls to eye us with a glare.

I blush and lower my voice. "If only we had a private compartment."

"Who needs privacy?" he says, his lips by my ear, his hand running up my inner thigh. "My fingers are dexterous enough to move without drawing much attention. You can keep quiet, can't you?"

I bite my lip and halt his wandering hand. "No, I can't."

He chuckles and ceases his seductive teasing. Then, belatedly, he adds, "To be clear, you turned down my proposal?"

"To fondle me in the public car of a train in the middle of the day? Yes."

"No, the other proposal. The wedding one."

My pulse quickens. I know he only proposed out of a misplaced sense of urgency, but it sends a warm thrill through me to hear the offer is still on the table. Even so, it's not one I can accept. "For now," I say, holding his eyes so he can see how earnest I'm being. "I want to take that step without any other influence at play."

"So you might say yes someday."

"I might," I say with a wink.

CHAPTER FORTY-TWO

DAPHNE

We disembark at the northernmost station and hail a cab to get as close as we can to the unseelie forest by carriage. After that, there's no other way to get to my hometown except for walking. Several signposts stand sentinel outside the woods as we approach, staggered every few yards, to remind travelers that they are about to enter unseelie territory. This entire forest is protected unseelie land where human rules do not apply. Hunters who dare step foot beyond these signposts will undoubtedly be torn limb from limb by the first dangerous fae they encounter and there will be no recompense to their families. Any conflicts that arise—whether between residents or visitors or any combination—are dealt with according to unseelie tradition, which is often a fight to the death.

I share a glance with Monty, ensuring he's ready for this. I prepared him as best I could on the train, reminding him that even though Cypress Hollow is modeled after a human village and will look rather cute, it is very much a place of ancient lore and fae-governed practices. The village is meant to give fae creatures who are interested in seelie culture but not seelie rules the ability to experience it without sacrificing their values.

He nods, giving me a dimpled grin. "Let's go."

Hand in hand, we enter the canopy of trees, the early evening sunlight dimming the deeper we go and casting speckles of golden light on the leaves and underbrush. It's such a beautiful palette of color. I'd give anything to capture this moment—the quiet stillness of the woods interrupted only by birdsong, the feel of Monty's hand in mine—and replicate it on canvas. Yellow ochre here. Cadmium red there. Burnt sienna and viridian—

"It was my fault, wasn't it?" Monty says, pulling me from my mental painting.

"What was your fault?" I release his hand as we reach a fallen tree. It landed at an angle, resting in the *V* of another tree. Too tempted to resist, I hop onto the log and begin to cross it.

Monty stays on the ground and strolls beside the beam. "The reason you were so upset that you buried your sorrows in booze last Lughnasadh."

I'm so surprised by his words that I nearly lose my balance. I spread my arms out wider and secure my footing before proceeding. "I wouldn't say it was *all* your fault. I'm the one who drank too much."

"You can tell me the truth, love," he says, and there's no judgment or apprehension in his tone. He truly wants to know.

I make my way to the end of the beam where it rests in the crook of the other tree, a good six feet off the ground. Monty stands at the base, arms wide. I don't need him to catch me, but that doesn't mean I'll refuse. I drop off the edge with control, and Monty catches me with ease, cradling me sideways in his arms. That's when I realize he doesn't plan on letting me go until I tell him the truth.

I give him a sheepish look. "Well, the thing is...I'd planned on inviting you home with me for my annual visit. Only as friends, of course. It had been so long since we'd seen each other, and I wanted to catch up. I also thought you'd enjoy Cypress Hollow and the festival's matchmaking ritual."

His expression fills with regret. "But I was an asshole and you never got the chance to invite me."

"I was more upset than I wanted to admit, even to myself." I don't want to say this next part because I don't want him to feel any guiltier than he already does. Yet he deserves to know. "I was feeling raw for weeks afterward. On edge. The end of our friendship felt like a fissure in my heart. In my confidence. Coming home felt like running away to safety. Clyde was extra attentive to me, and I clung to that. Under the haze of inebriation, I thought maybe it wouldn't be so bad to stay and take a mate. To give up my dreams of being an illustrator and return to my easy, predictable life where things don't change nearly as fast as they do in seelie society. Where every day is the same and I fit in without effort."

He pulls me tighter to his chest, nestling his face in my neck. "I'm so sorry I made you feel that way."

"It's truly not your fault," I say, hugging my arms around his neck. "I needed to learn a lesson in confidence. I needed to commit once and for all to the life I wanted."

He sets me on my feet but keeps his arms around my waist. "Thank you for telling me. And trusting I won't spiral into self-loathing over it."

"You're here now, and that's what matters. I wasn't planning on bringing you this time, but you're a stalker."

"I can't argue with that." We proceed walking. "I truly am sorry, though. I know I've already said it, but I regret that I was such an ass the day I got fired. I was so afraid that we'd gotten too close. I'd felt that fear ever since the night of the gala when I saw you in seelie form for the first time. I…I sensed the spark then."

I whip my gaze to him. "The spark? What spark?"

He rubs his neck in an adorably shy gesture. "You know how I told you I can sense a spark between potential couples? I felt it the night we stood on the balcony after the gala. You climbed upon the railing and caught cherry blossoms that were drifting on the breeze. That's when it hit me. That you were someone I could have feelings for one day. And that fucking terrified me."

Because, deep down, he's always been afraid of getting hurt.

Silence falls between us. I step closer to him and bump my shoulder into his. "So…you've liked me all along?"

"It was a spark," he says with a teasing roll of his eyes.

The underbrush gets denser the deeper we go. We follow game trails whenever we come across them, but the terrain becomes increasingly complex.

"Am I holding you back?" Monty asks as we climb over a series of rotted stumps on the trail. "Since you didn't know about my fae heritage a year ago, you planned on inviting me to your hometown in a human body. Would it be faster if you were in unseelie form? If I was too? Furthermore, won't the villagers react poorly if we show up like this?"

He makes a valid point. Our progress is certainly slower than I planned. I've never walked to my village on two legs. But still.

"I hoped to present myself like this," I say. "We don't have rules against fae entering our village in seelie form or even bringing human friends for visits, and I wanted to show them this side of me."

Monty assesses me with a thoughtful look. "I can see the

value in that, but I've also noticed you don't let yourself shift into your unseelie form very often."

I shake my head. "I promised myself I wouldn't use my unseelie form to run away anymore."

Monty's fingers encircle my wrist, and he stops me on the trail, gently pulling me to face him. "From what you've told me, you haven't run away in a long time. You've faced your fears and anxieties and continue to face them daily. You've gotten so strong, but I don't want that strength to be the reason you lose a piece of yourself. You love your unseelie form. You love climbing and frolicking and curling up in high places."

My chest tightens with yearning at his words. He's right. I do love that. All of that.

"You deserve to enjoy both sides of yourself, Daffy Dear."

I blow out a heavy breath. "I've been so afraid that returning to my unseelie form will make me want to stay in it. That it will make it easier for me to shrink down and hide when I feel nervous or too seen. But I suppose that's just another fear I need to face. Another lesson in confidence."

A grin breaks over his face. "That's my girl. My brave little beast."

An answering smile melts over my lips. I've really come to adore his praise. "And I suppose it would be much faster if we were in unseelie form. Assuming you can shift at will now?"

He winces. "About that...today was the first time I shifted intentionally, and it wasn't the easiest feat. Maybe it will get easier one day, but for now, I can only do it when I connect with my fae magic, and I've spent most of my life doing the opposite."

"How did you manage today?"

"Well, I was fucking angry about the Modesty Committee, and that sparked feelings of...of my passionate love for you."

He blushes when he says the last part, which is so charming I could bite him.

"Ah," I say with a nod. "We need to get you hot. Want to see my breasts?" I'm already unbuttoning my waistcoat while he stammers to form an incoherent reply. By the time I have my blouse open and my bralette raised, he's ceased even trying to argue.

His mouth drops as he drinks in the sight of me. "I'll never get tired of this view," he says, striding closer with the hunger of a man ready to pounce.

I halt him with a pointed look.

"Ah, right. Shifting, shifting." He stares longingly at my breasts a few beats more. "Yes, I can use that, just give me a moment."

I press my lips tight to keep myself from laughing at the amount of concentration that twists his features, paired with the fiery lust in his eyes. Just when I worry his efforts will come to naught, a shudder tears through his frame and he drops to all fours.

With a delighted squeal, I press my palms to my cheeks, staring down at the fennec fox he's become. I know I've already seen him like this once today, but he truly is criminally adorable. I crouch down to study him closer, from his enormous ears to his long whiskers. He's so cute it makes me want to squeeze his giant head, crush his tiny little bones, and chomp him to bits—out of love! Out of love, not hunger. I want to chomp him to bits *metaphorically*. It's hard to explain, but I am struck with the undeniable urge to squeeze him with all my might.

"My dear," he says, tone wry, "are you going to keep staring at me like you might have me for dinner or are you going to join me already?"

"Oh, right." I close my eyes, turn my attention over to my inner hunter, and shrink down into my pine marten form.

Monty's eyes go rounder. "Aw, look at you," he says, voice soft. "I haven't seen you like this in so long."

"Keep up if you can." I spring ahead, scampering down the trail. Monty catches up with me in a matter of seconds, and we race across stones and dirt and fallen trees. As we're running alongside a stream, I sense his eyes locked on me.

"You're really pretty, Daph."

I angle my head toward him. "Are you falling in love with me in unseelie form now too?"

"Maybe—*urp*!" Monty crashes face first into the dirt, his hind legs snagged on a stump he'd tried to leap over while looking at me.

I hiss with laughter.

He scrambles to right himself, not a hint of the elegant aristocrat, only the clumsy fox. "Don't judge my lack of agility. This is only my third time in unseelie form and only my second time running in it. My legs are tired from chasing you across town."

Despite his defense, I can't stop laughing, so I take off running again, and he keeps close to my side, baring his teeth in a vulpine smile.

It doesn't take long to reach Cypress Hollow, and we decide to remain in our unseelie forms as we enter. We pass beneath the trellised ivy-tangled archway that serves as the entrance to the town and step onto a brick walkway. The trees are only somewhat sparser here, but most of the architecture is built between, around, or inside the wide trunks. Strings of warm light weave overhead, strung from branches and towering boughs, creating a canopy of illumination. Nostalgia hums through my entire being at the sight of the market just ahead. It's in full swing every day until sundown. We join the busy throng of fae creatures bustling between buildings and stalls. The architecture is bright and colorful in every shade of yellow, blue, and green, the style closer to something one would find in a human farming town with deeply sloped roofs, exposed wood framing, and barn-style doors. The main difference is the size. Every building is in proportion to the average size of the fae creatures who reside here. Were we in our seelie bodies, it would look quite miniature.

Monty studies our surroundings with an awed look, his ears down and back as we pad across the brick walkway and between other furry bodies. "This is incredible. I can't believe you don't feel overwhelmed here."

I skip ahead, then frolic backward for a few paces so I can study the look on his face. "It was very overwhelming when I first moved here from the solitary quiet of my tree burrow. Now it's just home to me."

"Daphne, is that you?"

I recognize the wizened female voice at once. Whipping back around, I catch sight of a large black mustelid with a wide silver-gray stripe along her head and back. We may be of the same genus, but a honey badger is much larger than I am, and fiercer too. She has the highest kill rate in our village and is famed for eating venomous snakes twice her length with her afternoon tea.

"Elder Rhisha," I say, bowing my muzzle in respect.

"You're rather early," she says in her creaky, crotchety voice. "You normally only come back for Lughnasadh."

The first pinch of anxiety I've felt since entering the town strikes me now, reminding me what I came here to do. I hold her gaze without falter, trying not to focus on the sharp teeth that hang over the sides of her muzzle. "There is an issue I want to address as soon as possible. I should have done it sooner, and I'm not willing to put it off any longer."

She huffs. "Does it have to do with this friend you've brought this time?"

"Apologies," I say, stepping aside to give Elder Rhisha a better view of Monty. "May I introduce my..."

Shit, how do I introduce him? He's more than a friend, but is it poor taste to call him my beau or my lover when I'm engaged to her nephew?

"Monty," he finishes for me, lowering his muzzle.

She makes a raspy chuckle. "You need to have a talk with Clyde."

I shift from paw to paw. "Actually, I thought maybe I should talk to you first."

"I won't need to intervene, trust me. This is between the two of you." With another raspy laugh, she pads off, leaving me to wonder what she's so amused about.

I bare my teeth in my pine marten equivalent of a grimace. "I guess it's now or never."

CLYDE'S RESIDENCE is at the edge of town, a small A-frame house painted red. I spot him just outside it, sitting at a picnic table set before his front door, polishing a wooden mug. He's a woodworker and specializes in carving intricate mugs that he sells to the tavern and other villagers. I even caught sight of them at a boutique near the train station once. I've always envied his dexterity. I may not have ever succeeded at creating art without opposable thumbs, but others have, including Clyde. Since his is a practical art, it's admired in Cypress Hollow, unlike my sexy paintings.

We approach the table. Clyde freezes when he sees me,

nearly dropping his mug and cloth. He's a honey badger just like his aunt with the same wide build, same black fur with a silver-gray stripe down his head and back. He is not, however, nearly as intimidating. "D-Daphne, I wasn't expecting you."

"Hello, Clyde," I say, unable to hide the trepidation in my voice. I hope this conversation remains civil. While he must have been hurt by my abrupt departure after the ritual last year, he likely held out hope that I'd seal our mating this year. He has had a fierce crush on me for as long as I've known him.

"We need to talk," he says, lowering his voice. His eyes dart anxiously between me and Monty. "Quickly."

"Yes, we do," I say, "and I have every intention of making this quick. Clyde, I'm so, so sorry but I cannot be your mate. You've been a good friend to me for so long, but that's all we can ever be. Our handfasting was—"

"Who the fuck is she?" I snap my muzzle shut as my eyes swivel toward the source of the female voice. A stocky gray-brown marmot hobbles out of Clyde's front door on her hind legs, carrying a butcher knife in one of her front paws. She slams the blade point first onto the table, sinking it an inch deep as she stares at Clyde with a murderous glare. "You were goddamned *engaged*?"

This time, Clyde fully drops his mug and cloth and holds out both paws. "I was drunk, baby. I didn't even remember what happened until my aunt told me a month later." He swivels toward me. "I was just about to tell you. I can't go through with our handfasting either because I'm already mated."

My jaw drops. "Mated."

Clyde's mate turns her enraged glare to me now, gripping the handle of her knife and tugging it free from where it was embedded in the table. "I will fucking cut you if you so much as make eyes at my Clyde-baby."

"You should go," Clyde rushes to say. "She really will cut you."

His mate bares her teeth. "Oh, you're taking her side?"

"No, baby, it's just..."

I don't wait to hear a word more, sharing a knowing look with Monty before we take off as fast as we can. We dart between trees, yelping when a butcher knife strikes a trunk just to the right of us, sending shards of bark flying.

We run until we're out of breath, stopping only when we've put ample space between us and the village. Then we collapse at the base of a thick cedar, its wide draping branches shielding us from view. Soon our panting breaths turn to sounds of relief. Then laughter.

"What the hell was that?" Monty says, his furry figure suddenly spilling outward to take the shape of his seelie body. He leans against the trunk of the tree, throwing his head of messy waves back. "A marmot with a butcher knife? Is that kind of domestic dispute normal for your village?"

"Yeah," I say with a shrug and shift back into my seelie form as well. I'm sprawled before him, my weight propped on my forearms as I recline halfway.

A snort of laughter has my gaze returning to Monty. "Your tits are still out, love."

I glance down to see that he's right. I'd forgotten about baring my breasts for him earlier. I lift a hand to tug my bralette back down but Monty's palm stills my fingers. He's crawled over to me and now hovers above me, one hand propped near my waist, the other removing my hand from my bralette to pin it overhead. I fall back on a bed of soil and cedar leaves.

"Don't cover up on my account," he says, lowering his lips to mine. "I'll never deny a chance to worship these morsels."

He moves his mouth down to my collar, then to my breast, where he flicks out his tongue and swirls it over my peaked nipple. I squirm at the pleasure that jolts through me, burning at the apex of my thighs. He moves to the other nipple, suckling until I release a whimper. Then he returns his lips to mine, kissing me deeply. As he pulls away, he bites my bottom lip. I let out another soft whine.

He cradles my cheek. "My friend. My lover. My partner in violence. Have I told you how much I love you today?"

"You can tell me again."

His expression turns serious. "I love you, Daphne Heartcleaver."

"I love you, Monty Phillips."

He shakes his head. "I'm a Heartcleaver too now. I'm relinquishing the Phillips name. I'm free. *We're* free."

Delightful shock ripples through me. He's right. We're officially free from every obstacle that stood between us. His debt. His father's control. My handfasting. All that's left…is whatever the hell we want. What we want to do. What we want to become. Our careers. Our relationship. We're both free to live how we wish. To love how we wish. To support each other and correct each other when one of us is being an idiot—mostly Monty, I'm sure.

I fully relax onto my bed of soil and stare up at the man I love, backlit by the setting sun filtering through the cedar boughs. "Correction," I say. "I love you too, Monty Heartcleaver."

He lowers his lips to mine in a fierce kiss. A kiss that burns with fire and lust, friendship and love. A kiss that burns with the violence that is distinctly *us*.

EPILOGUE

ONE YEAR LATER

DAPHNE

I stand outside the entrance to Cypress Hollow. The trellised arch is decorated in braided wheat, sunflowers, and marigolds for Lughnasadh. For the first time, I'll have to duck under the archway to enter the village. Because, for the first time, I'm entering it on two legs.

A squeeze to my hand reminds me to have courage. I meet Monty's gaze and give him an anxious smile, returning the squeeze. His eyes say what his lips don't—that we don't have to stay in our seelie forms if we don't want to. We can shift into our animal forms and fit in with all the other unseelie creatures, just like we did when we came last year, before we were chased out by a homicidal marmot. I didn't bother coming back for the festival, for I wanted to give Clyde and his mate ample time to work out their problems before I showed my face again. This year, I'm determined to show the face I've never shown anyone here, save for Elder Rhisha the day I left with the other chosen girls to debut in society.

That was over a decade ago, and I've since come to integrate both sides of myself. I no longer *need* my hometown as my refuge, for I'm committed to following my dreams to be an illustrator amongst seelie society no matter what comes my way. That commitment has already paid off. I was officially promoted to illustrator at the beginning of this year. Edwina's brand-new sexy book covers, hidden behind their much more discreet dust jackets, were such a hit, I was immediately contracted to do the next four after the first set was released. I still make mistakes, say the wrong things, or second-guess myself, but I'm no longer tempted to run away and hide.

I can be seen and accepted for who I am. Monty taught me that.

I am the artist and the hunter. The woman and the fae.

So desperately, I want to experience that integration here too, in this village that is my second home.

"Ready, love?" Monty asks.

I exhale a steadying breath and give a sharp nod. "I'm ready."

"Me too," Araminta says from my other side, even though no one asked her. In fact, no one invited her on this trip at all. "It's going to be so nice not being hounded by my fans at every turn."

I cast a wry look at her. Despite her words, she doesn't look at all like someone trying not to stand out. She's dressed in her most extravagant mourning gown yet, with layers upon layers of black silk lined with the most intricate lace I've ever seen. The bodice boasts a high neck, leg-of-mutton sleeves, and black jewels for buttons. She wears her tinted spectacles and an oversized bonnet that matches her dress.

I'm not sure if she's quite as famous as she thinks she is, but she has had a very busy year. The Modesty Committee didn't negatively impact her modeling career for long. If anything, the Committee's bill to separate adult publications with explicit content from general-audience media only opened the door for more opportunities. Periodicals now had to either exclude adult content or create a separate alternate volume. And with such high demand for the lewd and scandalous, the latter became the most popular solution. Pinup magazines flourished, and now there is more ad space than ever with such a vast array of adult publications. Ari was unemployed for all of a month before she became inundated with work.

If she's looking for a place where no one has seen her adverts or centerfolds, it's here. And even though I didn't technically invite her on this trip, I am glad to have her. I just won't tell her that. She'd be insufferable if she knew how much I cherish her.

"Let's go, then," Monty says. "And let us hope we don't get stabbed by marmots today."

Ari whips her head toward us. "Is that something I should be wary of?"

Monty and I share a secret laugh as we pass under the archway.

As soon as we reach the market square, we find the festival in full swing. Cypress Hollow is never busier than it is during the seasonal holidays when the residents invite friends from other parts of the unseelie forest—or even from seelie cities—to attend. An eclectic blend of musicians form a band, playing a jubilant tune at the edge of a makeshift dance floor. Half of the musicians are fae creatures and residents of Cypress Hollow while the others are humanoid fae. There are several more bipedal figures scattered throughout; some are fae in seelie form, others are unseelie fae with naturally humanoid bodies, and a small few are humans, or maybe human-fae hybrids like Monty. Marigold garlands are draped amongst the strings of lights overhead, enhancing the warm glow of the midday sun that peeks through the dense canopy of trees.

We weave through the fray, circling the dance floor without joining in—I'm going to need a lot of alcohol before I can participate in that—and take in the sights around us. The village looks so different from five feet and some odd inches above ground. It's a view I've never had the pleasure of admiring Cypress Hollow from, and it's somehow even more charming than it looks from a pine marten's perspective. The houses are even more quaint than they normally are, especially as heavily decorated as they are with wreaths of sunflowers and apples, ornaments shaped from wheat hanging from windows, roofs, and awnings.

On the other side of the dance floor, countless stalls beckon us with everything from food to wares to activities like fortune telling and games.

"Oooh, matchmaking!" Araminta starts off for a stall featuring stands of braided ribbons in an assortment of different color combinations. At the center of the stall is a miniature archway set with a wooden door that has a hole at the center.

Memories of past booze-addled decision-making flood my mind, and I snag Ari's sleeve before she can take more than three steps. "No matchmaking," I say through my teeth. "Trust me."

She pouts but obeys with only a longing glance. Ari has certainly had more adventures in romance and heartache this past year than she needed. She doesn't need a yearlong engagement to a stranger.

I link one arm through Monty's—my other hand still firmly grasped to Ari's sleeve lest she get any funny ideas—

and drag my companions to the selection of stalls I'm already drooling over. Scents of candied meat and hearty bread fill the air, along with sweet wines and bitter ale.

Monty gives a good-natured roll of his eyes. "Yes, yes, dear, let's get your bacon."

We sample food from every stall I have my eye on, eating until we're full to bursting. My mind grows delightfully fuzzy from the bottle of pomegranate cordial I imbibed. Araminta is even more inebriated than I am, guzzling apple wine like it's water.

"Your hometown is the best!" she says with a wide grin as she cradles her bottle against her chest. Her bonnet hangs down her back now, her tinted spectacles perched on her head and tangled in her lilac hair.

"I'm fucking stuffed," Monty says, rubbing his belly as if it's bulging and not perfectly chiseled like always. If anything, he's only developed more defined musculature, thanks to his new profession. As predicted, the Modesty Committee heavily targeted the *Ask Gladys* column, which had grown especially salacious during Monty's tenure. Even though the Committee's bill opened new opportunities for separate publications, *Ask Gladys* was such a longtime staple of the *Gazette* that Monty's boss feared losing their readership if they moved it to a strictly adult periodical. Monty made the decision easy for the *Gazette*, turning in his resignation with no hard feelings. They did, however, publish his manuscript, thanks to its relatively tame content. That earned him a decent advance to stay afloat while he figured out what to do next.

It also gave him time to rediscover his love for boxing. Which just so happened to coincide with the introduction of a new variation on the sport. A mixed martial arts fighting style made its way across the ocean from Isola, a country Faerwyvae has had little influence from so far, and it immediately won the hearts of boxing fans. Monty was one of the early adopters of the sport, and he's begun to make a name for himself.

He was right when he said I'd only ever seen him holding back while fighting. Monty is a beast in the ring, and even though Isolan boxing isn't much bloodier than the standard kind, it's a thousand times more thrilling to watch.

Or maybe I just like watching Monty, whatever he does. Whether he's penning inappropriate articles, managing chaotic book tours, or beating his opponents to a pulp.

He arches a brow at me, and I realize I'm staring adoringly at him. "Did you accidentally drink a love potion instead of cordial, dear?" He is, of course, the only one of our trio who isn't buzzed on booze. He may not need to be quite as careful about outing his father's secret, for he's no longer bound to a bargain, but he maintains his sobriety nonetheless. He's still quite fond of his herbal cigarillos, which he takes a drag from now.

"I don't need a potion for that, dummy," I mutter.

"You say the sweetest things."

We leave the food stalls and enter the rows reserved for games and activities. I've yet to seek out any of my old friends, although I do plan on introducing myself to them in this body. First, I want time alone with my two companions. To experience this first with them. My first time visiting Cypress Hollow in seelie form. My first time bringing friends with me to our Lughnasadh festival.

"Wait…is that…" Monty quickens his pace.

When I finally see what has stolen his attention, I utter an excited squeal. "It's the shooting game!"

We stop outside the stall, studying the mossy green wall covered in bubbles, the tiny bud that will grow into a vine, the wooden air rifles. The game operator is still calling for contestants to join before the next round begins. Monty and

I exchange maniacal grins before we race toward the open seats.

"Oh, God," Ari says with a groan. "Not this again."

Tinny music plays as the game starts. Monty immediately hits his first three targets while I take a few messy shots before I familiarize myself with the weight of the gun and the deceptively inaccurate sight. Once I get comfortable, I hit my first target, popping one of the larger bubbles. My little green bud grows to a sprout, a good foot shorter than Monty's vine. That's all right. I still have time to catch up.

"Hey, Monty," I say, keeping my concentration sharp as I pop my next three targets, all smaller ones that are worth more vine growth than the larger ones.

"Yes, dearest?"

"Remember the last time we played this game?"

"How could I forget?" He pops two more bubbles, the absolute smallest on the board. His vine climbs higher.

"You mentioned something then." *Pop. Pop. Pop.* "About how you'd wondered about my lips. Particularly how they'd feel on your cock."

"I remember," he says with a grin, not missing a single target.

"You know how it feels now, don't you?"

"Yes, love. I have every pattern of that clever tongue memorized like the back of my cock. You truly don't need fifteen steps to fantastic fellatio." He takes his eyes off his target and gives me a smug wink, all the while popping his next target without even looking at it.

I grit my teeth. My methods aren't working to fluster him at all. So I amp up my efforts, rising from my stool and propping my foot on it. Then I lift the hem of my dress—glad I wore one of my comfortable yet plain day dresses for the festival—and bare my stockinged leg. My garters are extra ruffly, and Monty can't help but glance at them.

"Those are new."

"Sure are. Ari took me shopping for undergarments."

"I did," she says from behind us, clapping her hands as I pop my next five targets. "It was about time you got a corset."

That steals Monty's attention for longer. His eyes go wide. "You got a corset?"

"Yes, but I'm never going to wear it. Outside of the bedroom, that is." I pop three more targets while Monty clears his throat.

"Interesting choice. I like it." He pops his next several bubbles, his composure restored.

"There is one new article I decided to wear though. It's a type of underwear that doesn't cover one's butt cheeks. The back goes straight between them."

He whips his face to me so fast, he nearly drops his rifle. "You're wearing them? Right now?"

"I am, and I will never wear them again. Extremely uncomfortable. Do not recommend. If you want to tear them off me with your teeth, I'm more than happy to oblige."

"You sexy, wicked beast," he says. He licks his lips as if tempted to take me up on my offer then and there, but he begrudgingly returns his attention to his target. He hits five more, but my vine has outgrown his by several inches. Just another foot and it will reach the top.

"Hey Daph," he says.

"Hmm?" I refuse to look at him. Refuse to take my eyes off my target. Just a few more—

"Will you marry me?"

My next shot misses, and I blink a few times to process what Monty just said. I hazard the briefest glance, prepared to look away just as quickly, but that's when he gets down on one knee beside my stool. My stomach flips, and I know this is just a ruse, but...

But that's not what the ring in his hand says.

My breath catches as he stares up at me with a crooked smile, his dimples on full display.

"Daphne Heartcleaver," he says, his voice carrying over the tinny music and shots fired, all the way to my heart. "My feral love with the prettiest sharp teeth, the cutest pine marten face, and the meanest growl if awoken before six in the morning. You've taught me so much about myself that I never wanted to face. You saw a side of me I tried to hide from everyone. You pulled me out of darkness and loved me for the mangled, broken, hastily-stitched-back-together being I am. I spent my whole life looking for evidence that love was real. That it could last without hurting. That it could stay without changing or leaving.

"But it does hurt, in the best kind of way. And when it changes, it shifts into something new and different. I can't stop it from leaving, and I don't need to. I can only give it my heart and cherish it while it's mine. Will you be mine, Daffy Dear, forever and always? Or until the day you get so sick of me you decide to bite out my throat?" He says the last part with a wink.

I realize now I can either win or set down my rifle and accept the ring.

Tears glaze my eyes, and I know I couldn't hit my next targets even if I wanted to. Besides, the most important target is before me now, resting on one knee.

I set down my rifle and return to sitting on my stool. Sniffling, I nod and hold out my hand. "Yes," I manage to croak out. "Yes, I'll marry you, asshole."

He slides the ring onto my finger, a rose gold chrysanthemum on a yellow gold band, then rises halfway to press his lips to mine.

"Hooray!" comes Araminta's voice, followed by the tickle of something fluttering against my cheek. Monty and I break away to discover the spray of glittery black confetti, tossed from Ari's palms.

I swat it away, but it still lands everywhere, in my hair, down the front of my dress. "You told Ari about this?"

"Of course I didn't," Monty says. "You think she can keep a secret?"

"Then why does she have confetti?" When Monty only shrugs in answer, I face Araminta.

"Why wouldn't I have confetti?" is her only reply.

The tinny music turns to a celebratory tune as the first contestant grows their vine to the roof of the stall. "We both lost," I say without regret.

Monty arches a brow. "Did we?"

I return to face him. My love. My friend. And now my fiancé. "No, not at all."

THE NEXT MORNING, we make our way to the train station, our weekend of frivolity behind us. None of us are well rested considering Monty and I celebrated our engagement with a marathon of orgasms. Predictably, my thong underpants lasted no more than a minute once we were alone. Meanwhile, Araminta stayed out drinking until dawn with some new friends she made—fast-talking squirrels and chipmunks. Very much her people.

She's paying for it now, taking up an entire bench to herself in our coach and moaning about every bump in the road. I'm snuggled up against Monty, his arm around my shoulders. Despite our lack of sleep, I feel refreshed. Invigorated.

And a touch nervous too.

Because Monty isn't the only one who planned a surprise this weekend. I haven't a clue how mine will go.

Our coach arrives at the station, and we buy our return tickets before heading for the platform. As a hub between the line that leads south to Jasper and another that joins routes to the northern courts, it's a busy station, despite its modest size. It consists of a single brick building with an ivy-coated awning to protect waiting passengers from the elements. On the nearest side of the building is the platform that leads home to Jasper. On the far side is the one that connects the northern line.

With my arm linked through Monty's, I guide him to the other side.

He belatedly catches on and points a thumb over his shoulder. "Shouldn't we be there?"

"Why did we get here so early?" Ari squints down at her ticket. "Our train doesn't depart for another two hours."

"Actually," I say, anticipation buzzing through me, "we're right on time." Though I can't see the arriving train yet, the blare of its horn sounds in the distance.

Monty frowns down at me. "What's going on?"

I take a deep breath and swivel to face him. "I sort of have a surprise. I've been working on it for a while now."

"Surprise?" Ari says. "What surprise?"

I ignore her. Like Monty, I chose not to let Araminta in on what's about to happen next.

"It's rather last-minute," I say, "but it ended up being perfect. I just got the telegram last week, and we arranged it—"

"Arranged what?" Monty's face flashes between confusion and concern.

I worry my bottom lip. I have no idea if this was the right thing to keep from him, but I didn't want to get his hopes up or give him a reason to be anxious all weekend. But there's no putting it off any longer. I'll take his reaction, whatever it may be. "Monty, I found your mother."

MONTY

No other words could have surprised me more. All sense flees my mind, and when I open my mouth, I can't utter a single word. Daphne takes my hands in hers, grounding me. Anchoring me with her presence. Finally, I manage to speak my reply. "How?"

"It was a group effort," she says, her tone a mixture of anxious and excited. I catch sight of the approaching train rounding the corner in the distance, and my pulse kicks up. She rushes to explain. "Briony Blackwood used her succubus magic to invade your father's dreams and coax information from him. We learned your mother's name. It's Étaín."

Étaín. The name echoes through my mind, sending a sharp pang through my heart. It's a bittersweet agony, hearing my mother's name. The woman I never got to know, save for the time when I thought she was merely my fox friend.

"We also learned your father has been paying her a stipend for her upkeep," Daphne says. "I passed this on to Angela, and she spent weeks going through your father's ledgers looking for records of long-time payments."

Angie helped too? I was so terrified to tell her the truth about my lineage, about Father's infidelity that led to my conception, about the burden he placed on me. The reason we'd always had at least a small wedge between us, keeping me from being the best brother I could be. She was understandably shocked and hurt by the secrets that had been kept from her. Furthermore by my lack of trust in how she could handle the truth. She knew I couldn't outright tell her, but she desperately wished I'd helped her figure it out on her own. Yet it didn't take her long to forgive me. The same goes for Thorne and Briony. My best friend hated that I'd kept such a secret from him—that I'd pushed him away in the past, acted like a complete ass at times to purposefully keep his friendship at a distance. But he understood better than anyone. He knew firsthand how family secrets could poison one's heart.

But they've all forgiven me, and we've all grown closer.

I never could have imagined they'd come together to help find my mother.

Daphne speaks again. "Thanks to Angela's research, we found several leads, but none were to a person named Étaín. I figured she was getting paid by an intermediary, but none of the leads I contacted replied to my queries. That's when I reached out to a local detective who takes on private cases, even non-criminal ones. He's been working on finding her for months now. Last week, he sent a telegram saying he'd found her in a small village in the Fire Court. Not only that, but she was eager to meet you. She too had been bound by a bargain with your father, but she'd recently received a letter stating he'd revoked it and would instead rely on trust in her discretion."

"She...she wants to meet me." My eyes flick to the approaching train that slows as it pulls into the station. "She's on that train?"

"She is. Detective Whitwood is serving as her personal escort here." Her expression turns more apprehensive, bordering on apologetic. "I know your feelings for her might be complicated, and maybe it was wrong of me—"

"No, love," I say, pulling her to my chest. My heart slams

against my ribs, and with her ear pressed so closely to it, I know she can hear every anxious, terrified, joyful beat. She's right about my complicated feelings about my mother, but I've never once balked at the thought of seeing her again. Meeting her—*truly* meeting her—for the first time. I press a kiss to the top of Daphne's head. "You did good. You did really, really good."

She pulls away slightly, keeping her arms around my waist. "If things feel too tense, you can have a nice chat with her, and she can catch the next train back north. But if things go well, maybe we could invite her for a longer visit home with us?"

"Maybe," I say with a hopeful smile.

"The two of you should really stop keeping secrets from me," Ari says, reminding me of her presence. "Unlucky for you, I'm fresh out of confetti. How will we celebrate now?"

The train stops at the platform, sending my pulse racketing. "Oh, fuck," I mutter. "I'm about to meet my mother. To see my…my fox friend again."

"Deep breaths," Daphne says, framing my cheeks with her palms and giving them a soft slap. It's become a routine of ours when we need encouragement. "You can do this. I'm right here with you."

I nod, gathering my resolve. We face the train, hands linked. After a few anxious moments, passengers begin to disembark. My eyes search the stairs, the ground, and it occurs to me the tiny four-legged creature I remember might not be my mother's current form. There's no way my strait-laced father had an affair with a fennec fox, and she probably only ever appeared to me as one because it allowed her to sneak onto my family's property. Which means…

I cast a worried look at Daph. "I just realized I don't know what she looks like."

She squeezes my palm. "She'll be with Detective Whitwood, and I've met him. I at least know what *he* looks like."

That sets my nerves at ease, and I begin searching the passengers' faces, wondering if I'll recognize—

The world around me slows as I spot a pair of eyes as familiar to me as my own reflection. Pale hair in messy waves, pinned under a straw hat dressed in silk flowers. She's outfitted in a short-sleeved day dress in white linen, exactly the kind of lightweight ensemble one might wear in the Fire Court.

She reaches the bottom step, and a tall human male helps her down to the platform. I lose her when she joins the fray of the crowd, but it's her. I know it is.

Daphne and I start forward. The roar of my heartbeat is the only sound I hear, drowning out the bustle of the chattering passengers.

Then the crowd clears...

And she's there.

My mother.

Étaín.

Her eyes lock on mine, and we freeze. She...she looks so much like me. She's nearly as tall as I am with the same gray eyes, the same dimples that frame her smile. Like most fae, she maintains a youthful countenance, but there's vast wisdom in her eyes, paired with crow's feet at their corners that speak of her age. She must be hundreds of years older than even Daphne.

Étaín's chest heaves with a sob. There's no question on her face. She recognizes me.

I swallow the lump in my throat and give Daphne's hand a final squeeze before releasing it. Then I close the remaining distance between me and my mother. "Hello, Mother."

Another sob tears through her, and she pulls me into her

arms. I'm so stunned, so wholly unprepared for this, that I'm hardly aware of the detective who stands at her side. My heart cracks, and I remember how to breathe, how to move, how to return the affection I got so used to withholding from everyone around me. I fold my arms around my mother, and it feels as if something inside me locks into place at last.

This is where it all began.

The fox friend who left me, making me wonder what I'd done to lose her.

The mother who that fox turned out to be, leaving me so suddenly without telling me who she was.

The guilt that plagued me when I reflected on how I'd treated her, how I'd carried her, climbed trees with her, dressed her in flower crowns and bow ties.

The fear I developed that loved ones could leave at any time without more than a curt goodbye.

The cold behavior I'd engaged in, doing exactly what was done to me to keep myself from ever feeling that shock of loss again.

The blame I placed on myself so that I always had a concrete reason for being abandoned.

This is where it all began, but none of it matters anymore. I don't blame her, and I don't blame myself.

This is where it ends.

My cheeks are wet but my heart is light as Mother and I separate, just enough to look at each other again. There's so much I want to know about her. What has she been doing all this time? What is her life like? In what ways are we similar? In what ways are we different?

But first, there's a piece of my heart she needs to meet.

"Mother," I say, stepping to the side and extending a hand to where Daphne hovers a few feet away, wringing her hands. Daph places her palm in mine and lets me pull her close. "Allow me to introduce my fiancée."

This is where it ends, and this is where it begins again.

Forgiven.

Renewed.

Free.

BONUS EPILOGUE

ARAMINTA

Well, this is awkward. A happy family reunion plays out before my eyes, and I'm stuck with a raging hangover and a stranger at my side. I probably shouldn't have participated in a drinking contest with Trinity—she's a chipmunk—but I thought for sure I could outdrink her, considering I was in my seelie form while she was hardly bigger than my palm.

The detective clears his throat and faces me. Now that I'm looking at him head-on, I must admit he's nice to look at. Broad shoulders, a fine suit, a stern expression. His hair is a rich brown and his neatly trimmed beard gives him a look that's somehow rugged yet refined. His towering build isn't exactly favorable, as I prefer men skinny and closer to my height. They look so cute and weak when I can look them in the eye without tipping my head back. "Miss…" he says, his words ending in another throat clearing. "Forgive me, we've yet to be acquainted."

The last thing I want is to engage in small talk when my head is spinning, but I should be polite. It's what we do in society, and I'm a public figure nowadays. I dip into an elegant curtsy, ignoring the way my stomach sloshes. "Lady Araminta of the Shining Waters."

"Miss Waters," he says, and I bristle at the shortening of my perfect name. "I'd like to inquire about your dress."

"Oh," I say, pulling my head back. I didn't get the sense he sought an introduction out of interest or attraction to me, but as he scans my gown from neck to hem, he must be. I do a twirl to show off my figure and grace. "You mean this old thing? Do you like it?"

"Might I ask where you acquired it?" he says without so much as a smile.

I frown. That wasn't at all how I expected him to respond. I shift side to side, trying to catch sight of his hands, seeking a wedding band. Perhaps he isn't attracted to me at all and simply wants to procure a similar gown for his wife. Or daughter? Is this man old enough to produce children? I don't know how humans work. Too bad for him, this dress was not found by usual means. I swish my skirt from side to side. "I got it from a dead woman."

His expression flashes with something like horror—or anger?—before he steels it behind an icy mask.

I bark a laugh, realizing my mistake. "No, she wasn't dead when she was wearing it. I got it from her closet *after* she died."

His jaw tightens. "Did you know this woman?"

Another train pulls into the station at the opposite platform, the one that will head back to Jasper. My liquor-filled stomach lurches at the thought of boarding a train. Thankfully we won't be catching ours for another couple of hours.

"Miss Waters?"

I blink a few times to clear my head, remembering the

handsome detective's question. "Yes, I met her through the obituaries. That's where I do most of my shopping."

There's a glint in his eyes that might be excitement. Huh. So he can make other expressions. "What you're saying," he says, his voice low and controlled, "is that you regularly steal mourning gowns from the deceased."

"No, I don't *steal* them. I take the clothing before the will has been read. When they don't belong to anyone."

His lips twitch at one corner, the ghost of a grin that looks almost wicked. I kind of like it. Is he attracted to me after all? "You strategically take these gowns before the will of the deceased has been read, after learning about their deaths in the obituaries, including but not limited to this gown—a precious family heirloom once worn by the Queen of Isola, featuring rare Isolan lace and black diamond buttons?"

I lift my sleeve, examining the dark jewels. "Huh. I didn't know these were diamonds."

"Miss Waters," he says, "will you answer the question?"

I snap my gaze back to his. Oh, he *is* looking at me with desire, I'm sure of it now! He isn't exactly my type—too tall and a bit older than the college boys I like—but it's been a while since I've felt the thrill of being looked at this way. Like a prize. A conquest. I give him a proud smile. "Yes."

In a single stride, he steps up to me and takes my hand.

My heart leaps. For the love of the All of All, he moves fast! Making a move on me after hardly a minute of knowing each other?

I tip my head back, admiring his dark hair, the hazel hue of his irises. Maybe he's not too tall after all, if he can look down at me with such sinister desire—

He steps away, and I find myself stumbling after him.

Not of my own accord, but…

I stare down at my hand where a metal cuff surrounds my wrist. What the…

To be honest, I've always wanted to be restrained during lovemaking in some way, but I'm no longer certain this is a love confession. Is he a deranged fan? Is he going to lock me in his basement and have his way with me?

My gaze falls on his backside as he tugs me toward the other platform, and I'm not sure I hate the visuals going through my head.

No, of course I hate them. I can't go to his secret love lair until I've told my friends.

I root my heels in place and turn toward Daphne, Monty, and his mother. The three are too preoccupied in their conversation to notice me, especially with the platform growing busy again. I open my mouth to call out to them, but a large hand covers my lips.

"Not a word," the detective growls in my ear. "You're under arrest for serial theft. Do you know how long I've been looking for you, Miss Waters? You're under my authority now."

Couldn't he have waited to say that last part when we were in his sex dungeon? I'd be into it then—no, wait. What about the other part?

Theft? I shout against his hand, but only muffled sounds come out. I try to wriggle out of his grip, but he's too strong, and my efforts only earn me another cuffed hand. Now they're both secured behind my back. I gather a breath and prepare to shout for my friends again, but his hand returns. He faces me away from him and marches me toward the train. He doesn't take me to the passenger car where the others are starting to board, a few of whom cast shocked looks at the spectacle we're making, but instead takes me to a rear car. He exchanges a nod with a porter, who must recognize him, for he doesn't so much as question the brute as he hauls me onto the train and into a private compartment, shutting the door behind us.

He drops me on a cushioned bench and claims the one opposite me.

I stare at him with wide eyes, still unable to believe what's happening. My mind sharpens through the haze of my shock, reminding me I have one way out.

Pursing my lips to hide my devious grin, I turn my attention inward and…

I turn my attention inward…

Nothing.

I can't shift into my unseelie form. I can't access my fae magic.

The blood drains from my face as I give a tug to the cuffs. They must be enchanted with something that suppresses fae magic. I…I'm stuck here. With him.

Worst of all…

I'm under arrest.

"Settle in," he says, crossing his arms over his chest. "This is the last comfort you'll have before jail."

DAPHNE AND MONTY'S story may be complete, but Araminta and Detective Whitwood are poised for an epic romance. Fall in love with the next fantasy romcom in the ***Fae Flings and Corset Strings*** series with ***Elegance and Espionage.***

NOT READY TO LEAVE FAERWYVAE?

I HAVE SO MUCH MORE FOR YOU! Daphne and Monty's story may be complete, but Araminta and Detective Whitwood are poised for an epic romance. Fall in love with the next fantasy romcom in the ***Fae Flings and Corset Strings*** series with ***Elegance and Espionage.***

If you haven't read the first book in the ***Fae Flings and Corset Strings*** series yet, be sure to read ***A Rivalry of Hearts***!

All caught up on my ***Fae Flings*** series but craving more cozy fantasy romance vibes? Start ***Entangled with Fae*** next! Every book in this series is a standalone new adult fairytale retelling with a HEA guarantee. You'll see some familiar faces that you met in ***A Rivalry of Hearts*** and ***My Feral Romance***! Such as…

- Briony Rose and Thorne Blackwood! Read about their tense enemies-to-lovers romance where the tattooed villain (who's actually a soft-hearted baker) gets the girl in ***A Dream So Wicked: A Sleeping Beauty Retelling.***

- Gemma Bellefleur, who you met in ***A Rivalry of Hearts*** as Edwina's biggest fan! Read all about her before she became queen in ***Curse of the Wolf King: A Beauty and the Beast Retelling***.

If you're in a stabby and angsty mood, take a trip to Faerwyvae's past with ***The Fair Isle Trilogy***, an upper YA/NA enemies-to-lovers romantasy. It's set two decades before ***Fae Flings and Corset Strings*** and lays the foundation for much of the isle's magic and world building.

ACKNOWLEDGMENTS

When I wrote the acknowledgments for *A Rivalry of Hearts*, I mentioned how some books are just so magically easy to write.

This was not one of those books.

Monty and Daphne fought me every step of the way. Daphne in particular. She vetoed so many of my original plot points with a "I would never do that, you know this. You're the one who wrote me." And she was right.

Thankfully I had many people to support me while I argued with figments of my imagination. (Monty and Daph are super offended I called them that, by the way. They are real, thank you very much.)

Thank you Hanna Sandvig and Alisha Klapheke for reading my very first draft when I was convinced the book was terrible and was too terrified to let anyone read it. Hanna, you especially bullied me to just rip off the bandaid and get some eyeballs on it. And turns out, you didn't hate it!

Thank you to my husband and daughter for supporting me as always. You tolerated much incomprehensible mumbling about my story woes while I inchwormed my body across the floor during my "dark night of the soul" aka my mood after every five chapters during the drafting process.

Thank you to my agent, Kimberly Whalen, for being awesome and helping my books spread their wings to new formats and new corners of the world. You're amazing!

Thank you to Kristen at Your Editing Lounge and the rest

of my proofreading/typo hunting team for this book: Claire, Emily, and Bea. I'm so lucky to have you!

Thank you to my PA, Emily and Elyse at Luna Blooms, for helping me stay organized and navigate the most stressful parts of my book releases.

And most of all, thank you to all my readers! I don't think I've ever seen so much hype for one of my sequels as I have for this book. You really kept me going when writing got tough!

Happy reading!

Tessonja

ALSO BY TESSONJA ODETTE

Fae Flings and Corset Strings - fae romcom

A Rivalry of Hearts

My Feral Romance

Elegance and Espionage

Entangled with Fae - fae romance

Curse of the Wolf King: A Beauty and the Beast Retelling

Heart of the Raven Prince: A Cinderella Retelling

Kiss of the Selkie: A Little Mermaid Retelling

A Taste of Poison: A Snow White Retelling

A Dream So Wicked: A Sleeping Beauty Retelling

The Fair Isle Trilogy - fae fantasy

To Carve a Fae Heart

To Wear a Fae Crown

To Spark a Fae War

standalone fae romance novella set in faerwyvae

Married by Scandal

Prophecy of the Forgotten Fae - epic fantasy

A Throne of Shadows

A Cage of Crystal

A Fate of Flame

ya dystopian psychological thriller

Twisting Minds

ABOUT THE AUTHOR

Tessonja Odette is a Seattle-based author of fantasy romance, epic romantasy, and fairytale retellings. She especially loves to write about brooding fae and the fierce women who hate-to-love them. When she isn't writing, she's watching cat videos, petting dogs, having dance parties in the kitchen with her daughter, or pursuing her many creative hobbies. In her books, you'll find enemies-to-lovers, witty banter, cozy vibes, and a delicious dash of steam. Read more about Tessonja at www.tessonjaodette.com

instagram.com/tessonja
facebook.com/tessonjaodette
tiktok.com/@tessonja
x.com/tessonjaodette

Made in the USA
Las Vegas, NV
09 April 2025